# 50 Horror Stories

# 50 Horror Stories

Selected By
Al Sarrantonio
& Martin H. Greenberg

GOODWILL PUBLISHING HOUSE™
B-3, RATTAN JYOTI, 18, RAJENDRA PLACE, NEW DELHI-110008 (INDIA)
TEL.: 25750801, 25755519, 25820556 FAX : 91-11-25763428

This special low priced Indian reprint is published by arrangement with Sterling Publishing Company, Inc. New York, U.S.A.



*Published in India by*
**GOODWILL PUBLISHING HOUSE™**
B-3 Rattan Jyoti, 18 Rajendra Place
New Delhi-110008 (INDIA)
Tel. : 25750801, 25755519, 25820556
Fax : 91-11-25763428
E-mail : goodwillpub@vsnl.net
website : www.goodwillpublishinghouse.com

Printed at : Kumar Offset Printers, Delhi-110092

# CONTENTS

# INTRODUCTION

You hold in your hands a very special book.

It contains fifty carnival rides of terror.

You must remember: horror can come from any direction. It can be as subtle as a spider web's caress, or as vicious as the drop of an ax blade. It can be grim as the reaper, or as sardonic as, well, Sardonicus. It can wear the garments of science or superstition; can be dressed in the trappings of fantasy or the fancy-free.

But always it will terrify.

And one of the bluntest of its instruments is the short-short story, one of the most difficult of literary devices to master. Not only must each word be perfect—but each comma and period. Nothing can be wasted.

In the hands of master executioners, like the authors who fill this book—it can be deadly.

So . . .

Die—and die again—fifty times . . .

—Martin H. Greenberg
Al Sarrantonio

# The Adventure of My Grandfather

By Washington Irving

My grandfather was a bold dragoon, for it's a profession, d' ye see, that has run in the family. All my forefathers have been dragoons, and died on the field of honor, except myself, and I hope my posterity may be able to say the same; however, I don't mean to be vainglorious. Well, my grandfather, as I said, was a bold dragoon, and had served in the Low Countries. In fact, he was one of that very army, which according to my uncle Toby, swore so terribly in Flanders. He could swear a good stick himself; and moreover was the very man that introduced the doctrine Corporal Trim mentions of radical heat and radical moisture, or, in other words, the mode of keeping out the damps of ditchwater by burnt brandy. Be that as it may, it's nothing to the purport of my story. I only tell it to show you that my grandfather was a man not easily to be humbugged. He had seen service, or, according to his own phrase, he had seen the devil—and that's saying everything.

Well, gentlemen, my grandfather was on his way to England, for which he intended to embark from Ostend—bad luck to the place! for one where I was kept by storms and headwinds for three long days, and the devil of a jolly companion or pretty girl to comfort me. Well, as I was saying, my grandfather was on his way to England, or rather to Ostend—no matter which, it's all the same. So one evening, towards night fall, he rode jollily into Bruges.—Very like you all know Bruges, gentlemen; a queer old-fashioned Flemish town, once, they say, a great place for trade and money-making in old times, when the Mynheers were in their glory; but almost as large and as empty as an Irishman's pocket at the present day.—Well, gentlemen, it was at the time of the annual fair. All Bruges was crowded; and the canals swarmed with Dutch boats, and the streets swarmed with Dutch merchants; and there was hardly any getting along for goods, wares, and merchandises, and peasants in big breeches, and women in half a score of petticoats.

My grandfather rode jollily along, in his easy, slashing way, for he was a saucy, sun-shiny fellow—staring about him at the motley crowd, the old houses with gable ends to the street, and storks' nests in the chimneys; winking at the yafrows who showed their faces at the windows and joking the women right and left in the street; all of whom laughed, and took it in amazing good part; for though he did not know a word of the language, yet he had always a knack of making himself understood among the women.

Well, gentlemen, it being the time of the annual fair, all the town was crowded, every inn and tavern full, and my grandfather applied in vain from one to the other for admittance. At length he rode up to an old rickety inn, that looked ready to fall to pieces, and which all the rats would have run away from, if they could have found room in any other house to put their heads. It was just such a queer building as you see in Dutch pictures, with a tall roof that reached up into the clouds, and as many garrets, one over the other, as the seven heavens of Mahomet. Nothing had saved it from tumbling down but a stork's nest on the chimney, which always brings good luck to a house in the Low Countries; and at the very time of my grandfather's arrival, there were two of these long-legged birds of grace standing like ghosts on the chimney-top. Faith, but they've kept the house on its legs to this very day, for you may see it any time you pass through Bruges, as it stands there yet, only it is turned into a brewery of strong Flemish beer,—at least it was so when I came that way after the battle of Waterloo.

My grandfather eyed the house curiously as he approached. It might not have altogether struck his fancy, had he not seen in large letters over the door,

HEER VERKOOPT MAN GOEDEN DRANK

My grandfather had learnt enough of the language to know that the sign promised good liquor. "This is the house for me," said he, stopping short before the door.

The sudden appearance of a dashing dragoon was an event in an old inn frequented only by the peaceful sons of traffic. A rich burgher of Antwerp, a stately ample man in a broad Flemish hat, and who was the great man and great patron of the establishment, sat smoking a clean long pipe on one side of the door; a fat little distiller of Geneva, from Schiedam, sat smoking on the other; and the bottle-nosed host stood in the door, and the comely hostess, in crimped cap, beside him; and the hostess's daughter, a plump Flanders lass, with long gold pendants in her ears, was at a side-window.

"Humph!" said the rich burgher of Antwerp, with a sulky glance at the stranger.

"De duyvel!" said the fat little distiller of Schiedam.

The landlord saw, with the quick glance of a publican, that the new guest was not at all to the taste of the old ones; and, to tell the truth, he did not like my grandfather's saucy eye. He shook his head. "Not a garret in the house but was full."

"Not a garret!" echoed the landlady.

"Not a garret!" echoed the daughter.

The burgher of Antwerp, and the little distiller of Schiedam, continued to smoke their pipes sullenly, eying the enemy askance from under their broad hats, but said nothing.

My grandfather was not a man to be browbeaten. He threw the reins on his horse's neck, cocked his head on one side, stuck one arm akimbo,—"Faith and troth!" said he, "but I'll sleep in this house this very night."—As he said this he gave a slap on his thigh, by way of emphasis—the slap went to the landlady's heart.

He followed up the vow by jumping off his horse, and making his way past the staring Mynheers into the public room.—Maybe you've been in the bar-room of an old Flemish inn—faith, but a handsome chamber it was as you'd wish to see; with a brick floor, and a great fireplace, with the whole Bible history in glazed tiles; and then the mantelpiece, pitching itself head foremost out of the wall, with a whole regiment of cracked tea-pots and earthen jugs paraded on it; not to mention half a dozen great Delft platters, hung about the room by way of pictures; and the little bar in one corner, and the bouncing bar-maid inside of it, with a red calico cap, and yellow ear-drops.

My grandfather snapped his fingers over his head, as he cast an eye round the room,—"Faith, this is the very house I've been looking after," said he.

There was some further show of resistance on the part of the garrison; but my grandfather was an old soldier, and an Irishman to boot, and not easily repulsed, especially after he had got into the fortress. So he blarneyed the landlord, kissed the landlord's wife, tickled the landlord's daughter, chucked the bar-maid under the chin; and it was agreed on all hands that it would be a thousand pities, and a burning shame into the bargain, to turn such a bold dragoon into the streets. So they laid their heads together, that is to say, my grandfather and the landlady, and it was at length agreed to accommodate him with an old chamber that had been for some time shut up.

"Some say it's haunted," whispered the landlord's daughter; "but you are a bold dragoon, and I dare say don't fear ghosts."

"The devil a bit!" said my grandfather, pinching her plump cheek. "But if I should be troubled by ghosts, I've been to the Red

Sea in my time, and have a pleasant way of laying them, my darling."

And then he whispered something to the girl which made her laugh, and give him a good-humored box on the ear. In short, there was nobody knew better how to make his way among the petticoats than my grandfather.

In a little while, as was his usual way, he took complete possession of the house, swaggering all over it; into the stable to look after his horse, into the kitchen to look after his supper. He had something to say or do with every one; smoked with the Dutchmen, drank with the Germans, slapped the landlord on the shoulder, romped with his daughter and the bar-maid;—never, since the days of Alley Croaker, had such a rattling blade been seen. The landlord stared at him with astonishment; the landlord's daughter hung her head and giggled whenever he came near; and as he swaggered along the corridor, with his sword trailing by his side, the maids looked after him, and whispered to one another, "What a proper man!"

At supper, my grandfather took command of the *table-d' hôte* as though he had been at home; helped everybody, not forgetting himself; talked with every one, whether he understood their language or not; and made his way into the intimacy of the rich burgher of Antwerp, who had never been known to be sociable with any one during his life. In fact, he revolutionized the whole establishment, and gave it such a rouse, that the very house reeled with it. He outsat every one at table, excepting the little fat distiller of Schiedam, who sat soaking a long time before he broke forth; but when he did, he was a very devil incarnate. He took a violent affection for my grandfather; so they sat drinking and smoking, and telling stories, and singing Dutch and Irish songs, without understanding a word each other said, until the little Hollander was fairly swamped with his own gin and water, and carried off to bed, whooping and hickuping, and trolling the burden of a Low Dutch love-song.

Well, gentlemen, my grandfather was shown to his quarters up a large staircase, composed of loads of hewn timber; and through long rigmarole passages, hung with blackened paintings of fish, and fruit, and game, and country frolics, and huge kitchens, and portly burgomasters, such as you see about old-fashioned Flemish inns, till at length he arrived at his room.

An old-times chamber it was, sure enough, and crowded with all kinds of trumpery. It looked like an infirmary for decayed and superannuated furniture, where everything diseased or disabled was sent to nurse or to be forgotten. Or rather it might be taken for a general congress of old legitimate movables, where every kind and country had a representative. No two chairs were alike. Such high backs and low backs, and leather bottoms, and worsted bottoms, and straw bottoms, and no bottoms; and cracked marble tables with curiously carved legs, holding balls in their claws, as though they were going to play at ninepins.

My grandfather made a bow to the motley assemblage as he entered, and, having undressed himself, placed his light in the fireplace, asking pardon of the tongs, which seemed to be making love to the shovel in the chimney-corner, and whispering soft nonsense in its ear.

The rest of the guests were by this time sound asleep, for your Mynheers are huge sleepers. The housemaids, one by one, crept up yawning to their attics; and not a female head in the inn was laid on a pillow that night without dreaming of the bold dragoon.

My grandfather, for his part, got into bed, and drew over him one of those great bags of down, under which they smother a man in the Low Countries; and there he lay, melting between two feather beds, like an anchovy sandwich between two slices of toast and butter. He was a warm-complexioned man, and this smothering played the very deuce with him. So, sure enough, in a little time it seemed as if a legion of imps were twitching at him, and all the blood in his veins was in a fever-heat.

He lay still, however, until all the house was quiet excepting the snoring of the Mynheers from the different chambers; who answered one another in all kinds of tones and cadences, like so many bull-frogs in a swamp. The quieter the house became, the more unquiet became my grandfather. He waxed warmer and warmer, until at length the bed became too hot to hold him.

"Maybe the maid had warmed it too much?" said the curious gentleman, inquiringly.

"I rather think the contrary," replied the Irishman. "But, be that as it may, it grew too hot for my grandfather."

"Faith, there's no standing this any longer," says he. So he jumped out of bed, and went strolling about the house.

"What for?" said the inquisitive gentleman.

"Why, to cool himself, to be sure—or perhaps to find a more comfortable bed—or perhaps— But no matter what he went for—he never mentioned—and there's no use in taking up our time in conjecturing."

Well, my grandfather had been for some time absent from his room, and was returning, perfectly cool, when just as he reached the door, he heard a strange noise within. He paused and listened. It seemed as if some one were trying to hum a tune in defiance of the asthma. He recollected the report of the room being haunted; but he was no believer in ghosts, so he pushed the door gently open and peeped in.

Egad, gentlemen, there was a gambol carrying on within enough to have astonished St. Anthony himself. By the light of the fire he saw a pale weazen-faced fellow, in a long flannel gown and a tall white night-cap with a tassel to it, who sat by the fire with a bellows under his arm by way of bagpipe, from which he forced the asthmatical music that had bothered my grandfather. As he played, too, he kept twitching about with a thousand queer contortions, nodding his head, and bobbing about his tasselled night-cap.

My grandfather thought this very odd and mighty presumptuous, and was about to demand what business he had to play his wind-instrument in another gentleman's quarters, when a new cause of astonishment met his eye. From the opposite side of the room a long-backed, bandy-legged chair, covered with leather, and studded all over in a coxcombical fashion with little brass nails, got suddenly into motion, thrust out first a claw-foot, then a crooked arm, and at length, making a leg, slided gracefully up to an easy-chair of tarnished brocade, with a hole in its bottom, and led it gallantly out in a ghostly minuet about the floor.

The musician now played fiercer and fiercer, and bobbed his head and his night-cap about like mad. By degrees the dancing mania seemed to seize upon all the other pieces of furniture. The antique, long-bodied chairs paired off in couples and led down a country-dance; a three-legged stool danced a hornpipe, though horribly puzzled by its supernumerary limb; while the amorous tongs seized the shovel round the waist, and whirled it about the room in a German waltz. In short, all the movables got in motion; pirouetting hands across, right and left, like so many devils; all except a great clothes-press, which kept courtesying and courtesying in a corner, like a dowager, in exquisite time to the music; being rather too corpulent to dance, or perhaps at a loss for a partner.

My grandfather concluded the latter to be the reason; so being, like a true Irishman, devoted to the sex, and at all times ready for a frolic, he bounced into the room, called to the musician to strike up Paddy O'Rafferty, capered up to the clothes-press, and seized upon the two handles to lead her out: ——when-whirr! the whole revel was at an end. The chairs, tables, tongs and shovel, slunk in an instant as quietly into their places as if nothing had happened, and the musician vanished up the chimney, leaving the bellows behind him in his hurry. My grandfather found himself seated in the middle of the floor with the clothes-press sprawling before him, and the two handles jerked off, and in his hands.

"Then, after all, this was a mere dream," said the inquisitive gentlemen.

"The divil a bit of a dream!" replied the Irishman. "There never was a truer fact in this world. Faith, I should have liked to see any man tell my grandfather it was a dream."

Well, gentlemen, as the clothes-press was a mighty heavy body, and my grandfather likewise, particularly in rear, you may easily suppose that two such heavy bodies coming to the ground would make a bit of a noise. Faith, the old mansion shook as though it had mistaken it for an earthquake. The whole garrison was alarmed. The landlord, who slept below, hurried up with a candle to inquire the cause, but with all his haste his daughter had arrived at the scene of uproar before him. The landlord was followed by the landlady, who was followed by the bouncing bar-maid, who was followed by the simpering chambermaids, all holding together, as well as they could, such garments as they first laid hands on; but all in a terrible hurry to see what the deuce was to pay in the chamber of the bold dragoon.

My grandfather related the marvellous scene he had witnessed, and the broken handles of the prostrate clothes-press bore testimony to the fact. There was no contesting such evidence; particularly with a lad of my grandfather's complexion, who seemed able to make good every word either with sword or shillelah. So the landlord scratched his head and looked silly, as he was apt to do when puzzled. The landlady scratched—no, she did not scratch her head, but she knit her brow, and did not seem half pleased with the explanation. But the landlady's daughter corroborated it by recollecting that the last person who had dwelt in that chamber was a famous juggler who died of St. Vitus's dance, and had no doubt infected all the furniture.

This set all things to rights, particularly when the chambermaids declared that they had all witnessed strange carryings on in that room; and as they declared this "upon their honors," there could not remain a doubt upon this subject.

"And did your grandfather go to bed again in that room?" said the inquisitive gentleman.

"That's more than I can tell. Where he passed the rest of the night was a secret he never disclosed. In fact, though he had seen much service, he was but indifferently acquainted with geography, and apt to make blunders in his travels about inns at night, which it would have puzzled him sadly to account for in the morning."

"Was he ever apt to walk in his sleep?" said the knowing old gentleman.

"Never that I heard of."

There was a little pause after this rigmarole Irish romance, when the old gentleman with the haunted head observed, that the stories hitherto related had rather a burlesque tendency. "I recollect an adventure however," added he, "which I heard of during a residence in Paris, for the truth of which I can undertake to vouch, and which is of a very grave and singular nature."

## The Adventure of My Aunt

By Washington Irving

My aunt was a lady of large frame, strong mind, and great resolution: she was what might be termed a very manly woman. My uncle was a thin, puny little man, very meek and acquiescent, and no match for my aunt. It was observed that he dwindled and dwindled gradually away, from the day of his marriage. His wife's powerful mind was too much for him; it wore him out. My aunt, however, took all possible care of him: had half the doctors in town to prescribe for him; made him take all their prescriptions, and dosed him with physic enough to cure a whole hospital. All was in vain. My uncle grew worse and worse the more dosing and nursing he underwent, until in the end he added another to the long list of matrimonial victims who have been killed with kindness.

"And was it his ghost that appeared to her?" asked the inquisitive gentleman, who had questioned the former story-teller.

"You shall hear," replied the narrator.—My aunt took on mightily for the death of her poor dear husband. Perhaps she felt some compunction at having given him so much physic, and nursed him into the grave. At any rate, she did all that a widow could do to honor his memory. She spared no expense in either the quantity or quality of her mourning weeds; wore a miniature of him about her neck as large as a little sun-dial, and had a full-length portrait of him always hanging in her bed-chamber. All the world extolled her conduct to the skies; and it was determined that a woman who behaved so well to the memory of one husband deserved soon to get another.

It was not long after this that she went to take up her residence in an old country-seat in Derbyshire, which had long been in the care of merely a steward and housekeeper. She took most of her servants with her, intending to make it her principal abode. The house stood in a lonely wild part of the country, among the gray Derbyshire hills, with a murderer hanging in chains on a bleak height in full view.

The servants from town were half frightened out of their wits at the idea of living in such a dismal, pagan-looking place; especially when they got together in the servants' hall in the evening, and compared notes on all the hobgoblin stories picked up in the course of the day. They were afraid to venture alone about the gloomy, black-looking chambers. My lady's maid, who was troubled with nerves, declared she could never sleep alone in such a "gashly rummaging old building"; and the footman, who was a kind-hearted young fellow, did all in his power to cheer her up.

My aunt was struck with the lonely appearance of the house. Before going to bed, therefore, she examined well the fastnesses of the doors and windows; locked up the plate with her own hands, and carried the keys, together with a little box of money and jewels, to her own room; for she was a notable woman, and always saw to all things herself. Having put the keys under her pillow, and dismissed her maid, she sat by her toilet arranging her hair; for being, in spite of her grief for my uncle, rather a buxom widow, she was somewhat particular about her person. She sat for a little while looking at her face in the glass, first on one side, then on the other, as ladies are apt to do when they would ascertain whether they have been in good looks; for a roistering country squire of the neighborhood, with whom she had flirted when a girl, had called that day to welcome her to the country.

All of a sudden she thought she heard something move behind her. She looked hastily round, but there was nothing to be seen. Nothing but the grimly painted portrait of her poor dear man, hanging against the wall.

She gave a heavy sigh to his memory, as she was accustomed to do whenever she spoke of him in company, and then went on adjusting her night-dress, and thinking of the squire. Her sigh was reechoed, or answered by a long-drawn breath. She looked round again, but no one was to be seen. She ascribed these sounds to the wind oozing through the ratholes of the old mansion, and proceeded leisurely to put her hair in papers, when, all at once, she thought she perceived one of the eyes of the portrait move.

"The back of her head being towards it!" said the story-teller with the ruined head,—"good!"

"Yes, sir!" replied dryly the narrator, "her back being towards the portrait, but her eyes fixed on its reflection in the glass."—Well, as I was saying, she perceived one of the eyes of the portrait move. So strange a circumstance, as you may well suppose, gave her a sudden shock. To assure herself of the fact, she put one hand to her forehead as if rubbing it; peeped through her fingers, and moved the candle with the other hand. The light of the taper gleamed on the eye, and was reflected from it. She was sure it moved. Nay, more, it seemed to give her a wink, as she had sometimes known her husband to do when living! It struck a momentary chill to her heart; for she was a lone woman, and felt herself fearfully situated.

The chill was but transient. My aunt, who was almost as resolute a personage as your uncle, sir, (turning to the old story-teller,) became instantly calm and collected. She went on adjusting her dress. She even hummed an air, and did not make even a single false note. She casually overturned a dressing-box; took a candle and picked up the articles one by one from the floor; pursued a rolling pin-cushion that was making the best of its way under the bed; then opened the door; looked for an instant into the corridor, as if in doubt whether to go; and then walked quietly out.

She hastened down-stairs, ordered the servants to arm themselves with the weapons first at hand, placed herself at their head, and returned almost immediately.

Her hastily levied army presented a formidable force. The steward had a rusty blunder-buss, the coachman a loaded whip, the footman a pair of horse-pistols, the cook a huge chopping-knife, and the butler a bottle in each hand. My aunt led the van with a red-hot poker, and in my opinion she was the most formidable of the party. The waiting-maid, who dreaded to stay alone in the servants' hall, brought up the rear, smelling to a broken bottle of volatile salts, and expressing her terror of the ghostesses. "Ghosts!" said my aunt, resolutely. "I'll singe their whiskers for them!"

They entered the chamber. All was still and undisturbed as when she had left it. They approached the portrait of my uncle.

"Pull down that picture!" cried my aunt. A heavy groan, and a sound like the chattering of teeth, issued from the portrait. The servants shrunk back; the maid uttered a faint shriek, and clung to the footman for support.

"Instantly!" added my aunt, with a stamp of the foot.

The picture was pulled down, and from a recess behind it, in which had formerly stood a clock, they hauled forth a round-shouldered, black-bearded varlet, with a knife as long as my arm, but trembling all over like an aspen-leaf.

"Well, and who was he? No ghost, I suppose," said the inquisitive gentleman.

"A Knight of the Post," replied the narrator, "who had been smitten with the worth of the wealthy widow; or rather a marauding Tarquin, who had stolen into her chamber to violate her purse, and rifle her strong box, when all the house should be asleep. In plain terms," continued he, "the vagabond was a loose idle fellow of the neighborhood, who had once been a servant in the house, and had been employed to assist in arranging it for the reception of its mistress. He confessed that he had contrived this hiding-place for his nefarious purpose, and had borrowed an eye from the portrait by way of a reconnoitring-hole."

"And what did they do with him? —did they hang him?" resumed the questioner.

"Hang him!—how could they?" exclaimed a beetle-browed barrister, with a hawk's nose. "The offence was not capital. No robbery, no assault had been committed. No forcible entry or breaking into the premises——"

"My aunt," said the narrator, "was a woman of spirit, and apt to take the law in her own hands. She had her own notions of cleanliness also. She ordered the fellow to be drawn through the horse-pond, to cleanse away all offences, and then to be well rubbed down with an oaken towel."

"And what became of him afterwards?" said the inquisitive gentleman."

"I do not exactly know. I believe he was sent on a voyage of improvement to Botany Bay."

"And your aunt," said the inquisitive gentleman; "I'll warrant she took care to make her maid sleep in the room with her after that."

"No, sir, she did better; she gave her hand shortly after to the roistering squire; for she used to observe, that it was a dismal thing for a woman to sleep alone in the country."

"She was right," observed the inquisitive gentleman, nodding sagaciously; "but I am sorry they did not hang that fellow!"

It was agreed on all hands that the last narrator had brought his tale to the most satisfactory conclusion, though a country clergyman present regretted that the uncle and aunt, who figured in the different stories, had not been married together; they certainly would have been well matched.

"But I don't see, after all," said the inquisitive gentleman, "that there was any ghost in this last story."

"Oh! If it's ghosts you want, honey," cried the Irish Captain of Dragoons, "if it's ghosts you want, you shall have a whole regiment of them. And since these gentlemen have given the adventures of their uncles and aunts, faith, and I'll even give you a chapter out of my own family-history."

## The Adventure of the German Student

By Washington Irving

On a stormy night, in the tempestuous times of the French revolution, a young German was returning to his lodgings, at a late hour, across the old part of Paris. The lightning gleamed, and the loud claps of thunder rattled through the lofty narrow streets—but I should now tell you something about this young German.

Gottfried Wolfgang was a young man of good family. He had studied for some time at Göttingen, but being of a visionary and enthusiastic character, he had wandered into those wild and speculative doctrines which have so often bewildered German students. His secluded life, his intense application, and the singular nature of his studies, had an effect on both mind and body. His health was impaired; his imagination diseased. He had been indulging in fanciful speculations on spiritual essences, until, like Swedenborg, he had an ideal world of his own around him. He took up a notion, I do not know from what cause, that there was an evil influence hanging over him; an evil genius or spirit seeking to ensnare him and ensure his perdition. Such an idea working on his melancholy temperament, produced the most gloomy effects. He became haggard and desponding. His friends discovered the mental malady preying upon him, and determined that the best cure was a change of scene; he was sent, therefore, to finish his studies amidst the splendors and gayeties of Paris.

Wolfgang arrived at Paris at the breaking out of the revolution. The popular delirium at first caught his enthusiastic mind, and he was captivated by the political and philosophical theories of the day: but the scenes of blood which followed shocked his sensitive nature, disgusted him with society and the world, and made him more than ever a recluse. He shut himself up in a solitary apartment in the *Pays Latin,* the quarter of students. There, in a gloomy street not far from the monastic walls of the Sorbonne, he pursued his favorite speculations. Sometimes he spent hours together in the great libraries of Paris, those catacombs of departed authors, rummaging among their hordes of dusty and obsolete works in quest of food for his unhealthy appetite. He was, in a manner, a literary ghoul, feeding in the charnel-house of decayed literature.

Wolfgang, though solitary and reclusive, was of an ardent temperament, but for a time it operated merely upon his imagination. He was too shy and ignorant of the world to make any advances to the fair, but he was a passionate admirer of female beauty, and in his lonely chamber would often lose himself in reveries on forms and faces which he had seen, and his fancy would deck out images of loveliness far surpassing the reality.

While his mind was in this excited and sublimated state, a dream produced an extraordinary effect upon him. It was of a female face of transcendent beauty. So strong was the impression made, that he dreamt of it again and again. It haunted his thoughts by day, his slumbers by night; in fine, he became passionately enamoured of this shadow of a dream. This lasted so long that it became one of those fixed ideas which haunt the minds of melancholy men, and are at times mistaken for madness.

Such was Gottfried Wolfgang, and such his situation at the time I mentioned. He was returning home late one stormy night, through some of the old and gloomy streets of the *Marais,* the ancient part of Paris. The loud claps of thunder rattled among the high houses of the narrow streets. He came to the Place de Grève, the square where public executions are performed. The lightning quivered about the pinnacles of the ancient Hôtel de Ville, and shed flickering gleams over the open space in front. As Wolfgang was crossing the square, he shrank back with horror at finding himself close by the guillotine. It was the height of the reign of terror, when this dreadful instrument of death stood ever ready, and its scaffold was continually running with the blood of the virtuous and the brave. It had that very day been actively employed in the work of carnage, and there it stood in grim array, amidst a silent and sleeping city, waiting for fresh victims.

Wolfgang's heart sickened within him, and he was turning shuddering from the horrible engine, when he beheld a shadowy form, cowering as it were at the foot of the steps which led up to the scaffold. A succession of vivid flashes of lightning revealed it more distinctly. It was a female figure, dressed in black. She was seated on one of the lower steps of the scaffold, leaning forward, her face hid in her lap; and her long dishevelled tresses hanging to the ground, streaming with the rain which fell in torrents. Wolfgang paused. There was something awful in this solitary monument of woe. The female had the appearance of being above the common order. He knew the times to be full of vicissitude, and that many a fair head, which had once been pillowed on down, now wandered houseless. Perhaps this was some poor mourner whom the dreadful axe had rendered desolate, and who sat here heart-broken on the strand of existence, from which all that was dear to her had been launched into eternity.

He approached, and addressed her in the accents of sympathy. She raised her head and gazed wildly at him. What was his astonishment at beholding, by the bright glare of the lightning, the very face which had haunted him in his dreams. It was pale and disconsolate, but ravishingly beautiful.

Trembling with violent and conflicting emotions, Wolfgang again accosted her. He spoke something of her being exposed at such an hour of the night, and to the fury of such a storm, and offered to conduct her to her friends. She pointed to the guillotine with a gesture of dreadful signification.

"I have no friend on earth!" she said.

"But you have a home," said Wolfgang.

"Yes—in the grave!"

The heart of the student melted at the words.

"If a stranger dare make an offer," said he, "without danger of being misunderstood, I would offer my humble dwelling as a shelter; myself as a devoted friend. I am friendless myself in Paris, and a stranger in the land; but if my life could be of service, it is at your disposal, and should be sacrificed before harm or indignity should come to you."

There was an honest earnestness in the young man's manner that had its effect. His foreign accent, too, was in his favor; it showed him not to be a hackneyed inhabitant of Paris. Indeed, there is an eloquence in true enthusiasm that is not to be doubted. The homeless stranger confided herself implicitly to the protection of the student.

He supported her faltering steps across the Pont Neuf, and by the place where the statue of Henry the Fourth had been overthrown by the populace. The storm had abated, and the thunder rumbled at a distance. All Paris was quiet; that great volcano of human passion slumbered for a while, to gather fresh strength for the next day's eruption. The student conducted his charge through the ancient streets of the *Pays Latin,* and by the dusky walls of the Sorbonne, to the great dingy hotel which he inhabited. The old portress who admitted them stared with surprise at the unusual sight of the melancholy Wolfgang with a female companion.

On entering his apartment, the student, for the first time, blushed at the scantiness and indifference of his dwelling. He had but one chamber—an old-fashioned saloon—heavily carved, and fantastically furnished with the remains of former magnificence, for it was one of those hotels in the quarter of the Luxembourg palace, which had once belonged to nobility. It was lumbered with books and papers, and all the usual apparatus of a student, and his bed stood in a recess at one end.

When lights were brought, and Wolfgang had a better opportunity of contemplating the stranger, he was more than ever intoxicated by her beauty. Her face was pale, but of a dazzling fairness, set off by a profusion of raven hair that hung clustering about it. Her eyes were large and brilliant, with a singular expression approaching almost to wildness. As far as her black dress permitted her shape to be seen, it was of perfect symmetry. Her whole appearance was highly striking, though she was dressed in the simplest style. The only thing approaching to an ornament which she wore, was a broad black band round her neck, clasped by diamonds.

The perplexity now commenced with the student how to dispose of the helpless being thus thrown upon his protection. He thought of abandoning his chamber to her, and seeking shelter for himself elsewhere. Still he was so fascinated by her charms, there seemed to be such a spell upon his thoughts and senses, that he could not tear himself from her presence. Her manner, too, was singular and unaccountable. She spoke no more of the guillotine. Her grief had abated. The attentions of the student had first won her confidence, and then, apparently, her heart. She was evidently an enthusiast like himself, and enthusiasts soon understand each other.

In the infatuation of the moment, Wolfgang avowed his passion for her. He told her the story of his mysterious dream, and how she had possessed his heart before he had even seen her. She was strangely affected by his recital, and acknowledged to have felt an impulse towards him equally unaccountable. It was the time for wild theory and wild actions. Old prejudices and superstitions were done away; everything was under the sway of the "Goddess of Reason." Among other rubbish of the old times, the forms and ceremonies of marriage began to be considered superfluous bonds for honorable minds. Social compacts were the vogue. Wolfgang was too much of a theorist not to be tainted by the liberal doctrines of the day.

"Why should we separate?" said he; "our hearts are united; in the eye of reason and honor we are as one. What need is there of sordid forms to bind high souls together?"

The stranger listened with emotion: she had evidently received illumination at the same school.

"You have no home or family," continued he, "let me be everything to you, or rather let us be everything to one another. If form is necessary, form shall be observed—there is my hand. I pledge myself to you forever."

"Forever?" said the stranger, solemnly.

"Forever!" repeated Wolfgang.

The stranger clasped the hand extended to her: "Then I am yours," murmured she, and sank upon his bosom.

The next morning the student left his bride sleeping, and sallied forth at an early hour to seek more spacious apartments suitable to the change in his situation. When he returned, he found the stranger lying with her head hanging over the bed, and one arm thrown over it. He spoke to her, but received no reply. He advanced to awaken her from her uneasy posture. On taking her hand, it was cold—there was no pulsation—her face was pallid and ghastly. In a word, she was a corpse.

Horrified and frantic, he alarmed the house. A scene of confusion ensued. The police was summoned. As the officer of police entered the room, he started back on beholding the corpse.

"Great heaven!" cried he, "how did this woman come here?"

"Do you know anything about her?" said Wolfgang eagerly.

"Do I?" exclaimed the officer: "she was guillotined yesterday."

He stepped forward; undid the black collar round the neck of the corpse, and the head rolled on the floor!

The student burst into a frenzy. "The fiend! the fiend has gained possession of me!" shrieked he; "I am lost forever."

They tried to soothe him, but in vain. He was possessed with the frightful belief that an evil spirit had reanimated the dead body to ensnare him. He went distracted, and died in a mad-house.

Here the old gentleman with the haunted head finished his narrative.

"And is this really a fact?" said the inquisitive gentleman.

"A fact not to be doubted," replied the other. "I had it from the best authority. The student told it me himself. I saw him in a madhouse in Paris."

## Ants

By Chet Williamson

Ben Piersall first saw them at the bottom of the drive, where the asphalt had been torn away by the combination of the harsh winter and the big tires of the oil delivery truck. They had a substantial hill in progress, six inches across at the center and an inch high.

Ants. Ants he didn't need. The goddamned moles were bad enough. His lawn already had more soft spots than a week-old melon. So he drew back his foot and kicked, making the dirt fly up in a waist-high arc.

That got them. They poured from the hole like a thick black thread, running in panic at the cataclysm that had ripped off the top of their city. Ben chuckled and began to stomp. In a minute the tiny scurrying motions had ended, though a few survivors still ran for cover and a multitude of wounded writhed in the furrows made by Ben's Vibram soles.

He turned and walked smiling toward the house, the mail tucked under his arm. That was fun—but not as much fun as when he was a kid and had dripped candle wax on the ants one at a time. In a few seconds you could peel the dried wax off the sidewalk and put a petrified ant in your pocket. Ben used to take a bunch to school, where they made unheralded appearances in the urinal, Mrs. Donovan's pencil cup, and Sheila Brown's milk.

But time had passed, he'd grown up, gotten married, gotten divorced, gotten tired. Small pleasures were all he could afford now. Alimony and child support allowed little else. A case of beer a week, an occasional movie, a *very* occasional roll with Mindy, the waitress at the Anchor, and whatever else he could find to amuse himself . . . like stomping ants. At least he'd been able to keep the house.

Inside, he opened a Bud and flopped on the sofa with a copy of

*Ms.* Harriet's two-year subscription was still going strong. He frowned at the article titles and picked up *Sports Illustrated* instead.

He had barely opened the magazine when his nose started to itch. He looked down its broad length and noticed a small black dot at the point where his vision crossed. Thinking it might be a misplaced period on the page, he wiggled both his eyes and the magazine, but, instead of disappearing, the dot took a few tentative steps upward on the oily film that coated Ben's proboscis.

"An ant!" he yelled, and smashed himself lustily on the nose. When he examined what stuck to his fingers, he found that it was indeed an ant, or rather crushed bits of ant head, ant thorax, and ant legs. "Ee-yuch," he said, and snapped the debris away.

Halfway through his article on football draft choices his head started to itch, right at the thin patch he called his crown and Harriet had called his bald spot. Whatever the appellation, it itched like a bitch, so he scratched madly and came away with something beneath his nail that was too dark to be dandruff. Too dark and too wiggly.

"Another one? Jesus H!" and he crushed the interloper, flinging its corpse to join its friend in the thick and tangled jungle of ten year old shag carpet. "Where the hell did *he* come from?" mused Ben, looking about for an answer. When he glanced at the left foot he'd so dapperly propped on the coffee table, he found it. His boot was swarming with little black bodies that were quickly disappearing between pant cuff and sock.

"Gaaah!" he shouted as the hairlike legs pattered over the skin of his calf. "Heeheeyahah!" He sat up faster than when the detective Harriet had hired surprised him at the Sunrise Motel, and started to smack his legs together vigorously.

When the tickling had diminished, he examined the source of the problem, unlacing the boot and turning it over. The thick depressions of the Vibram soles still sheltered dozens of the little hangers on. Ben, now smacking his thighs, ran outside, where he smashed the boot against the sidewalk, and kept smashing until nothing remained but a nondescript blob of formic acid.

"That'll show ya, little buggers . . . wow!" he cried, as a survivor fastened its appendage to *Ben's* appendage. Ben danced about frantically, his hand thrust between waistband and belly, until he finally snagged the ant and crushed it. Then, leaving his boots outside, he went into the house, where he immediately shed his clothes, threw them in the washing machine, and ran into the bathroom.

In the shower, he made the water as hot as he could stand it, rubbed and scrubbed his skin raw with Harriet's old loofah, and dug his fingers into his scalp until it tingled on the edge of pain. Then he rinsed thoroughly, turned off the faucet, and stepped into the mat. There, goddammit, that was better. No more ants on him now.

But as he toweled himself dry, he became aware of a slight itching in his hair. He scratched, and a small ant fell out. Then another, and another.

Gasping, he staggered back, his legs bumping against the side of the tub so that he toppled backwards into it, his bare buttocks striking the porcelain with a loud smack. He still had the towel, and now he saw that it was swarming with ants, dozens and dozens of them making an ever changing pattern on the blue cloth. Throwing it from him, he stood up in the tub, naked and trembling. They were entering the bathroom by the hundreds, so thick that they seemed like a living mass of tar rolling toward the edge of the bath.

Ben grabbed the faucet handles and wrenched them on, sending hot water streaming over his body, washing down the drain the few ants that had made it into the tub. Several more dropped over the edge and were swept straight into the plumbing. After that the others stopped, and Ben could read an angry wariness in the multitude of black specks that stood between him and the door.

A minute passed while the water roared down and the room filled with steam. Then a single ant started up the wall, and others followed until a blob of darkness two feet square moved to the ceiling, over and across the room, and stopped directly above the cowering form of Ben Piersall.

Ants lay like a sheet on the floor, clung overhead to the ceiling, flowed in a wave under the crack of the door—hundreds, thousands, *tens* of thousands of ants . . .

"Stop!" Ben Piersall cried, his voice lengthened and curved by his terror and the thunder of the shower. "Please stop! I'm sorry! I'll do whatever you want, whatever . . ." He collapsed sobbing in the bottom of the tub, each hot droplet of water stinging him like a tiny mandible.

The ants watched, and smiled a collective smile.

Later that afternoon, people at the Acme Market started to wonder about Ben Piersall. They wondered why he looked so pale and nervous, they wondered why he bought six cases of pancake syrup, and they wondered, on such a hot summer day, how Ben Piersall could wear a thick, black, shiny scarf wrapped tightly around his neck and still be shivering.

# The Assembly of the Dead

By Chet Williamson

The man was inordinately fat. He brought to mind the more bloated of the corpses Hutchinson had seen in the morgue the day before. But the living man's smile was broader, his skin not as gray. His bow was deeper than Hutchinson thought his girth would allow. The *quayabera* the man wore was huge, and simply embroidered. Beneath its sleeve Hutchinson noticed a gold Seiko watch that crimped the flesh of the wrist.

"Mister Hutchinson?" the man said. His voice was light, and surprisingly gentle. Hutchinson nodded, and the man went on in Spanish. "May I speak with you for a moment? In private?"

Hutchinson turned to the young man from the embassy and to the younger, uniformed soldier, and motioned them ahead.

"There is something, someone you seek here," the man said to Hutchinson when they were alone.

"Yes."

"He is a relative?"

"No. The relative of a . . ." Hutchinson used the English word. ". . . a constituent."

"Please?"

"Someone in my district," he explained, and the man nodded.

"Locke," the man said.

"Thomas Locke. Yes."

"You know that he is dead."

"I had heard that."

"You wish his body?"

"His family does."

"I can get Mister Locke's body for you."

Hutchinson looked at the man for a moment before speaking again. "Are you certain?"

"Please?"

"That it's him."

The man reached into a pocket and pulled out a small parcel wrapped in brown paper and twine. It was the size of a thick paperback book. "Take this. You will see. Then come and meet me." The man gave Hutchinson the directions, and told him how much money to bring. "Come alone," the man said.

"Alone?"

"You will not be harmed."

The man turned and walked away. Hutchinson rejoined the young diplomat and the soldier, and went back to the hotel. Together, he and the diplomat went to his room, where Hutchinson unwrapped the small package. Inside was a plastic bag which contained a bloodless, nearly white piece of a human hand, the little and ring fingers still attached. The diplomat turned ashen. Hutchinson's face did not change.

From his briefcase, Hutchinson drew a sheet of shiny paper divided into ten squares. In the center of each was a single fingerprint. He manipulated the piece of hand in the plastic bag until the two fingertips were outside, past the zip-loc seal. Hutchinson lifted the hand close to his eyes, and the young diplomat looked away.

"They look the same," Hutchinson said at last.

"They'd be . . . a mirror image," the diplomat said.

"Yes. Even so . . . I don't have a pad, an ink pad. But they look the same. First two fingers left hand."

"We'll send someone with you."

"He told me to come alone."

"They don't expect you to. They just say that."

"No. I have to."

"You can't be alone here." The diplomat paused. "It isn't safe."

"It's not that far," Hutchinson said.

That night, Hutchinson and the diplomat met for dinner in the hotel restaurant. The last time Hutchinson had been there, two years before, the table at which he sat had commanded a view of the street and the courtyard beyond. Now the glass was missing, and plywood planks hid the outside from view.

The diplomat sipped a Tom Collins. "It didn't bother you much, did it?"

"What?"

"The fingers. That hand."

"I've seen as much before," Hutchinson said, draining his scotch and softly crunching a pearl of ice.

"You in Vietnam?"

Hutchinson nodded. "You?"

"No. 4-F."

"Lucky."

"I don't know. It's become a status symbol now to have been there." The diplomat sipped again.

"Maybe so. I guess it got me elected."

The diplomat shook his head. "Christ, these people. I think I've been here too long. All I can see is the sickness. Selling a body . . ."

"Capitalism," Hutchinson said. "That's what we're trying to protect. Seems to be flourishing. That's all that fat man is, a good capitalist."

"Sometimes you don't sound like a congressman."

"Goods and services? Supply and demand? I sound *just* like a congressman. I've studied. Done my homework." There was a grim humor in Hutchinson's smile. "This country," he said, "*is* undoubtedly full of shit."

"But it doesn't bother you."

"No. I told you it doesn't."

The next day Hutchinson drove to where the man had said he would meet him. It was a mile outside of the city, down a side road of dirt to a small village. Hutchinson saw women and naked children, and very few men. Some soldiers with rifles sat beneath trees, scarcely looking up as he drove past.

He stopped, as directed, outside the only brick building in the village. The man he had spoken to the day before came out of the door and walked to the car, his hand extended. Hutchinson took it. It was cool and dry. "You have brought the money?" the man asked.

Hutchinson nodded.

"Drive your car behind the building. There is a shed there. See. Where I go."

The man walked around the side of the brick building, and Hutchinson followed in his car. A one-story shed roofed with corrugated metal stood in the shade of trees at the jungle's edge. Long grass grew around it, nearly hiding it from sight. Hutchinson brought the car as close as he could without miring it in the tall fronds.

"Come," the man said, and passed through the door. Inside, a refrigeration unit throbbed hollowly, and Hutchinson saw cases of canned goods with American labels. He could see his own breath, and the larger, denser clouds from the man who led him. The man stopped by a covered form, and pulled back a canvas tarpaulin.

"This is Thomas Locke," he said.

The body had been dismembered. Hutchinson looked at the left hand first, saw the thumb and two remaining fingers, and felt certain the piece in the hotel's freezer would match. The face, empty and expressionless, resembled his photographs of Thomas Locke.

As for the other pieces—the torso, still joined to the upper right arm and thighs, the right forearm and hand, and the two disjointed feet and lower legs—he was not sure. But then he remembered.

"The left foot," he said, pointing to it.

"Yes?"

"It is not Thomas Locke's."

"It is not?" The man's florid face shone with innocence, and he knelt by the gray-green, broken-toed appendage.

"No. Locke walked with a limp. He had no left foot. It was artificial. He used a cane."

"Ah." The man nodded, eying the foot critically. "Well." Then he looked up and smiled. "Is death not wonderful here? We can make lame men whole. As is Mister Locke before his God." The smile faded. "You will pay me still?"

"Yes."

"That is fine then. For enough money, we can find wings, and make Mister Locke an angel." The man straightened up. "I will have my friends put the body in your car."

"Not the foot," Hutchinson said.

"No," the man agreed. "Not the foot."

After the pieces were wrapped in canvas and placed in Hutchinson's trunk, he paid the man, and they left the shed. In the doorway, Hutchinson paused and looked back to where the foot still lay on the stone floor, flanked by the brown cardboard boxes of canned goods. The soldiers did not look up as Hutchinson drove out of the village, back to the city.

That night in the hotel, Hutchinson prepared for bed. When it came time to remove his socks, he sat on the bed as always, and started to roll the left sock over his ankle. Then he stopped for a moment. When he continued, he moved more slowly, deliberately. He let the sock drop quietly onto the carpet, and looked at his bare foot, gently touching the toes, kneading the sole, as if inspecting a piece of fruit in the marketplace. Then he quickly turned off the light, and finished undressing in the dark.

As the night lengthened, his feet grew large, unwieldy, until they were thick slabs of meat, heavy stones that became no lighter when he flung back the sheet and lay naked, pooled in sweat. When morning came, they were immovable.

He waited, breathing deeply, for them to come back to life. Eventually they did, allowing him to walk unsteadily into the bathroom. By the time he breakfasted, they felt fine, though he did not forget what they had become in the night.

Two days later he was home in the Georgetown apartment he

shared with his wife. She made them an excellent dinner, and afterward they went to bed and made love. Sometime before dawn, she was awakened by the sound of his ragged breathing. "What's wrong?" she whispered, thinking of bad dreams and turning on the light to banish them.

Hutchinson lay on his back, shiny with sweat, his head pressed into the pillow, his jaw jutting ceilingward. "My foot's asleep," he said through clenched teeth.

"Does it hurt?" she asked him, wondering at the tears in his eyes, thinking how out of place they seemed there, then realizing that she had never seen him cry, not even at their daughter's funeral.

## At the Bureau

By Steve Rasnic Tem

I've been the administrator of these offices for twenty-five years now. I wish my employees were as steady. Most of them last only six months or so before they start complaining of boredom. It's next to impossible to find good help. But I've always been content here.

My wife doesn't understand how I could remain with the job this long. She says it's a dead end; I'm at the top of my pay scale, there'll be no further promotions, or increase in responsibilities. I've no place to go but down, she says. Her complaints about my job always lead to complaints about the marriage itself, of course. No children. Few friends. All the magic's gone, she says. But I've always been content.

When I started in the office we handled building permits. After a few years we were switched to peddling, parade, demolition licenses. Two years ago it was dog licenses. Last year they switched us to nothing but fishing permits.

Not too many people fish these days; the streams are too polluted. Last month I sold one permit. None the two months before. They plan to change our function again, I'm told, but a final decision apparently hasn't been made. I really don't care, as long as my offices continue to run smoothly.

A photograph of my wife taken the day of our marriage has sat on my desk the full twenty-five years, watching over me. At least she doesn't visit the office. I'm grateful for that.

Last week they reopened the offices next door. About time, I thought; the space had been vacant for five years. Ours was the last office still occupied in the old City Building. I was afraid maybe we too would be moved.

But I haven't been able as yet to determine just what it is exactly they do next door. They've a small staff, just one lone man at a telephone, I think. No one comes in or out of the office all day, until five, when he goes home.

I feel it's my business to find out what he does over there, and what it is he wants from me. A few days ago I looked up from my newspaper and saw a shadow on the frosted glass of our front door. Imagine my irritation when I rushed out into the hallway only to see his door just closing. I walked over there, intending to knock, and ask him what it was he wanted, but I saw his shadow within the office, bent over his desk. For some reason this stopped me, and I returned to my own office.

The next day the same thing happened. Then the day after that. I then refused to leave my desk. I wouldn't chase a shadow; he would not use me in such a fashion. I soon discovered that when I didn't go to the door, the shadow remained in my frosted glass all day long. He was standing outside my door all day long, every day.

Once there were two shadows. That brought me to my feet immediately. But when I jerked the door open I discovered two city janitors, sent to scrape off the words "Fish Permits" from my sign, "Bureau Of Fish Permits." When I asked them what the sign was to be changed to, they told me they hadn't received those instructions yet. Typical, I thought; nor had I been told.

Of course, after the two janitors had left, the single shadow was back again. It was there until five.

The next morning I walked over to his office door. The lights were out; I was early. I had hoped that the sign painters had labeled his activity for me, but his sign had not yet been filled in. "Bureau Of . . ." There were a few black streaks where the paint had been scraped away years ago, bare fragments of the letters that I couldn't decipher.

I'm not a man given to emotion. But the next day I lost my temper. I saw the shadow before the office door and I exploded. I ordered him away from my door at the top of my voice. When three hours had passed and he still hadn't left, I began to weep. I pleaded with him. But he was still there.

The next day I moaned. I shouted obscenities. But he was always there.

Perhaps my wife is right; I'm not very decisive, I don't like to make waves. But it's been days. He is always there.

Today I discovered the key to another empty office adjacent to mine. It fits a door between the two offices. I can go from my office to this vacant office without being seen from the hallway. At last, I can catch this crazy man in the act.

I sit quietly at my desk, pretending to read the newspaper. He hasn't moved for hours, except to occasionally peer closer at the frosted glass in my door, simulating binoculars with his two hands to his eyes.

I take off my coat and put it on the back of my chair. A strategically placed flower pot will give the impression of my head. I crawl over to the door to the vacant office, open it as quietly as possible, and slip through.

Cobwebs trace the outlines of the furniture. Files are scattered everywhere, some of the papers beginning to mold. The remains of someone's lunch are drying on one desk. I have to wonder at the city's janitorial division.

Unaccountably, I worry over the grocery list my wife gave me, now lying on my desk. I wonder if I should go back after it. Why? It bothers me terribly, the list unattended, unguarded on my desk. But I must push on. I step over a scattered pile of newspapers by the main desk, and reach the doorway leading into the hall.

I leap through the doorway with one mighty swing, prepared to shout the rude man down, in the middle of his act.

The hall is empty.

I am suddenly tired. I walk slowly to the man's office door, the door to the other bureau. I stand waiting.

I can see his shadow through the office door. He sits at his desk, apparently reading a newspaper. I step closer, forming my hands into imaginary binoculars. I press against the glass, right below the phrase, "Bureau Of," lettered in bold, black characters.

He orders me away from his door. He weeps. He pleads. Now he is shouting obscenities.

I've been here for days.

# Babylon: 70 M.

By Donald A. Wollheim

"How many miles to Babylon?
Threescore miles and ten.
Can I get there by candlelight?
Yes, and back again.
If your heels are nimble and light,
You may get there by candlelight."

Sitting in his study, by the open window, Barry Kane heard the woman in the garden of the adjoining house reading *Mother Goose* rhymes to her little girl. He hadn't been paying attention consciously; it had just been a part of the noises of everyday living. His mind had been reflecting on the small urn he had just unpacked. But the word 'Babylon' struck his ear and sparked his attention; the little jingle jerked his mind away from the black, time-encrusted relic before him, and onto the woman's clear enunciation outside.

Barry frowned a bit, still idly turning the stone jug in his hand. Now that was an odd one, he thought. It was vaguely familiar; he supposed that he had run across it himself in his own childhood—and, as children do, simply had listened to it for its rhythm and ignored its meaning. Like so many of Mother Goose's poems it seemed to make not much sense.

He tried to focus his attention again on the urn. He'd only unwrapped it a few minutes ago from its careful packings and sawdust. The expedition had shipped it to him from Baghdad, along with other interesting bits they had dug out of Babylon's ruins. An odd coincidence that that particular bit of nursery nonsense should have been overheard at just this time. He wondered idly if the mother outside would be surprised to know that so close to her was a piece that had just arrived from that very Babylon.

Only "threescore miles and ten" too, Barry thought. Why didn't he up and go then? Although he'd rated as an expert on the ancient civilizations of Asia Minor, actually he'd never been abroad. But now that he knew how close it was, why . . .

He shook his head sharply. What *was* he thinking about, he asked himself angrily. Daydreaming of all things! Babylon was perhaps ten thousand or more miles away from where he sat, not the mere seventy of the rhyme. He couldn't get there in a hundred candlelights, nor many times that number. But for a moment it had seemed so clear, so simple, that he'd actually wondered why he'd never made the trip.

He smiled bleakly to himself. *Wish it really were easy.* But back to work. He took a soft brush from his desk and began to dust the little urn gently. An interesting piece. Probably not valuable, for it looked like a fairly common votary urn, as might have been found in any Babylonian household. Well . . . he amended his thoughts, studying its engraved sides, maybe not just any . . . it didn't quite fit the standard designs.

He turned it around in interest. No, it certainly didn't fit the usual patterns after all. And—why should it? If it had, the expedition wouldn't probably have bothered to air-express it to him. It had to be something they hadn't been able to classify properly, and so had hoped that he would be able to look it up in the more detailed library and references available here at the college.

So then what was it? He turned it over and squirmed uncomfortably in his seat, feeling an irritated mood come over him. He suddenly felt restless. The urn could possibly have held a votary light. It might have been possible to put a little oil in it and fire it; but it didn't quite seem to fit that bill. He bent over, looked sharply at the hollowed-out interior, poked a finger into it and scratched the side with his nail.

He looked at his fingernail with surprise. Wax. There was a slight trace of wax inside the stone urn. Maybe it was a candle-holder . . . but that, he told himself immediately, was silly. They didn't have candles in 2500 B.C.

On the other hand there was no reason to believe that the expedition had just dug it up. They might have found it for sale in some dark shop or dingy market place booth in Baghdad. It might have been used by some Iraqi for years before it found a place in the merchant's stall. There were many instances of ancient objects that had been found on the desert by wandering Arabs, who had used them for their own living purposes when they had seemed useful. Of course nowadays the Arabs were on the lookout for such stuff, to sell to the curious Westerners. But years ago, a century or two meant little in those ancient lands . . . Yes, he supposed it might have served sometime during the past four thousand years as a candlestick.

*Can I get there by candlelight?* Well, by this candlelight, maybe Babylon had indeed been only walking distance. Barry studied the engravings.

They displayed the usual Babylonian bas-relief technique: a bearded god walking stiffly, holding an object in one hand, the other raised to shield it. On the other side of the small cylindrical urn, opposite the walking god, was a giant coiled and winged snake upon whose head rose two curving horns and from whose mouth a flame was emitted. Not unconventional, thought Barry, yet he'd never quite seen the like.

Why—the object the man was carrying was a light. Barry was astonished at this realization. The god was walking with a light in his hand. And there was something else, his expert eyes now noticed: at the back of the god's feet were tiny wings. The artist had meant to convey that the figure was moving rapidly. *If your heels are nimble and light,* Barry's mind interjected idiotically.

"Oh, stuff!" Barry said aloud, surprising himself. What *was* getting into him. He was becoming dreamy. What if the man did have winged heels? That was coincidence; you might find a hundred such examples.

What I need, Barry thought, is a little exercise. I'm getting silly sitting here on a lovely sunny day like this. My mind is falling asleep. He stood up, carefully set the little black urn down, started for the door. At the door he stopped, paused a moment with an odd feeling that there must be something better to do than walking, then finally left his study, closed the door, and went for a walk.

As he passed his neighbor still seated in her yard with her child, Barry nodded politely. She still had the big Mother Goose book open on her lap.

He walked along the sunny streets of the college town with wide strides. He liked to walk, found it good exercise to calm the nerves and steady the thoughts. He began to analyse his irritation.

Somehow that nursery rhyme had got beneath his skin. It had been coincidence of course, but still, it made you think, it did.

Barry had done some work in his own student years on Middle English literature and some of his research had crossed the Mother Goose lore. He knew that many of the apparently pointless verses had once had very definite meanings. Time had erased their references and what now remained were apparently silly jingles.

For instance there was the one about Little Jack Horner, which referred to an actual personage of that name. This person, some sort of minor official in England five hundred years ago, had won himself a "plum" in the royal Christmas honors for doing some sort of secret toadying never made public. The verse had been made up in mockery by his enemies and popularized around the taverns.

Perhaps more obvious was the one about "Hark, hark, the dogs do bark," and the beggars who came to town, having some among them in *silken gowns.* This was essentially the same deal—nobility coming to beg favors of the king at Christmas-time. The people in inns and marketplaces had a way of disguising their digs at their social betters in such a fashion as to avoid *lese majesté.*

And of course the one about Banbury Cross which referred to Lady Godiva's ride.

Barry remembered his amazement at the grim story behind what had seemed one of the silliest—that about Goosey, Goosey Gander and the old man who "would not say his prayers." This was a memorial of murder most black on a day of great evil. Yet, *How many miles to Babylon . . .*

He walked steadily through the streets, thinking about it. He worked the rhyme over, tore it apart, but still he could not fathom its possible original meaning. Finally he turned back and strode home. Once returned, he felt refreshed from the air and the exercise; he sat down again at his desk, renewed his attack on the little black urn.

He worked on it for the remainder of the afternoon, digging out his files, studying pictures of similar vessels and of Babylonian deities and demons. By nightfall he had to admit he'd not gotten near to solution. Nothing fitted the designs exactly, although several seemed superficially close.

He went in to supper, found himself drifting back in thought to the urn and to the silly rhyme alternately. He was annoyed at his failure to get his mind off the side issue. He could ask some of the Lit. faculty about the verse, he thought. Probably they could tell him its origin and meaning in a minute. But not tonight.

After eating, he read the evening paper, turned on the television, watched a comedian for an hour, found him neither funny nor relaxing, turned off the machine, decided to go to bed. He was still oddly irritated, still keyed up by the obstacle to his intellect. After all, with Babylon only threescore miles and ten away . . . "by candlelight" that is, his mind corrected himself as he entered the bedroom.

What silly thoughts! Maybe by morning he'd get that jingle out of his head and be able to look at the relic in a less clouded light. He undid his tie, hesitated. "Maybe I'd better have another glance at that thing," he murmured to himself. He left the bedroom, passed through the dark hall, and entered his study.

He switched the desk light on and took the little urn in his hand, studying the figure. The man was indeed walking somewhere by candlelight. And his heels *were* nimble and light.

Yet even so, Barry's mind slipped in a new twist, what man could walk seventy miles in the time it would take a candle to burn down? Assuming even that it was a large candle, it would last at most four or five hours. That meant walking at least fifteen miles an hour. He had heard somewhere that a man could run at that rate for perhaps a few seconds, but certainly not for hours.

And then of course it wasn't really seventy miles—it was twice that, because you have to get back again, too. And by the same candlelight incidentally.

That definitely put it out of possible class.

Another idea struck Barry. Maybe if he put a candle into the black stone relic and lit it, perhaps it would put some sort of special angle on the engravings and bring out some unnoticed secret details. He'd heard of such things in Egyptian statuary. Anyway, it would be an amusing experiment.

He looked around. There was a candle sticking in an ornamental silver holder on the mantel in the study. He took it down, tried the candle into the hollowed space and found it just fit, tight and neat.

He reached into his pocket for his lighter, flicked it, and lit the candle. Then, to complete the effect, he switched off the desk light.

The candlelight flickered in the room, throwing moving shadows all about. Barry stared at the black urn but it was in darkness from the glow above.

"How many miles to Babylon?" he said under his breath. And quick as a flash his mind answered:

"Three score miles and ten."

Why, of course, he thought, *of course!* It should have been *obvious,* but he asked aloud: "Can I get there by candlelight?"

*Yes, and back again.* It was so certain that he arose from his seat, holding the candle in its black Babylonian container, and, shielding it with his other hand from drafts, strode confidently to the door, out the hall, opened the front door, and walked out into the street.

It was all so incredibly clear now. You could go anywhere you wished if you just saw it the right way. Why, he marveled, there are two ways of getting anywhere—the difficult, ordinary way everyone stuck to—and the *obvious* way.

"If your heels are nimble and light," he said happily to himself, and increased his pace springily. "My heels are nimble and light—I'm a naturally fast walker," he laughingly told himself. His body was tingling with excitement, his mind seemed clearer than ever before. Why hadn't he ever seen how simple it was, how fast one could go places this way, this simple clear *shortcut* way!

"You may get there by candlelight," he laughed aloud, holding the candle high before him, shielding it with outstretched hand and pacing breathlessly through the night. The flickering yellow flame cast little light about. He could see almost nothing in the blackness about him. Somehow he didn't expect to. Not by the shortcut; you won't get scenery. The idea is to get there and I shall. Only seventy miles, Barry thought, and I must be eating that up fast. I'll get there before this candle is half gone.

He walked faster, the light flickering before him, the opaque dark all about. Beneath his feet was the crunch of dirt and then the swishing resiliency of sand.

Suddenly before him loomed a wall. He stopped, almost bumping into it. His breath was fast; he had been walking hard, but he was in perfect spirits. It was a bit cold out here, he thought, not as warm as it should be.

But it gets cold quickly on the desert, he thought. He held the candle up. The wall was old, it was sandswept and time-worn. It was ancient, and it was—he saw from the faint traceries of weather-worn carvings—Babylonian. He looked up feeling suddenly faint and uneasy.

There were stars above him and in their pale glow he saw that he was standing out on a desert, in the midst of a barren desert, broken here and there by bits of projecting stone, partial walls broken by time, bits of excavated basements. A thin cold wind was blowing from somewhere and there was nothing living in sight.

The candle flickered in his hand. His hand suddenly shook as with the ague, as with terror. He stared about. The candle flickered again. Something, something was breathing on it, breathing over his shoulder from behind him.

If the candle went out, he'd never get back. And as the thought struck him, at that very moment the candle—only half burned—flickered again. A nauseating breath blew past his shoulder and the candle went out.

In a split second Barry Kane remembered the other half of the engraving on the black urn, the half turned away from the walking god with the nimble heels and the light, the thing towards which his nimble steps were surely directed. He turned his head quickly, looked over his shoulder.

Now he knew that there was another significance to the injunction, *if your heels are nimble and light.* It didn't just apply to the getting there; it also meant getting back. And he'd dallied too long in Babylon.

For the ancient Babylonian sculptor had been a good artist. The engraving was true to life.

## Berenice

By Edgar Allan Poe

> Dicebant mihi sodales,
> si sepulchrum amicae visitarem,
> curas meas aliquar tulum fore levatas.
>
> —*Ebn Zaiat*

Misery is manifold. The wretchedness of earth is multiform. Overreaching the wide horizon as the rainbow, its hues are as various as the hues of that arch—as distinct too, yet as intimately blended. Overreaching the wide horizon as the rainbow! How is it that from beauty I have derived a type of unloveliness?—from the covenant of peace, a simile of sorrow? But, as in ethics, evil is a consequence of good, so, in fact, out of joy is sorrow born. Either the memory of past bliss is the anguish of to-day, or the agonies which *are,* have their origin in the ecstasies which *might have been.*

My baptismal name is Egaeus; that of my family I will not mention. Yet there are no towers in the land more time-honored than my gloomy, gray, hereditary halls. Our line has been called a race of visionaries; and in many striking particulars—in the character of the family mansion—in the frescos of the chief saloon—in the tapestries of the dormitories—in the chiselling of some buttresses in the armory—but more especially in the gallery of antique paintings—in the fashion of the library chamber—and, lastly, in the very peculiar nature of the library's contents—there is more than sufficient evidence to warrant the belief.

The recollections of my earliest years are connected with that chamber, and with its volumes—of which latter I will say no more. Here died my mother. Herein was I born. But it is mere idleness to say that I had not lived before—that the soul has no previous existence. You deny it? —let us not argue the matter. Convinced myself, I seek not to convince. There is, however, a remembrance of aërial forms—of spiritual and meaning eyes—of sounds, musical yet sad; a remembrance which will not be excluded; a memory like a shadow—vague, variable, indefinite, unsteady; and like a shadow, too, in the impossibility of my getting rid of it while the sunlight of my reason shall exist.

In that chamber was I born. Thus awakening from the long night of what seemed, but was not, nonentity, at once into the very regions of fairy land—into a palace of imagination—into the wild dominions of monastic thought and erudition—it is not singular that I gazed around me with a startled and ardent eye—that I loitered away my boyhood in books, and dissipated my youth in revery; but it *is* singular, that as years rolled away, and the noon of manhood found me still in the mansion of my fathers—it *is* wonderful what a stagnation there fell upon the springs of my life—wonderful how total an inversion took place in the character of my commonest thought. The realities of the world affected me as visions, and as visions only, while the wild ideas of the land of dreams became, in turn, not the material of my every-day existence, but in very deed that existence utterly and solely in itself.

Berenice and I were cousins, and we grew up together in my paternal halls. Yet differently we grew—I, ill of health, and buried in gloom—she, agile, graceful, and overflowing with energy; hers the ramble on the hillside—mine, the studies of the cloister; I, living within my own heart, and addicted, body and soul, to the most intense and painful meditation—she, roaming carelessly through life, with no thought of the shadows in her path, or the silent flight of the raven-winged hours. Berenice!—I call upon her name—Berenice!—and from the gray ruins of memory a thousand tumultuous recollections are startled at the sound! Ah, vividly is her image before me now, as in the early days of her light-heartedness and joy! Oh, gorgeous yet fantastic beauty! Oh, sylph amid the shrubberies of Arnheim! Oh, Naiad among its fountains! And then—then all is mystery and terror, and a tale which should not be told. Disease—a fatal disease, fell like the simoon upon her frame; and even, while I gazed upon her, the spirit of change swept over her, pervading her mind, her habits, and her character, and, in a manner the most subtle and terrible, disturbing even the identity of her person! Alas! the destroyer came and went!—and the victim—where is she? I knew her not—or knew her no longer as Berenice!

Among the numerous train of maladies superinduced by that fatal and primary one which effected a revolution of so horrible a kind in the moral and physical being of my cousin, may be mentioned as the most distressing and obstinate in its nature, a species of epilepsy not unfrequently terminating in *trance* itself—trance very nearly resembling positive dissolution, and from which her manner of recovery was, in most instances, startingly abrupt. In the meantime, my own disease—for I have been told that I should call it by no other appellation—my own disease, then, grew rapidly upon me, and assumed finally a monomaniac character of a novel and extraordinary form—hourly and momently gaining vigor—and at length obtaining over me the most incomprehensible ascendency. This monomania, if I must so term it, consisted in a morbid irritability of those properties of the mind in metaphysical science termed the *attentive*. It is more than probable that I am not understood; but I fear, indeed, that it is in no manner possible to convey to the mind of the merely general reader, an adequate idea of that nervous *intensity of interest* with which, in my case, the powers of meditation (not to speak technically) busied and buried themselves, in the contemplation of even the most ordinary objects of the universe.

To muse for long unwearied hours, with my attention riveted to some frivolous device on the margin or in the typography of a book; to become absorbed, for the better part of a summer's day, in a quaint shadow falling aslant upon the tapestry or upon the floor; to lose myself, for an entire night, in watching the steady flame of a lamp, or the embers of a fire; to dream away whole days over the perfume of a flower; to repeat, monotonously, some common word, until the sound, by dint of frequent repetition, ceased to convey any idea whatever to the mind; to lose all sense of motion or physical existence, by means of absolute bodily quiescence long and obstinately persevered in: such were a few of the most common and least pernicious vagaries induced by a condition of the mental faculties, not, indeed, altogether unparalleled, but certainly bidding defiance to any thing like analysis or explanation.

Yet let me not be misapprehended. The undue, earnest, and morbid attention thus excited by objects in their own nature frivolous, must not be confounded in character with that ruminating propensity common to all mankind, and more especially indulged in by persons of ardent imagination. It was not even, as might be at first supposed, an extreme condition, or exaggeration of such propensity, but primarily and essentially distinct and different. In the one instance, the dreamer, or enthusiast, being interested by an object usually *not* frivolous, imperceptibly loses sight of this object in a wilderness of deductions and suggestions issuing therefrom, until, at the conclusion of a day-dream *often replete with luxury,* he finds the *incitamentum,* or first cause of his musings, entirely vanished and forgotten. In my case, the primary object was *invariably frivolous,* although assuming, through the medium of my distempered vision, a refracted and unreal importance. Few deductions, if any, were made; and those few pertinaciously returning in upon the original object as a centre. The meditations were *never* pleasurable; and at the termination of the revery, the first cause, so far from being out of sight, had attained that supernaturally exaggerated interest which was the prevailing feature of the disease. In a word, the powers of mind more particularly exercised were, with me, as I have said before, the *attentive,* and are, with the daydreamer, the *speculative.*

My books, at this epoch, if they did not actually serve to irritate the disorder, partook, it will be perceived, largely, in their imaginative and inconsequential nature, of the characteristic qualities of the disorder itself. I well remember, among others, the treatise of the noble Italian, Coelius Secundus Curio, "*De Amplitudine Beati Regni Dei*"; St. Austin's great work, "The City of God"; and Tertullian's "*De Carne Christi,*" in which the paradoxical sentence, "*Mortuus est Dei filius; credibile est quia ineptum est; et sepultus resurrexit; certum est quia impossible est,*" occupied my undivided time, for many weeks of laborious and fruitless investigation.

Thus it will appear that, shaken from its balance only by trivial things, my reason bore resemblance to that ocean-crag spoken of by Ptolemy Hephestion, which steadily resisting the attacks of human violence, and the fiercer fury of the waters and the winds, trembled only to the touch of the flower called Asphodel. And although, to a careless thinker, it might appear a matter beyond doubt, that the alteration produced by her unhappy malady, in the *moral* condition of Berenice, would afford me many objects for the exercise of that intense and abnormal meditation whose nature I have been at some trouble in explaining, yet such was not in any degree the case. In the lucid intervals of my infirmity, her calamity, indeed, gave me pain, and, taking deeply to heart that total wreck of her fair and gentle life, I did not fail to ponder, frequently and bitterly, upon the wonder-working means by which so strange a revolution had been so suddenly brought to pass. But these reflections partook not of the idiosyncrasy of my disease, and were such as would have occurred, under similar circumstances, to the ordinary mass of mankind. True to its own character, my disorder revelled in the less important but more startling changes wrought in the *physical* frame of Berenice—in the singular and most appalling distortion of her personal identity.

During the brightest days of her unparalleled beauty, most surely I had never loved her. In the strange anomaly of my existence, feelings with me, *had never been* of the heart, and my passions *always were* of the mind. Through the gray of the early morning—among the trellised shadows of the forest at noonday—and in the silence of my library at night—she had flitted by my eyes, and I had seen her—not as the living and breathing Berenice, but as the Berenice of a dream; not as a being of the earth, earthy, but as the abstraction of such a being; not as a thing to admire, but to analyze; not as an object of love, but as the theme of the most abstruse although desultory speculation. And *now*—now I shuddered in her presence, and grew pale at her approach; yet, bitterly lamenting her fallen and desolate condition, I called to mind that she had loved me long, and, in an evil moment, I spoke to her of marriage.

And at length the period of our nuptials was approaching, when, upon an afternoon in the winter of the year—one of those unseasonably warm, calm, and misty days which are the nurse of the beautiful Halcyon,[1]—I sat (and sat, as I thought, alone) in the inner apartment of the library. But, uplifting my eyes, I saw that Berenice stood before me.

Was it my own excited imagination—or the misty influence of the atmosphere—or the uncertain twilight of the chamber—or the gray draperies which fell around her figure—that caused in it so vacillating and indistinct an outline? I could not tell. She spoke no word; and I—not for worlds could I have uttered a syllable. An icy chill ran through my frame; a sense of insufferable anxiety oppressed me; a consuming curiosity pervaded my soul; and, sinking back upon the chair, I remained for some time breathless and motionless, with my eyes riveted upon her person. Alas! its emaciation was excessive, and not one vestige of the former being lurked in any single line of the contour. My burning glances at length fell upon the face.

The forehead was high, and very pale, and singularly placid; and the once jetty hair fell partially over it, and overshadowed the hollow temples with innumerable ringlets, now of a vivid yellow, and jarring discordantly, in their fantastic character, with the reigning

[1] For as Jove, during the winter season, gives twice seven days of warmth, men have called this clement and temperate time the nurse of the beautiful Halcyon.—*Simonides.*

melancholy of the countenance. The eyes were lifeless, and lustreless, and seemingly pupilless, and I shrank involuntarily from their glassy stare to the contemplation of the thin and shrunken lips. They parted; and in a smile of peculiar meaning, *the teeth* of the changed Berenice disclosed themselves slowly to my view. Would to God that I had never beheld them, or that, having done so, I had died!

The shutting of a door disturbed me, and looking up, I found that my cousin had departed from the chamber. But from the disordered chamber of my brain, had not, alas! departed, and would not be driven away, the white and ghastly *spectrum* of the teeth. Not a speck on their surface—not a shade on their enamel—not an indenture in their edges—but what that brief period of her smile had sufficed to brand in upon my memory. I saw them *now* even more unequivocally than I beheld them *then*. The teeth!—the teeth!—they were here, and there, and everywhere, and visibly and palpably before me; long, narrow, and excessively white, with the pale lips writhing about them, as in the very moment of their first terrible development. Then came the full fury of my *monomania,* and I struggled in vain against its strange and irresistible influence. In the multiplied objects of the external world I had no thoughts but for the teeth. For these I longed with a frenzied desire. All other matters and all different interests became absorbed in their single contemplation. They—they alone were present to the mental eye, and they, in their sole individuality, became the essence of my mental life. I held them in every light. I turned them in every attitude. I surveyed their characteristics. I dwelt upon their peculiarities. I pondered upon their conformation. I mused upon the alteration in their nature. I shuddered as I assigned to them, in imagination, a sensitive and sentient power, and, even when unassisted by the lips, a capability of moral expression. Of Mademoiselle Salle it has been well said: "*Que tous ses pas étaient des sentiments,*" and of Berenice I more seriously believed *que tous ses dents étaient des idées. Des idées!*—ah, here was the idiotic thought that destroyed me! *Des idées!*—ah, *therefore* it was that I coveted them so madly! I felt that their possession could alone ever restore me to peace, in giving me back to reason.

And the evening closed in upon me thus—and then the darkness came, and tarried, and went—and the day again dawned—and the mists of a second night were now gathering around—and still I sat motionless in that solitary room—and still I sat buried in meditation—and still the *phantasma* of the teeth maintained its terrible ascendancy, as, with the most vivid and hideous distinctness, it floated about amid the changing lights and shadows of the chamber. At length there broke in upon my dreams a cry as of horror and dismay; and thereunto, after a pause, succeeded the sound of troubled voices, intermingled with many low moanings of sorrow or of pain. I arose from my seat, and throwing open one of the doors of the library, saw standing out in the antechamber a servant maiden, all in tears, who told me that Berenice was—no more! She had been seized with epilepsy in the early morning, and now, at the closing in of the night, the grave was ready for its tenant, and all the preparations for the burial were completed.

I found myself sitting in the library, and again sitting there alone. It seemed to me that I had newly awakened from a confused and exciting dream. I knew that it was now midnight, and I was well aware, that since the setting of the sun, Berenice had been interred. But of that dreary period which intervened I had no positive, at least no definite, comprehension. Yet its memory was replete with horror—horror more horrible from being vague, and terror more terrible from ambiguity. It was a fearful page in the record of my existence, written all over with dim, and hideous, and unintelligible recollections. I strived to decipher them, but in vain; while ever and anon, like the spirit of a departed sound, the shrill and piercing shriek of a female voice seemed to be ringing in my ears. I had done a deed—what was it? I asked myself the question aloud, and the whispering echoes of the chamber answered me—"*What was it?*"

On the table beside me burned a lamp, and near it lay a little box. It was of no remarkable character, and I had seen it frequently before, for it was the property of the family physician; but how came it *there,* upon my table, and why did I shudder in regarding it? These things were in no manner to be accounted for, and my eyes at length dropped to the open pages of a book, and to a sentence underscored therein. The words were the singular but simple ones of the poet Ebn Zaiat:—"*Dicebant mihi sodales si sepulchrum amicae visitarem, curas meas aliquantulum fore levatas.*" Why, then, as I perused them, did the hairs of my head erect themselves on end, and the blood of my body become congealed within my veins?

There came a light tap at the library door—and, pale as the tenant of a tomb, a menial entered upon tiptoe. His looks were wild with terror, and he spoke to me in a voice tremulous, husky, and very low. What said he? —some broken sentences I heard. He told of a wild cry disturbing the silence of the night—of the gathering together of the household—of a search in the direction of the sound; and then his tones grew thrillingly distinct as he whispered me of a violated grave—of a disfigured body enshrouded, yet still breathing—still palpitating—*still alive!*

He pointed to my garments; they were muddy and clotted with gore. I spoke not, and he took me gently by the hand: it was indented with the impress of human nails. He directed my attention to some object against the wall. I looked at it for some minutes: it was a spade. With a shriek I bounded to the table, and grasped the box that lay upon it. But I could not force it open; and, in my tremor, it slipped from my hands, and fell heavily, and burst into pieces; and from it, with a rattling sound, there rolled out some instruments of dental surgery, intermingled with thirty-two small, white, and ivory-looking substances that were scattered to and fro about the floor.

## Beyond the Wall

By Ambrose Bierce

Many years ago, on my way from Hongkong to New York, I passed a week in San Francisco. A long time had gone by since I had been in that city, during which my ventures in the Orient had prospered beyond my hope; I was rich and could afford to revisit my own country to renew my friendship with such of the companions of my youth as still lived and remembered me with the old affection. Chief of these, I hoped, was Mohun Dampier, an old schoolmate with whom I had held a desultory correspondence which had long ceased, as is the way of correspondence between men. You may have observed that the indisposition to write a merely social letter is in the ratio of the square of the distance between you and your correspondent. It is a law.

I remembered Dampier as a handsome, strong young fellow of scholarly tastes, with an aversion to work and a marked indifference to many of the things that the world cares for, including wealth, of which, however, he had inherited enough to put him beyond the reach of want. In his family, one of the oldest and most aristocratic in the country, it was, I think, a matter of pride that no member of it had ever been in trade nor politics, nor suffered any kind of distinction. Mohun was a trifle sentimental, and had in him a singular element of superstition, which led him to the study of all manner of occult subjects, although his sane mental health safeguarded him against fantastic and perilous faiths. He made daring incursions into the realm of the unreal without renouncing his residence in the partly surveyed and charted region of what we are pleased to call certitude.

The night of my visit to him was stormy. The Californian winter was on, and the incessant rain plashed in the deserted streets, or, lifted by irregular gusts of wind, was hurled against the houses with incredible fury. With no small difficulty my cabman found the right place, away out toward the ocean beach, in a sparsely populated suburb. The dwelling, a rather ugly one, apparently, stood in the center of its grounds, which as nearly as I could make out in the gloom were destitute of either flowers or grass. Three or four trees, writhing and moaning in the torment of the tempest, appeared to be trying to escape from their dismal environment and take the chance of finding a better one out at sea. The house was a two-story brick structure with a tower, a story higher, at one corner. In a window of that was the only visible light. Something in the appearance of the place made me shudder, a performance that may have been assisted by a rill of rain-water down my back as I scuttled to cover in the doorway.

In answer to my note apprising him of my wish to call, Dampier had written, "Don't ring—open the door and come up." I did so. The staircase was dimly lighted by a single gas-jet at the top of the second flight. I managed to reach the landing without disaster and entered by an open door into the lighted square room of the tower. Dampier came forward in gown and slippers to receive me, giving me the greeting that I wished, and if I had held a thought that it might more fitly have been accorded me at the front door the first look at him dispelled any sense of his inhospitality.

He was not the same. Hardly past middle age, he had gone gray and had acquired a pronounced stoop. His figure was thin and angular, his face deeply lined, his complexion dead-white, without a touch of color. His eyes, unnaturally large, glowed with a fire that was almost uncanny.

He seated me, proffered a cigar, and with grave and obvious sincerity assured me of the pleasure that it gave him to meet me. Some unimportant conversation followed, but all the while I was dominated by a melancholy sense of the great change in him. This he must have perceived, for he suddenly said with a bright enough smile, "You are disappointed in me—*non sum qualis eram.*"

I hardly knew what to reply, but managed to say: "Why, really, I don't know: your Latin is about the same."

He brightened again. "No," he said, "being a dead language, it grows in appropriateness. But please have the patience to wait: where I am going there is perhaps a better tongue. Will you care to have a message in it?"

The smile faded as he spoke, and as he concluded he was looking into my eyes with a gravity that distressed me. Yet I would not surrender myself to his mood, nor permit him to see how deeply his prescience of death affected me.

"I fancy that it will be long," I said, "before human speech will cease to serve our need; and then the need, with its possibilities of service, will have passed."

He made no reply, and I too was silent, for the talk had taken a dispiriting turn, yet I knew not how to give it a more agreeable character. Suddenly, in a pause of the storm, when the dead silence was almost startling by contrast with the previous uproar, I heard a gentle tapping, which appeared to come from the wall behind my chair. The sound was such as might have been made by a human hand, not as upon a door by one asking admittance, but rather, I thought, as an agreed signal, an assurance of someone's presence in an adjoining room; most of us, I fancy, have had more experience of such communications than we should care to relate. I glanced at Dampier. If possibly there was something of amusement in the look he did not observe it. He appeared to have forgotten my presence, and was staring at the wall behind me with an expression in his eyes that I am unable to name, although my memory of it is as vivid today as was my sense of it then. The situation was embarrassing; I rose to take my leave. At this he seemed to recover himself.

"Please be seated," he said; "it is nothing—no one is there."

But the tapping was repeated, and with the same gentle, slow insistence as before.

"Pardon me," I said, "it is late. May I call tomorrow?"

He smiled—a little mechanically, I thought. "It is very delicate of you," said he, "but quite needless. Really, this is the only room in the tower, and no one is there. At least——" He left the sentence incomplete, rose, and threw up a window, the only opening in the wall from which the sound seemed to come. "See."

Not clearly knowing what else to do I followed him to the window and looked out. A street-lamp some little distance away gave enough light through the murk of the rain that was again falling in torrents to make it entirely plain that "no one was there." In truth there was nothing but the sheer blank wall of the tower.

Dampier closed the window and signing me to my seat resumed his own.

The incident was not in itself particularly mysterious; any one of a dozen explanations was possible (though none has occurred to me), yet it impressed me strangely, the more, perhaps, from my friend's effort to reassure me, which seemed to dignify it with a certain significance and importance. He had proved that no one was there, but in that fact lay all the interest; and he proffered no explanation. His silence was irritating and made me resentful.

"My good friend," I said, somewhat ironically, I fear, "I am not disposed to question your right to harbor as many spooks as you find agreeable to your taste and consistent with your notions of companionship; that is no business of mine. But being just a plain man of affairs, mostly of this world, I find spooks needless to my peace and comfort. I am going to my hotel, where my fellow-guests are still in the flesh."

It was not a very civil speech, but he manifested no feeling about it. "Kindly remain," he said. "I am grateful for your presence here. What you have heard to-night I believe myself to have heard twice before. Now I *know* it was no illusion. That is much to me—more than you know. Have a fresh cigar and a good stock of patience while I tell you the story."

The rain was now falling more steadily, with a low, monotonous susurration, interrupted at long intervals by the sudden slashing of the boughs of the trees as the wind rose and failed. The night was well advanced, but both sympathy and curiosity held me a willing listener to my friend's monologue, which I did not interrupt by a single word from beginning to end.

"Ten years ago," he said, "I occupied a ground-floor apartment in one of a row of houses, all alike, away at the other end of the town, on what we call Rincon Hill. This had been the best quarter of San Francisco, but had fallen into neglect and decay, partly because the primitive character of its domestic architecture no longer suited the maturing tastes of our wealthy citizens, partly because certain public improvements had made a wreck of it. The row of dwellings in one of which I lived stood a little way back from the street, each having a miniature garden, separated from its neighbors by low iron fences and bisected with mathematical precision by a box-bordered gravel walk from gate to door.

"One morning as I was leaving my lodging I observed a young girl entering the adjoining garden on the left. It was a warm day in

June, and she was lightly gowned in white. From her shoulders hung a broad straw hat profusely decorated with flowers and wonderfully beribboned in the fashion of the time. My attention was not long held by the exquisite simplicity of her costume, for no one could look at her face and think of anything earthly. Do not fear; I shall not profane it by description; it was beautiful exceedingly. All that I had ever seen or dreamed of loveliness was in that matchless living picture by the hand of the Divine Artist. So deeply did it move me that, without a thought of the impropriety of the act, I unconsciously bared my head, as a devout Catholic or well-bred Protestant uncovers before an image of the Blessed Virgin. The maiden showed no displeasure; she merely turned her glorious dark eyes upon me with a look that made me catch my breath, and without other recognition of my act passed into the house. For a moment I stood motionless, hat in hand, painfully conscious of my rudeness, yet so dominated by the emotion inspired by that vision of incomparable beauty that my penitence was less poignant than it should have been. Then I went my way, leaving my heart behind. In the natural course of things I should probably have remained away until nightfall, but by the middle of the afternoon I was back in the little garden, affecting an interest in the few foolish flowers that I had never before observed. My hope was vain; she did not appear.

"To a night of unrest succeeded a day of expectation and disappointment, but on the day after, as I wandered aimlessly about the neighborhood, I met her. Of course I did not repeat my folly of uncovering, nor venture by even so much as too long a look to manifest an interest in her; yet my heart was beating audibly. I trembled and consciously colored as she turned her big black eyes upon me with a look of obvious recognition entirely devoid of boldness or coquetry.

"I will not weary you with particulars; many times afterward I met the maiden, yet never either addressed her or sought to fix her attention. Nor did I take any action toward making her acquaintance. Perhaps my forbearance, requiring so supreme an effort of self-denial, will not be entirely clear to you. That I was heels over head in love is true, but who can overcome his habit of thought, or reconstruct his character?

"I was what some foolish persons are pleased to call, and others, more foolish, are pleased to be called—an aristocrat; and despite her beauty, her charms and graces, the girl was not of my class. I had learned her name—which it is needless to speak—and something of her family. She was an orphan, a dependent niece of the impossible elderly fat woman in whose lodging-house she lived. My income was small and I lacked the talent for marrying; it is perhaps a gift. An alliance with that family would condemn me to its manner of life, part me from my books and studies, and in a social sense reduce me to the ranks. It is easy to deprecate such considerations as these and I have not retained myself for the defense. Let judgment be entered against me, but in strict justice all my ancestors for generations should be made co-defendants and I be permitted to plead in mitigation of punishment the imperious mandate of heredity. To a mésalliance of that kind every globule of my ancestral blood spoke in opposition. In brief, my tastes, habits, instinct, with whatever of reason my love had left me—all fought against it. Moreover, I was an irreclaimable sentimentalist, and found a subtle charm in an impersonal and spiritual relation which acquaintance might vulgarize and marriage would certainly dispel. No woman, I argued, is what this lovely creature seems. Love is a delicious dream; why should I bring about my own awakening?

"The course dictated by all this sense and sentiment was obvious. Honor, pride, prudence, preservation of my ideals—all commanded me to go away, but for that I was too weak. The utmost that I could do by a mighty effort of will was to cease meeting the girl, and that I did. I even avoided the chance encounters of the garden, leaving my lodging only when I knew that she had gone to her music lessons, and returning after nightfall. Yet all the while I was as one in a trance, indulging the most fascinating fancies and ordering my entire intellectual life in accordance with my dream. Ah, my friend, as one whose actions have a traceable relation to reason, you cannot know the fool's paradise in which I lived.

"One evening the devil put it into my head to be an unspeakable idiot. By apparently careless and purposeless questioning I learned from my gossipy landlady that the young woman's bedroom ajoined my own, a party-wall between. Yielding to a sudden and coarse impulse I gently rapped on the wall. There was no response, naturally, but I was in no mood to accept a rebuke. A madness was upon me and I repeated the folly, the offense, but again ineffectually, and I had the decency to desist.

"An hour later, while absorbed in some of my infernal studies, I heard, or thought I heard, my signal answered. Flinging down my books I sprang to the wall and as steadily as my beating heart would permit gave three slow taps upon it. This time the response was distinct, unmistakable: one, two, three—an exact repetition of my signal. That was all I could elicit, but it was enough—too much.

"The next evening, and for many evenings afterward, that folly went on, I always having 'the last word.' During the whole period I was deliriously happy, but with the perversity of my nature I persevered in my resolution not to see her. Then, as I should have expected, I got no further answers. 'She is disgusted,' I said to myself, 'with what she thinks my timidity in making no more definite advances'; and I resolved to seek her and make her acquaintance and —what? I did not know, nor do I now know, what might have come of it. I know only that I passed days and days trying to meet her, and all in vain; she was invisible as well as inaudible. I haunted the streets where we had met, but she did not come. From my window I watched the garden in front of her house, but she passed neither in nor out. I fell into the deepest dejection, believing that she had gone away, yet took no steps to resolve my doubt by inquiry of my landlady, to whom, indeed, I had taken an unconquerable aversion from her having once spoken of the girl with less of reverence than I thought befitting.

"There came a fateful night. Worn out with emotion, irresolution and despondency, I had retired early and fallen into such sleep as was still possible to me. In the middle of the night something—some malign power bent upon the wrecking of my peace forever—caused me to open my eyes and sit up, wide awake and listening intently for I knew not what. Then I thought I heard a faint tapping on the wall—the mere ghost of the familiar signal. In a few moments it was repeated: one, two, three—no louder than before, but addressing a sense alert and strained to receive it. I was about to reply when the Adversary of Peace again intervened in my affairs with a rascally suggestion of retaliation. She had long and cruelly ignored me; now I would ignore her. Incredible fatuity—may God forgive it! All the rest of the night I lay awake, fortifying my obstinacy with shameless justifications and—listening.

"Late the next morning, as I was leaving the house, I met my landlady, entering.

" 'Good morning, Mr. Dampier,' she said. 'Have you heard the news?'

"I replied in words that I had heard no news; in manner, that I did not care to hear any. The manner escaped her observation.

" 'About the sick young lady next door,' she babbled on. 'What! you did not know? Why, she has been ill for weeks. And now——'

"I almost sprang upon her. 'And now,' I cried, 'now what?'

" 'She is dead.'

"That is not the whole story. In the middle of the night, as I learned later, the patient, awakening from a long stupor after a week of delirium, had asked—it was her last utterance—that her bed be moved to the opposite side of the room. Those in attendance had thought the request a vagary of her delirium, but had complied. And there the poor passing soul had exerted its failing will to restore a broken connection—a golden thread of sentiment between its innocence and a monstrous baseness owning a blind, brutal allegiance to the Law of Self.

"What reparation could I make? Are there masses that can be said for the repose of souls that are abroad such nights as this—spirits 'blown about by the viewless winds'—coming in the storm and darkness with signs and portents, hints of memory and presages of doom?

"This is the third visitation. On the first occasion I was too skeptical to do more than verify by natural methods the character of the incident; on the second, I responded to the signal after it had been several times repeated, but without result. Tonight's recurrence completes the 'fatal triad' expounded by Parapelius Necromantius. There is no more to tell."

When Dampier had finished his story I could think of nothing relevant that I cared to say, and to question him would have been a hideous impertinence. I rose and bade him good night in a way to convey to him a sense of my sympathy, which he silently acknowledged by a pressure of the hand. That night, alone with his sorrow and remorse, he passed into the Unknown.

## The Boarded Window

By Ambrose Bierce

In 1830, only a few miles away from what is now the great city of Cincinnati, lay an immense and almost unbroken forest. The whole region was sparsely settled by people of the frontier—restless souls who no sooner had hewn fairly habitable homes out of the wilderness and attained to that degree of prosperity which to-day we should call indigence than, impelled by some mysterious impulse of their nature, they abandoned all and pushed farther westward, to encounter new perils and privations in the effort to regain the meagre comforts which they had voluntarily renounced. Many of them had already forsaken that region for the remoter settlements, but among those remaining was one who had been of those first arriving. He lived alone in a house of logs surrounded on all sides by the great forest, of whose gloom and silence he seemed a part, for no one had ever known him to smile nor speak a needless word. His simple wants were supplied by the sale or barter of skins of wild animals in the river town, for not a thing did he grow upon the land which, if needful, he might have claimed by right of undisturbed possession. There were evidences of "improvement"—a few acres of ground immediately about the house had once been cleared of its trees, the decayed stumps of which were half concealed by the new growth that had been suffered to repair the ravage wrought by the ax. Apparently the man's zeal for agriculture had burned with a failing flame, expiring in penitential ashes.

The little log house, with its chimney of sticks, its roof of warping clapboards weighted with traversing poles and its "chinking" of clay, had a single door and, directly opposite, a window. The latter, however, was boarded up—nobody could remember a time when it was not. And none knew why it was so closed; certainly not because of the occupant's dislike of light and air, for on those rare occasions when a hunter had passed that lonely spot the recluse had commonly been seen sunning himself on his doorstep if heaven had provided sunshine for his need. I fancy there are few persons living to-day who ever knew the secret of that window, but I am one, as you shall see.

The man's name was said to be Murlock. He was apparently seventy years old, actually about fifty. Something besides years had had a hand in his aging. His hair and long, full beard were white, his gray, lustreless eyes sunken, his face singularly seamed with wrinkles which appeared to belong to two intersecting systems. In figure he was tall and spare, with a stoop of the shoulders—a burden bearer. I never saw him; these particulars I learned from my grandfather, from whom also I got the man's story when I was a lad. He had known him when living near by in that early day.

One day Murlock was found in his cabin, dead. It was not a time and place for coroners and newspapers, and I suppose it was agreed that he had died from natural causes or I should have been told, and should remember. I know only that with what was probably a sense of the fitness of things the body was buried near the cabin, alongside the grave of his wife, who had preceded him by so many years that local tradition had retained hardly a hint of her existence. That closes the final chapter of this true story—excepting, indeed, the circumstance that many years afterward, in company with an equally intrepid spirit, I penetrated to the place and ventured near enough to the ruined cabin to throw a stone against it, and ran away to avoid the ghost which every well-informed boy thereabout knew haunted the spot. But there is an earlier chapter —that supplied by my grandfather.

When Murlock built his cabin and began laying sturdily about with his ax to hew out a farm—the rifle, meanwhile, his means of support—he was young, strong and full of hope. In that eastern country whence he came he had married, as was the fashion, a young woman in all ways worthy of his honest devotion, who shared the dangers and privations of his lot with a willing spirit and light heart. There is no known record of her name; of her charms of mind and person tradition is silent and the doubter is at liberty to entertain his doubt; but God forbid that I should share it! Of their affection and happiness there is abundant assurance in every added day of the man's widowed life; for what but the magnetism of a blessed memory could have chained that venturesome spirit to a lot like that?

One day Murlock returned from gunning in a distant part of the forest to find his wife prostrate with fever, and delirious. There was no physician within miles, no neighbor; nor was she in a condition to be left, to summon help. So he set about the task of nursing her back to health, but at the end of the third day she fell into unconsciousness and so passed away, apparently, with never a gleam of returning reason.

From what we know of a nature like his we may venture to sketch in some of the details of the outline picture drawn by my grandfather. When convinced that she was dead, Murlock had sense enough to remember that the dead must be prepared for burial. In performance of this sacred duty he blundered now and again, did certain things incorrectly, and others which he did correctly were done over and over. His occasional failures to accomplish some simple and ordinary act filled him with astonishment, like that of a drunken man who wonders at the suspension of familiar natural laws. He was surprised, too, that he did not weep—surprised and a little ashamed; surely it is unkind not to weep for the dead. "To-morrow," he said aloud, "I shall have to make the coffin and dig the grave; and then I shall miss her, when she is no longer in sight; but now—she is dead, of course, but it is all right—it *must* be all right, somehow. Things cannot be so bad as they seem."

He stood over the body in the fading light, adjusting the hair and putting the finishing touches to the simple toilet, doing all mechanically, with soulless care. And still through his consciousness ran an undersense of conviction that all was right—that he should have her again as before, and everything explained. He had had no experience in grief; his capacity had not been enlarged by use. His heart could not contain it all, nor his imagination rightly conceive it. He did not know he was so hard struck; *that* knowledge would come later, and never go. Grief is an artist of powers as various as the instruments upon which he plays his dirges for the dead, evoking from some the sharpest, shrillest notes, from others the low, grave chords that throb recurrent like the slow beating of a distant drum. Some natures it startles; some it stupefies. To one it comes like the stroke of an arrow, stinging all the sensibilities to a keener life: to another as the blow of a bludgeon, which in crushing benumbs. We may conceive Murlock to have been that way affected, for (and here we are upon surer ground than that of conjecture) no sooner had he finished his pious work than, sinking into a chair by the side of the table upon which the body lay, and noting how white the profile showed in the deepening gloom, he laid his arms upon the table's edge, and dropped his face into them, tearless yet and unutterably weary. At that moment came in through the open window a long, wailing sound like the cry of a lost child in the far deeps of the darkening wood! But the man did not move. Again, and nearer than before, sounded that unearthly cry upon his failing sense. Perhaps it was a wild beast; perhaps it was a dream. For Murlock was asleep.

Some hours later, as it afterward appeared, this unfaithful watcher awoke and lifting his head from his arms intently listened —he knew not why. There in the black darkness by the side of the dead, recalling all without a shock, he strained his eyes to see—he knew not what. His senses were all alert, his breath was suspended, his blood had stilled its tides as if to assist the silence. Who—what had waked him, and where was it?

Suddenly the table shook beneath his arms, and at the same moment he heard, or fancied that he heard, a light, soft step—another—sounds as of bare feet upon the floor!

He was terrified beyond the power to cry out or move. Perforce he waited—waited there in the darkness through seeming centuries of such dread as one may know, yet live to tell. He tried vainly to speak the dead woman's name, vainly to stretch forth his hand across the table to learn if she were there. His throat was powerless, his arms and hands were like lead. Then occurred something most frightful. Some heavy body seemed hurled against the table with an impetus that pushed it against his breast so sharply as nearly to overthrow him, and at the same instant he heard and felt the fall of something upon the floor with so violent a thump that the whole house was shaken by the impact. A scuffling ensued, and a confusion of sounds impossible to describe. Murlock had risen to his feet. Fear had by excess forfeited control of his faculties. He flung his hands upon the table. Nothing was there!

There is a point at which terror may turn to madness; and madness incites to action. With no definite intent, from no motive but the wayward impulse of a madman, Murlock sprang to the wall, with a little groping seized his loaded rifle, and without aim discharged it. By the flash which lit up the room with a vivid illumination, he saw an enormous panther dragging the dead woman toward the window, its teeth fixed in her throat! Then there were darkness blacker than before, and silence; and when he returned to consciousness the sun was high and the wood vocal with songs of birds.

The body lay near the window, where the beast had left it when frightened away by the flash and report of the rifle. The clothing was deranged, the long hair in disorder, the limbs lay anyhow. From the throat, dreadfully lacerated, had issued a pool of blood not yet entirely coagulated. The ribbon with which he had bound the wrists was broken; the hands were tightly clenched. Between the teeth was a fragment of the animal's ear.

## Boxes

By Al Sarrantonio

They went to see the man who collected boxes.

There were two of them, Nathan and Roger, and they went in the afternoon after lunch and armed with flashlights and code kits. They carried Boy Scout Handbooks in their ski coat pockets, and candybars and a railroad flare which Roger had stolen from his father's workbench. Nathan had a whistle ring and two sticks of gum which he hoarded to himself. They went in October, when the sun was orange-red and large as a hanging jack-o'-lantern, and they went in the afternoon when the leaves danced circles at their feet in the curt wind and when the chill of winter death was beginning to settle in on porches and doorsteps. They went with caps on their heads, and the energetic joy of the young bloomed in their cheeks and in their bright angel eyes.

Sidewalks disappeared under their running feet. Nathan leaped at the near-nude branch of a tree, missing it with an ooof. Roger leaped behind him and touched it.

The wind whistled the dark day's passing.

The man who collected boxes lived at the far end of the farthest block. His house—lonely, square, and brooding—suddenly reared up before them, and they skidded to a halt.

Roger looked at Nathan.

This was the dividing line, the place where innocent adventure stopped and the breaking of rules began. Bicycles were not even allowed to be ridden to this spot. Cats shied away. The lawn around the house of the man who collected boxes was immaculately trimmed, green even in this late time of the year. No dog did his business here.

No tree grew here.

Nathan and Roger shied away from the perfect, straight front walk, crept instead across the forbidden lawn. Breathing lightly, they drew up to the side of the house. Gingerbread brown it was, and seemed still wet to the touch it looked so freshly painted. So fresh that Roger found himself reaching to touch it. Nathan slapped at his hand and motioned for him to be quiet. Roger smiled.

Around to the back they crept, stopping underneath the one window. Shivers went through them both.

They raised their heads.

Inside, dimly lit, were the colors of Christmas morning. Red and green, gold and bronze, silver, blue.

Boxes.

There they were. Stacked one upon the other, butted up against walls, on tables and chairs, filling almost every inch of space. Boxes. Enameled and lacquered, painted in watercolor, pastel, and crayon, of wood, of cardboard, of tin and beaten brass, round, square, oval, triangle, large, little, tiny, nested, oblong, flat, high, decorated with stencils or drawings, some plain, some elaborately carved, lidded, unlidded, hinged, fitted, some with brass pulls, some with brass handles, some with moldings of party colors, others green felt-lined, red felt-lined, violet felt-lined, black felt-lined, flat-topped and dome-topped, pyramid-topped, untopped, some with secret compartments, keys, spring locks, one with a tiny steel padlock, with stained-glass insets, clear-glass insets, round peek holes, false tops, one with stubby teak legs, one with the face of a monkey tattooed to its front, one with the head of a camel carved from its lid-pull, one with trick eyes set into its side that seemed to follow you back and forth, one with a knife spring-jacked into its bottom, ready to fly up on opening, one with tactile poison along its ridged lip, one with the face of a happy clown on its cover that changed to a frown when you turned it upside down. A bright pink one with peeling paint. A chocolate-colored one with a crack in one corner. One that had never been opened—and never could be. One that had never been closed. One encrusted with precious gems: rubies, a topaz, sapphires, a thumb-sized diamond, eight-sided.

Nathan and Roger stared, fascinated, into the room and their eyes made a glue bond with these boxes. This was part of the dream of their plan. To see these boxes. To peer into this forbidden window and witness the treasures of the man who collected boxes.

To be among them.

There was no communication between Nathan and Roger. Their souls were united and separate in this decision. They had come to observe and now they must touch. Boy Scout Handbooks were fumbled out of slick ski parka pockets and paged through. How to open a stuck window? As expected, there was nothing on how to open a closed window, especially one that did not belong to the scout doing the opening. Handbooks went back into pockets, and Roger, in a sudden and triumphant flash of thought, produced a small scout knife, attached to his keychain. It pulled open into a one-inch blade. Nathan was doubtful, but Roger overrode his doubt with enthusiasm.

Eyes peered over the window ledge again.

Boxes beckoned.

With care and the special skill of an amateur, Roger slipped the knife blade under the rubber seal of the outside window and tried to pry it out. Nathan suddenly grabbed his arm, stopping him. He pointed. There was a catch on the horizontal window, and it was in the open position.

Roger pocketed his tiny knife and pulled the window to the side.

It opened with a smooth hiss.

Nathan and Roger exchanged glances.

Behind them, the wind whipped up. An early moon had risen, and shone a pale crescent at their backs. The red sun was sinking. The sky had deepened a notch on the blue color scale, toward eventual black. The air bit cold.

Nathan looked at Roger and thought suddenly of home. Of Dad at six o'clock, coming home with a quart of milk, of the paperboy, of television, of the warm couch and the sharp smell of supper and Mom moving about in the next room. Of sister upstairs, playing her records too loud. Of an apple or late-peach pie, cooling by the kitchen window; the window open a crack to cool the pie but keep the chill out. Of his schoolbooks waiting in his room, neatly stacked; the neon lamp waiting to be buzzed on. Dad reading his paper and the smell of coffee. A warm bed with a crazyquilt coverlet Mom made last winter. The ticking sound of heat coming up in the baseboard. Thoughts of Halloween coming and Thanksgiving coming and Christmas coming. Kickball at recess tomorrow. Late-peach pie and cold milk.

Nathan turned to go and Roger took his arm. A look of reproach crossed his face. Somewhere at the other end of the block a dog barked once, twice. Roger held on to Nathan's arm, pulled his gaze back to the window.

To the boxes inside.

The dog barked again but Nathan did not hear it. Roger looked at him and smiled. Nathan made a step with his hands, locking them together and cradling Roger's foot, hoisting him up and over the ledge. There was momentary silence, and then Roger's face appeared on the other side. He was still smiling. He reached down for Nathan, who now locked his hands in Roger's hands and pulled himself up, over, and in.

Nathan righted himself and heard Roger sliding the window shut behind them.

There was almost nowhere to turn or step. There were boxes to the ceiling. Nathan tried to move deeper into the room and nearly knocked over a large box with carved pull knobs and black polka dots painted on its yellow surface. It tilted and began to fall toward a pile of black lacquer boxes which were stacked upon a cardboard storage box with rope handles. Nathan grabbed at it with both hands, noting its smooth and dustless finish, and righted it.

Roger, meanwhile, had found a pathway of sorts through the boxes and was disappearing behind a bronze-cornered trunk. Nathan hurried to catch up to him.

They both found themselves in a hurricane eye in the center of the room, a tiny cleared out spot walled in on all sides by boxes. It was very dim here, since the fading outside light was cut off by a row of bloodred cubes of diminishing size, starting at the bottom at about three feet square and finishing at the top with a pyramid topper of a tiny box a half inch on a side. There was enough light to see, though, and Roger cut off Nathan's attempt to snap on his flashlight, indicating that it would ruin the effect by having their own light infringe on this treasure room.

Nathan demurred, then agreed.

They sat, Indian style, in their spot and reveled in the boxes. Roger leaned over to his right, plucking at an oval tin circled with painted swans. He opened it, gazed into its bright reflective insides, and closed it again. Nathan stared up at the skyline of boxes around them, and thought how wonderful a dream this would make. There were more colors and pleasing shapes here than anywhere on earth —there must be—and he could think of no place that was more dreamlike. Roger brushed his fingers over the mottled surface of an ebony shoebox-sized box and sighed.

Light became a little dimmer.

There was a sound, and Nathan and Roger were startled. They had forgotten that they had broken into the house of the man who collected boxes; they had forgotten altogether that there was a man connected with these boxes. That had been part of the original adventure—to see the boxes, but above all to see the man who collected them. This they would be able to tell their friends—that they had not only seen the boxes but, most of all, that they had seen the man in the perfect house who kept them.

The sound came again.

It was almost a scrabbling sound—like tiny fiddler crabs loose in a wooden boat and ticking all over its inside surface. An ancient and wheezing sound—old age with claws, moving with slow careful grace and constant, inevitable movement towards its destination.

Nathan and Roger were trapped.

The sound was all around them—slow, inexorable—and, though they were on their feet and fingering their Scout Handbooks, there was nowhere to turn. Nathan could not locate the pathway back to the window; indeed, that pathway had seemed to disappear and even the line of bloodred pyramid boxes no longer stood in quite the same line. The tin box Roger had handled was nowhere to be seen.

There was the sound of a box opening.

Somewhere behind them, or in front of them, or to their left or right. A large box with a large and ponderous lid was being opened. There was a heavy, wheezy breathing. A rattling, dry cough. Another wheezing breath, and then a whispered grunt and the closing of the box lid.

A shuffling sound, the click of a light switch, a shuffling sound once more.

The room was suffused with a dull amber glow, like that in a dusty antique shop. The colors of the boxes deepened and softened.

A dry cough and the shuffling continued.

Abruptly, from behind a box with the grey-painted form of an elephant on it, the man who collected boxes appeared.

Nathan and Roger drew back.

The man who collected boxes shuffled toward them and lifted his heavy head. There were wrinkles there, so many that his eyes were almost lost to view behind them. His hair was the color of white dandelion and looked as though it would, like dandelion, fly away if breathed upon. His hands were veined and trembling, his bones gaunt.

He lifted his head, slowly, and looked out at them through the black shadows of his eyes.

He tried to speak.

He lifted his hand, painfully, and opened his mouth, but only a rasp emerged, dry as yellowed newspaper.

His hand lowered itself to his side.

Nathan looked at Roger.

At that moment, the dog at the end of the block barked again, and Nathan heard it, muffled as it was. He looked at Roger. It was six o'clock.

Late-peach pie would be cooling.

Nathan felt Roger's hand on his arm, but he pulled away. In the pale yellow light he found the slight opening between a dull blue nest of boxes and a charcoal-colored case; he slipped sideways between them and made his way through the maze of boxes to the window, sliding it open. It showed a dark rectangle of the outside world.

He climbed quickly out, hesitating on the ledge.

The dog barked once more, sharply.

He jumped down onto perfect grass.

Behind him as he ran, he heard the shuffle of shoes, and then the clean sound of one lid closing, and then another.

## The Candidate

By Henry Slesar

A man's worth can be judged by the calibre of his enemies. Burton Grunzer, encountering the phrase in a pocket-sized biography he had purchased at a newsstand, put the book in his lap and stared reflectively from the murky window of the commuter train. Darkness silvered the glass and gave him nothing to look at but his own image, but it seemed appropriate to his line of thought. How many people were enemies of that face, of the eyes narrowed by a myopic squint denied by vanity the correction of spectacles, of the nose he secretly called patrician, of the mouth that was soft in relaxation and hard when animated by speech or smiles or frowns? How many enemies? Grunzer mused. A few he could name, others he could guess. But it was their calibre that was important. Men like Whitman Hayes, for instance; there was a 24-carat opponent for you. Grunzer smiled, darting a sidelong glance at the seat-sharer beside him, not wanting to be caught indulging in a secret thought. Grunzer was thirty-four; Hayes was twice as old, his white hairs synonymous with experience, an enemy to be proud of. Hayes knew the food business, all right, knew it from every angle: he'd been a wagon jobber for six years, a broker for ten, a food company executive for twenty before the old man had brought him into the organization to sit on his right hand. Pinning Hayes to the mat wasn't easy, and that made Grunzer's small but increasing triumphs all the sweeter. He congratulated himself. He had twisted Hayes's advantages into drawbacks, had made his long years seem tantamount to senility and outlived usefulness; in meetings, he had concentrated his questions on the new supermarket and suburbia phenomena to demonstrate to the old man that times had changed, that the past was dead, that new merchandising tactics were needed, and that only a younger man could supply them. . . .

Suddenly, he was depressed. His enjoyment of remembered victories seemed tasteless. Yes, he'd won a minor battle or two in the company conference room; he'd made Hayes's ruddy face go crimson, and seen the old man's parchment skin wrinkle in a sly grin.

But what had been accomplished? Hayes seemed more self-assured than ever, and the old man more dependent upon his advice. . . .

When he arrived home, later than usual, his wife Jean didn't ask questions. After eight years of a marriage in which, childless, she knew her husband almost too well, she wisely offered nothing more than a quiet greeting, a hot meal, and the day's mail. Grunzer flipped through the bills and circulars, and found an unmarked letter. He slipped it into his hip pocket, reserving it for private perusal, and finished the meal in silence.

After dinner, Jean suggested a movie and he agreed; he had a passion for violent action movies. But first, he locked himself in the bathroom and opened the letter. Its heading was cryptic: *Society for United Action.* The return address was a post office box. It read:

*Dear Mr. Grunzer:*

*Your name has been suggested to us by a mutual acquaintance. Our organization has an unusual mission which cannot be described in this letter, but which you may find of exceeding interest. We would be gratified by a private discussion at your earliest convenience. If I do not hear from you to the contrary in the next few days, I will take the liberty of calling you at your office.*

It was signed, *Carl Tucker, Secretary.* A thin line at the bottom of the page read: *A Nonprofit Organization.*

His first reaction was a defensive one; he suspected an oblique attack on his pocketbook. His second was curiosity: he went to the bedroom and located the telephone directory, but found no organization listed by the letterhead name. *Okay, Mr. Tucker,* he thought wryly, *I'll bite.*

When no call came in the next three days, his curiosity was increased. But when Friday arrived, he forgot the letter's promise in the crush of office affairs. The old man called a meeting with the bakery products division. Grunzer sat opposite Whitman Hayes at the conference table, poised to pounce on fallacies in his statements. He almost had him once, but Eckhardt, the bakery products manager, spoke up in defense of Hayes's views. Eckhardt had only been with the company a year, but he had evidently chosen sides already. Grunzer glared at him, and reserved a place for Eckhardt in the hate chamber of his mind.

At three o'clock, Carl Tucker called.

"Mr. Grunzer?" The voice was friendly, even cheery. "I haven't heard from you, so I assume you don't mind my calling today. Is there a chance we can get together sometime?"

"Well, if you could give me some idea, Mr. Tucker—"

The chuckle was resonant. "We're not a charity organization, Mr. Grunzer, in case you got that notion. Nor do we sell anything. We're more or less a voluntary service group: our membership is over a thousand at present."

"To tell you the truth," Grunzer frowned, "I never heard of you."

"No, you haven't, and that's one of the assets. I think you'll understand when I tell you about us. I can be over at your office in fifteen minutes, unless you want to make it another day."

Grunzer glanced at his calendar. "Okay, Mr. Tucker. Best time for me is right now."

"Fine! I'll be right over."

Tucker was prompt. When he walked into the office, Grunzer's eyes went dismayed at the officious briefcase in the man's right hand. But he felt better when Tucker, a florid man in his early sixties with small, pleasant features, began talking.

"Nice of you to take the time, Mr. Grunzer. And believe me, I'm not here to sell you insurance or razor blades. Couldn't if I tried; I'm a semi-retired broker. However, the subject I want to discuss is rather—intimate, so I'll have to ask you to bear with me on a certain point. May I close the door?"

"Sure," Grunzer said, mystified.

Tucker closed it, hitched his chair closer and said:

"The point is this. What I have to say must remain in the strictest confidence. If you betray that confidence, if you publicize our society in any way, the consequences could be most unpleasant. Is that agreeable?"

Grunzer, frowning, nodded.

"Fine!" The visitor snapped open the briefcase and produced a stapled manuscript. "Now, the society has prepared this little spiel about our basic philosophy, but I'm not going to bore you with it. I'm going to go straight to the heart of our argument. You may not agree with our first principle at all, and I'd like to know that now."

"How do you mean, first principle?"

"Well . . ." Tucker flushed slightly. "Put in the crudest form, Mr. Grunzer, the Society for United Action believes that—*some* people are just not fit to live." He looked up quickly, as if anxious to gauge the immediate reaction. "There, I've said it," he laughed, somewhat in relief. "Some of our members don't believe in my direct approach; they feel the argument has to be broached more discreetly. But frankly, I've gotten excellent results in this rather crude manner. How do you feel about what I've said, Mr. Grunzer?"

"I don't know. Guess I never thought about it much."

"Were you in the war, Mr. Grunzer?"

"Yes. Navy." Grunzer rubbed his jaw. "I suppose I didn't think the Japs were fit to live, back then. I guess maybe there are other cases. I mean, you take capital punishment, I believe in that. Murderers, rape-artists, perverts, hell, I certainly don't think *they're* fit to live."

"Ah," Tucker said. "So you really accept our first principle. It's a question of category, isn't it?"

"I guess you could say that."

"Good. So now I'll try another blunt question. Have you—personally—ever wished someone dead? Oh, I don't mean those casual, fleeting wishes everybody has. I mean a real, deep-down, uncomplicated wish for the death of someone *you* thought was unfit to live. Have you?"

"Sure," Grunzer said frankly. "I guess I have."

"There are times, in your opinion, when the removal of someone from this earth would be beneficial?"

Grunzer smiled. "Hey, what is this? You from Murder, Incorporated or something?"

Tucker grinned back. "Hardly, Mr. Grunzer, hardly. There is absolutely no criminal aspect to our aims or our methods. I'll admit we're a 'secret' society, but we're no Black Hand. You'd be amazed at the quality of our membership; it even includes members of the legal profession. But suppose I tell you how the society came into being?

"It began with two men; I can't reveal their names just now. The year was 1949, and one of these men was a lawyer attached to the district attorney's office. The other man was a state psychiatrist. Both of them were involved in a rather sensational trial, concerning a man accused of a hideous crime against two small boys. In their opinion, the man was unquestionably guilty, but an unusually persuasive defense counsel, and a highly suggestible jury, gave him his freedom. When the shocking verdict was announced, these two, who were personal friends as well as colleagues, were thunderstruck and furious. They felt a great wrong had been committed, and they were helpless to right it. . . .

"But I should explain something about this psychiatrist. For some years, he had made studies in a field which might be called anthropological psychiatry. One of these researches related to the voodoo practice of certain groups, the Haitian in particular. You've probably heard a great deal about voodoo, or Obeah as they call it in Jamaica, but I won't dwell on the subject lest you think we hold tribal rites and stick pins in dolls. . . . But the chief feature of his study was the uncanny *success* of certain strange practices. Naturally, as a scientist, he rejected the supernatural explanation and sought the rational one. And of course, there was only one answer. When the *vodun* priest decreed the punishment or death of a malefactor, it was the malefactor's own convictions concerning the efficacy of the death wish, his own faith in the voodoo power, that eventually made the wish come true. Sometimes, the process was organic—his body reacted psychosomatically to the voodoo curse, and he would sicken and die. Sometimes, he would die by 'accident' —an accident prompted by the secret belief that once cursed, he *must* die. Eerie, isn't it?"

"No doubt," Grunzer said, dry-lipped.

"Anyway, our friend, the psychiatrist, began wondering aloud if *any* of us have advanced so far along the civilized path that we couldn't be subject to this same sort of 'suggested' punishment. He proposed that they experiment on this choice subject, just to see.

"How they did it was simple," he said. "They went to see this man, and they announced their intentions. They told him they were going to *wish him dead.* They explained how and why the wish would become reality, and while he laughed at their proposal, they could see the look of superstitious fear cross his face. They promised him that regularly, every day, they would be wishing for his death, until he could no longer stop the mystic juggernaut that would make the wish come true."

Grunzer shivered suddenly, and clenched his fist. "That's pretty silly," he said softly.

"The man died of a heart attack two months later."

"Of course. I knew you'd say that. But there's such a thing as coincidence."

"Naturally. And our friends, while intrigued, weren't satisfied. *So they tried it again.*"

"Again?"

"Yes, again. I won't recount who the victim was, but I will tell you that this time they enlisted the aid of four associates. This little band of pioneers was the nucleus of the society I represent today."

Grunzer shook his head. "And you mean to tell me there's a *thousand* now?"

"Yes, a thousand and more, all over the country. A society whose one function is to *wish people dead.* At first, membership was purely voluntary, but now we have a system. Each new member of the Society for United Action joins on the basis of submitting one potential victim. Naturally, the society investigates to determine whether the victim is deserving of his fate. If the case is a good one, the *entire* membership then sets about to *wish him dead.* Once the task has been accomplished, naturally, the new member must take part in all future concerted action. That and a small yearly fee, is the price of membership."

Carl Tucker grinned.

"And in case you think I'm not serious, Mr. Grunzer—" He dipped into the briefcase again, this time producing a blue-bound volume of telephone directory thickness. "Here are the facts. To date, two hundred and twenty-nine victims were named by our selection committee. Of those, *one hundred and four* are no longer alive. Coincidence, Mr. Grunzer?

"As for the remaining one hundred and twenty-five—perhaps that indicates that our method is not infallible. We're the first to admit that. But new techniques are being developed all the time. I assure you, Mr. Grunzer, *we will get them all.*"

He flipped through the blue-bound book.

"Our members are listed in this book, Mr. Grunzer. I'm going to give you the option to call one, ten or a hundred of them. Call them and see if I'm not telling the truth."

He flipped the manuscript toward Grunzer's desk. It landed on the blotter with a thud. Grunzer picked it up.

"Well?" Tucker said. "Want to call them?"

"No." He licked his lips. "I'm willing to take your word for it, Mr. Tucker. It's incredible, but I can see how it works. Just *knowing* that a thousand people are wishing you dead is enough to shake hell out of you." His eyes narrowed. "But there's one question. You talked about a 'small' fee—"

"It's fifty dollars, Mr. Grunzer."

"Fifty, huh? Fifty times a thousand, that's pretty good money, isn't it?"

"I assure you, the organization is not motivated by profit. Not the kind you mean. The dues merely cover expenses, committee work, research and the like. Surely you can understand that?"

"I guess so," he grunted.

"Then you find it interesting?"

Grunzer swiveled his chair about to face the window.

*God!* he thought.

*God!* if it *really* worked!

But how could it? If wishes became deeds, he would have slaughtered dozens in his lifetime. Yet, that was different. His wishes were always secret things, hidden where no man could know them. But this method was different, more practical, more terrifying. Yes, he could see how it might work. He could visualize a thousand minds burning with the single wish of death, see the victim sneering in disbelief at first, and then slowly, gradually, surely succumbing to the tightening, constricting chain of fear that it *might* work, that so many deadly thoughts could indeed emit a mystical, malevolent ray that destroyed life.

Suddenly, ghostlike, he saw the ruddy face of Whitman Hayes before him.

He wheeled about and said:

"But the victim has to *know* all this, of course? He has to know the society exists, and has succeeded, and is wishing for *his* death? That's essential, isn't it?"

"Absolutely essential," Tucker said, replacing the manuscripts in his briefcase. "You've touched on the vital point, Mr. Grunzer. The victim must be informed, and that, precisely, is what I have done." He looked at his watch. "Your death wish began at noon today. The society has begun to work. I'm very sorry."

At the doorway, he turned and lifted both hat and briefcase in one departing salute.

"Goodbye, Mr. Grunzer," he said.

## Cemetery Dance

By Richard T. Chizmar

Elliott Fosse, age thirty-three, small-town accountant. Waiting alone. Dead of winter. After midnight. The deserted gravel parking lot outside of Winchester County Cemetery.

Elliott stared out the truck window at the frozen darkness. His thoughts raced back to the handwritten note in his pants pocket. He reached down and squeezed the denim. The pants were new—bought for work not a week ago and still stiff to the touch—but Elliott could feel the reassuring crinkle of paper inside the pocket.

While the woman on the radio droned on about a snow warning for the entire eastern sector of the state, storm winds rumbled outside, buffeting the truck. Elliott's breath escaped in visible puffs and, despite the lack of heat in the truck, he wiped beads of moisture from his face. With the same hand, he snatched a clear pint bottle from the top of the dash and guzzled, tilting it upward long after it ran dry. He tossed the bottle on the seat next to him—where it clinked against two others—and reached for the door handle.

The wind grabbed him, lashing at his exposed face, and immediately the sweat on his cheeks frosted over. He quickly pulled the flashlight from his pocket and straightened his jacket collar, shielding his neck. The night sky was starless, enveloping the cemetery like a huge, black circus tent. His bare hands shook uncontrollably, the flashlight beam fluttering over the hard ground. Somewhere, almost muffled by the whine of the wind, he heard a distant clanking—a dull sound echoing across the grounds. He hesitated, tried to recognize the source, but failed.

*Snow coming soon,* he thought, gazing upward.

He touched a hand to the lopsided weight in his coat pocket and slowly climbed the cracked steps leading to the monument gate. During visiting hours, the gate marked the cemetery's main entrance and was always guarded by a grounds keeper; a short, roundish fellow with a bright red beard. But, at one in the morning, the grounds were long closed and abandoned.

The liquor in Elliott's system was no match for the strength of the storm. His legs ached with every step. His eyes and ears stung from the frigid blasts of wind. He longed to rest, but the contents of the note in his pocket pushed him onward. As he reached the last step, he was greeted by a rusty, fist-sized padlock banging loudly against the twin gates. It sounded like a bell tolling, warning the countryside of some unseen danger.

He rested for a moment, supporting himself against the gate, grimacing from the sudden shock of cold steel. He rubbed his hands together, then walked toward a narrow opening, partly concealed by a clump of scrubby thorn bushes, where the fence stopped just short of connecting with the gate's left corner. Easing his body through the space, Elliott felt the familiar tingle of excitement return. He had been here many times before . . . many times.

But tonight was different.

Creeping among the faded white headstones, Elliott noticed for the first time that their placement looked rather peculiar, as if they'd been dropped from the sky in some predetermined pattern. From above, he ruminated, the grounds must look like an overcrowded housing development.

Glancing at the sky again, thinking: *Big snow on the way, and soon.* He moved slower now, still confident, but careful not to pass the gravestone.

He had been there before, so many times, but he remembered the first time most vividly—fifteen years ago, during the day.

*Everyone had been there. A grim Elliott standing far behind Kassie's parents, hidden among the mourning crowd. Her father, standing proudly, a strong hand on each son's shoulder. The mother, clad in customary black, standing next to him, choking back the tears.*

*Immediately following the service, the crowd had left the cemetery to gather at her parent's home, but Elliott had stayed. He had waited in the upper oak grove, hidden among the trees. When the workers had finished the burial, he had crept down the hill and sat, talking with his love on the fresh grave. And it had been magical, the first time Kassie really talked to him, shared herself with him. He'd felt her inside him that day and known that it had been right—her death, his killing, a blessing.*

High above the cemetery, a rotten tree limp snapped, crashed to the ground below. Elliott's memory of Kassie's funeral vanished. He stood motionless, watching the bare trees shake and sway in the wind, dead branches scraping and rattling against each other. A hazy vision of dancing skeletons and demons surfaced in his mind. *It's called the cemetery dance,* the demons announced, glistening worms squirming from their rotten, toothless mouths. *Come dance with us, Elliott,* they invited, waving long, bony fingers. *Come.* And he wanted to go. They sounded so inviting. *Come dance the cemetery dance . . .*

He shook the thoughts away—*too much liquor, that's all it was*—and walked into a small gully, dragging his feet through the thin blanket of fallen leaves. He recognized the familiar row of stone markers ahead and slowed his pace. Finally, he stopped, steadied the bright beam on the largest slab.

The marker was clean and freshly cared for, the frozen grass around it still neatly trimmed. There were two bundles of cut flowers leaning against it. Elliott recognized the fresh bundle he'd left just yesterday during his lunch break. He crept closer, bending to his knees. Tossing the flashlight aside, he eased next to the white granite stone, touching the deep grooves of the inscription, slowly caressing each letter, stopping at her name.

"Kassie," he whispered, the word swept away with the wind. "I found it, love." He dug deep in his front pocket, pulled out a crumpled scrap of lined white paper. "I couldn't believe you came to me again after all these years. I couldn't believe it . . . but I found the note on my pillow where you left it."

Sudden tears streamed down his face. "I always believed you'd forgive me. I truly did. You know I had to do it . . . it was the only way. You wouldn't even look at me back then," he pleaded. "I *tried* to make you notice me, but you wouldn't . . ."

The cemetery came to life around him, breathing for the dead. The wind gained strength, plastering leaves against tree trunks and headstones. Elliott gripped the paper tightly in his palm, protecting it from the night's constant pull.

"I'm coming now, love," he laughed with nervous relief. "We can be together, forever." He pulled his hand from his coat pocket and looked skyward. *Snow coming, now. Anytime.* A sudden gust of wind sent another branch crashing to the ground where it shattered into hundreds of jagged splinters.

Two gravestones away from it, Elliott collapsed hard to the earth, fingers curled around the pistol's rubber handgrip, locked there now. The single gunshot echoed across the cemetery until the storm swallowed it. Bits of glistening brain tissue sprayed the air, and mixed with the wooden splinters, showering the corpse. His mangled head rocked once, then lolled to the side, spilling more shiny gray matter onto the grassy knoll.

For just one moment, an ivory sliver of moonbeam slipped through the darkness, quickly disappeared. As the crumpled scrap of paper—scrawled in Elliott's own handwriting—was lifted into the wind's possession, the towering trees, once again, found their dancing partners. And it began to snow.

## The Certificate

By Avram Davidson

The winter sunrise was still two hours away when Dr. Roger Freeman came to stand in front of the great door. By good fortune—incredibly good fortune—he had not been questioned in his furtive progress from the dormitory. If he had been stopped, or if his answer had been either disbelieved or judged inadequate, he might have been sent back to the dorm for punishment. The punishment would have been over, of course, in time for him to go to work at ten in the morning, but a man could suffer through several thousand eternities of Hell in those few hours. And no more than a low muffled groaning and a subdued convulsive movement of the body to show what was going on. You were able to sleep through it—if it was happening to someone else.

The great door was set well in from the street, and the cutting edge of the wind was broken by it.

Freeman was grateful for that. It was two years ago that he'd applied for a new overcoat, and the one he still had was ragged even then. Perhaps—if this was not to be his year for escape—in another year he would get the coat. He crowded into a corner and tried not to think of the cold.

After a little while another man joined him, then another, then a woman, than a couple. By sunrise there was a long line. They were all willing to risk it, risk punishment for being out before work, or for being late to work. Some merely wanted clothes. Some wanted permission to visit relatives in another locale. You could wait years for either. Or, you could wait years and not get either. And some, like Freeman, hoped against hope for a chance at escape.

Dr. Freeman stared at the door. The design was as intricate as it was incomprehensible. No doubt it made sense to the Hedderans. If you could understand it you might gain some understanding of the nature of their distant home. If you cared. It was fifty years since they had arrived, and men still knew almost nothing about them.

They were here. They would never go away. That was enough.

The man behind Dr. Freeman collapsed. No one paid any attention to him. After a moment there was a high, brief, humming. The man twitched, opened his eyes. He got to his feet.

And then the door opened.

*"Proceed in the order,"* the voice directed—a thick, flat Hedderan voice; harsh, yet glutinous. No one tried to push ahead, the lesson had been too well learned. Dr. Freeman got on the third escalator, rode down two levels. There had been a time when you rode *up*—but that was before the Hedderans came. They didn't like tall buildings—at least it seemed so. They'd never explained—that, or anything else. What they did not like they simply destroyed.

Dr. Freeman looked behind him as he approached the office. There must have been at least a dozen people behind him. They looked at him wolfishly. So few certificates were granted, and he was first in line. He looked away. He'd stayed awake all night in order to *be* the first. No one had the right to resent him. And the next man in line was young. What did he expect . . . ?

The door opened, the voice said, *"Proceed one at a single time."* Fifty years, and the Hedderans still hadn't mastered the language. They didn't have to, of course. Roger Freeman entered the office, took the application form from the slot in the wall-machine found in every office, sat down at the table. When was the last time he had sat in a chair? No matter.

The form was in Hedderan, of course. The voice said, *"Name."* The voice said, *"Number."*

He wrote it down, Roger Freeman . . . 655-673-60-60-2. Idly he glanced at the cluster of Hedderan characters. If one could take the application form away, with Hedderan questions and English answers, perhaps—if there was time—a key could be found for translating. But it was impossible to take it away. If you spoiled it, you were out. You could apply only once a year. And if you *did* find out how to read their language, what then? Freeman's brother Bob had talked of rebellion—but that was years ago . . . and he didn't like to think what had happened to Bob. And besides, he hadn't *time*—he had to be at work by ten.

From ten in the morning until ten at night (the Hedderans had their own ways of reckoning time) he worked at a machine, pulling hard on levers. Some he had to bend down to reach, some he had to mount steps to reach. Up and down, up and down. He didn't know what the machine did, or even how it worked. And he no longer cared. He no longer cared about anything—except a new overcoat (or, at least, a *newer* one, not worn so thin), and his chances of escape.

*Age. Occupation. Previous Occupation.* Previous to the arrival of the Hedderans, that was. Fifty years ago. He had been a physician. An obsolete skill. Inside of every man nowadays there was a piece of . . . something . . . presumably it communicated with a machine somewhere deep in the Hedderan quarters. If you broke a bone or bled or even if you just fainted (as the young man behind him in line had), you were set right almost in the second. No one was ill for long—even worn-out organs were regenerated. Too few men had been left alive, and the Hedderans needed those who were left too much to let them sicken or die.

At last the long form was filled out. The harsh voice said, *"Now at once to Office Ten, Level Four."*

Dr. Freeman hastily obeyed. When they said 'at once,' they meant just that. The punishment might come like a single whiplash —or it might go on and on. You never knew. Maybe the Hedderans knew. But they never told. The man next behind the outer door scuttled in as Freeman left. The others waited. Not more than three could expect to be processed before it would be time to return to work.

Office Ten, Level Four, asked him the same questions, but in a different order. He was then directed to Office Five, Level Seventeen. Here his two forms were fed into a machine, returned with markings stamped on them in Hedderan.

*"Office Eight, Level Two,"* the voice said. There, he fed his applications into the slot. After a moment they came back—unmarked.

*"Name Roger Freeman. Number 655-673-60-60-2. You have a single time application outstanding. Unpermitted two. You will cancel this one. Or you will cancel that one."*

Frantically he searched his mind. What application did he have outstanding? When was this rule made? The overcoat! If he went ahead with this new application and it was refused, he'd have to wait till next year to reinstate the one for the coat. And then more years of waiting . . . It was cold, the dormitory was ill-heated, he had no blanket. His present coat was very worn. Services for humans were minimal.

But he *had* to proceed with this new application. He was first in line . . .

*"Speak,"* the thick, flat voice directed. *"Answer. Speak. Now."*

Gobbling his words in haste, Freeman said, "I cancel the one outstanding."

*"Insert forms."*

He did. Waited.

*"Proceed to Office Ten, Level Four."*

That was the second place he'd been to. A mistake? No matter, he had to go. Once again he entered. And waited.

A grunting noise caught his eye. He looked up, started, cowered. A Hedderan, his baffle-screen turned off, was gazing at him. The blank, grey, faceted eyes in the huge head, and the body, like a deformed foetus . . . then the baffle-screen went on again. Freeman shuddered. One rarely saw them. It had been years.

A piece of paper slid from the machine. He took it up, waiting for the command to proceed—where? Unless it could be accomplished before ten, there was no chance of escape for him this year. None whatever. He stared dully at the strange characters. The cold indifferent voice said, *"Name Roger Freeman. Number 655-673-60-60-2. Declared surplus. Application for death certificate is granted. Proceed for certificate to Office One, Level Five. At once."*

Tears rolled down Dr. Freeman's cheeks. "At last," he sobbed, joyfully. "At last . . ."

And then he hastily left. He had achieved his escape after all—but only if he got there before ten o'clock.

## Cheapskate

By Gary Raisor

Dad drives too fast when he's upset, and Mom says that one day he's going to cause a terrible accident. Maybe even kill somebody. Dad always says the same thing to her: Elizabeth, why don't you cut off my goddamn balls, sling them over the rear-view mirror, and just be done with it?

Boy! Dad must be pissed right now. Because his face is all purple and everything is really whizzing by.

I guess it's mostly my fault that Dad is angry. You see, yesterday, I turned eleven and I was expecting a special present. But I didn't get what I asked for—they gave me a stupid old camera instead.

Can you believe that?

All I wanted was a pair of roller skates. I mean, it wasn't like I didn't drop enough hints.

Mom tried her best to smooth things over with a talk about how this had been a tough year for Dad, what with the economy being in the toilet and all. So I tried to act thrilled about the camera, but I don't think anybody was fooled.

Everything would've been fine, except they decided to dump me with the sitter. I heard them whispering about going to some big party where Mom worked. That was when I started to get mad. If Dad had enough money to take Mom to a dumb old party, then he had money for my roller skates.

I was upstairs, working on a plan, when I heard the sitter come in. Her name is Mary Ann, and Eddie, who lives down the street, said he heard she was a nympho. But nobody pays much attention to Eddie, cause he's been brain-damaged ever since Monica Pfieffer and two of her friends mooned him at the last school picnic.

Things were so boring I lay on the bed and listened while Mom and Mary Ann talked about the new sofa in the living room. Girls sure do get excited about the goofiest stuff.

Mom thinks Mary Ann is sweet, and Dad likes her, too. But I think Dad likes her because she wears mostly jogging shorts. He watches her like our dog, Skippy, watches my plate.

Only Skippy don't drool as much.

Mom told Mary Ann to make herself comfortable while she ran out to the store and picked up a few things. Mom had been gone about two minutes when Dad came out of his study and started sucking up to Mary Ann, asking her dumb stuff like how she liked college and if she had any new boy friends. They were laughing and giggling, so I thought I'd better turn on the TV before I barfed.

I was coming downstairs for a coke when I noticed how quiet it was in the living room.

So I peeked around the corner . . .

They were both sitting on the new sofa. Only Dad had his hands under Mary Ann's top, and he was breathing harder than the last time he tried to wrestle away Mom's Master Card.

I was gonna sneak back up the stairs, but then I got an idea. It was pure genius. After all, Dad *had* bought me a camera to take pictures . . .

Today, while Mom was gone to bunco, I showed one to Dad. He took one look and his face went all pale and sweaty, like he was about to faint or throw up. He kept asking why I would do such a terrible thing. Over and over. It was real monotonous.

Finally I told him to relax, that if he came across with the new roller skates, Mom wouldn't have to see the pictures. He went kinda crazy when I said that. Started making lots of threats. I gotta admit I was scared, but, after a while, he calmed down. Except for a big vein in his forehead that kept jumping around.

Then he asked, real quiet like, if this was going to be a one-time deal or if there would be other demands.

I said I didn't know. We'd have to see how my next birthday went. He sighed, just like he does when Mom gets the upper hand, and I knew he was gonna give in. All the air oozed out of him and he sort of slumped over.

So we went out and picked up a real nifty pair of roller skates, and Dad said I could even wear them home. But I don't think we're going to make it home. Dad is driving too fast and he's not keeping his eyes on the road. Mostly, he keeps looking back through the rear window and smiling. I guess he's checking to make sure the rope is still tied. He's speeding up again . . . *and I don't think these skates can go much faster!*

## The China Bowl

By E. F. Benson

I had long been on the look-out for one of the small houses at the south end of that delectable oblong called Barrett's Square, but for many months there was never revealed to me that which I so much desired to see—namely, a notice-board advertising that one of these charming little abodes was to be let.

At length, however, in the autumn of the current year, in one of my constant passages through the square, I saw what my eye had so long starved for, and within ten minutes I was in the office of the agent in whose hands the disposal of No. 29 had been placed.

A communicative clerk informed me that the present lessee, Sir Arthur Bassenthwaite, was anxious to get rid of the remainder of his lease as soon as possible, for the house had painful associations for him, owing to the death of his wife, which had taken place there not long before. He was a wealthy man, so I was informed, Lady Bassenthwaite having been a considerable heiress, and was willing to take what is professionally known as a ridiculously low price, in order to get the house off his hand without delay. An order 'to view' was thereupon given me, and a single visit next morning was sufficient to show that this was precisely what I had been looking for.

Why Sir Arthur should be so suddenly anxious to get rid of it, at a price which certainly was extremely moderate, was no concern of mine, provided the drains were in good order, and within a week the necessary business connected with the transference of the lease was arranged. The house was in excellent repair, and less than a month from the time I had first seen the notice-board up, I was ecstatically established there.

I had not been in the house more than a week or two when, one afternoon, I was told that Sir Arthur had called, and would like to see me if I was disengaged. He was shown up, and I found myself in the presence of one of the most charming men I have ever had the good fortune to meet.

The motive of his call, it appeared, was of the politest nature, for he wished to be assured that I found the house comfortable and that it suited me. He intimated that it would be a pleasure to him to see round, and together we went over the whole house, with the exception of one room. This was the front bedroom on the third floor, the largest of the two spare rooms, and at the door, as I grasped the handle, he stopped me.

'You will excuse me,' he said, 'for not coming in here. The room, I may tell you, has the most painful associations for me.'

This was sufficiently explicit; I made no doubt that it was in this room that his wife had died.

It was a lovely October afternoon, and, having made the tour of the house, we went out into the little garden with its tiled walk that lay at the back, and was one of the most attractive features of the place. Low brick walls enclosed it, separating it on each side from my neighbours, and at the bottom from the pedestrian thoroughfare that ran past the back of the row of houses.

Sir Arthur lingered here some little while, lost, I suppose, in regretful memories of the days when perhaps he and his companion planned and executed the decoration of the little plot. Indeed, he hinted as much when, shortly after, he took his leave.

'There is so much here,' he said, 'that is very intimately bound up with me. I thank you a thousand times for letting me see the little garden again.'

And once more, as he turned to go into the house, his eyes looked steadfastly and wistfully down the bright borders.

The regulations about the lighting of houses in London had some little while previously demanded a more drastic dusk, and a night or two later, as I returned home after dinner through the impenetrable obscurity of the streets, I was horrified to find a bright light streaming cheerfully from the upper windows in my house, with no blinds to obscure it.

It came from the front bedroom on the third floor, and, letting myself in, I proceeded hurriedly upstairs to quench this forbidden glow. But when I entered, I found the room in darkness, and, on turning up the lights myself, I saw that the blinds were drawn down, so that even if it had been lit, I could not have seen from outside the illumination which had made me hasten upstairs.

An explanation easily occurred to me: no doubt the light I had seen did not come from my house, but from windows of a house adjoining. I had only given one glance at it, and with this demonstration that I had been mistaken, I gave no further conscious thought to the matter. But subconsciously I felt that I knew that I had made no mistake: I had not in that hurried glance confused the windows of the house next door with my own; it was this room that had been lit.

I had moved into the house, as I have said, with extraordinary expedition, and for the next day or two I was somewhat busily engaged, after my day's work was over, in sorting out and largely destroying accumulations of old books and papers, which I had not had time to go through before my move. Among them I came across an illustrated magazine which I had kept for some forgotten reason, and turning over the pages to try to ascertain why I had preserved it, I suddenly came across a picture of my own back-garden. The title at the top of the page showed me that the article in question was an interview with Lady Bassenthwaite, and her portrait and that of her husband made a frontispiece to it.

The coincidence was a curious one, for here I read about the house which I now occupied, and saw what it had been like in the reign of its late owners. But I did not spend long over it, and added the magazine to the pile of papers destined for destruction. This grew steadily, and when I had finished turning out the cupboard which I had resolved to empty before going to bed, I found it was already an hour or more past midnight.

I had been so engrossed in my work that I had let the fire go out, and myself get hungry, and went into the dining-room, which opened into the little back-garden, to see if the fire still smouldered there, and a biscuit could be found in the cupboard. In both respects I was in luck, and whilst eating and warming myself, I suddenly thought I heard a step on the tiled walk in the garden outside.

I quickly went to the window and drew aside the thick curtain, letting all the light in the room pour out into the garden, and there, beyond doubt, was a man bending over one of the beds. Startled by this illumination, he rose, and without looking round, ran to the end of the little yard and, with surprising agility, vaulted on to the top of the wall and disappeared.

But at the last second, as he sat silhouetted there, I saw his face in the shaded light of a gas-lamp outside, and, to my indescribable astonishment, I recognized Sir Arthur Bassenthwaite. The glimpse was instantaneous, but I was sure I was not mistaken, any more than I had been mistaken about the light which came from the bedroom that looked out on to the square.

But whatever tender associations Sir Arthur had with the garden that had once been his, it was not seemly that he should adopt such means of indulging them. Moreover, where Sir Arthur might so easily come, there, too, might others whose intentions were less concerned with sentiment than with burglary.

In any case, I did not choose that my garden should have such easy access from outside, and next morning I ordered a pretty stiff barrier of iron spikes to be erected along the outer wall. If Sir Arthur wished to muse in the garden, I should be delighted to give him permission, as, indeed, he must have known from the cordiality which I was sure I showed him when he called, but this method of his seemed to me irregular. And I observed next evening, without any regret at all, that my order had been promptly executed. At the same time I felt an invincible curiosity to know for certain if it was merely for the sake of a solitary midnight vigil that he had come.

I was expecting the arrival of my friend Hugh Grainger the next week, to stay a night or two with me, and since the front spare room, which I proposed to give him, had not at present been slept in, I gave orders that a bed should be made up there the next night for me, so that I could test with my own vile body whether a guest would be comfortable there.

This can only be proved by personal experience. Though there may be a table apparently convenient to the head of the bed, though the dressing-table may apparently be properly disposed, though it seem as if the lighting was rightly placed for reading in bed, and for the quenching of it afterwards without disturbance, yet practice and not theory is the only method of settling such questions, and next night accordingly I both dressed for dinner in this front spare room, and went to bed there.

Everything seemed to work smoothly; the room itself had a pleasant and restful air about it, and the bed exceedingly comfortable, I fell asleep almost as soon as I had put out the electric light, which I had found adequate for reading small print. To the best of my knowledge, neither the thought of the last occupant of the room nor of the light that I believed I had seen burning there one night entered my head at all.

I fell asleep, as I say, at once, but instantly that theatre of the brain, on the boards of which dreams are transacted, was brightly illuminated for me, and the curtain went up on one of those appalling nightmare-pieces which we can only vaguely remember afterwards.

There was the sense of flight—clogged, impotent flight from before some hideous spiritual force—the sense of powerlessness to keep away from the terror that gained on me, the strangling desire to scream, and soon the blessed dawning consciousness that it was but with a dream that I wrestled.

I began to know that I was lying in bed, and that my terrors were imaginary, but the trouble was not over yet, for with all my efforts I could not raise my head from the pillow nor open my eyes.

Then, as I drew nearer to the boundaries of waking, I became aware that even when the spell of my dream was altogether broken I should not be free. For through my eyelids, which I knew had closed in a darkened room, there now streamed in a vivid light, and remembering for the first time what I had seen from the square outside, I knew that when I opened them they would look out on to a lit room, peopled with who knew what phantoms of the dead or living.

I lay there for a few moments after I had recovered complete consciousness, with eyes still closed, and felt the trickle of sweat on my forehead. That horror I knew was not wholly due to the self-coined nightmare of my brain; it was the horror of expectancy more than of retrospect. And then curiosity, sheer stark curiosity, to know what was happening on the other side of the curtain of my eyelids prevailed, and I sat and looked.

In the armchair just opposite the foot of my bed sat Lady Bassenthwaite, whose picture I had seen in the illustrated magazine. It simply was she; there could be no doubt whatever about it. She was dressed in a bedgown, and in her hand was a small fluted china bowl with a cover and a saucer. As I looked she took the cover off, and began to feed herself with a spoon. She took some half-dozen mouthfuls, and then replaced the cover again. As she did this she turned full face towards where I lay, looking straight at me, and already the shadow of death was fallen on her. Then she rose feebly, wearily, and took a step towards the bed. As she did this, the light in the room, from whatever source it came, suddenly faded, and I found myself looking out into impenetrable darkness.

My curiosity for the present was more than satisfied, and in a couple of minutes I had transferred myself to the room below.

Hugh Grainger, the ruling passion of whose life is crime and ghosts, arrived next day, and I poured into an eager ear the whole history of the events here narrated.

'Of course, I'll sleep in the room,' he said at the conclusion. 'Put another bed in it, can't you, and sleep there, too. A couple of simultaneous witnesses of the same phenomena are ten times more valuable than one. Or do you funk?' he added as a kind afterthought.

'I funk, but I will,' I said.

'And are you sure it wasn't all part of your dream?' he asked.

'Absolutely positive.'

Hugh's eye glowed with pleasure.

'I funk, too,' he said. 'I funk horribly. But that's part of the allurement. It's so difficult to get frightened nowadays. All but a few things are explained and accounted for. What one fears is the unknown. No one knows yet what ghosts are, or why they appear, or to whom.'

He took a turn up and down the room.

'And what do you make of Sir Arthur creeping into your garden at night?' he asked. 'Is there any possible connection?'

'Not as far as I can see. What connection could there be?'

'It isn't very obvious certainly. I really don't know why I asked. And you liked him?'

'Immensely. But not enough to let him get over my garden wall at midnight,' said I.

Hugh laughed.

'That would certainly imply a considerable degree of confidence and affection,' he said.

I had caused another bed to be moved into Hugh's room, and that night, after he had put out the light, we talked awhile and then relapsed into silence. It was cold, and I watched the fire on the hearth die down from flame into glowing coal, and from glow into clinkering ash, while nothing disturbed the peaceful atmosphere of the quiet room. Then it seemed to me as if something broke in, and instead of lying tranquilly awake, I found a certain horror of expectancy, some note of nightmare begin to hum through my waking consciousness. I heard Hugh toss and turn and turn again, and at length he spoke.

'I say, I'm feeling fairly beastly,' he said, 'and yet there's nothing to see or hear.'

'Same with me,' said I.

'Do you mind if I turn up the light a minute, and have a look round?' he asked.

'Not a bit.'

He fumbled at the switch, the room leapt into light, and he sat up in bed frowning. Everything was quite as usual, the bookcase, the chairs, on one of which he had thrown his clothes; there was nothing that differentiated this room from hundreds of others where the occupants lay quietly sleeping.

'It's queer,' he said, and switched off the light again.

There is nothing harder than to measure time in the dark, but I do not think it was long that I lay there with the sense of nightmare growing momentarily on me before he spoke again in an odd, cracked voice.

'It's coming,' he said.

Almost as soon as he spoke I saw that the thick darkness of the room was sensibly thinning. The blackness was less complete, though I could hardly say that light began to enter. Then by degrees I saw the shape of chairs, the lines of the fireplace, the end of Hugh's bed begin to outline themselves, and as I watched the darkness vanished altogether, as if a lamp had been turned up. And in the chair at the foot of Hugh's bed sat Lady Bassenthwaite, and again putting aside the cover of her dish, she sipped the contents of the bowl, and at the end rose feebly, wearily, as in mortal sickness. She looked at Hugh, and turning, she looked at me, and through the shadow of death that lay over her face, I thought that in her eyes was a demand, or at least a statement of her case. They were not angry, they did not cry for justice, but the calm inexorable gaze of justice that must be done was there . . . Then the light faded and died out.

I heard a rustle from the other bed and the springs creaked.

'Good Lord,' said Hugh, 'where's the light?'

His fingers fumbled and found it, and I saw that he was already out of bed, with streaming forehead and chattering teeth.

'I know now,' he said. 'I half guessed before. Come downstairs.'

Downstairs we went, and he turned up all the passage lights as we passed. He led the way into the dining room, picking up the poker and the shovel as he went by the fireplace, and he threw open the door into the garden. I switched up the light, which threw a bright square of illumination over the garden.

'Where did you see Sir Arthur?' he said. 'Where? Exactly where?'

Still not guessing what he sought, I pointed out to him the spot, and loosening the earth with the poker, he dug into the bed. Once again he plunged the poker down, and as he removed the earth I heard the shovel grate on something hard. And then I guessed.

Already Hugh was at work with his fingers in the earth, and slowly and carefully he drew out fragments of a broken china cover. Then, delving again, he raised from the hole a fluted china bowl. And I knew I had seen it before, once and twice.

We carried this indoors and cleaned the earth from it. All over the bottom of the bowl was a layer of some thick porridge-like substance, and a portion of this I sent next day to a chemist, asking him for his analysis of it. The basis of it proved to be oatmeal, and in it was mixed a considerable quantity of arsenic.

Hugh and I were together in my little sitting room close to the front door, where on the table stood the china bowl with the fragments of its cover and saucer, when this report was brought to us, and we read it together. The afternoon was very dark and we stood close to the window to decipher the minute handwriting, when there passed the figure of Sir Arthur Bassenthwaite. He saw me, waved his hand, and a moment afterwards the front door bell rang.

'Let him come in,' said Hugh. 'Let him see that on the table.'

Next moment my servant entered, and asked if the caller might see me.

'Let him see it,' repeated Hugh. 'The chances are that we shall know if he sees it unexpectedly.'

There was a moment's pause while in the hall, I suppose, Sir Arthur was taking off his coat. Outside, some few doors off, a traction engine, which had passed a minute before, stopped, and began slowly coming backwards again, crunching the newly-laid stones. Sir Arthur entered.

'I ventured to call,' he began, and then his glance fell on the bowl. In one second the very aspect of humanity was stripped from his face. His mouth drooped open, his eyes grew monstrous and protruding, and what had been the pleasant, neat-featured face of a man was a mask of terror, a gargoyle, a nightmare countenance. Even before the door that had been open to admit him was closed, he had turned and gone with a crouching, stumbling run from the room, and I heard him at the latch of the front door.

Whether what followed was design or accident, I shall never know, for from the window I saw him fall forward, almost as if he threw himself there, straight in front of the broad crunching wheels of the traction engine, and before the driver could stop, or even think of stopping, the iron roller had gone over his head.

## The Cobweb

By Saki

The farmhouse kitchen probably stood where it did as a matter of accident or haphazard choice; yet its situation might have been planned by a master-strategist in farmhouse architecture. Dairy and poultry-yard, and herb garden, and all the busy places of the farm seemed to lead by easy access into its wide flagged haven, where there was room for everything and where muddy boots left traces that were easily swept away. And yet, for all that it stood so well in the centre of human bustle, its long, latticed window, with the wide window-seat, built into an embrasure beyond the huge fireplace, looked out on a wild spreading view of hill and heather and wooded combe. The window nook made almost a little room in itself, quite the pleasantest room in the farm as far as situation and capabilities went. Young Mrs. Ladbruk, whose husband had just come into the farm by way of inheritance, cast covetous eyes on this snug corner, and her fingers itched to make it bright and cozy with chintz curtains and bowls of flowers, and a shelf or two of old china. The musty farm parlour, looking out to a prim, cheerless garden imprisoned within high, blank walls, was not a room that lent itself readily either to comfort or decoration.

"When we are more settled I shall work wonders in the way of making the kitchen habitable," said the young woman to her occasional visitors. There was an unspoken wish in those words, a wish which was unconfessed as well as unspoken. Emma Ladbruk was the mistress of the farm; jointly with her husband she might have her say, and to a certain extent her way, in ordering its affairs. But she was not mistress of the kitchen.

On one of the shelves of an old dresser, in company with chipped sauce-boats, pewter jugs, cheese-graters, and paid bills, rested a worn and ragged Bible, on whose front page was the record, in faded ink, of a baptism dated ninety-four years ago. "Martha Crale" was the name written on that yellow page. The yellow, wrinkled old dame who hobbled and muttered about the kitchen, looking like a dead autumn leaf which the winter winds still pushed hither and thither, had once been Martha Crale; for seventy odd years she had been Martha Mountjoy. For longer than any one could remember she had pattered to and fro between oven and wash-house and dairy, and out to chicken-run and garden, grumbling and muttering and scolding, but working unceasingly. Emma Ladbruk, of whose coming she took as little notice as she would of a bee wandering in at a window on a summer's day, used at first to watch her with a kind of frightened curiosity. She was so old and so much a part of the place, it was difficult to think of her exactly as a living thing. Old Shep, the white-nozzled, stiff-limbed collie, waiting for his time to die, seemed almost more human than the withered, dried-up old woman. He had been a riotous, roystering puppy, mad with the joy of life, when she was already a tottering, hobbling dame; now he was just a blind, breathing carcase, nothing more, and she still worked with frail energy, still swept and baked and washed, fetched and carried. If there were something in these wise old dogs that did not perish utterly with death, Emma used to think to herself, what generations of ghost-dogs there must be out on those hills, that Martha had reared and fed and tended and spoken a last good-bye word to in that old kitchen. And what memories she must have of human generations that had passed away in her time. It was difficult for any one, let alone a stranger like Emma, to get her to talk of the days that had been; her shrill, quavering speech was of doors that had been left unfastened, pails that had got mislaid, calves whose feeding-time was overdue, and the various little faults and lapses that chequer a farmhouse routine. Now and again, when election time came round, she would unstore her recollections of the old names round which the fight had waged in the days gone by. There had been a Palmerston, that had been a name down Tiverton way; Tiverton was not a far journey as the crow flies, but to Martha it was almost a foreign country. Later there had been Northcotes and Aclands, and many other newer names that she had forgotten; the names changed, but it was always Libruls and Toories, Yellows and Blues. And they always quarrelled and shouted as to who was right and who was wrong. The one they quarrelled about most was a fine old gentleman with an angry face—she had seen his picture on the walls. She had seen it on the floor too, with a rotten apple squashed over it, for the farm had changed its politics from time to time. Martha had never been on one side or the other; none of "they" had ever done the farm a stroke of good. Such was her sweeping verdict, given with all a peasant's distrust of the outside world.

When the half-frightened curiosity had somewhat faded away, Emma Ladbruk was uncomfortably conscious of another feeling towards the old woman. She was a quaint old tradition, lingering about the place, she was part and parcel of the farm itself, she was something at once pathetic and picturesque—but she was dreadfully in the way. Emma had come to the farm full of plans for little reforms and improvements, in part the result of training in the newest ways and methods, in part the outcome of her own ideas and fancies. Reforms in the kitchen region, if those deaf ears could have been induced to give them even a hearing, would have met with short shrift and scornful rejection, and the kitchen region spread over the zone of dairy and market business and half the work of the household. Emma, with the latest science of dead-poultry dressing at her fingertips, sat by, an unheeded watcher, while old Martha trussed the chickens for the market-stall as she had trussed them for nearly fourscore years—all leg and no breast. And the hundred hints anent effective cleaning and labour-lightening and the things that make for wholesomeness which the young woman was ready to impart or to put into action dropped away into nothingness before that wan, muttering, unheeding presence. Above all, the coveted window corner, that was to be a dainty, cheerful oasis in the gaunt old kitchen, stood now choked and lumbered with a litter of odds and ends that Emma, for all her nominal authority, would not have dared or cared to displace; over them seemed to be spun the protection of something that was like a human cobweb. Decidedly Martha was in the way. It would have been an unworthy meanness to have wished to see the span of that brave old life shortened by a few paltry months, but as the days sped by Emma was conscious that the wish was there, disowned though it might be, lurking at the back of her mind.

She felt the meanness of the wish come over her with a qualm of self-reproach one day when she came into the kitchen and found an unaccustomed state of things in that usually busy quarter. Old Martha was not working. A basket of corn was on the floor by her side, and out in the yard the poultry were beginning to clamour a protest of overdue feeding-time. But Martha sat huddled in a shrunken bunch on the window seat, looking out with her dim old eyes as though she saw something stranger than the autumn landscape.

"Is anything the matter, Martha?" asked the young woman.

"'Tis death, 'tis death a-coming," answered the quavering voice; "I knew 'twere coming. I knew it. 'Tweren't for nothing that old Shep's been howling all morning. An' last night I heard the screech-owl give the death-cry, and there were something white as run across the yard yesterday; 'tweren't a cat nor a stoat, 'twere something. The fowls knew 'twere something; they all drew off to one side. Ay, there's been warnings. I knew it were a-coming."

The young woman's eyes clouded with pity. The old thing sitting there so white and shrunken had once been a merry, noisy child, playing about in lanes and hay-lofts and farmhouse garrets; that had been eighty odd years ago, and now she was just a frail old body cowering under the approaching chill of the death that was coming at last to take her. It was not probable that much could be done for her, but Emma hastened away to get assistance and counsel. Her husband, she knew, was down at a tree-felling some little distance off, but she might find some other intelligent soul who knew the old woman better than she did. The farm, she soon found out, had that faculty common to farmyards of swallowing up and losing its human population. The poultry followed her in interested fashion, and swine grunted interrogations at her from behind the bars of their sties, but barnyard and rickyard, orchard and stables and dairy, gave no reward to her search. Then, as she retraced her steps towards the kitchen, she came suddenly on her cousin, young Mr. Jim, as every one called him, who divided his time between amateur horse-dealing, rabbit-shooting, and flirting with the farm maids.

"I'm afraid old Martha is dying," said Emma. Jim was not the sort of person to whom one had to break news gently.

"Nonsense," he said; "Martha means to live to a hundred. She told me so, and she'll do it."

"She may be actually dying at this moment, or it may just be the beginning of the break-up," persisted Emma, with a feeling of contempt for the slowness and dulness of the young man.

A grin spread over his good-natured features.

"It don't look like it," he said, nodding towards the yard. Emma turned to catch the meaning of his remark. Old Martha stood in the middle of a mob of poultry scattering handfuls of grain around her. The turkey-cock, with the bronzed sheen of his feathers and the purple-red of his wattles, the game-cock with the glowing metallic lustre of his Eastern plumage, the hens, with their ochres and buffs and umbers and their scarlet combs, and the drakes, with their bottle-green heads, made a medley of rich colour, in the centre of which the old woman looked like a withered stalk standing amid the riotous growth of gaily-hued flowers. But she threw the grain deftly amid the wilderness of beaks, and her quavering voice carried as far as the two people who were watching her. She was still harping on the theme of death coming to the farm.

"I knew 'twere a-coming. There's been signs an' warnings."

"Who's dead, then, old Mother?" called out the young man.

"'Tis young Mister Ladbruk," she shrilled back; "they've just a-carried his body in. Run out of the way of a tree that was coming down an' ran hisself on to an iron post. Dead when they picked un up. Ay, I knew 'twere coming."

And she turned to fling a handful of barley at a belated group of guinea-fowl that came racing toward her.

The farm was a family property, and passed to the rabbit-shooting cousin as the next-of-kin. Emma Ladbruk drifted out of its history as a bee that had wandered in at an open window might flit its way out again. On a cold grey morning she stood waiting with her boxes already stowed in the farm cart, till the last of the market produce should be ready, for the train she was to catch was of less importance than the chickens and butter and eggs that were to be offered for sale. From where she stood she could see an angle of the long latticed window that was to have been cozy with curtains and gay with bowls of flowers. Into her mind came the thought that for months, perhaps for years, long after she had been utterly forgotten, a white, unheeding face would be seen peering out through those latticed panes, and a weak muttering voice would be heard quavering up and down those flagged passages. She made her way to a narrow barred casement that opened into the farm larder. Old Martha was standing at a table trussing a pair of chickens for the market stall as she had trussed them for nearly fourscore years.

## Come to the Party

By Frances Garfield

Dusk was fast overcoming the autumn twilight. Nora felt no closer to Steve Thomas's country house than they'd been half an hour earlier. She snuggled closer to big Jeff in the back seat and tried to see the road ahead. The headlights bravely probed a path, but the darkness seemed to nestle nearer and gloomier to either side.

Willie, in the front seat beside Sam, bent her ginger head above a crude, penciled map, which the four had begun to fear was false.

"Steve just doesn't know how to draw maps," Willie half moaned. "And he promised to put up signals to show where to turn off onto his private road. Why ever did I pick a publisher who throws his parties on the far side of nowhere?"

"But, my dear, this publisher picked you out," reminded silver-haired Sam at the wheel. "A dozen others turned you down—"

"Please. Why bring that up?" Willie appealed. But he went on.

"Here was Steve with his little regional publishing house, pretty much on the far side of nowhere itself, a county away. Regional, and he wanted a regional novel for the Christmas trade. And he liked yours very much. And here we are, on our way to cheer you on while you autograph a thousand or so flyleaves."

Sam loved his writer wife, and showed it by his teasing. Nora knew he smiled his special smile of affectionate amusement, blue eyes slanted and twinkling.

"He said there might be about a dozen guests," protested Willie. "He said he'd invited some special friends who might like my book and buy it. And tell all their friends—so they'd buy it too. For Christmas gifts. Word-of-mouth advertising, Steve called it."

"Yes. Cheaper than published advertising," remarked Sam.

"There's that little white church again," said Jeff, big and trying to sound cheerful. "How many times have we passed it? Three? Or maybe four?"

"Four, I'm sure," put in Nora. "And there's the little gray house that keeps following us."

"Damn," said Sam. "This curve looming ahead is boringly familiar. We seem to be in orbit—"

A grotesquely painted van charged into the glare of headlights, squarely in the center of the road. Sam cursed and wrenched the wheel. The car swayed onto the grassy shoulder. The tremendous van shot past, its driver goggling out, blocky white teeth gleaming from a dark thicket of beard. Then he was gone, and Sam twisted back onto the road.

"Whew," gasped Willie. "Thank God you were driving, Sam, not me."

Nora tossed her thick, black hair out of her eyes. Her hand tingled where Jeff had gripped it so powerfully. She could still see that staring, shaggy face.

"It'll be a great party if we ever get there," she said in a feeble attempt at humor. "Look, isn't that the church again?"

"I wonder if anybody will find the place," ventured Willie.

"Pessimist," chuckled Sam. He loved everything about Willie, including her novel about a woman's passion for both her husband and her husband's brother. Nora had overheard a neighbor woman ask Sam which of the characters he was supposed to be. "A little of both," he had said, with a perfectly straight face, slant blue eyes twinkling as usual.

"There'll be people there all right," promised burly Jeff. "And Nora and I are here to give you moral support, Willie." He, too, admired the book, had helped Willie read proof on it. The four were close friends, always enjoyed each other, never bored together.

"That van looks better behind us than in front of us," said Sam. "Maybe he's lost out here, too, rolling round and round. Look a mist is coming up."

An owl hooted in the distance, strangely loud and clear above the motor's purr. No houses showed now, only great twisted trees crowded at the sides of the road, branches laced overhead. Willie gave a sudden, happy squeak.

"Look—a bit of tinsel on a post," she cried. "That's bound to be Steve's signal."

"And a driveway just past it," said Sam, turning deftly. "A long one, too."

They followed turns, rises, and falls in the bumpy road. Dark thickets massed to right and left. They heard nothing, no sound but the motor. Nora saw a grotesquely hunched tree that reminded her of a cedar of Lebanon she remembered from Winchester Cathedral. Weird.

"Turn there," directed Willie, pointing ahead. And Sam turned.

"Geez, how well you obey Willie," laughed Nora. "One word from me and Jeff does the exact opposite."

Jeff said nothing. He stared out of the window, lips clamped; his cheek had a taut crease where there should be a dimple.

Sam bumped the car over the coarse outflung roots of a great oak, and stopped on the tall grass. Ahead of them showed a great, bleakly drab house. Wavering lights from the tall windows tinted the dim evening. A broad chimney, rosy in the dusk, climbed the side wall. Large pillars rose along a wide porch.

"Okay." Jeff touched Nora's shoulder, and she felt his great hand tremble. "Let's go on in."

Willie smoothed her cap of ginger curls and freshened her lipstick. Nora shook her long, dark hair and moved to follow Jeff. "Odd," she said. "I don't see any other cars."

"They've probably been and gone," joked Sam, coming along behind with Willie. "It took us long enough to find the place."

They mounted the steps. A dark, heavy door loomed. Sam swung the huge knocker, and the door opened.

"Come in. Come in," came a booming voice.

They went in.

The man at the door was outrageously handsome, blond and tall, dressed in a tuxedo, shirtfront all foamy with lace, self-consciously cordial. "Glad you came," he greeted them.

"We had some problems," said Nora. "Where's Steve?"

"Oh, never mind Steve for a moment. My name's Patrick. Come on in and join the crowd."

The hubbub inside was unbelievable. Nora took hold of Jeff's coat, seeking reassurance. For what reason she didn't know. They had come into a huge, swarming room, a multitude of bodies. All kinds—tall, thin, short, fat, every one of them completely strange to her. Maybe Willie knew some of them, she thought. They could be part of Steve's publishing company. She stepped back to let Willie lead the way.

"Keep straight ahead," Patrick advised from behind. He was dismayingly handsome, and Nora speculated for a moment whether his hair had been permanented. "Food and drink over there," he smiled. "You'll find some friends there, probably."

"With my sort of friends, that's just where I'll find them," said Jeff, grinning now.

The four wove in and out among packed groups. Everybody was talking to everybody else and nobody seemed to notice them. A dull red fire glowed on a broad hearth, but did not seem to send out any heat. Several extremely thin men stood there and listened to a grossly heavy man. His face was bearded, toothy. Nora remembered the driver of that killer van. High along an inner wall ran a balcony. Faces looked down, the faces, perhaps, of children. One gnawed on what might have been a chicken wing.

"It's positively unreal," Nora whispered to Jeff, and it was. They seemed to walk through people, as though people dissolved from in front of them. "My imagination's going haywire," she said, and squeezed his hand for comfort.

Willie's brilliant, curly head had led the way to a butler's pantry. It, too, thronged with people, filling trays with barbecued chicken, cold cuts, sliced cheese. Baskets of crackers and little cakes sat here and there. In the midst of everything, a gigantic glass bowl of rosy liquid.

"Pink wine," whispered Sam, crinkling his nose. "The cheapest."

For a moment, they thought they saw Steve Thomas's beautiful wife balancing an empty tray toward a rear door, perhaps the kitchen. "Hey, Florence," Willie called out. But whoever it was didn't turn. She vanished so abruptly, they couldn't be sure if they'd seen her.

Sam picked up a plate and piled it high with salad and meat. "Let's dig in," he said. "That ride would give a skeleton an appetite. I'll even try this sorry wine—it's not worthy of Steve. Or is it? I think he outdid himself this time."

"There's Em Selden, there by the fireplace," said Nora to Jeff.

"Where?"

"No, she's gone. Maybe it wasn't Em. Anyway, let's stick together. What a strange bunch of people."

As she spoke, she thought she heard singing somewhere. A radio, a record player? It died away as she wondered.

"Look," said Willie, putting down her plate. "At the end of the hall. It looks like Patrick, summoning me. I'd better go see—maybe it's time for me to autograph some books."

Briskly she headed for the long hallway, striding fast on green high-heeled sandals and swinging the skirt of her flowered green dress. There were chairs lining the hall. They seemed to be heaped with mink coats. "Hmm," Nora heard her murmur as she left. "None of Steve's authors could afford those."

Nora chewed on a strangely tasteless slice of sausage as she watched Willie out of sight. "I hope she sells enough books to make this trip worthwhile."

"You're not having fun?" worried Sam.

"That means you aren't happy either." Nora looked from platter to platter. "What happened to the chicken wings? They're my favorite food?"

"If I had a pair of chicken wings, I might just fly out of here," said Jeff. Nora laughed, but Jeff didn't join her.

The crowd had grown thicker, noisier. The air seemed damp and close; it had a smell like a roomful of old clothes. Sam frowned and brushed back his silver hair.

"Let's go somewhere quiet," he said.

"How about up on the balcony with the kids?" suggested Nora.

But the balcony seemed empty, lost in dark shadows. Maybe a hint of movement. Or maybe not.

"How much of this putrid wine did you drink, Jeff?" asked Sam.

"No more than I could help. I hope Willie's in her element, autographing books."

"I'm going to go see," said Sam.

He moved toward the hallway where Willie had vanished. The crowd let him through without seeming to make way.

"At least Steve had the sense to stay away from his own party," growled Jeff. "Look there in the corner. Isn't that Genevieve and Joe?"

Nora peered. "Let's go see."

They pressed their way through a huddle of people, who made a path for them. Nobody looked familiar. Except, against a far wall—the bearded van driver? The voices, all s's and all loud, hurt their ears. The air thickened, and was hard to breathe.

"Here we are," said Jeff, reaching the corner.

But nobody stood there. Nobody. Only a flicker from the fireplace that did not seem to give off heat.

"I'll be damned," Jeff muttered. "Do we have a single friend in this room?"

They looked around. Halfway across the room drifted a face,

wan as lemon custard, peering from under the brim of a worn, shapeless felt hat. The body seemed lost in foggy darkness—they imagined a long black caftan. Behind him, or it, there grimaced the bearded driver.

"Jeff," said Nora, "I don't like it here."

"It's just that you don't know anybody," said Jeff. But his dimples did not show. "But you're right. The whole thing's a crashing bore. Let me go check with Willie and Sam. Maybe we can sneak out if they're through."

"Yes, go look for them." Nora tried to smile.

"I'll be right back."

Away he tramped, huge among the others. She watched him enter the hallway between the piled fur coats. Watched his dark head disappear. Then she stood alone, nobody noticing her, nobody talking to her. She felt dull, sticky, as though she hung in a mass of warm jelly.

Haze crawled in the air of the crowded room. It smelled, not like tobacco, not like that other familiar-grown marijuana smell. Nora did not belong there. She knew it. She hadn't been invited, really; she and Jeff had only come with Willie and Sam. For moral support. She wished they had stayed at home. Or wished, anyway, she had gone along with Jeff to find the others.

I'll follow them, she said to herself. Follow them. Maybe they're ready to go.

The hallway seemed to narrow as she entered. Those piles of furs closed in around her. Maybe the little white rabbit in the Alice book had felt closed in like that. And the hallway was shadow-barred, with open doorways shedding light along the side.

Nora looked in at a door. Music seeped out. Something in there like a little old-fashioned organ. It seemed to be playing, all by itself, a tune like a hymn, but dissonant, repelling. Voices echoed through the next doorway. Nora went there.

"Come in," somebody called. "We've been waiting."

A man in a very dark suit put out a very white hand to her. His chalky face grinned with dark, narrow teeth. His hand was clammy as it touched hers. "Come in," he said again.

Staring past him, she saw dull paneled walls, a hanging lamp that sprouted a shaky flame, a closely drawn knot of people. They, too, wore dark clothes, tight-fitted to gaunt bodies. They seemed to have faces of pale clay. Their eyes looked little and beady. They spoke from thick red lips, unintelligibly.

But on the floor lay three others, instantly recognizable—a bit of green cloth. Jeff's great, limp body. The red curls of Willie, the silver hair of Sam. None of them moved.

"Come in," a chorus, bidding.

All hands rose toward her, beckoning.

Nora screamed thinly and whirled to run.

Run anywhere, away from that little room, anywhere. A door stood at the end of the hallway. Escape. That was all she could think of. She gasped stranglingly. At the door, she clawed for the knob. She strove hard against the panel, and the door grumbled open.

She filled her lungs with fresh air. Somehow, miraculously, she was outside. Where to go? It didn't matter. Only get away.

She ran in the dark night, stumbling over the heavy coiled roots of trees, tearing her sheer hose. A slipper came off and desperately she kicked the other away. She kept running. Stones hurt her bare feet, biting painfully at her ankles. A mockingbird sang, strangely comforting. She was escaping. Away from that house.

A broad, open lawn loomed ahead of her. A beautiful house, standing tall and proud against sentinel pines. She floundered to one knee, dragged herself up again and to the door, beating at it with her fists.

"Why, Nora!"

There stood Steve Thomas, opening to her. Steve was slim, impeccable. His curled black hair was carefully groomed, a smile was on his face.

"For heaven's sake. Where have you been? Where are the others?"

She flung herself into his arms, and he held her close to quiet her trembling. "Where are they?" he asked again.

"I don't know," she chattered. "I saw them on the floor—over there at your party—"

"What are you talking about?"

She fought her choking sobs. "Over in that big house, right over there—"

"My God, Nora, there hasn't been a house there for years." Steve held her closer. "You're imagining things. No house. It burned down, long before I came here."

"B-burned down?"

"I've heard a crazy story. A bunch of far-out people, who had a belief of some sort about human sacrifice. And one night, when they celebrated it, lightning struck and burned the place to the ground, with everybody inside."

"But—"

"Look, Nora. There's nothing there. Nothing whatever."
Nora made herself look.
There *was* nothing there. Nothing whatever.

## A Curious Dream

By Mark Twain

### Containing a Moral

Night before last I had a singular dream. I seemed to be sitting on a doorstep (in no particular city perhaps) ruminating, and the time of night appeared to be about twelve or one o'clock. The weather was balmy and delicious. There was no human sound in the air, not even a footstep. There was no sound of any kind to emphasize the dead stillness, except the occasional hollow barking of a dog in the distance and the fainter answer of a further dog. Presently up the street I heard a bony clack-clacking, and guessed it was the castanets of a serenading party. In a minute more a tall skeleton, hooded, and half clad in a tattered and moldy shroud, whose shreds were flapping about the ribby latticework of its person, swung by me with a stately stride and disappeared in the gray gloom of the starlight. It had a broken and worm-eaten coffin on its shoulder and a bundle of something in its hand. I knew what the clack-clacking was then; it was this party's joints working together, and his elbows knocking against his sides as he walked. I may say I was surprised. Before I could collect my thoughts and enter upon any speculations as to what this apparition might portend, I heard another one coming—for I recognized his clack-clack. He had two-thirds of a coffin on his shoulder, and some foot and head boards under his arm. I mightily wanted to peer under his hood and speak to him, but when he turned and smiled upon me with his cavernous sockets and his projecting grin as he went by, I thought I would not detain him. He was hardly gone when I heard the clacking again, and another one issued from the shadowy half-light. This one was bending under a heavy gravestone, and dragging a shabby coffin after him by a string. When he got to me he gave me a steady look for a moment or two, and then rounded to and backed up to me, saying:

"Ease this down for a fellow, will you?"

I eased the gravestone down till it rested on the ground, and in doing so noticed that it bore the name of "John Baxter Copmanhurst," with "May, 1839," as the date of his death. Deceased sat wearily down by me, and wiped his os frontis with his major maxillary—chiefly from former habit I judged, for I could not see that he brought away any perspiration.

"It is too bad, too bad," said he, drawing the remnant of the shroud about him and leaning his jaw pensively on his hand. Then he put his left foot up on his knee and fell to scratching his ankle-bone absently with a rusty nail which he got out of his coffin.

"What is too bad, friend?"

"Oh, everything, everything. I almost wish I never had died."

"You surprise me. Why do you say this? Has anything gone wrong? What is the matter?"

"Matter! Look at this shroud—rags. Look at this gravestone, all battered up. Look at that disgraceful old coffin. All a man's property going to ruin and destruction before his eyes, and ask him if anything is wrong? Fire and brimstone!"

"Calm yourself, calm yourself," I said. "It *is* too bad—it is certainly too bad, but then I had not supposed that you would much mind such matters, situated as you are."

"Well, my dear sir, I *do* mind them. My pride is hurt, and my comfort is impaired—destroyed, I might say. I will state my case—I will put it to you in such a way that you can comprehend it, if you will let me," said the poor skeleton, tilting the hood of his shroud back, as if he were clearing for action, and thus unconsciously giving himself a jaunty and festive air very much at variance with the grave character of his position in life—so to speak—and in prominent contrast with his distressful mood.

"Proceed," said I.

"I reside in the shameful old graveyard a block or two above you here, in this street—there, now, I just expected that cartilage would let go!—third rib from the bottom, friend, hitch the end of it to my spine with a string, if you have got such a thing about you, though a bit of silver wire is a deal pleasanter, and more durable and becoming, if one keeps it polished—to think of shredding out and going to pieces in this way, just on account of the indifference and neglect of one's posterity!"—and the poor ghost grated his teeth in a way that gave me a wrench and a shiver—for the effect is mightily increased by the absence of muffling flesh and cuticle. "I reside in that old graveyard, and have for these thirty years; and I tell you things are changed since I first laid this old tired frame there, and turned over, and stretched out for a long sleep, with a delicious sense upon me of being *done* with bother, and grief, and anxiety, and doubt, and fear, forever and ever, and listening with comfortable and increasing satisfaction to the sexton's work, from the startling clatter of his first spadeful on my coffin till it dulled away to the faint patting that shaped the roof of my new home—delicious! My! I wish you could try it to-night!" and out of my reverie deceased fetched me a rattling slap with a bony hand.

"Yes, sir, thirty years ago I laid me down there, and was happy. For it was out in the country then—out in the breezy, flowery, grand old woods, and the lazy winds gossiped with the leaves, and the squirrels capered over us and around us, and the creeping things visited us, and the birds filled the tranquil solitude with music. Ah, it was worth ten years of a man's life to be dead then! Everything was pleasant. I was in a good neighborhood, for all the dead people that lived near me belonged to the best families in the city. Our posterity appeared to think the world of us. They kept our graves in the very best condition; the fences were always in faultless repair, head-boards were kept painted or whitewashed, and were replaced with new ones as soon as they began to look rusty or decayed; monuments were kept upright, railings intact and bright, the rose-bushes and shrubbery trimmed, trained, and free from blemish, the walks clean and smooth and graveled. But that day is gone by. Our descendants have forgotten us. My grandson lives in a stately house built with money made by these old hands of mine, and I sleep in a neglected grave with invading vermin that gnaw my shroud to build them nests withal! I and friends that lie with me founded and secured the prosperity of this fine city, and the stately bantling of our loves leaves us to rot in a dilapidated cemetery which neighbors curse and strangers scoff at. See the difference between the old time and this—for instance: Our graves are all caved in now; our head-boards have rotted away and tumbled down; our railings reel this way and that, with one foot in the air, after a fashion of unseemly levity; our monuments lean wearily, and our gravestones bow their heads discouraged; there be no adornments any more—no roses, nor shrubs, nor graveled walks, nor anything that is a comfort to the eye; and even the paintless old board fence that did make a show of holding us sacred from companionship with beasts and the defilement of heedless feet, has tottered till it overhangs the street, and only advertises the presence of our dismal resting-place and invites yet more derision to it. And now we cannot hide our poverty and tatters in the friendly woods, for the city has stretched its withering arms abroad and taken us in, and all that remains of the cheer of our old home is the cluster of lugubrious forest trees that stand, bored and weary of a city life, with their feet in our coffins, looking into the hazy distance and wishing they were there. I tell you it is disgraceful!

"You begin to comprehend—you begin to see how it is. While our descendants are living sumptuously on our money, right around us in the city, we have to fight hard to keep skull and bones together. Bless you, there isn't a grave in our cemetery that doesn't leak—not one. Every time it rains in the night we have to climb out and roost in the trees—and sometimes we are wakened suddenly by the chilly water trickling down the back of our necks. Then I tell you there is a general heaving up of old graves and kicking over of old monuments, and scampering of old skeletons for the trees! Bless me, if you had gone along there some such nights after twelve you might have seen as many as fifteen of us roosting on one limb, with our joints rattling drearily and the wind wheezing through our ribs! Many a time we have perched there for three or four dreary hours, and then come down, stiff and chilled through and drowsy, and borrowed each other's skulls to bail out our graves with—if you will glance up in my mouth now as I tilt my head back, you can see that my head-piece is half full of old dry sediment—how top-heavy and stupid it makes me sometimes! Yes, sir, many a time if you had happened to come along just before the dawn you'd have caught us bailing out the graves and hanging our shrouds on the fence to dry. Why, I had an elegant shroud stolen from there one morning—think a party by the name of Smith took it, that resides in a plebeian graveyard over yonder—I think so because the first time I ever saw him he hadn't anything on but a check shirt, and the last time I saw him, which was at a social gathering in the new cemetery, he was the best-dressed corpse in the company—and it is a significant fact that he left when he saw me; and presently an old woman from here missed her coffin—she generally took it with her when she went anywhere, because she was liable to take cold and bring on the spasmodic rheumatism that originally killed her if she exposed herself to the night air much. She was named Hotchkiss—Anna Matilda Hotchkiss—you might know her? She has two upper front teeth, is tall, but a good deal inclined to stoop, one rib on the left side gone, has one shred of rusty hair hanging from the left side of her head, and one little tuft just above and a little forward of her right ear, has her underjaw wired on one side where it had worked loose, small bone of left forearm gone—lost in a fight—has a kind of swagger in her gait and a 'gallus' way of going with her arms akimbo and her nostrils in the air—has been pretty free and easy, and is all damaged and battered up till she looks like a queensware crate in ruins—maybe you have met her?"

"God forbid!" I involuntarily ejaculated, for somehow I was not looking for that form of question, and it caught me a little off my guard. But I hastened to make amends for my rudeness, and say, "I simply meant I had not had the honor—for I would not deliberately speak discourteously of a friend of yours. You were saying that you were robbed—and it was a shame, too—but it appears by what is left of the shroud you have on that it was a costly one in its day. How did—"

A most ghastly expression began to develop among the decayed features and shriveled integuments of my guest's face, and I was beginning to grow uneasy and distressed, when he told me he was only working up a deep, sly smile, with a wink in it, to suggest that about the time he acquired his present garment a ghost in a neighboring cemetery missed one. This reassured me, but I begged him to confine himself to speech thenceforth, because his facial expression was uncertain. Even with the most elaborate care it was liable to miss fire. Smiling should especially be avoided. What *he* might honestly consider a shining success was likely to strike me in a very different light. I said I liked to see a skeleton cheerful, even decorously playful, but I did not think smiling was a skeleton's best hold.

"Yes, friend," said the poor skeleton, "the facts are just as I have given them to you. Two of these old graveyards—the one that I resided in and one further along—have been deliberately neglected by our descendants of to-day until there is no occupying them any longer. Aside from the osteological discomfort of it—and that is no light matter this rainy weather—the present state of things is ruinous to property. We have got to move or be content to see our effects wasted away and utterly destroyed. Now, you will hardly believe it, but it is true, nevertheless, that there isn't a single coffin in good repair among all my acquaintance—now that is an absolute fact. I do not refer to low people who come in a pine box mounted on an express-wagon, but I am talking about your high-toned, silver-mounted burial-case, your monumental sort, that travel under black plumes at the head of a procession and have choice of cemetery lots—I mean folks like the Jarvises, and the Bledsoes and Burlings, and such. They are all about ruined. The most substantial people in our set, they were. And now look at them—utterly used up and poverty-stricken. One of the Bledsoes actually traded his monument to a late barkeeper for some fresh shavings to put under his head. I tell you it speaks volumes, for there is nothing a corpse takes so much pride in as his monument. He loves to read the inscription. He comes after a while to believe what it says himself, and then you may see him sitting on the fence night after night enjoying it. Epitaphs are cheap, and they do a poor chap a world of good after he is dead, especially if he had hard luck while he was alive. I wish they were used more. Now I don't complain, but confidentially I *do* think it was a little shabby in my descendants to give me nothing but this old slab of a gravestone—and all the more that there isn't a compliment on it. It used to have

'GONE TO HIS JUST REWARD'

on it, and I was proud when I first saw it, but by and by I noticed that whenever an old friend of mine came along he would hook his chin on the railing and pull a long face and read along down till he came to that, and then he would chuckle to himself and walk off, looking satisfied and comfortable. So I scratched it off to get rid of those fools. But a dead man always takes a deal of pride in his monument. Yonder goes half a dozen of the Jarvises now, with the family monument along. And Smithers and some hired specters went by with his awhile ago. Hello, Higgins, good-by, old friend! That's Meredith Higgins—died in '44—belongs to our set in the cemetery—fine old family—great-grandmother was an Injun—I am on the most familiar terms with him—he didn't hear me was the reason he didn't answer me. And I am sorry, too, because I would have liked to introduce you. You would admire him. He is the most disjointed, sway-backed, and generally distorted old skeleton you ever saw, but he is full of fun. When he laughs it sounds like rasping two stones together, and he always starts it off with a cheery screech like raking a nail across a window-pane. Hey, Jones! That is old Columbus Jones—shroud cost four hundred dollars—entire trousseau, including monument, twenty-seven hundred. This was in the spring of '26. It was enormous style for those days. Dead people came all the way from the Alleghanies to see his things—the party that occupied the grave next to mine remembers it well. Now do you see that individual going along with a piece of a head-board under his arm, one leg-bone below his knee gone, and not a thing in the world on? That is Barstow Dalhousie, and next to Columbus Jones he was the most sumptuously outfitted person that ever entered our cemetery. We are all leaving. We cannot tolerate the treatment we are receiving at the hands of our descendants. They open new cemeteries, but they leave us to our ignominy. They mend the streets, but they never mend anything that is about us or belongs to us. Look at that coffin of mine—yet I tell you in its day it was a piece of furniture that would have attracted attention in any drawing-room in this city. You may have it if you want it—I can't afford to repair it. Put a new bottom in her, and part of a new top, and a bit of fresh lining along the left side, and you'll find her about as comfortable as any receptacle of her species you ever tried. No thanks—no, don't mention it—you have been civil to me, and I would give you all the property I have got before I would seem ungrateful. Now this winding-sheet is a kind of a sweet thing in its way, if you would like to— No? Well, just as you say, but I wished to be fair and liberal—there's nothing mean about *me*. Good-by, friend, I must be going. I may have a good way to go to-night—don't know. I only know one thing for certain, and that is that I am on the emigrant trail now, and I'll never sleep in that crazy old cemetery again. I will travel till I find respectable quarters, if I have to hoof it to New Jersey. All the boys are going. It was decided in public conclave, last night, to emigrate, and by the time the sun rises there won't be a bone left in our old habitations. Such cemeteries may suit my surviving friends, but they do not suit the remains that have the honor to make these remarks. My opinion is the general opinion. If you doubt it, go and see how the departing ghosts upset things before they started. They were almost riotous in their demonstrations of distaste. Hello, here are some of the Bledsoes, and if you will give me a lift with this tombstone I guess I will join company and jog along with them—mighty respectable old family, the Bledsoes, and used to always come out in six-horse hearses and all that sort of thing fifty years ago when I walked these streets in daylight. Good-by, friend."

And with his gravestone on his shoulder he joined the grisly procession, dragging his damaged coffin after him, for notwithstanding he pressed it upon me so earnestly, I utterly refused his hospitality. I suppose that for as much as two hours these sad outcasts went clacking by, laden with their dismal effects, and all that time I sat pitying them. One or two of the youngest and least dilapidated among them inquired about midnight trains on the railways, but the rest seemed unacquainted with that mode of travel, and merely asked about common public roads to various towns and cities, some of which are not on the map now, and vanished from it and from the earth as much as thirty years ago, and some few of them never *had* existed anywhere but on maps, and private ones in real-estate agencies at that. And they asked about the condition of the cemeteries in these towns and cities, and about the reputation the citizens bore as to reverence for the dead.

This whole matter interested me deeply, and likewise compelled my sympathy for these homeless ones. And it all seeming real, and I not knowing it was a dream, I mentioned to one shrouded wanderer an idea that had entered my head to publish an account of this curious and very sorrowful exodus, but said also that I could not describe it truthfully, and just as it occurred, without seeming to trifle with a grave subject and exhibit an irreverence for the dead that would shock and distress their surviving friends. But this bland and stately remnant of a former citizen leaned him far over my gate and whispered in my ear, and said:

"Do not let that disturb you. The community that can stand such graveyards as those we are emigrating from can stand anything a body can say about the neglected and forsaken dead that lie in them."

At that very moment a cock crowed, and the weird procession vanished and left not a shred or a bone behind. I awoke, and found myself lying with my head out of the bed and "sagging" downward considerably—a position favorable to dreaming dreams with morals in them, maybe, but not poetry.

NOTE The reader is assured that if the cemeteries in his town are kept in good order, this Dream is not leveled at his town at all, but is leveled particularly and venomously at the *next* town.

## Dark Wings

By Phyllis Eisenstein

The house seemed large and empty now that her parents were dead. And yet it was also so soothingly quiet that Lydia would sometimes just stand in the high-ceilinged dining room and relish the silence. No shrill voice came floating from the upper story, no gravelly, grating one from the oak-paneled study, no orders, demands, advice, admonishments. The electricity was gone from the air, leaving nothing but solitude.

She had dreamed of such peace, dreamed as the years and her

youth ebbed away, eroded by a struggle she was too weak to win. Dutiful and self-sacrificing, people had called her—nurse, maid, cook, buffer between her parents and the outside world. But behind her back, she knew, they had clucked their tongues over the poor dried-up spinster. What did they know of the guilts and fears that her parents had instilled in her, of the elaborate net of obligation they had spun about her, till she was bound to them with ties that only death could sever? And death had come at last, like a knight on his pale charger, and borne away two coffins that set her free. Still, people clucked their tongues because Lydia lived much as before, alone in her parents' house, alone in her heart. If anything, she was quieter than ever.

Yet some things had changed for her. She painted a great deal more these days, uninterrupted. She had moved her studio from the basement to the big bedroom upstairs, where the light splashed in from windows on three sides. On fine days she would open those windows and let the sea air wash away the smell of paint. In the evenings she walked by the shore, sharing it with tourists and young lovers, and there were no responsibilities to call her home at any particular time. Some nights she would be there long after the noises of traffic had faded to nothing, till only the bell of a distant buoy remained for company. She hardly thought about anything at those times, only enjoyed the dark and the starlight on the waves, and the blessed, blessed silence.

On one such night she saw the bird for the first time. The moon had risen as she watched, its light splashed like a pale and shimmering highway crossing the restless ocean toward Europe. Like a shadow upon that path, the bird caught her eye, its dark wings limned by silvery radiance. For a moment it glided over the waves, pinions motionless in the still night air, and then it swooped upward and vanished in the darkness.

She stood awhile by the shore, straining her eyes for another glimpse of the creature, hoping it would wheel and make a second pass over the glittering water. It was a hawk of some sort, perhaps even an eagle—size and distance were deceptive out over the ocean, where there were no references to judge by. She wanted it to be an eagle, for they were rare in these parts and protected. She had only seen a live eagle here once before, when she was a small child. But though she waited till the moon was high and shrunken, she saw the bird no more, though perhaps she heard the beat of its wings far above her head. Or perhaps she only heard the cool surf beating at the rocks below her feet. At night by the sea, time, distance, and direction all seemed to muddle together, playing tricks on the eyes, the ears, and the mind.

At home she could not sleep for thinking about the bird, and before dawn she was in the studio by yellow, artificial light, with a fresh canvas and dark acrylic pigments spread over her palette. Swiftly, she recreated the impression of the scene, the silver moon-path, the dark bird an instantaneous silhouette, and all surrounded by an impenetrable black that seemed to suck light away from the hard, sharp stars. Blue-black she used, instead of true black—Prussian blue, that velvety shade so dark that only a careful eye could tell it from black, but warmer somehow, softer, deeper. The sky and the bird, Prussian blue. But when dawn added its radiance to her lamps, she saw that she had not captured the mood of that moment. The canvas was dull and dim. Her dilated pupils had perceived a patch of luminous, ethereal night in a vaster darkness, but the paints had given her only the latter.

Light, she thought, as she cleaned the palette and brushes. Light. But all she could remember was the plumage of the bird, blacker than black under the silver moon.

She slept.

Later in the day she walked down to the shore, earlier than usual. This time she carried binoculars hurriedly purchased in town, and she scanned the seaward sky from north to south, searching for a familiar silhouette. Gulls she saw, gulls in plenty, soaring, swooping for food, perching on rocks. Fat gulls, grey on top and white beneath. But no hawks, no eagles. She turned the binoculars westward toward the rooftops of the town, just visible beyond the intervening trees. She saw flecks that might be pigeons, crows, even sparrows, near and far. Ordinary birds. Nowhere did she see the short head, broad tail, and flared wings that marked her quarry.

She ate a quick dinner and returned to the painting by the waning, rosy glow of dusk. One could not evoke the depths of night, she thought, under a bright sun. She lightened her palette, reworked the moon and sea and even the dark air between them, trying to capture the radiance against which the bird had seemed so intense a shadow. Past midnight she realized that there was a contradiction in her mind, a double image of that instant, in which the sky was bright and dark at the same time. She could feel it, but the painting was only a poor reflection of that feeling, two-dimensional and—by now—muddy. She cleaned the palette and brushes and set the canvas aside against the wall. Stifling a yawn, she mounted a fresh, blank canvas on the easel.

The bird this time, nothing else. She sketched quickly, placing tail and flared pinions, adding details that she *felt* rather than remembered. The light was moonlight of course, but there was no sky, no ocean, only the dark wingspan and the merest suggestion of curved beak and piercing eye. And when she reached the limits of both her recollection and her invention, she went downstairs to the study and looked eagles up in the encyclopedia. She knew now that it had been an eagle; she wouldn't allow it to be anything else. The encyclopedia illustrations gave her some inspiration and corrected a few of her assumptions, and she hurried back upstairs to make adjustments.

By dawnlight again, she viewed her new effort with a critical eye. She had never painted birds before; at most, they had been pieces of background in her few landscapes, a brushstroke or two in the sky. The black eagle showed her lack of familiarity with his kind; he was naïve and awkward, though bold. If she squinted, she could see a family resemblance to the bird on the back of a dollar bill.

At twilight she walked by the shore, searching the darkening sky for him, staying on till the moon was high, that night and many after. Night upon night, as the moon waned and the stars brightened by contrast. Night upon night, in fair weather and foul, when the waves were slick as glass, when the waves were wild things clutching for the sky. She waited for another glimpse, straining at clouds or a late gull or a speck of flotsam on the water. She waited late, late, and past midnight she returned home and worked on one or the other of the paintings, striving to recreate the bird.

She had never gone to town much, less since the deaths of her parents. Now she had no use for the place at all; she had her groceries delivered and paid her bills by mail. Every scrap of her spare time was spoken for, by paint or binoculars or the sleep that she grudgingly allowed herself. Only the postman saw her, dropping off a few bills, catalogues, advertisements a couple of times a week. And the people who walked by the sea. But the weather was beginning to grow chilly for both tourists and lovers; soon the moon waxed full again, and only Lydia stood on the shore to watch it touch the waves with silver.

She heard the bird now, sometimes—she was sure of that, though she never saw his broad, dark wings. She heard him beat the air once, twice, high above her head, and then there was silence as he soared and she stared upward, trying to pierce the blackness with her human eyes. She thought he could probably see her well enough, eagles' eyes being so much sharper than humans', and she tried to imagine how she must appear to him—her face a pale speck amid the darkness of rocks and scrubby grass. A small thing, earth-bound, of no significance to a creature who sailed the dark ocean of air. What would it be like, she wondered, to have wings and look down upon the creatures who could only walk?

The paintings had proliferated by this time. They lined the studio, view after view of the subject she had seen only once. Yet there was a clear image of him in her mind's eye, as if she could reconstruct his whole form from the sound of his wings. His eye, she knew, was golden, like a great amber bead set above the corner of his beak. The beak was dark as his plumage, like polished jet. And to display their true span, the great black pinions would require a canvas larger than any Lydia had ever worked. She contemplated ordering the proper size from Boston, stretching it and preparing it herself. She measured the door of the studio to be sure the finished product could be carried out of the room, and then she made the phone call.

Autumn was waning by the time the painting was well begun. The sea breeze that washed her studio was chill by day now, and gusty, though she still opened the windows to it, and painted wearing an old sweater. When she walked by the shore, she could see scarlet leaves floating among the restless waves. The color of the ocean was changing, too, and the color of the sky; the daytime world was beginning to grey out for winter. Only at night were the changes invisible. At night the buoy still clanged far out on the water and the moon still splashed its shimmering highway to Europe almost at Lydia's feet. At night ebony wings beat the air, and Lydia strained for a glimpse, just a single brief glimpse of the bird that glided somewhere, somewhere, in the vast, unchanging darkness.

The days grew shorter as the chilling wind ruffled the waves to a restive froth, and the nights were long—long for walking by the choppy water, long for painting by lamplight. Lydia slept the whole short day through now, seeing thc sun only at dawn and dusk. The bird preferred the night hours, and Lydia had begun to understand that preference. Day was jarring, stark, revealing too much of reality. Night was kind and soothing, hiding the world's flaws in velvet. At night Lydia could look into her dimly lit mirror and see the girl she had once been, the girl whose skin bore no sign of wrinkling, whose hair was yet untouched by grey, whose life still lay ahead of her. That girl could walk on the shore and dream dreams; she could look upon the moonlit highway to Europe and imagine herself traveling it, light as a feather, eastward, over the horizon.

She finished the painting half a dozen times. At dawn she would step back from it, cock her head to one side, and nod to herself. She would clean the brushes and palette carefully, then, and go to bed satisfied. But when she woke at dusk, the light of the setting sun showed her flaws, approximations, incompleteness, and she would eat a quick breakfast and go out to the shore again in search of her model, and inspiration. Inspiration she would find, in the clang of the buoy or the whisper of the wind, or the faint rustle of wingbeats high, high. But the model would not show himself, not even his shadow, and she would return home and work determinedly through the dark hours until she laid the brushes aside again come dawn.

Half a dozen times, she finished and slept—and then one blustery sunset found her with nothing left to do.

Not that the painting was perfect. She eyed it critically from every angle, brushes poised in her fingers, palette in the crook of her arm. She approached it several times, as if to lay another stroke upon the canvas, then drew back. The paint was very thick in some places. But she knew another layer would not make it better. The painting was beyond her ability to improve. She set her brushes aside and went out to walk.

Lydia understood the limits of her skill. She did not expect the canvas to be a photographic reproduction of the image in her mind's eye. She knew she would have to be satisfied with the faintest hint of the beauty and grace and power of the original. And down by the shore, in the pale light of the full moon, she had to weep for her own limitations. She wept, and she shivered a little because the night was very chill, and her coat was not quite heavy enough.

High above her head, she heard his wings.

She knew the sound instantly and looked up, straining to pierce the darkness, her tears a chilly patch upon each eye, blurring her vision for a moment. As a blur, she saw him silhouetted against the moon, and then she blinked and brought him into sharp focus. He was poised above the shimmering path that the moon laid down on the surface of the sea, his great wings motionless as he glided lower, lower, almost touching the white-topped waves. An eagle—yes, she had been right all the time, right in every detail, even to the amber eye that glittered with moonlight, glittered as it regarded her.

He swooped toward her, his great dark wings blotting out the moon, the sky, the world. She gazed at him in wonder, in adoration; the painting had not matched his true size, not remotely. He was the grandfather of eagles, she thought—the god of eagles. She felt a great gust of air as he hovered over her a moment. And then, as delicately as she might cradle a kitten, his great talons locked about her waist and hips. Her hair blew wild as his pinions cupped air to rise again, and then her feet floated free of the earth. Upward they soared—upward—and the rushing wind was a tonic to Lydia's soul. She felt light, young, and beautiful as the bird himself. Looking down, she could see the silver moonpath flowing far below.

Eastward they flew. Eastward toward Europe.

As the first rays of sunlight spread out over the ocean, Lydia saw the island. The only land visible from horizon to horizon, it was dominated by a huge mountain and, as they drew closer, she realized that the summit of that mountain was their destination. This did not surprise her; where else, she reasoned, would an eagle rest?

Closer still, and she saw the nest, big as her parents' house, built of bushes and driftwood and spars from sailing ships, some with ropes and tattered canvas still clinging to them. And then, at the last moment, just before her feet touched the soft, shadowed interior of the nest, just before they brushed the lining of feathers torn from the bird's own downy breast, and his mate's, she struggled. Poor dried-up spinster, she struggled—weakly—as she fell toward those small, dark, gaping beaks.

## Dead Call

By William F. Nolan

Len had been dead for a month when the phone rang.

Midnight. Cold in the house and me dragged up from sleep to answer the call. Helen gone for the weekend. Me, alone in the house. And the phone ringing . . .

"Hello."

"Hello, Frank."

"Who is this?"

"You know *me.* It's Len . . . ole Len Stiles."

Cold. Deep and intense. The receiver dead-cold matter in my hand.

"Leonard Stiles died four weeks ago."

"Four weeks, three days, two hours and twenty-seven minutes ago—to be exact."

"I want to know who you are?"

A chuckle. The same dry chuckle I'd heard so many times.

"C'mon, ole buddy—after twenty years. Hell, you *know* me."

"This is a damned poor joke!"

"No joke, Frank. You're there, alive. And I'm here, dead. And you know something, old buddy . . . I'm really *glad* I did it."

"Did . . . what?"

"Killed myself. Because . . . death is just what I hoped it would be. Beautiful . . . gray . . . quiet . . . no pressures."

"Len Stiles's death was an accident . . . a concrete freeway barrier . . . His car—"

"I *aimed* my car for that barrier," the phone voice told me. "Pedal to the floor. Doing over ninety when I hit . . . No accident, Frank." The voice cold . . . cold. "I *wanted* to be dead. And no regrets."

I tried to laugh, make light of this—matching his chuckle with my own. "Dead men don't use telephones."

"I'm not really using the phone, not in a physical sense. It's just that I chose to contact you this way. You might say it's a matter of 'psychic electricity.' As a detached spirit I'm able to align my cosmic vibrations to match the vibrations of this power line. Simple, really."

"Sure. A snap. Nothing to it."

"Naturally, you're skeptical. I expected you to be. But . . . listen carefully to me, Frank."

And I listened—with the phone gripped in my hand in that cold night house—as the voice told me things that *only* Len could know . . . intimate details of shared experiences extending back through two decades. And when he'd finished I was certain of one thing:

He *was* Len Stiles.

"But, how . . . I still don't . . ."

"Think of this phone as a 'medium'—a line of force through which I can bridge the gap between us." The dry chuckle again. "Hell, you gotta admit it beats holding hands around a table in the dark—yet the principle is the same."

I'd been standing by my desk, transfixed by the voice. Now I moved behind the desk, sat down, trying to absorb this dark miracle. My muscles were wire-taut, my fingers cramped about the black receiver. I dragged in a slow breath, the night dampness of the room pressing at me.

"All right . . . I don't . . . believe in ghosts, don't . . . pretend to understand any of this, but . . . I'll accept it. I *must* accept it."

"I'm glad, Frank—because it's important that we talk." A long moment of hesitation. Then the voice, lower now, softer. "I know how lousy things have been, ole buddy."

"What do you mean?"

"I just know how things are going for you. And . . . I want to help. As your friend, I want you to know that I understand."

"Well . . . I'm really not . . ."

"You've been feeling bad, haven't you? Kind of 'down', right?"

"Yeah . . . a little, I guess."

"And I don't blame you. You've got reasons. Lots of reasons. For one . . . there's your money problem."

"I'm expecting a raise. Shendorf promised me one—within the next few weeks."

"You won't get it, Frank. I *know.* He's lying to you. Right now, at this moment, he's looking for a man to replace you at the company. Shendorf's planning to fire you."

"He never liked me . . . We never got along from the day I walked into that office."

"And your wife . . . all the arguments you've been having with her lately . . . It's a pattern, Frank. Your marriage is all over. Helen's going to ask you for a divorce. She's in love with another man."

"*Who,* dammit? What's his name?"

"You don't know him. Wouldn't change things if you did. There's nothing you can do about it now. Helen just . . . doesn't love you anymore. These things happen to people."

"We've been . . . drifting apart for the last year—but I didn't know why. I had no idea that she . . ."

"And then there's Jan. She's back on it, Frank. Only it's worse now. A lot worse."

I knew what he meant—and the coldness raked along my body. Jan was nineteen, my oldest daughter—and she'd been into drugs for the past three years. But she'd promised to quit.

"What do you know about Jan? Tell me!"

"She's into the heavy stuff, Frank. She's hooked bad. It's too late for her."

"What the hell are you saying?"

"I'm saying she's lost to you . . . She's rejected you, and there's no reaching her. She *hates* you . . . blames you for everything."

"I won't *accept* that kind of blame! I did my best for her."

"It wasn't enough, Frank. We both know that. You'll never see Jan again."

The blackness was welling within me, a choking wave through my body.

"Listen to me, old buddy. Things are going to get worse, not better. I know. I went through my own kind of hell when I was alive."

"I'll . . . start over . . . leave the city—go East, work with my brother in New York."

"Your brother doesn't want you in his life. You'd be an intruder . . . an alien. He never writes you, does he?"

"No, but that doesn't mean—"

"Not even a card last Christmas. No letters or calls. He doesn't *want* you with him, Frank, believe me."

And then he began to tell me other things . . . He began to talk about middle age and how it was too late now to make any kind of new beginning . . . He spoke of disease . . . loneliness . . . of rejection and despair. And the blackness was complete.

"There's only one real solution to things, Frank—just *one.* That gun you keep in your desk upstairs. Use it, Frank. Use the gun."

"I couldn't do that."

"But why not? What other choice have you got? The solution is *there.* Go upstairs and use the gun. I'll be waiting for you afterwards. You won't be alone. It'll be like the old days . . . we'll be together . . . Death is beautiful, Frank. I *know.* Life is ugly, but death is beautiful . . . Use the gun, Frank . . . the gun . . . use the gun . . . the gun . . . the gun . . ."

I've been dead for a month now, and Len was right. It's fine here. No pressures. No worries. Gray and quiet and beautiful . . .

I know how lousy things have been going for you. And they *won't* get any better.

Isn't that your phone ringing?

Better answer it.

It's important that we talk.

## Different Kinds of Dead

By Ed Gorman

Around eight that night, snow started drifting on the narrow Nebraska highway Ralph Sheridan was traveling. Already he could feel the rear end of the new Buick begin sliding around on the freezing surface of the asphalt, and could see that he would soon have to pull over and scrape the windshield. Snow was forming into gnarly bumps on the safety glass.

The small-town radio station he was listening to confirmed his worst suspicions: the weather bureau was predicting a genuine March blizzard, with eight to ten inches of snow and drifts up to several feet.

Sheridan sighed. A thirty-seven-year-old bachelor who made his living as a traveling computer salesman—he worked especially hard at getting farmers to buy his wares—he spent most of the year on the road, putting up in the small shabby plains motels that from a distance always reminded him of doghouses. A brother in Cleveland was all the family he had left, everybody else was dead. The only other people he stayed in touch with were the men he'd been in Viet Nam with. There had been women, of course, but somehow it never worked out—this one wasn't his type, that one laughed too loudly, this one didn't have the same interests as he. And while his friends bloomed with mates and children, there was for Sheridan just the road, beers in bars with other salesmen, and nights alone in motel rooms with paper strips across the toilet seats.

The Buick pitched suddenly toward the ditch. An experienced driver and a calm man, Sheridan avoided the common mistake of slamming on the brakes. Instead, he took the steering wheel in both hands and guided the hurtling car along the edge of the ditch. While he had only a foot of earth keeping him from plunging into the gully on his right, he let the car find its own traction. Soon enough, the car was gently heading back onto the asphalt.

It was there, just when the headlights focused on the highway again, that he saw the woman.

At first, he tried sensibly enough to deny she was even there. His first impression was that she was an illusion, a mirage of some sort created by the whirling, whipping snow and the vast black night.

But no, there really was a beautiful, red-haired woman standing in the center of the highway. She wore a trench coat and black high-heeled shoes. She might have been one of the women on the covers of the private eye paperbacks he'd read back in the sixties.

This time, he did slam on the brakes; otherwise, he would have run over her. He came to a skidding stop less than three feet from her.

His first reaction was gratitude. He dropped his head to the wheel and let out a long sigh. His whole body trembled. She could easily have been dead by now.

He was just raising his head when harsh wind and snow and cold blew into the car. The door on the passenger side had opened.

She got inside, saying nothing, closing the door when she was seated comfortably.

Sheridan looked over at her. Close up, she was even more beautiful. In the yellow glow of the dashboard, her features were so exquisite they had the refined loveliness of sculpture. Her tumbling, radiant hair only enhanced her face.

She turned to him finally and said, in a low, somewhat breathy voice, "You'd better not sit here in the middle of the highway long. It won't be safe."

He drove again. On either side of the highway he could make out little squares of light—the yellow windows of farmhouses lost in the furious gloom of the blizzard. The car heater warmed them nicely. The radio played some sexy jazz that somehow made the prairie and the snow and the weather alert go away.

All he could think of was those private eye novels he'd read as a teenager. This was what always happened to the Hammer himself, ending up with a woman like this.

"Do you mind?" she asked.

Before he had time to answer, she already had the long white cigarette between her full red lips and was lighting it. Then she tossed her head back and French inhaled. He hadn't seen anybody do that in years.

"Your car get ditched somewhere" he asked finally, realizing that these were his first words to her.

"Yes," she said, "somewhere."

"So you were walking to the nearest town?"

"Something like that."

"You were walking in the wrong direction." He paused. "And you're traveling alone?"

She glanced over at him again with her dark, lovely gaze. "Yes. Alone." Her voice was as smoky as her cigarette.

He drove some more, careful to keep both hands on the wheel, slowing down whenever the rear of the car started to slide.

He wasn't paying much attention to the music at this point—they were going up a particularly sleek and dangerous hill—but then the announcer's voice came on and said, "Looks like the police have really got their hands full tonight. Not only with the blizzard, but now with a murder. Local banker John T. Sloane was found murdered in his downtown apartment twenty minutes ago. Police report an eyewitness say he heard two gunshots and then saw a beautiful woman leaving Sloane's apartment. The eyewitness reportedly said that the woman strongly resembled Sloane's wife, Carlotta. But police note that that's impossible, given the fact that Carlotta died mysteriously last year in a boating accident. The eyewitness insists that the resemblance between the redheaded woman leaving Sloane's apartment tonight and the late Mrs. Sloane is uncanny. Now back to our musical program for the evening."

A bosso nova came on.

Beautiful. Redheaded. Stranded alone. Looking furtive. He started glancing at her, and she said, "I'll spare you the trouble. It's me. Carlotta Stone."

"You? But the announcer said—"

She turned to him and smiled. "That I'm dead? Well, so I am."

Not until then did Sheridan realize how far out in the boonies he was. Or how lacerating the storm had become. Or how helpless he felt inside a car with a woman who claimed to be dead.

"Why don't you just relax?"

"Please don't patronize me, Mr. Sheridan."

"I'm not patroniz— Say, how did you know my name?"

"I know a lot of things."

"But I didn't tell you my name and there's no way you could read my registration from there and—"

She French inhaled—then exhaled—and said, "As I said, Mr. Sheridan, I know a lot of things." She shook her head. "I don't know how I got like this."

"Like what?"

"Dead."

"Oh."

"You still don't believe me, do you?"

He sighed. "We've got about eight miles to go. Then we'll be in Porterville. I'll let you out at the Greyhound depot there. Then you can go about your business and I can go about mine."

She touched his temple with long, lovely fingers. "That's why you're such a lonely man, Mr. Sheridan. You never take any chances. You never let yourself get involved with anybody."

He smiled thinly, "Especially with dead people."

"Maybe you're the one who's dead, Mr. Sheridan. Night after night alone in cheap little hotel rooms, listening to the country western music through the wall, and occasionally hearing people make love. No woman. No children. No real friends. It's not a very good life, is it, Mr. Sheridan?"

He said nothing. Drove.

"We're both dead, Mr. Sheridan. You know that?"

He still said nothing. Drove.

After a time, she said, "Do you want to know how tonight happened, Mr. Sheridan?"

"No."

"I made you mad, didn't I, Mr. Sheridan, when I reminded you of how lonely you are?"

"I don't see where it's any of your business."

Now it was her turn to be quiet. She stared out at the lashing snow. Then she said, "The last thing I could remember before tonight was John T. holding me under water till I drowned off the side of our boat. By the way, that's what all his friends called him. John T." She lit one cigarette off another. "Then earlier tonight I felt myself rise through darkness and suddenly I realized was taking form. I was rising from the grave and taking form. And there was just one place I wanted to go. The apartment he kept in town for his so-called business meetings. So I went there tonight and killed him."

"You won't die."

"I beg your pardon?"

"They won't execute you for doing it. You just tell them the same story you told me, and you'll get off with second degree. Maybe even not guilty by reason of insanity."

She laughed. "Maybe if you weren't so busy watching the road, you'd notice what's happening to me, Mr. Sheridan."

She was disappearing. Right there in his car. Where her left arm had been was now just a smoldering red-tipped cigarette that seemed to be held up on invisible wires. A part of her face was starting to disappear, too.

"About a quarter mile down the highway, let me out if you would."

He laughed. "What's there? A graveyard?"

"As a matter of fact, yes."

By now her legs had started disappearing.

"You don't seem to believe it, Mr. Sheridan, but I'm actually trying to help you. Trying to tell you to go out and live while you're still alive. I wasted my life on my husband, sitting around at home while he ran around with other women, hoping against hope that someday he'd be faithful and we'd have a good life together. It never happened, Mr. Sheridan. I wasted my whole life."

"Sounds like you paid him back tonight. Two gunshots, the radio said."

Her remaining hand raised the cigarette to what was left of her mouth. She inhaled deeply. When she exhaled the smoke was a lovely gray color. "I was hoping there would be some satisfaction in it. There isn't. I'm as lonely as I ever was."

He wondered if that was a small, dry sob he heard in her voice.

"Right here," she said.

He had been cautiously braking the last minute and a half. He brought the car comfortably over to the side of the road. He put on his emergency flashers in case anybody was behind him.

Up on the hill to his right, he saw it. A graveyard. The tombstones looked like small children huddled against the whipping snow.

"After I killed him, I just started walking," she said. "Walking. Not even knowing where I was going. Then you came along." She stabbed the cigarette out in the ashtray. "Do something about your life, Mr. Sheridan. Don't waste it the way I have."

She got out of the car and leaned back in. "Goodbye, Mr. Sheridan."

He sat there, watching her disappear deep into the gully, then reappear on the other side and start walking up the slope of the hill.

By the time she was halfway there, she had nearly vanished altogether.

Then, moments later, she was gone utterly.

At the police station, he knew better than to tell the cops about the ghost business. He simply told them he'd seen a woman fitting the same description out on the highway about twenty minutes ago.

Grateful for his stopping in, four cops piled into two different cars and they set out under blood red flashers into the furious white night.

Mr. Sheridan found a motel—his usual one in this particular burg—and took his usual room. He stripped, as always, to his boxer shorts and t-shirt and got snug in bed beneath the covers and watched a rerun of an old sitcom.

He should have been laughing—at least all the people on the laugh track seemed to be having a good time—but instead he did something he rarely did. He began crying. Oh, not big wailing tears, but hard tiny silver ones. Then he shut off both TV and the lights and lay in the solitary darkness thinking of what she'd said to him.

*No woman. No children. No love.*

Only much later, when the wind near dawn died and the snow near light subsided, only then did Sheridan sleep, his tears dried out but feeling colder than he ever had.

Lonely cold. Dead cold.

## Displaced Person

By Eric Frank Russell

He glided out of the gathering dusk and seated himself at the other end of my bench and gazed absently across the lakes toward the Sherry Netherland. The setting sun had dribbled blood in the sky. Central Park was enjoying its eventide hush: there was only the rustle of leaves and grasses, the cooing of distant and shadowy couples, the muted toot of a bus way over on Fifth.

When the bench quivered its announcement of company I had glanced along it expecting to find some derelict seeking a flop. The difference between the anticipated and the seen was such that I looked again, long, carefully, out one corner of my eye so that he wouldn't notice it.

Despite the gray half-tones of twilight, what I saw was a study in black and white. He had thin, sensitive features as white as his gloves and his shirt-front. His shoes and suit were not quite as black as his finely curved eyebrows and well-groomed hair. His eyes were blackest of all; that solid, supernal darkness that can be no deeper or darker. Yet they were alive with an underlying glow.

He had no hat. A slender walking stick of ebony rested against his legs. A black silk-lined cloak hung from his shoulders. If he'd been doing it for the movies he couldn't have presented a better picture of a distinguished foreigner.

My mind speculated about him the way minds do when momentarily they've nothing else to bother them. A European refugee, it decided. A great surgeon, or sculptor or something like that. Perhaps a writer, or a painter. More likely the latter.

I stole another look at him. In the lowering light his pale profile was hawklike. The glow behind his eyes was strengthening with the dark. His cloak lent him majesty. The trees were stretching their arms toward him as if to give comfort through the long, long night.

No hint of suffering marked that face. It had nothing in common with the worn, lined faces I had seen in New York, features stamped forever with the brand of the Gestapo. On the contrary, it held a mixture of boldness and serenity. Impulsively I decided that he was a musician. I could imagine him conducting a choir of fifty thousand voices.

"I am fond of music," he said in low, rich tones.

He turned his face toward me, revealed a pronounced peak in his hair.

"Really?" The unexpectedness of it had me muddled. "What sort?" I asked feebly.

"This." He used his ebony stick to indicate the world at large. "The sigh of ending day."

"Yes, it is soothing," I agreed.

We were silent awhile. Slowly the horizon soaked up the blood in the sky. A wan moon floated over the towers.

"You're not a native of New York?" I prompted.

"No." Resting long, slender hands upon his stick, he gazed meditatively forward. "I am a displaced person."

"I'm sorry."

"Thank you," he said.

I couldn't sit there and leave him flat like that. The choice was to continue or go. There was no need to go. I continued.

"Care to tell me about it?"

His head came round and he studied me as if only now aware of my presence. That weird light in his orbs could almost be felt. He smiled gradually, tolerantly, showing perfect teeth.

"I would be wasting your time."

"Not at all. I'm wasting it anyway."

Smiling again, he used his stick to draw unseeable circles in front of his black shoes.

"In these days it is an all too familiar story," he said. "A leader became so blinded by his own glory that no longer could he perceive his own blunders. He developed delusions of grandeur, posed as the final arbiter on everything from birth to death, and thereby brought into being a movement for his overthrow. He created the seeds of his own destruction. It was inevitable in the circumstances."

"You bet!" I supported wholeheartedly. "To hell with dictators!"

The stick slipped from his grasp. He picked it up, juggled it idly, resumed his circle-drawing.

"The revolt didn't succeed?" I suggested.

"No." He looked at the circles as if he could see them. "It proved too weak and too early. It was crushed. Then came the purge." His glowing eyes surveyed the sentinel trees. "I organized that opposition. I still think it was justified. But I dare not go back."

"Fat lot you should care about that. You'll fit in here like Reilly."

"I don't think so. I'm not welcome here either." His voice was deeper. "Not wanted—anywhere."

"You don't look like Trotsky to me," I cracked. "Besides, he's dead. Cheer up. Don't be morbid. You're in a free country now."

"No man is free until he's beyond his enemy's reach." He glanced at me with an irritating touch of amusement. "When one's foe has gained control of every channel of propaganda, uses them exclusively to present his own case and utterly suppress mine, and damns the truth in advance as the worst of lies, there is no hope for me."

"That's your European way of looking at things. I don't blame you for it, but you've got to snap out of it. You're in America now. We've free speech here. A man can say what he likes, write what he likes."

"If only that were true."

"It is true," I asserted, my annoyance beginning to climb. "Here, you can call the Rajah of Bam a hyphenated soandso if you want. Nobody can stop you, not even a cop. We're free, like I told you."

He stood up, towering amid embracing trees. From my sitting position his height seemed tremendous. The moon lit his face in pale ghastliness.

"Would that I had one-tenth of your comforting faith."

With that, he turned away. His cape swung behind him, billowing in the night breeze until it resembled mighty wings.

"My name," he murmured softly, "is Lucifer."

After that, there was only the whisper of the wind.

# The Disintegration of Alan

By Melissa Mia Hall

I can pinpoint almost the very second it began, the disintegration of Alan. It was the morning of October one; I had just glanced at the digital clock. Seven A.M., five or four minutes past. A Wednesday. In Greystone Bay. His right hand. He was reaching for the sugar at the breakfast table and as I watched his familiar hand pass through a diagonal shaft of sunlight, I saw his thumb fragment into nothingness. For a moment I thought it was due to my nearsighted eyes. I blinked groggily, coffee cup halfway to my lips.

"Alan?"

He thought I was beginning the old antisugar routine.

I swallowed heavily and set the cup down, staring at the space where his thumb had been. The index finger next to it looked like it would follow the thumb any moment, the fingertip shortening to the first joint. I exhaled slowly, resting my eyes on the crumpled newspaper beside my chair. I adjusted my glasses and returned my gaze to Alan.

He watched me curiously. The wrist of the disintegrating arm rested by his plate.

"Anything wrong, sweetie pie?"

"It's just—"

"Don't worry, if it bothers you that much, I won't take any sugar."

"Alan—"

"Now, Gabrielle, don't be a nuisance—"

Biting my lip, I continued to stare.

"What's with you?"

"I don't know," I said truthfully. I picked up my coffee and turned my head toward the window over the sink. "Go ahead, put some sugar in your coffee."

"I don't want to," he said.

"I said, go ahead."

"And I said I don't want to!"

"Why not?" I looked at him again. The disintegration had progressed. I wondered why it had begun at such an unlikely spot and not at his feet or his head. Then I realized the insanity of such reflections. Heat rose in my cheeks.

Alan's left hand reached toward the sugar bowl.

My heart sank. "Alan, why are you using your left hand?"

He shrugged his broad shoulders and the solidity of his chest only emphasized the absurdity of what I saw occurring before me. "Why not?"

"You're right-handed," I said.

Beads of perspiration broke out along his forehead. He scratched his mustache nervously and then tugged at his white collar—all with his left hand.

"Alan, what has happened to your right hand—your arm?"

His handsome, well-ordered face crumpled into confusion. "Nothing's wrong. I don't know what you mean. You're always finding something wrong with me. I don't know—I'm sick—sick to death." He pushed back his chair and stood up. "Call the office and tell them I'm not coming into work today." He glared at me, but the force of his chaotic anger had already dissipated. He looked constipated.

"Alan, really—"

"Shut up. I mean it." His mouth turned down at the ends and quivered. "I want to be alone." With that, he went to the doorway.

"Alan—please tell me what's going on."

"Nothing; it's the flu or something," he said, a touch of the shriek in his tone.

"Your arm—"

"What about my arm? There's nothing wrong about my arm!" He lifted the affected appendage and waved it around. It was grotesque.

I gasped. "Alan, can't you see—it's disappearing!"

"It is not!" he said before stomping down the hallway.

I sat in my chair and considered the situation. It was ridiculous, horrifying, and repulsive. Funny, too—well, a little. I hit my spoon against the tabletop. A sharp pain needled my temples.

The clock rang out. Time to leave for work. I had to call the *Gazette* and tell them Alan wasn't coming in. It didn't take long. I had to call in too. No way I could go to work either. I dialed the number. My secretary answered, her Brooklyn accent bright and sure over the line. I told her that I wouldn't be in and all the other things I was supposed to. I hung up the phone again and took off my shoes.

Down the hall, past the bedroom, to the studio I went. The

drawing board was just as I had left it. I sat before a half-drawn pencil sketch of Alan. I had tried—

I looked at it a long time. Finally I covered the sketch and played on a new piece of paper, blending lines and shapes without meaning. It was midmorning before I got up and stretched my legs. They'd almost fallen asleep. I had to go see about Alan.

He didn't call out to my query when I knocked on the door. I pushed it open slowly. Our room was paneled in dark wood and had never been very light. That morning was no exception. My eyes had to adjust to the dimness before I could see what was left of him, sitting in the striped armchair by the window. He looked at me and shrugged. His head, shoulders, and a portion of his torso were all that remained.

I wanted to vomit but did not. I held my hands to my mouth. What could I say?

He gazed at me vacantly, as if he could see me, but did not know me or the reason why I was there. He might have been thinking. Of other things. As I watched him I could detect recognition struggling in his eyes.

His mouth opened. "I'm sick. Please leave me alone for a while. I'll be okay if you'll just leave me alone."

He was afraid.

I was sweating. I took off my jacket and pushed back my hair. Then I went to him and tried to touch him. He jerked backward.

"Alan—please—"

"Gabrielle, why?"

I reached out again, trembling. My hands slid through. It's not always easy to face a reality like that.

He had been real. We had made love; we had taken baths together; we had hiked in the Vermont mountains. He liked Gatorade and tennis. I hated tennis. He liked beer. We saved beer cans. There was a huge bag of them out in the garage. The color orange was his favorite. He preferred Kleenex to Puffs. He didn't like the same kind of music I did and resented me singing along with the radio when we were in the car together. He always wore his hair parted on the right side. He liked watching the boats in the harbor. I liked sailing them.

There was nothing I could do. Soon he would be gone entirely. I thought of the police. Could such a thing be explained? "My husband disintegrated this morning and I thought you'd like to know." A giggle mushroomed from the madness and spilled out. I couldn't help it. Poor Alan. He twitched at that giggle.

"I'm sorry, Alan."

I would tell the police he just left me. Men do that sometimes. Nothing you can do to stop them—I don't think.

I straightened up, folded my arms. I regarded him with a sudden clarity. I was a camera remembering rolls of film that had passed through my chamber. Images, yes, yes—flash forward and flash back.

"Alan, is there anything I can do?"

"Well—" His head swiveled back and forth. He was trying to think of something.

I stared at the space where his bottom had been. I had not seen that disappear. It was unfortunate. Manic laughter pushed in my throat, wanting out. I clamped my lips and waited. I would be generous, kind.

"Yes, Alan?"

Childlike, shrill, he said something I couldn't quite understand.

"What?"

"I said, I guess I'm going away."

To just fade away, like that?

"Must it be like this—" Perhaps his image would firm up again—strong Alan, stalwart reporter. My stomach churned or maybe it growled. I hadn't eaten much breakfast and it was noon or after.

His mouth worked like a fish out of water. He'd always been rather clumsy.

"I don't want you to think I don't care about you, Gab."

I flinched. I hated him to call me Gab.

"Aw, Gabby, I really don't know why this has to happen. I thought we had a swell marriage and I've had a neat life, with the paper and all. But you know—I never really had control. This isn't that much a surprise."

His big blue eyes were mistlike. Sunlight glowed through his hair.

There was nothing I could do. I tried to kiss him. It was like kissing air. I couldn't even smell the after-shave he used to put on every morning.

The futility of life descended upon me. But I had to be brave.

"Wish it would get over with," he said. His voice was whistle-thin.

"Do you have anything else to say? Any—last words?" I gasped back the sobs.

"It's not my fault."

Childish of him. Always that petulant tilt to his lips—that too vivid, colorful face. What color? He was pale.

"Didn't you love me?" I asked, blushing at my boldness. It was now or never.

He looked at me like he didn't understand.

I left the bedroom. I thought I could hear him crying.

The studio was my sanctuary. I went to the drawing board and sat down. I looked out at Blind Point, at the ocean beyond. I pulled out the portrait of Alan and studied it intently to see if I could save it. Frowning, I took my favorite artgum eraser and finished erasing it.

I have always been a competent artist and I know a failure when I see one.

## Down by the Sea near the Great Big Rock

By Joe R. Lansdale

Down by the sea near the great big rock, they made their camp and toasted marshmallows over a small, fine fire. The night was pleasantly chill and the sea spray cold. Laughing, talking, eating the gooey marshmallows, they had one swell time; just them, the sand, the sea and the sky, and the great big rock.

The night before they had driven down to the beach, to the camping area; and on their way, perhaps a mile from their destination, they had seen a meteor shower, or something of that nature. Bright lights in the heavens, glowing momentarily, seeming to burn red blisters across the ebony sky.

Then it was dark again, no meteoric light, just the natural glow of the heavens—the stars, the dime-size moon.

They drove on and found an area of beach on which to camp, a stretch dominated by pale sands and big waves, and the great big rock.

Toni and Murray watched the children eat their marshmallows and play their games, jumping and falling over the great big rock, rolling in the cool sand. About midnight, when the kids were crashed out, they walked along the beach like fresh-found lovers, arm in arm, shoulder to shoulder, listening to the sea, watching the sky, speaking words of tenderness.

"I love you so much," Murray told Toni, and she repeated the words and added, "and our family too."

They walked in silence now, the feelings between them words enough. Sometimes Murray worried that they did not talk as all the marriage manuals suggested, that so much of what he had to say on the world and his work fell on the ears of others, and that she had so little to truly say to him. Then he would think: What the hell? I know how I feel. Different messages, unseen, unheard, pass between us all the time, and they communicate in a fashion words cannot.

He said some catch phrase, some pet thing between them, and Toni laughed and pulled him down on the sand. Out there beneath that shiny-dime moon, they stripped and loved on the beach like young sweethearts, experiencing their first night together after long expectation.

It was nearly two A.M. when they returned to the camper, checked the children and found them sleeping comfortably as kittens full of milk.

They went back outside for awhile, sat on the rock and smoked and said hardly a word. Perhaps a coo or a purr passed between them, but little more.

Finally they climbed inside the camper, zipped themselves into their sleeping bag and nuzzled together on the camper floor.

Outside the wind picked up, the sea waved in and out, and a slight rain began to fall.

Not long after Murray awoke and looked at his wife in the crook of his arm. She lay there with her face a grimace, her mouth opening and closing like a guppie, making an "uhhh, uhh," sound.

A nightmare perhaps. He stroked the hair from her face, ran his fingers lightly down her cheek and touched the hollow of her throat and thought: What a nice place to carve out some fine, white meat . . .

—*What in hell is wrong with me?* Murray snapped inwardly, and he rolled away from her, out of the bag. He dressed, went outside and sat on the rock. With shaking hands on his knees, buttocks resting on the warmth of the stone, he brooded. Finally he dismissed the possibility that such a thought had actually crossed his mind, smoked a cigarette and went back to bed.

He did not know that an hour later Toni awoke and bent over

him and looked at his face as if it were something to squash. But finally she shook it off and slept.

The children tossed and turned. Little Roy squeezed his hands open, closed, open, closed. His eyelids fluttered rapidly.

Robyn dreamed of striking matches.

Morning came and Murray found that all he could say was, "I had the oddest dream."

Toni looked at him, said, "Me too," and that was all.

Placing lawn chairs on the beach, they put their feet on the rock and watched the kids splash and play in the waves; watched as Roy mocked the sound of the JAWS music and made fins with his hands and chased Robyn through the water as she scuttled backwards and screamed with false fear.

Finally they called the children from the water, ate a light lunch, and, leaving the kids to their own devices, went in for a swim.

The ocean stroked them like a mink-gloved hand. Tossed them, caught them, massaged them gently. They washed together, laughing, kissing—

—Then tore their lips from one another as up on the beach they heard a scream.

Roy had his fingers gripped about Robyn's throat, had her bent back over the rock and was putting a knee in her chest. There seemed no play about it. Robyn was turning blue.

Toni and Murray waded for shore, and the ocean no longer felt kind. It grappled with them, held them, tripped them with wet, foamy fingers. It seemed an eternity before they reached shore, yelling at Roy.

Roy didn't stop. Robyn flopped like a dying fish.

Murray grabbed the boy by the hair and pulled him back, and for a moment, as the child turned, he looked at his father with odd eyes that did not seem his, but looked instead as cold and firm as the great big rock.

Murray slapped him, slapped him so hard Roy spun and went down, stayed there on hands and knees, panting.

Murray went to Robyn, who was already in Toni's arms, and on the child's throat were blue-black bands like thin, ugly snakes.

"Baby, baby, are you okay?" Toni said over and over. Murray wheeled, strode back to the boy, and Toni was now yelling at him, crying, "Murray, Murray, easy now. They were just playing and it got out of hand."

Roy was on his feet, and Murray, gritting his teeth, so angry he could not believe it, slapped the child down.

"MURRAY," Toni yelled, and she let go of the sobbing Robyn and went to stay his arm, for he was already raising it for another strike. "That's no way to teach him not to hit, not to fight."

Murray turned to her, almost snarling, but then his face relaxed and he lowered his hand. Turning to the boy, feeling very criminal, Murray reached down to lift Roy by the shoulder. But Roy pulled away, darted for the camper.

"Roy," he yelled, and started after him. Toni grabbed his arm.

"Let him be," she said. "He got carried away and he knows it. Let him mope it over. He'll be all right." Then softly: "I've never known you to get that mad."

"I've never been so mad before," he said honestly.

They walked back to Robyn, who was smiling now. They all sat on the rock, and about fifteen minutes later Robyn got up to see about Roy. "I'm going to tell him it's okay," she said. "He didn't mean it." She went inside the camper.

"She's sweet," Toni said.

"Yeah," Murray said, looking at the back of Toni's neck as she watched Robyn move away. He was thinking that he was supposed to cook lunch today, make hamburgers, slice onions; big onions cut thin with a freshly sharpened knife. He decided to go get it.

"I'll start lunch," he said flatly, and stalked away.

As he went, Toni noticed how soft the back of his skull looked, so much like an over-ripe melon.

She followed him inside the camper.

Next morning, after the authorities had carried off the bodies, taken the four of them out of the bloodstained, fire-gutted camper, one detective said to another:

"Why does it happen? Why would someone kill a nice family like this? And in such horrible ways . . . set fire to it afterwards?"

The other detective sat on the huge rock and looked at his partner, said tonelessly, "Kicks maybe."

That night, when the moon was high and bright, gleaming down like a big spotlight, the big rock, satiated, slowly spread its flippers out, scuttled across the sand, into the waves, and began to swim toward the open sea. The fish that swam near it began to fight.

## Dragon Sunday

By Ruth Berman

The desire for dragons is insidious. With the best intentions of remaining aware that you would be scared shitless by a real dragon and too obsessed with getting the hell out of the way of the flames to respond to the beauty of firelight reflected on blue or green or purple metallic scales, still—the desire remains.

You sit there on the yellow carpet, safe inside the beige walls, and desire dragons.

Which is all right, although wasteful of time and energy if you can't get dragons, but potentially dangerous if you can.

And it's all very well to consider that half the beauty of a vast body supported against the sky by wide leathery wings clangorously striking the air is in the fact that it's aerodynamically impossible. The sensual solidity of the imaginary is touching, and dragons are lovable quite simply because they look real and aren't. Until one Sunday you open the door to bring in the paper, and instead of funnies on the mat there are dragons all over the sky.

If they are.

They look real, seen in glimpses through plastic slats held apart by uncertain fingers (after the door is slammed shut). The bright sky is full of them, and there is even one ramping in the swimming pool, splashing water all over the courtyard. The slats clatter as the fingers let them go, and they fall back together.

So you pick up the telephone. Luckily, the dial tone is there, and it whines at you dutifully. Only you can't think where to call. There isn't anybody in LA you really know well enough to call up and say, "Hey, I know this is going to sound funny, but can you see any dragons out your window?" You could, of course, call any one of the people from the office. On the other hand, in the interests of keeping the job, maybe you'd better not.

A high *skree* shrills in the air from somewhere beyond the window, and other calls echo it from all over the sky.

Perhaps a call home would help. But long-distance is a strain on the budget, even on weekends. And anyway, they wouldn't know anything about what's going on in the sky. Not the one here. No, clearly, the thing to do is call the manager and complain.

The phone is still working, and she answers it on the third ring. "Hello?"

"Hi, this is 31 B."

"Uh-huh?" she says encouragingly.

"Yes. There seem to be these dragons all around, and—"

"Oh, that's too bad."

She is a conscientious manager.

"I'll get the exterminator to come out Monday. Will that be okay?"

"Well, but . . . Yeah, I guess so."

"Uh-huh." She waits, in case there are any other complaints to hand.

"Thanks. G'bye."

"Bye-bye."

There are several possibilities: (A) She misheard and thought the problem was roaches; (B) She thought it was just a bit of typically peculiar tenant's humor; (C) She thought she was humoring someone who'd just gone off his rocker, and she's going to call a hospital. Or, of course (D): Well, what else can you do about dragons except call in an exterminator? Knights don't do that sort of work anymore.

Another frightened glance out the picture window reveals the dragon in the swimming pool just leaping out. Its wings cup the air, and it rises leisurely, circling upward and throwing flecks of water against the white stucco walls as its tail swirls around after it.

There still remains the TV set. Nothing happens when the on knob is pulled out. But then nothing does happen when the on knob is pulled out. Bending over and putting an ear against it makes audible a humming deep inside it. The TV is working, and there is time for a glass of water before it does anything about it.

Even with water your throat feels dry.

Time for the news.

"—og alert," says the TV, still pictureless. "Motorists on the Hollywood Freeway report that the Capitol Records Building is invisible. Meteorological records indicate that this is the worst smog recorded in five years. Not since . . ." And so on. No dragons.

Perhaps later, after the weather.

The picture joins up. It does a little ballet and settles into a view of the Freeway without the Capitol Records Building. Without much of anything except on-ramp, overpass, off-ramp, and smoggy sky. Even the FWY signs are obscured.

But the smog . . .

That sky is smoggy. The TV says so. That sky is smoggy, and this sky is blue. Which is impossible. Which is crazy. Which makes sense.

Naturally, if you're crazy enough to imagine dragons, you imagine them a blue sky. A dragon demands a blue sky.

The thing to do is to go get psychiatric care. Fortunately, County General is in walking distance. And driving it'll take less than no time.

So you go out, and the nearest dragon *skrees* and descends upon you, its scales flashing as it curves against the sunny sky, and the light is reflected off it, flashing reptilian stainedglass on the stucco.

It lands with all its claws in your back, and its mouth open, flaming.

Smoke blots out the sky.

Drops of light from dragonscales can still be seen, a little while, until dragonfire obliterates . . .

## Duck Hunt

By Joe R. Lansdale

There were three hunters and three dogs. The hunters had shiny shotguns, warm clothes and plenty of ammo. The dogs were each covered in big blue spots and were sleek and glossy and ready to run. No duck was safe.

The hunters were Clyde Barrow, James Clover and little Freddie Clover who was only fifteen and very excited to be asked along. However, Freddie did not really want to see a duck, let alone shoot one. He had never killed anything but a sparrow with his BB gun and that had made him sick. But he was nine then. Now he was ready to be a man. His father told him so.

With this hunt he felt he had become part of a secret organization. One that smelled of tobacco smoke and whiskey breath; sounded of swear words, talk about how good certain women were, the range and velocity of rifles and shotguns, the edges of hunting knives, the best caps and earflaps for winter hunting.

In Mud Creek the hunt made the man.

Since Freddie was nine he had watched with more than casual

interest, how when a boy turned fifteen in Mud Creek, he would be invited to The Hunting Club for a talk with the men. Next step was a hunt, and when the boy returned he was a boy no longer. He talked deep, walked sure, had whiskers bristling on his chin and could take up with the assurance of not being laughed at, cussing, smoking and watching women's butts as a matter of course.

Freddie wanted to be a man too. He had pimples, no pubic hair to speak of (he always showered quickly at school to escape derisive remarks about the size of his equipment and the thickness of his foliage), scrawny legs and little, gray, watery eyes that looked like ugly planets spinning in white space.

And truth was, Freddie preferred a book to a gun.

But came the day when Freddie turned fifteen and his father came home from the Club, smoke and whiskey smell clinging to him like a hungry tick, his face slightly dark with beard and tired-looking from all-night poker.

He came into Freddie's room, marched over to the bed where Freddie was reading *THOR,* clutched the comic from his son's hands, sent it fluttering across the room with a rainbow of comic panels.

"Nose out of a book," his father said. "Time to join the Club."

Freddie went to the Club, heard the men talk ducks, guns, the way the smoke and blood smelled on cool morning breezes. They told him the kill was the measure of a man. They showed him heads on the wall. They told him to go home with his father and come back tomorrow bright and early, ready for his first hunt.

His father took Freddie downtown and bought him a flannel shirt (black and red), a thick jacket (fleece lined), a cap (with ear flaps) and boots (waterproof). He took Freddie home and took a shotgun down from the rack, gave him a box of ammo, walked him out back to the firing range and made him practice while he told his son about hunts and the war and about how men and ducks died much the same.

Next morning before the sun was up, Freddie and his father had breakfast. Freddie's mother did not eat with them. Freddie did not ask why. They met Clyde over at the Club and rode in his jeep down dirt roads, clay roads and trails, through brush and briars until they came to a mass of reeds and cattails that grew thick and tall as Japanese bamboo.

They got out and walked. As they walked, pushing aside the reeds and cattails, the ground beneath their feet turned marshy. The dogs ran ahead.

When the sun was two hours up, they came to a bit of a clearing in the reeds, and beyond them Freddie could see the break-your-heart-blue of a shiny lake. Above the lake, coasting down, he saw a duck. He watched it sail out of sight.

"Well boy?" Freddie's father said.

"It's beautiful," Freddie said.

"Beautiful, hell, are you ready?"

"Yes, sir."

On they walked, the dogs way ahead now, and finally they stood within ten feet of the lake. Freddie was about to squat down into hiding as he had heard of others doing, when a flock of ducks burst up from a mass of reeds in the lake and Freddie, fighting off the sinking feeling in his stomach, tracked them with the barrel of the shotgun, knowing what he must do to be a man.

His father's hand clamped over the barrel and pushed it down. "Not yet," he said.

"Huh?" said Freddie.

"It's not the ducks that do it," Clyde said.

Freddie watched as Clyde and his father turned their heads to the right, to where the dogs were pointing noses, forward, paws upraised—to a thatch of underbrush. Clyde and his father made quick commands to the dogs to stay, then they led Freddie into the brush, through a twisting maze of briars and out into a clearing where all the members of The Hunting Club were waiting.

In the center of the clearing was a gigantic duck decoy. It looked ancient and there were symbols carved all over it. Freddie could not tell if it were made of clay, iron or wood. The back of it was scooped out, gravy-bowllike, and there was a pole in the center of the indention; tied to the pole was a skinny man. His head had been caked over with red mud and there were duck feathers sticking in it, making it look like some kind of funny cap. There was a ridiculous, wooden duck bill held to his head by thick elastic straps. Stuck to his butt was a duster of duck feathers. There was a sign around his neck that read DUCK.

The man's eyes were wide with fright and he was trying to say or scream something, but the bill had been fastened in such a way he couldn't make any more than a mumble.

Freddie felt his father's hand on his shoulder. "Do it," he said. "He ain't nobody to anybody we know. Be a man."

"Do it! Do it! Do it!" came the cry from The Hunting Club.

Freddie felt the cold air turn into a hard ball in his throat. His scrawny legs shook. He looked at his father and The Hunting Club. They all looked tough, hard and masculine.

"Want to be a titty baby all your life?" his father said.

That put steel in Freddie's bones. He cleared his eyes with the back of his sleeve and steadied the barrel on the derelict's duck's head.

"Do it!" came the cry. "Do it! Do it! Do it!"

At that instant he pulled the trigger. A cheer went up from The Hunting Club, and out of the clear cold sky, a dark blue norther blew in and with it came a flock of ducks. The ducks lit on the great idol and on the derelict. Some of them dipped their bills in the derelict's wetness.

When the decoy and the derelict were covered in ducks, all The Hunting Club lifted their guns and began to fire.

The air became full of smoke, pellets, blood and floating feathers.

When the gunfire died down and the ducks died out, The Hunting Club went forward and bent over the decoy, did what they had to do. Their smiles were red when they lifted their heads. They wiped their mouths gruffly on the backs of their sleeves and gathered ducks into hunting bags until they bulged. There were still many carcases lying about.

Fred's father gave him a cigarette. Clyde lit it.

"Good shooting, son," Fred's father said and clapped him manfully on the back.

"Yeah," said Fred, scratching his crotch, "got that sonofabitch right between the eyes, pretty as a picture."

They all laughed.

The sky went lighter, and the blue norther that was rustling the reeds and whipping feathers about blew up and out and away in an instant. As the men walked away from there, talking deep, walking sure, whiskers bristling on all their chins, they promised that tonight they would get Fred a woman.

## The Dust

By Al Sarrantonio

There was more of the dust.

The house was kept clean; Mother had cleaned it herself for a long time and then, when she had begun to get old and tired and

Father had finally agreed with her that she was indeed old and tired, they had retained someone to come up the hill twice a week to clean immaculately; but no matter how much cleaning was done, the dust remained. Seven of the eight floor and ceiling corners in any room might be spotless, but the eighth would have the dust, tucked neatly in and watching him. Ronnie knew why it watched him, and he hated the dust.

When Mother and Father went out, which they did four or five or sometimes—lately—even six times a week, Ronnie was left with the old lonely house to himself. In fact, Mother and Father locked him in. They went to town, Ronnie knew, to be away from him, and from the memory of the things that had happened with the dust when they lived in another town in another place thirty full years ago. When he had been called Slow Ronnie instead of just Ronnie, and had hated it. When he had begun to hate the dust because of what it did to him.

He had tried to tell Mother and Father about the dust, had been trying to tell them how the house was never really clean for thirty years, but they wouldn't listen to him. Or didn't want to. Mother just looked at him sadly out of her moon eyes, or sometimes shook her head or hid her face in her hands, and Father merely mumbled about the "problems of this boy." Ronnie knew Mother and Father argued about him, about putting him somewhere else away from people and away from them; sometimes he heard Mother's wailings in the night and Father's muffled arguments of "Better this way" or "Cheaper in the long run for us" and he knew that someday, perhaps someday soon, they would come to him with their tearful or blank faces and tell him that they could no longer keep him, that they were too old for it. But he understood all this. He only longed to make them understand about the dust, and about how it must be cleaned away before it consumed them all.

The house was high and dark, set in the side of a wooded hill up away from the town. It was what some might call dreary, but Ronnie loved every bit of it. And knew every bit of it, from the cold deep cellar to the musty gables at each end of the attic, including the Room in the Attic and the Secret Room. He knew where every shadow was, except for the shadows of the dust which kept changing, and he knew every sharp corner and hideyhole and how many steps there were in each of the stairways. He liked the house even better at night, when the shadows were thicker, and you could hide anything, even the dust, in them, and the sixty-watt bulbs that Father preferred (because they were cheaper) barely illuminated the large spaces between them. When it was cold in the winter, and nighttime dark, like it was this night, and when Mother and Father were out, which they were, it was his favorite time because he could almost lose himself in those dark spaces and make believe that even the dust didn't exist; that nothing existed but Ronnie—not Slow Ronnie—and that the night and the sharp clear cold belonged to him alone and that whatever happened thirty years ago never happened and that he had only started existing here and now in this blackness. It was wonderful because he was here all alone.

Except for the dust.

The dust was out there, he could see it, even on this perfect night. He could not even shut the dust out now. And that made him angry and frightened, because on other nights like this, of which there were only four or five each year, he had been able to get rid of the dust, push it out beyond his circle of darkness and back away from the illumination of sixty-watt bulbs to a sulking corner deep across the room, or away and into another room entirely, where it would gather and brood and wait for the daylight to see and follow him again. But this night he could feel it within the circle, clinging to itself and knowing that it had won a new battle and followed him nearly to the heart of his most secret places. There was nowhere he could go now to be alone, except the Room in the Attic and the Secret Room (which even Mother and Father didn't know about), his special rooms where even the dust never followed.

"Go away," he said to the space inside the circle, where the dust lurked.

There was a silent shifting.

"Go away," he said again.

There was another shifting, a sound like many threads being drawn across wood, behind him.

"I said go away! You can't come here!"

Suddenly, there were memories. It was thirty years ago, and the dust was all around him. Pressing him in dryly, more dust than he had ever seen before, covering him, blocking his vision, making him cough and his eyes begin to water.

There was laughter.

More than one voice. A lot of voices. Out beyond the dust, not laughter like when Spike or Pauly stood on their heads and sang "I'm Popeye the Sailor Man," but mean laughter, laughter that had been waiting below the surface to spring on him, and had only needed a bit of running away to get out at him. He was fighting at the dust with his fingers and hands, coughing and beginning to cry, trying to get out of the dust to see where he was, where the laughter was coming from, where the dust was coming from.

There was more and more dust, blinding him now, and then he was pushing at it crazily and it was going away, finally pulling back and away from him and he could see and breathe again.

That was when they called him Slow Ronnie.

There were five or six of them, almost all of his friends, the ones who had let him follow them around and carry their baseball equipment and, because he was so big, play touch football as a substitute in the fall after school. They had been waiting for him around the corner from Woolworth's, waiting for him to meet them, to come around the corner so they could drop the sacks of dirt and dust that Pauly had rigged up above the wrought-iron sign that hung on the corner with an orange firebox light on it, and they had pulled the string and were still laughing at him.

"Slow Ronnie," they were screeching. "Sloooooow Ronnie!" Waving their hands and taunting him while they said it. Almost all of them his friends, except for a new one he had never seen before, taller and sharp-faced.

"*Sloooooow* Ronnie," they kept saying as he wheezed and cried and brushed trembling at the dust.

Then he looked through his tears at the new one, the tall one with the bright sharp eyes, and a rage seized him.

"*I'm not slow!*" he screamed, and then he remembered the muscles in his arms going tight and hard and the breaking of a glass window and sharp red pieces of glass. Then no more. When he was awake again he was in a hospital tied down to a white bed and Mother and Father, their faces also white, looked down from above him. Father's face was whiter, and blanker.

The memories went away.

"Go away!" he screamed at the dust again. He was within his cold circle, and the dust was trying to come at him again. He was not Slow Ronnie, he knew that; he would never be Slow Ronnie again and as long as he could keep the dust away, and the boy with the sharp hard eyes and smile, he would never be Slow Ronnie again. The boy was a long way away, in time and distance, but the dust was here and he had to keep it away or he would be Slow Ronnie again.

"I am not Slow Ronnie!"

The dust gathered, making a hissing noise, on either side of him. A small ball of it slid by, brushing at his shoe.

"No!"

He stood, making swimming motions with his arms, threatening the dust to stay back. He had told Mother and Father about the dust, and they hadn't listened to him, and now this was happening. He could see into the circle of weak amber light in front of him, and he saw that the dust, all of the dust, was forming. It was covering the floor, like whispering gray snow, clumps and bunches moving here and there across it, and it was pushing toward him. It was into the circle now, and he knew that finally, after growing in separate strength all these years, the dust was coming for him again, coming to make him gasp and scream helplessly, to fill his mouth and nose with absolute and terrible dryness, to make him into Slow Ronnie once more. He could not accept that, he would not let the dust do that to him again.

He shouted "Keep back!" and ran from the room, out into the shadows of the hallway, his shadows, toward the stairway. The dust, as his feet touched it, rose up in wavy fingers and tried to clutch at him, but he screamed and swatted down at it, and ran on. There was dust in the hallway too, flowing out of every doorway to meet in a splash at the center of the hall; Ronnie leaped over it and onto the stairs, taking them two steps at a time. Below him, the dust rose and drew together, flowing up the stairs after him.

Ronnie ran to the attic ladder, climbing it and dropping the door behind him and then frantically pulling at the door to the inner attic room, moving his arm this way and that in the darkness, searching for the overhead light cord. He found it, and the weak bulb clicked on. The room was empty, and Ronnie let out a long and shuddering breath. The Room in the Attic was still safe, and closing and bolting the door behind him, he sat down in the center.

He listened.

There were sounds, soft clicks and rustlings, but these were the sounds that were always in his room. These were the sounds of his house, moving and sighing and settling contentedly about itself, and there was nothing of the dust about them. The dust did not come here, to this room; it did not belong and never had and all the sounds of the house, and the house itself, had always kept it out. This was the room that Ronnie went to when he was feeling sad, or when the dust in the other rooms began to bother him too much, or when the weather wasn't cold and shadowy like it was tonight. It was almost his favorite room in the house. There was hardly any furniture, and what furniture and storage there was was oddly shaped and threw long, deep and special shadows. Soothing shadows that blended with the creaking sounds and made the room always seem cold and dark. The dust never came in here.

The dust was coming in now.

Ronnie jumped up as he saw that the dust was sliding slowly but inexorably under the door. There was a great weight of dust behind the door, the lock was rattling heavily with the pressure of it, and there was a steady, roiling portion of it squeezing into the room and building inside.

Building to engulf him.

There was only one place for him to go, one place where the dust would never go because it didn't even know about it—no one knew about it, not Mother nor Father nor anyone else—and therefore couldn't follow. His Secret Room. The one that only he and the house were alive to, where he could think about anything, and the house would soothe him and the dust would not be there to watch.

He would go to that room and be safe.

There was a place under an old table in the Room in the Attic where the wall was not solid. Behind this was the Secret Room. On the outside of the house it showed as a tiny gable with no window, an obvious mistake of architecture. It was not even high enough to stand in, and was nearly airtight and completely dustless; one had to crouch low to get through its door, and step down into it as its floor was almost two feet below that of the Room in the Attic. There was not even a light in it, and Ronnie kept a flashlight hidden on a hook under the table by the door. The door itself was a paneled section of wood which fit snugly and undoorlike into the rest of the paneled wall.

It was a dark and secret and dustless place.

Ronnie crawled under the table and lifted his flashlight from its hook. He looked behind to see the dust building massively, high, roiling and blocklike, and pushing toward him. If he didn't go into the secret place, give the dust the chance of seeing where it was, it would press over him and suffocate him. It would choke him until he couldn't think and he became Slow Ronnie again. He began to cough just thinking about it.

He turned, shaking, to the secret door to the Secret Room and pulled at the latch.

Crouching low, his flashlight snapped on, he pulled open the door and began to step down.

The dust was waiting for him.

Heaving, gray, and shadowless, it filled the entire Secret Room.

And the dust was pressing at him from behind, as it overflowed the Room in the Attic.

A sudden peace came over him, a silent raging peace, as the dust pressed down and up on him, holding him to itself, and the house murmured to him, and the boy with the sharp eyes and face was there before him in the dust, embracing him.

Outside, he heard the muffled hum of Mother and Father's returning car.

He knew who they would find.

## The Evil Clergyman

By H. P. Lovecraft

I was shown into the attic chamber by a grave, intelligent-looking man with quiet clothes and an iron-gray beard, who spoke to me in this fashion:

"Yes, *he* lived here—but I don't advise your doing anything. Your curiosity makes you irresponsible. *We* never come here at night, and it's only because of *his* will that we keep it this way. You know what *he* did. That abominable society took charge at last, and we don't know where *he* is buried. There was no way the law or anything else could reach the society.

"I hope you won't stay till after dark. And I beg of you to let that thing on the table—the thing that looks like a match-box—alone. We don't know what it is, but we suspect it has something to do with what *he* did. We even avoid looking at it very steadily."

After a time the man left me alone in the attic room. It was very dingy and dusty, and only primitively furnished, but it had a neatness which showed it was not a slum-denizen's quarters. There were shelves full of theological and classical books, and another bookcase containing treatises on magic—Paracelsus, Albertus Magnus, Trithemius, Hermes Trismegistus, Borellus, and others in strange alphabets whose titles I could not decipher. The furniture was very plain. There was a door, but it led only into a closet. The only egress was the aperture in the floor up to which the crude, steep staircase led. The windows were of bull's-eye pattern, and the black oak beams bespoke unbelievable antiquity. Plainly, this house was of the Old World. I seemed to know where I was, but cannot recall what I then knew. Certainly the town was *not* London. My impression is of a small seaport.

The small object on the table fascinated me intensely. I seemed to know what to do with it, for I drew a pocket electric light—or what looked like one—out of my pocket and nervously tested its flashes. The light was not white but violet, and seemed less like true light than like some radio-active bombardment. I recall that I did not regard it as a common flashlight—indeed, I *had* a common flashlight in another pocket.

It was getting dark, and the ancient roofs and chimney-pots outside looked very queer through the bull's-eye windowpanes. Finally I summoned up courage and propped the small object up on the table against a book—then turned the rays of the peculiar violet light upon it. The light seemed now to be more like a rain or hail of small violet particles than like a continuous beam. As the particles struck the glassy surface at the center of the strange device, they seemed to produce a crackling noise like the sputtering of a vacuum tube through which sparks are passed. The dark glassy surface displayed a pinkish glow, and a vague white shape seemed to be taking form at its center. Then I noticed that I was not alone in the room—and put the ray-projector back in my pocket.

But the newcomer did not speak—nor did I hear any sound whatever during all the immediately following moments. Everything was shadowy pantomime, as if seen at a vast distance through some intervening haze—although on the other hand the newcomer and all subsequent comers loomed large and close, as if both near and distant, according to some abnormal geometry.

The newcomer was a thin, dark man of medium height attired in the clerical garb of the Anglican church. He was apparently about thirty years old, with a sallow, olive complexion and fairly good features, but an abnormally high forehead. His black hair was well cut and neatly brushed, and he was clean-shaven though blue-chinned with a heavy growth of beard. He wore rimless spectacles with steel bows. His build and lower facial features were like other clergymen I had seen, but he had a vastly higher forehead, and was darker and more intelligent-looking—also more subtly and concealedly *evil*-looking. At the present moment—having just lighted a faint oil lamp—he looked nervous, and before I knew it he was casting all his magical books into a fireplace on the window side of the room (where the wall slanted sharply) which I had not noticed before. The flames devoured the volumes greedily—leaping up in strange colors and emitting indescribably hideous odors as the strangely hieroglyphed leaves and wormy bindings succumbed to the devastating element. All at once I saw there were others in the room—grave-looking men in clerical costume, one of whom wore the bands and knee-breeches of a bishop. Though I could hear nothing, I could see that they were bringing a decision of vast import to the first-comer. They seemed to hate and fear him at the same time, and he seemed to return these sentiments. His face set itself into a grim expression, but I could see his right hand shaking as he tried to grip the back of a chair. The bishop pointed to the empty case and to the fireplace (where the flames had died down amidst a charred, noncommittal mass), and seemed filled with a peculiar loathing. The first-comer then gave a wry smile and reached out with his left hand toward the small object on the table. Everyone then seemed frightened. The procession of clerics began filing down the steep stairs through the trap-door in the floor, turning and making menacing gestures as they left. The bishop was last to go.

The first-comer now went to a cupboard on the inner side of the room and extracted a coil of rope. Mounting a chair, he attached one end of the rope to a hook in the great exposed central beam of black oak, and began making a noose with the other end. Realizing he was about to hang himself, I started forward to dissuade or save him. He saw me and ceased his preparations, looking at me with a kind of *triumph* which puzzled and disturbed me. He slowly stepped down from the chair and began gliding toward me with a positively wolfish grin on his dark, thin-lipped face.

I felt somehow in deadly peril, and drew out the peculiar ray-projector as a weapon of defense. Why I thought it could help me, I do not know. I turned it on—full in his face, and saw the sallow features glow first with violet and then with pinkish light. His expression of wolfish exultation began to be crowded aside by a look of profound fear—which did not, however, wholly displace the exultation. He stopped in his tracks—then, flailing his arms wildly in the air, began to stagger backward. I saw he was edging toward the open stair-well in the floor, and tried to shout a warning, but he did not hear me. In another instant he had lurched backward through the opening and was lost to view.

I found difficulty in moving toward the stair-well, but when I did get there I found no crushed body on the floor below. Instead there was a clatter of people coming up with lanterns, for the spell of phantasmal silence had broken, and I once more heard sounds and saw figures as normally tri-dimensional. Something had evidently drawn a crowd to this place. Had there been a noise I had not heard? Presently the two people (simple villagers, apparently) farthest in the lead saw me—and stood paralyzed. One of them shrieked loudly and reverberantly:

"Ahrrh! . . . It be'ee, zur? Again?"

Then they all turned and fled frantically. All, that is, but one. When the crowd was gone I saw the grave-bearded man who had brought me to this place—standing alone with a lantern. He was gazing at me gaspingly and fascinatedly, but did not seem afraid. Then he began to ascend the stairs, and joined me in the attic. He spoke:

"So you *didn't* let it alone! I'm sorry. I know what has happened. It happened once before, but the man got frightened and shot himself. You ought not to have made *him* come back. You know what *he* wants. But you mustn't get frightened like the other man he got. Something very strange and terrible has happened to you, but it didn't get far enough to hurt your mind and personality. If you'll keep cool, and accept the need for making certain radical readjustments in your life, you can keep right on enjoying the world, and the fruits of your scholarship. But you can't live here—and I don't think you'll wish to go back to London. I'd advise America.

"You mustn't try anything more with that—thing. Nothing can be put back now. It would only make matters worse to do—or summon—anything. You are not as badly off as you might be—but you must get out of here at once and stay away. You'd better thank Heaven it didn't go further. . . .

"I'm going to prepare you as bluntly as I can. There's been a certain change—in your personal appearance. *He* always causes that. But in a new country you can get used to it. There's a mirror up at the other end of the room, and I'm going to take you to it. You'll get a shock—though you will see nothing repulsive."

I was now shaking with a deadly fear, and the bearded man almost had to hold me up as he walked me across the room to the mirror, the faint lamp (i.e., that formerly on the table, not the still fainter lantern he had brought) in his free hand. This is what I saw in the glass:

A thin, dark man of medium stature attired in the clerical garb of the Anglican church, apparently about thirty, and with rimless, steel-bowed glasses glistening beneath a sallow, olive forehead of abnormal height.

It was the silent first-comer who had burned his books.

For all the rest of my life, in outward form, I was to be that man!

# Examination Day

By Henry Slesar

The Jordans never spoke of the exam, not until their son, Dickie, was twelve years old. It was on his birthday that Mrs. Jordan first mentioned the subject in his presence, and the anxious manner of her speech caused her husband to answer sharply.

"Forget about it," he said. "He'll do all right."

They were at the breakfast table, and the boy looked up from his plate curiously. He was an alert-eyed youngster, with flat blond hair and a quick, nervous manner. He didn't understand what the sudden tension was about, but he did know that today was his birthday, and he wanted harmony above all. Somewhere in the little apartment there were wrapped, beribboned packages waiting to be opened, and in the tiny wall-kitchen, something warm and sweet was being prepared in the automatic stove. He wanted the day to be happy, and the moistness of his mother's eyes, the scowl on his father's face, spoiled the mood of fluttering expectation with which he had greeted the morning.

"What exam?" he asked.

His mother looked at the tablecloth. "It's just a sort of Government intelligence test they give children at the age of twelve. You'll be getting it next week. It's nothing to worry about."

"You mean a test like in school?"

"Something like that," his father said, getting up from the table. "Go read your comic books, Dickie."

The boy rose and wandered toward that part of the living room which had been "his" corner since infancy. He fingered the topmost comic of the stack, but seemed uninterested in the colorful squares of fast-paced action. He wandered toward the window, and peered gloomily at the veil of mist that shrouded the glass.

"Why did it have to rain *today?*" he said. "Why couldn't it rain tomorrow?"

His father, now slumped into an armchair with the Government newspaper, rattled the sheets in vexation. "Because it just did, that's all. Rain makes the grass grow."

"Why, Dad?"

"Because it does, that's all."

Dickie puckered his brow. "What makes it green, though? The grass?"

"Nobody knows," his father snapped, then immediately regretted his abruptness.

Later in the day, it was birthday time again. His mother beamed as she handed over the gaily-colored packages, and even his father managed a grin and a rumple-of-the-hair. He kissed his mother and shook hands gravely with his father. Then the birthday cake was brought forth, and the ceremonies concluded.

An hour later, seated by the window, he watched the sun force its way between the clouds.

"Dad," he said, "how far away is the sun?"

"Five thousand miles," his father said.

Dickie sat at the breakfast table and again saw moisture in his mother's eyes. He didn't connect her tears with the exam until his father suddenly brought the subject to light again.

"Well, Dickie," he said, with a manly frown, "you've got an appointment today."

"I know, Dad. I hope——"

"Now it's nothing to worry about. Thousands of children take this test every day. The Government wants to know how smart you are, Dickie. That's all there is to it."

"I get good marks in school," he said hesitantly.

"This is different. This is a—special kind of test. They give you this stuff to drink, you see, and then you go into a room where there's a sort of machine——"

"What stuff to drink?" Dickie said.

"It's nothing. It tastes like peppermint. It's just to make sure you answer the questions truthfully. Not that the Government thinks you won't tell the truth, but this stuff makes *sure*."

Dickie's face showed puzzlement, and a touch of fright. He looked at his mother, and she composed her face into a misty smile.

"Everything will be all right," she said.

"Of course it will," his father agreed. "You're a good boy, Dickie; you'll make out fine. Then we'll come home and celebrate. All right?"

"Yes, sir," Dickie said.

They entered the Government Educational Building fifteen minutes before the appointed hour. They crossed the marble floors of the great pillared lobby, passed beneath an archway and entered an automatic elevator that brought them to the fourth floor.

There was a young man wearing an insignia-less tunic, seated at a polished desk in front of Room 404. He held a clipboard in his hand, and he checked the list down to the Js and permitted the Jordans to enter.

The room was as cold and official as a courtroom, with long benches flanking metal tables. There were several fathers and sons already there, and a thin-lipped woman with cropped black hair was passing out sheets of paper.

Mr. Jordan filled out the form, and returned it to the clerk. Then he told Dickie: "It won't be long now. When they call your name, you just go through the doorway at that end of the room." He indicated the portal with his finger.

A concealed loudspeaker crackled and called off the first name. Dickie saw a boy leave his father's side reluctantly and walk slowly toward the door.

At five minutes of eleven, they called the name of Jordan.

"Good luck, son," his father said, without looking at him. "I'll call for you when the test is over."

Dickie walked to the door and turned the knob. The room inside was dim, and he could barely make out the features of the gray-tunicked attendant who greeted him.

"Sit down," the man said softly. He indicated a high stool beside his desk. "Your name's Richard Jordan?"

"Yes, sir."

"Your classification number is 600-115. Drink this, Richard."

He lifted a plastic cup from the desk and handed it to the boy. The liquid inside had the consistency of buttermilk, tasted only vaguely of the promised peppermint. Dickie downed it, and handed the man the empty cup.

He sat in silence, feeling drowsy, while the man wrote busily on a sheet of paper. Then the attendant looked at his watch, and rose to stand only inches from Dickie's face. He unclipped a penlike object from the pocket of his tunic, and flashed a tiny light into the boy's eyes.

"All right," he said. "Come with me, Richard."

He led Dickie to the end of the room, where a single wooden armchair faced a multi-dialed computing machine. There was a microphone on the left arm of the chair, and when the boy sat down, he found its pinpoint head conveniently at his mouth.

"Now just relax, Richard. You'll be asked some questions, and you think them over carefully. Then give your answers into the microphone. The machine will take care of the rest."

"Yes, sir."

"I'll leave you alone now. Whenever you want to start, just say 'ready' into the microphone."

"Yes, sir."

The man squeezed his shoulder, and left.

Dickie said, "Ready."

Lights appeared on the machine, and a mechanism whirred. A voice said:

"Complete this sequence. One, four, seven, ten . . ."

Mr. and Mrs. Jordan were in the living room, not speaking, not even speculating.

It was almost four o'clock when the telephone rang. The woman tried to reach it first, but her husband was quicker.

"Mr. Jordan?"

The voice was clipped; a brisk; official voice.

"Yes, speaking."

"This is the Government Educational Service. Your son, Richard M. Jordan, Classification 600-115, has completed the Government examination. We regret to inform you that his intelligence quotient has exceeded the Government regulation, according to Rule 84, Section 5, of the New Code."

Across the room, the woman cried out, knowing nothing except the emotion she read on her husband's face.

"You may specify by telephone," the voice droned on, "whether you wish his body interred by the Government or would you prefer a private burial place? The fee for Government burial is ten dollars.

## The Faceless Thing

By Edward D. Hoch

Sunset: golden flaming clouds draped over distant canyons barely seen in the dusk of the dying day; farmland gone to rot; fields in the foreground given over wildly to the running of the rabbit and the woodchuck; the farmhouse gray and paint-peeled, sleeping possibly but more likely dead—needing burial.

It hadn't changed much in all those years. It hadn't changed; only died.

He parked the car and got out, taking it all in with eyes still intent and quick for all their years. Somehow he hadn't really thought it would still be standing. Farmhouses that were near collapse fifty years ago shouldn't still be standing; not when all the people, his mother and father and aunt and the rest, were all long in their graves.

He was an old man, had been an old man almost as long as he could remember. Youth to him was only memories of this farm, so many years before, romping in the hay with his little sister at his side; swinging from the barn ropes, exploring endless dark depths out beyond the last field. After that, he was old—through misty college days and marriage to a woman he hadn't loved, through a business and political career that carried him around the world. And never once in all those years had he journeyed back to this place, this farmhouse now given over to the weeds and insects. They were all dead; there was no reason to come back . . . no reason at all.

Except the memory of the ooze.

A childhood memory, a memory buried with the years, forgotten sometimes but always there, crowded into its own little space in his mind, was ready to confront him and startled him with its vividness.

The ooze was a place beyond the last field, where water always collected in the springtime and after a storm; water running over dirt and clay and rock, merging with the soil until there was nothing underfoot but a black ooze to rise above your boots. He'd followed the stream rushing with storm water, followed it to the place where it cut into the side of the hill.

It was the memory of the tunnel, really, that had brought him back—the dark tunnel leading nowhere, gurgling with rain-fed water, barely large enough for him to fit through. A tunnel floored with unseen ooze, peopled by unknown danger; that was a place for every boy.

Had he been only ten that day? Certainly he'd been no more than eleven, leading the way while his nine-year-old sister followed. "This way. Be careful of the mud." She'd been afraid of the dark, afraid of what they might find there. But he'd called encouragement to her; after all, what could there be in all this ooze to hurt them?

How many years? Fifty?

"What *is* it, Buddy?" She'd always called him Buddy. What is it, Buddy? Only darkness, and a place maybe darker than dark, with a half-formed shadow rising from the ooze. He'd brought along his father's old lantern, and he fumbled to light it.

"Buddy!" she'd screamed—just once—and in the flare of the match he'd seen the thing, great and hairy and covered with ooze; something that lived in the darkness here, something that hated the light. In that terrifying instant it had reached out for his little sister and pulled her into the ooze.

That was the memory, a memory that came to him sometimes only at night. It had pursued him down the years like a fabled hound, coming to him, reminding him, when all was well with the world. It was like a personal demon sent from Hades to torture him. He'd never told anyone about that thing in the ooze, not even his mother. They'd cried and carried on when his sister was found the next day, and they'd said she'd drowned. He was not one to say differently.

And the years had passed. For a time, during his high school days, he read the local papers—searching for some word of the thing, some veiled news that it had come out of that forgotten cavern. But it never did; it liked the dark and damp too much. And, of course, no one else ever ventured into the stream bed. That was a pursuit only for the very young and very foolish.

By the time he was twenty, the memory was fading, merging with other thoughts, other goals, until at times he thought it only a child's dream. But then at night it would come again in all its vividness, and the thing in the ooze would beckon him.

A long life, long and crowded . . . One night he'd tried to tell his wife about it, but she wouldn't listen. That was the night he'd realized how little he'd ever loved her. Perhaps he'd only married her because, in a certain light, she reminded him of that sister of his youth. But the love that sometimes comes later came not at all to the two of them. She was gone now, like his youth, like his family and friends. There was only this memory remaining. The memory of a thing in the ooze.

Now the weeds were tall, beating against his legs, stirring nameless insects to flight with every step. He pressed a handkerchief against his brow, sponging the sweat that was forming there. Would the dark place still be there, or had fifty years of rain and dirt sealed it forever?

"Hello there," a voice called out. It was an old voice, barely carrying with the breeze. He turned and saw someone on the porch of the deserted farmhouse. An old woman, ancient and wrinkled.

"Do I know you?" he asked, moving closer.

"You may," she answered. "You're Buddy, aren't you? My, how old I've gotten. I used to live at the next farm, when you were just a boy. I was young then myself. I remember you."

"Oh! Mrs. . . . ?" The name escaped him, but it wasn't important.

"Why did you come back, Buddy? Why, after all these years?"

He was an old man. Was it necessary to explain his actions to this woman from the past? "I just wanted to see the place," he answered. "Memories, you know."

"Bitter memories. Your little sister died here, did she not?" The old woman should have been dead, should have been dead and in her grave long ago.

He paused in the shade of the porch roof. "She died here, yes, but that was fifty years ago."

"How old we grow, how ancient! Is that why you returned?"

"In a way. I wanted to see the spot."

"Ah! The little brook back there beyond the last field. Let me walk that way with you. These old legs need exercise."

"Do you live here?" he asked, wanting to escape her now but knowing not how.

"No, still down the road. All alone now. Are you all alone, too?"

"I suppose so." The high grass made walking difficult.

"You know what they all said at the time, don't you? They all said you were fooling around, like you always did, and pushed her into the water."

There was a pain in his chest from breathing so hard. He was an old man. "Do you believe that?"

"What does it matter?" she answered. "After all these fifty years, what does it matter?"

"Would you believe me," he began, then hesitated into silence. Of course she wouldn't believe him, but he had to tell now. "Would you believe me if I told you what happened?"

She was a very old woman and she panted to keep up even his slow pace. She was ancient even to his old eyes, even in his world where now everyone was old. "I would believe you," she said.

"There was something in the ooze. Call it a monster, a demon, if you want. I saw it in the light of a match, and I can remember it as if it were yesterday. It took her."

"Perhaps," she said.

"You don't believe me."

"I said I would. This sun is hot today, even at twilight."

"It will be gone soon. I hate to hurry you, old woman, but I must reach the stream before dark."

"The last field is in sight."

Yes, it was in sight. But how would he ever fit through that small opening, how would he face the thing, even if by some miracle it still waited there in the ooze? Fifty years was a long long time.

"Wait here," he said as they reached the little stream at last. It hadn't changed much, not really.

"You won't find it." He lowered his aged body into the bed of the stream, feeling once again the familiar forgotten ooze closing over his shoes.

"No one has to know," she called after him. "Even if there was something, that was fifty years ago."

But he went on, to the place where the water vanished into the rock. He held his breath and groped for the little flashlight in his pocket. Then he ducked his head and followed the water into the black.

It was steamy here, steamy and hot with the sweat of the earth. He flipped on the flashlight with trembling hands and followed its narrow beam with his eyes. The place was almost like a room in the side of the hill, a room perhaps seven feet high, with a floor of mud and ooze that seemed almost to bubble as he watched.

"Come on," he said softly, almost to himself. "I know you're there. You've got to be there."

And then he saw it, rising slowly from the ooze. A shapeless thing without a face, a thing that moved so slowly it might have been dead. An old, very old thing. For a long time he watched it, unable to move, unable to cry out. And even as he watched, the thing settled back softly into the ooze, as if even this small exertion had tired it.

"Rest," he said, very quietly. "We are all so old now."

And then he made his way back out of the cave, along the stream, and finally pulled himself from the clinging ooze. The ancient woman was still waiting on the bank, with fireflies playing about her in the dusk.

"Did you find anything?" she asked him.

"Nothing," he answered.

"Fifty years is a long time. You shouldn't have come back."

He sighed and fell into step beside her. "It was something I had to do."

"Come up to my house, if you want. I can make you a bit of tea."

His breath was coming better now, and the distance back to the farmhouse seemed shorter than he'd remembered. "I think I'd like that," he said. . . .

## The Facts in the Case of M. Valdemar

By Edgar Allan Poe

Of course I shall not pretend to consider it any matter for wonder, that the extraordinary case of M. Valdemar has excited discussion. It would have been a miracle had it not—especially under the circumstances. Through the desire of all parties concerned, to keep the affair from the public, at least for the present, or until we had further opportunities for investigation—through our endeavors to effect this—a garbled or exaggerated account made its way into society, and became the source of many unpleasant misrepresentations; and, very naturally, of a great deal of disbelief.

It is now rendered necessary that I give the *facts*—as far as I comprehend them myself. They are, succinctly, these:

My attention, for the last three years, had been repeatedly drawn to the subject of Mesmerism; and, about nine months ago, it occurred to me, quite suddenly, that in the series of experiments made hitherto, there had been a very remarkable and most unaccountable omission:—no person had as yet been mesmerized *in articulo mortis.* It remained to be seen, first, whether, in such condition, there existed in the patient any susceptibility to the magnetic influence; secondly, whether, if any existed, it was impaired or increased by the condition; thirdly, to what extent, or for how long a period, the encroachments of Death might be arrested by the process. There were other points to be ascertained, but these most excited my curiosity—the last in especial, from the immensely important character of its consequences.

In looking around me for some subject by whose means I might test these particulars, I was brought to think of my friend, M. Ernest Valdemar, the well-known compiler of the "Bibliotheca Forensica," and author (under the *nom de plume* of Issachar Marx) of the Polish versions of "Wallenstein" and "Gargantua." M. Valdemar, who has resided principally at Harlem, N. Y., since the year of 1839, is (or was) particularly noticeable for the extreme spareness of his person—his lower limbs much resembling those of John Randolph; and, also, for the whiteness of his whiskers, in violent contrast to the blackness of his hair—the latter, in consequence, being very generally mistaken for a wig. His temperament was markedly nervous, and rendered him a good subject for mesmeric experiment. On two or three occasions I had put him to sleep with little difficulty, but was disappointed in other results which his peculiar constitution had naturally led me to anticipate. His will was at no period positively, or thoroughly, under my control, and in regard to *clairvoyance,* I could accomplish with him nothing to be relied upon. I always attributed my failure at these points to the disordered state of his health. For some months previous to my becoming acquainted with him, his physicians had declared him in a confirmed phthisis. It was his custom, indeed, to speak calmly of his approaching dissolution, as of a matter neither to be avoided nor regretted.

When the ideas to which I have alluded first occurred to me, it was of course very natural that I should think of M. Valdemar. I knew the steady philosophy of the man too well to apprehend any scruples from *him;* and he had no relatives in America who would be likely to interfere. I spoke to him frankly upon the subject; and, to my surprise, his interest seemed vividly excited. I say to my surprise; for, although he had always yielded his person freely to my experiments, he had never before given me any tokens of sympathy with what I did. His disease was of that character which would admit of exact calculation in respect to the epoch of its termination in death; and it was finally arranged between us that he would send for me about twenty-four hours before the period announced by his physicians as that of his decease.

It is now rather more than seven months since I received, from M. Valdemar himself, the subjoined note:

*"My Dear P——*

*"You may as well come* now. *D—— and F—— are agreed that I cannot hold out beyond to-morrow midnight; and I think they have hit the time very nearly.*

*Valdemar"*

I received this note within half an hour after it was written, and in fifteen minutes more I was in the dying man's chamber. I had not seen him for ten days, and was appalled by the fearful alteration which the brief interval had wrought in him. His face wore a leaden hue; the eyes were utterly lustreless; and the emaciation was so extreme, that the skin had been broken through by the cheekbones. His expectoration was excessive. The pulse was barely perceptible. He retained, nevertheless, in a very remarkable manner, both his mental power and a certain degree of physical strength. He spoke with distinctness—took some palliative medicines without aid—and, when I entered the room, was occupied in penciling memoranda in a pocket-book. He was propped up in the bed by pillows. Doctors D—— and F—— were in attendance.

After pressing Valdemar's hand, I took these gentlemen aside, and obtained from them a minute account of the patient's condition. The left lung had been for eighteen months in a semi-osseous or cartilaginous state, and was, of course, entirely useless for all purposes of vitality. The right, in its upper portion, was also partially, if not thoroughly, ossified, while the lower region was merely a mass of purulent tubercles, running one into another. Several extensive perforations existed; and, at one point, permanent adhesion to the ribs had taken place. These appearances in the right lobe were of comparatively recent date. The ossification had proceeded with very unusual rapidity; no sign of it had been discovered a month before, and the adhesion had only been observed during the three previous days. Independently of the phthisis, the patient was suspected of aneurism of the aorta; but on this point the osseous symptoms rendered an exact diagnosis impossible. It was the opinion of both physicians that M. Valdemar would die about midnight on the morrow (Sunday.) It was then seven o'clock on Saturday evening.

On quitting the invalid's bedside to hold conversation with myself, Doctors D—— and F—— had bidden him a final farewell. It had not been their intention to return; but, at my request, they agreed to look in upon the patient about ten the next night.

When they had gone, I spoke freely with M. Valdemar on the subject of his approaching dissolution, as well as, more particularly, of the experiment proposed. He still professed himself quite willing and even anxious to have it made, and urged me to commence it at once. A male and a female nurse were in attendance; but I did not feel myself altogether at liberty to engage in a task of this character with no more reliable witnesses than these people, in case of sudden accident, might prove. I therefore postponed operations until about eight the next night, when the arrival of a medical student, with whom I had some acquaintance (Mr. Theodore L——l), relieved me from further embarrassment. It had been my design, originally, to wait for the physicians; but I was induced to proceed, first, by the urgent entreaties of M. Valdemar, and secondly, by my conviction that I had not a moment to lose, as he was evidently sinking fast.

Mr. L——l was so kind as to accede to my desire that he would take notes of all that occurred; and it is from his memoranda that what I now have to relate is, for the most part, either condensed or copied *verbatim.*

It wanted about five minutes of eight when, taking the patient's hand, I begged him to state, as distinctly as he could, to Mr. L——l, whether he (M. Valdemar) was entirely willing that I should make the experiment of mesmerizing him in his then condition.

He replied feebly, yet quite audibly: "Yes, I wish to be mesmerized"—adding immediately afterward: "I fear you have deferred it too long."

While he spoke thus, I commenced the passes which I had already found most effectual in subduing him. He was evidently influenced with the first lateral stroke of my hand across his forehead; but, although I exerted all my powers, no further perceptible effect was induced until some minutes after ten o'clock, when Doctors D—— and F—— called, according to appointment. I explained to them, in a few words, what I designed, and as they opposed no objection, saying that the patient was already in the death agony, I proceeded without hesitation—exchanging, however, the lateral passes for downward ones, and directing my gaze entirely into the right eye of the sufferer.

By this time his pulse was imperceptible and his breathing was stertorious, and at intervals of half a minute.

This condition was nearly unaltered for a quarter of an hour. At the expiration of this period, however, a natural although a very deep sigh escaped from the bosom of the dying man, and the stertorious breathing ceased—that is to say, its stertoriousness was no longer apparent; the intervals were undiminished. The patient's extremities were of an icy coldness.

At five minutes before eleven, I perceived unequivocal signs of the mesmeric influence. The glassy roll of the eye was changed for that expression of uneasy *inward* examination which is never seen except in cases of sleep-waking, and which it is quite impossible to mistake. With a few rapid lateral passes I made the lids quiver, as in incipient sleep, and with a few more I closed them altogether. I was not satisfied, however, with this, but continued the manipulations vigorously, and with the fullest exertion of the will, until I had completely stiffened the limbs of the slumberer, after placing them in a seemingly easy position. The legs were at full length; the arms were nearly so, and reposed on the bed at a moderate distance from the loins. The head was very slightly elevated.

When I had accomplished this, it was fully midnight, and I requested the gentlemen present to examine M. Valdemar's condition. After a few experiments, they admitted him to be in an unusually perfect state of mesmeric trance. The curiosity of both the physicians was greatly excited. Dr. D—— resolved at once to remain with the patient all night, while Dr. F—— took leave with a promise to return at daybreak. Mr. L——l and the nurses remained.

We left M. Valdemar entirely undisturbed until about three o'clock in the morning, when I approached him and found him in precisely the same condition as when Dr. F—— went away—that is to say, he lay in the same position; the pulse was imperceptible; the breathing was gentle (scarcely noticeable, unless through the application of a mirror to the lips); the eyes were closed naturally; and the limbs were as rigid and as cold as marble. Still, the general appearance was certainly not that of death.

As I approached M. Valdemar I made a kind of half effort to influence his right arm into pursuit of my own, as I passed the latter gently to and fro above his person. In such experiments with this patient, I had never perfectly succeeded before, and assuredly I had little thought of succeeding now; but to my astonishment, his arm very readily, although feebly, followed every direction I assigned it with mine. I determined to hazard a few words of conversation.

"M. Valdemar," I said, "are you asleep?" He made no answer, but I perceived a tremor about the lips, and was thus induced to repeat the question, again and again. At its third repetition, his whole frame was agitated by a very slight shivering; the eyelids unclosed themselves so far as to display a white line of a ball; the lips moved sluggishly, and from between them, in a barely audible whisper, issued the words:

"Yes;—asleep now. Do not wake me!—let me die so!"

I here felt the limbs, and found them as rigid as ever. The right arm, as before, obeyed the direction of my hand. I questioned the sleep-waker again:

"Do you still feel pain in the breast, M. Valdemar?"

The answer now was immediate, but even less audible than before:

"No pain—I am dying!"

I did not think it advisable to disturb him further just then, and nothing more was said or done until the arrival of Dr. F——, who came a little before sunrise, and expressed unbounded astonishment at finding the patient still alive. After feeling the pulse and applying a mirror to the lips, he requested me to speak to the sleep-waker again. I did so, saying:

"M. Valdemar, do you still sleep?"

As before, some minutes elapsed ere a reply was made; and during the interval the dying man seemed to be collecting his energies to speak. At my fourth repetition of the question, he said very faintly, almost inaudibly:

"Yes; still asleep—dying."

It was now the opinion, or rather the wish, of the physicians, that M. Valdemar should be suffered to remain undisturbed in his present apparently tranquil condition, until death should supervene—and this, it was generally agreed, must now take place within a few minutes. I concluded, however, to speak to him once more, and merely repeated my previous question.

While I spoke, there came a marked change over the countenance of the sleep-waker. The eyes rolled themselves slowly open, the pupils disappearing upwardly; the skin generally assumed a cadaverous hue, resembling not so much parchment as white paper; and the circular hectic spots which, hitherto, had been strongly defined in the centre of each cheek, *went out* at once. I use this expression, because the suddenness of their departure put me in mind of nothing so much as the extinguishment of a candle by a puff of the breath. The upper lip, at the same time, writhed itself away from the teeth, which it had previously covered completely; while the lower jaw fell with an audible jerk, leaving the mouth widely extended, and disclosing in full view the swollen and blackened tongue. I presume that no member of the party then present had been unaccustomed to death-bed horrors; but so hideous beyond conception was the appearance of M. Valdemar at this moment, that there was a general shrinking back from the region of the bed.

I now feel that I have reached a point of this narrative at which every reader will be startled into positive disbelief. It is my business, however, simply to proceed.

There was no longer the faintest sign of vitality in M. Valdemar; and concluding him to be dead, we were consigning him to the charge of the nurses, when a strong vibratory motion was observable in the tongue. This continued for perhaps a minute. At the expiration of this period, there issued from the distended and motionless jaws a voice—such as it would be madness in me to attempt describing. There are, indeed, two or three epithets which might be considered as applicable to it in part; I might say, for example, that the sound was harsh, and broken and hollow; but the hideous whole is indescribable, for the simple reason that no similar sounds have ever jarred upon the ear of humanity. There were two particulars, nevertheless, which I thought then, and still think, might fairly be stated as characteristic of the intonation—as well adapted to convey some idea of its unearthly peculiarity. In the first place, the voice seemed to reach our ears—at least mine—from a vast distance, or from some deep cavern within the earth. In the second place, it impressed me (I fear, indeed, that it will be impossible to make myself comprehended) as gelatinous or glutinous matters impress the sense of touch.

I have spoken both of "sound" and of "voice." I mean to say that the sound was one of distinct—of even wonderfully, thrillingly distinct—syllabification. M. Valdemar *spoke*—obviously in reply to the question I had propounded to him a few minutes before. I had asked him, it will be remembered, if he still slept. He now said:

"Yes;—no;—I *have been* sleeping—and now—now—*I am dead.*"

No person present even affected to deny, or attempted to repress, the unutterable, shuddering horror which these few words, thus uttered, were so well calculated to convey. Mr. L——l (the student) swooned. The nurses immediately left the chamber, and could not be induced to return. My own impressions I would not pretend to render intelligible to the reader. For nearly an hour, we busied ourselves, silently—without the utterance of a word—in endeavors to revive Mr. L——l. When he came to himself, we addressed ourselves again to an investigation of M. Valdemar's condition.

It remained in all respects as I have last described it, with the exception that the mirror no longer afforded evidence of respiration. An attempt to draw blood from the arm failed. I should mention, too, that this limb was no further subject to my will. I endeavored in vain to make it follow the direction of my hand. The only real indication, indeed, of the mesmeric influence, was now found in the vibratory movement of the tongue, whenever I addressed M. Valdemar a question. He seemed to be making an effort to reply, but had no longer sufficient volition. To queries put to him by any other person than myself he seemed utterly insensible—although I endeavored to place each member of the company in mesmeric *rapport* with him. I believe that I have now related all that is necessary to an understanding of the sleep-waker's state at this epoch. Other nurses were procured; and at ten o'clock I left the house in company with the two physicians and Mr. L——l.

In the afternoon we all called again to see the patient. His condition remained precisely the same. We had now some discussion as to the propriety and feasibility of awakening him; but we had little difficulty in agreeing that no good purpose would be served by so doing. It was evident that, so far, death (or what is usually termed death) had been arrested by the mesmeric process. It seemed clear to us all that to awaken M. Valdemar would be merely to insure his instant, or at least his speedy, dissolution.

From this period until the close of last week—*an interval of nearly seven months*—we continued to make daily calls at M. Valdemar's house, accompanied, now and then, by medical and other friends. All this time the sleep-waker remained *exactly* as I have last described him. The nurses' attentions were continual.

It was on Friday last that we finally resolved to make the experiment of awakening, or attempting to awaken him; and it is the (perhaps) unfortunate result of this latter experiment which has given rise to so much discussion in private circles—to so much of what I cannot help thinking unwarranted popular feeling.

For the purpose of relieving M. Valdemar from the mesmeric trance, I made use of the customary passes. These for a time were unsuccessful. The first indication of revival was afforded by a partial descent of the iris. It was observed, as especially remarkable, that this lowering of the pupil was accompanied by the profuse outflowing of a yellowish ichor (from beneath the lids) of a pungent and highly offensive odor.

It was now suggested that I should attempt to influence the patient's arm as heretofore. I made the attempt and failed. Dr. F—— then intimated a desire to have me put a question. I did so, as follows:

"M. Valdemar, can you explain to us what are your feelings or wishes now?"

There was an instant return of the hectic circles on the cheeks: the tongue quivered, or rather rolled violently in the mouth (although the jaws and lips remained rigid as before), and at length the same hideous voice which I have already described, broke forth:

"For God's sake!—quick!—quick!—put me to sleep—or, quick!—waken me!—quick!—*I say to you that I am dead!*"

I was thoroughly unnerved, and for an instant remained undecided what to do. At first I made an endeavor to recompose the patient; but, failing in this through total abeyance of the will, I retraced my steps and as earnestly struggled to awaken him. In this attempt I soon saw that I should be successful—or at least I soon fancied that my success would be complete—and I am sure that all in the room were prepared to see the patient awaken.

For what really occurred, however, it is quite impossible that any human being could have been prepared.

As I rapidly made the mesmeric passes, amid ejaculations of "dead! dead!" absolutely *bursting* from the tongue and not from the lips of the sufferer, his whole frame at once—within the space of a single minute, or less, shrunk—crumbled—absolutely *rotted* away beneath my hands. Upon the bed, before that whole company, there lay a nearly liquid mass of loathsome—of detestable putrescence.

## Feeding Time

By James Gunn

Angela woke up with the sickening realization that today was feeding time. She slipped out of bed, hurried to the desk, and leafed nervously through her appointment book. She sighed with relief; it was all right—today was her appointment.

Angela took only forty-five minutes to put on her makeup and dress: it was feeding time. As she descended in the elevator, walked swiftly through the lobby, and got into a taxi, she didn't even notice the eyes that stopped and swiveled after her: feeding time.

Angela was haunted by a zoo.

She was also haunted by men, but this was understandable. She was the kind of blond, blue-eyed angel men pray to—or for—and she had the kind of measurements—36-26-36—that make men want to take up mathematics.

But Angela had no time for men—not today. Angela was haunted by a zoo, and it was feeding time.

Dr. Bachman had a gray-bearded, pink-skinned, blue-eyed kindliness that was his greatest stock in trade. Underneath, there was something else not quite so kindly which had been influential in his choice of professions. Now, for a moment, his professional mask—his *persona,* as the Jungians call it—slipped aside.

"A zoo?" he repeated, his voice clear, deep, and cultured, with just a trace of accent; Viennese without a doubt. He caught himself quickly. "A zoo. Exactly."

"Well, not exactly a zoo," said Angela, pursing her red lips thoughtfully at the ceiling. "At least not an ordinary zoo. It's really only one animal—if you could call him an animal."

"What do you call him?"

"Oh, I never call him," Angela said quickly, giving a delicious little shiver. "He might come."

"Hmmmm," hmmmmed Dr. Bachman neutrally.

"But you don't mean that," Angela said softly. "You mean if he isn't an animal, what is he? What he is—is a monster."

"What kind of monster?" Dr. Bachman asked calmly.

Angela turned on one elbow and looked over the back of the couch at the psychoanalyst. "You say that as if you met monsters every day. But then I guess you do." She sighed sympathetically. "It's a dangerous business, being a psychiatrist."

"Dangerous?" Dr. Bachman repeated querulously, caught off guard a second time. "What do you mean?"

"Oh, the people you meet—all the strange ones—and their problems—"

"Yes, yes, of course," he said hurriedly. "But about the monster—?"

"Yes, Doctor," Angela said in her obedient tone and composed herself again on the couch. She looked at the corner of the ceiling as if she could see him clinging there. "He's not a nightmare monster, though he's frightening enough. He's too real; there are no blurred edges. He has purple fur—short, rather like the fur on some spiders—and four legs, not evenly distributed like a dog's or a cat's but grouped together at the bottom. They're very strong—much stronger than they need to be. He can jump fifteen feet straight up into the air."

She turned again to look at Dr. Bachman. "Are you getting all this?"

Hastily, the psychoanalyst turned his notebook away, but Angela had caught a glimpse of his doodling.

"Goodie!" she said, clapping her hands in delight. "You're drawing a picture."

"Yes, yes," he said grumpily. "Go on."

"Well, he has only two arms. He has six fingers on each hand, and they're flexible, as if they had no bones in them. They're elastic, too. They can stretch way out—as if to pick fruit that grows on a very tall vine."

"A vegetarian," said Dr. Bachman, making his small joke.

"Oh no, Doctor!" Angela said, her eyes wide. "He eats everything, but meat is what he likes the best. His face is almost human except it's green. He has very sharp teeth." She shuddered. "Very sharp. Am I going too fast?"

"Don't worry about me!" snapped the psychoanalyst. "It is your subconscious we are exploring, and it must go at its own speed."

"Oh dear," Angela said with resignation. "The subconscious. It's going to be another one of those."

"You don't believe this nightmare has any objective reality?" Dr. Bachman asked sharply.

"That would make me insane, wouldn't it? Well, I guess there's no help for it. That's what I think."

Dr. Bachman tugged thoughtfully at his beard. "I see. Let's go back. How did this illusion begin?"

"I think it began with the claustrophobia."

Dr. Bachman shrugged. "A morbid fear of confined places is not unusual."

"It is when you're out in the open air. The fear had no relationship to my surroundings. All of a sudden I'd feel like I was in a fairly large room which had a tremendous weight of rock or masonry above it. I was in the midst of a crowd of people. For moments it became so real that my actual surroundings faded out."

"But the feeling came and went."

"Yes. Then came the smell. It was a distinctive odor—musty and strong like the lion house in the winter, only wrong, somehow. But it made me think of the zoo."

"Naturally you were the only one who smelled it."

"That's right. I was self-conscious, at first. I tried to drown out the odor with perfume, but that didn't help. Then I realized that no one else seemed to smell it. Like the claustrophobia, it came and went. But each time it returned it was stronger. Finally I went to a psychiatrist—a Dr. Aber."

"That was before the illusion became visual?"

"That was sort of Dr. Aber's fault—my seeing the monster, I mean."

"It is to be expected."

"When nothing else worked, Dr. Aber tried hypnosis. 'Reach

into your subconscious,' he said. 'Open the door to the past!' Well, I reached out. I opened the door. And that's when it happened."

"What happened?" Dr. Bachman leaned forward.

"I saw the monster."

"Oh." He leaned back again, disappointed.

"People were close, but the monster was closer. The odor was stifling as he stared through the door—and saw me. I slammed the door shut, but it was too late. The door was there. I knew it could be opened. And he knew it could be opened. Now I was really afraid."

"Afraid?"

"That the monster might get through the door."

The psychoanalyst tugged at his beard. "You have an explanation for this illusion?"

"You won't laugh?"

"Certainly not!"

"I think, through some strange accident of time, I've become linked to a zoo that will exist in the distant future. The monster—wasn't born on Earth. He's an alien—from Jupiter, perhaps, although I don't think so. Through the door I can see part of a sign; I can read this much."

Angela turned and took the notebook from his surprised fingers and printed quickly:

M'BA
(*Larmis*
Nativ
Vega

"Just like in the zoo," she said, handing the book back. "There's a star named Vega."

"Yes," said the psychoanalyst heavily. "And you are afraid that this—alien will get through the door and—"

"That's it. He can open it now, you see. He can't exist here; that would be impossible. But something from the present can exist in the future. And the monster gets hungry—for meat."

"For meat?" Dr. Bachman repeated, frowning.

"Every few weeks," Angela said, shivering, "it's feeding time."

Dr. Bachman tugged at his beard, preparing the swift, feline stroke which would lay bare the traumatic relationship at the root of the neurosis. He said, incisively, "The monster resembles your father, is that not so?"

It was Angela's turn to frown. "That's what Dr. Aber said. I'd never have noticed it on my own. There might be a slight resemblance."

"This Dr. Aber—he did you no good?"

"Oh, I wouldn't want you to think that," Angela protested quickly. "He helped. But the help was—temporary, if you know what I mean."

"And you would like something more permanent."

"That would be nice," Angela admitted. "But I'm afraid it's too much to hope for."

"No. It will take time, but eventually we will work these subconscious repressions into your conscious mind, where they will be cleansed of their neurotic value."

"You think it's all in my head?" Angela said wistfully.

"Certainly," the psychoanalyst said briskly. "Let us go over the progress of the illusion once more: first came the claustrophobia, then the smell, then, through Dr. Aber's bung—treatment, I should say, the dreams—"

"Oh, not dreams, doctor," Angela corrected. "When I sleep, I don't dream of monsters. I dream"—she blushed prettily—"of men. The thing in the zoo—I can see him whenever I close my eyes." She shivered. "He's getting impatient."

"Hungry?"

Angela beamed at him. "Yes. It's almost feeding time. He gets fed, of course. By the keeper, I suppose. But that's just grains and fruits and things like that. And he gets hungry for meat."

"And then?"

"He opens the door."

"And I suppose he sticks his elastic fingers through the door."

Angela gave him a look of pure gratitude. "That's right."

"And you're afraid that one day he will get hungry enough to eat you."

"That's it, I guess. Wouldn't you be? Afraid, that is? There's all the legends about dragons and Minotaurs and creatures like that. They always preferred a diet of young virgins; and where there's all that talk—"

"If that were your only concern," Dr. Bachman commented dryly, "it seems to me that you could make yourself ineligible with no great difficulty."

Angela giggled. "Why, Doctor! What a suggestion!"

"Hmmmm. So! To return. Every few weeks comes feeding time. And you, feeling nervous and afraid, come to me for help."

"You put it so well."

"And now it's feeding time."

"That's right." Angela's nostrils dilated suddenly. "He's getting close to the door. Don't you smell him, doctor?"

Dr. Bachman sniffed once and snorted. "Certainly not. Now tell me about your father."

"Well," Angela began reluctantly, "he believed in reincarnation—"

"No, no," the psychoanalyst said impatiently. "The important things. How you felt about him when you were a little girl. What he said to you. How you hated your mother."

"I'm afraid there won't be time. He's got one of his hands on the door already."

Despite himself, Dr. Bachman glanced back over his shoulder. "The monster?" His beard twitched nervously. "Nonsense. About your father—"

"The door's opened!" Angela cried out. "I'm scared, doctor. It's feeding time!"

"I won't be tricked again," the psychoanalyst said sternly. "If we're to get anywhere with this analysis, I must have complete—"

"Doctor! Watch out! The fingers—Dr. Bachman! Doctor! Doc—!"

Angela sighed. It was a strange sigh, half hopelessness and half relief. She picked up her purse.

"Doctor?" she said tentatively to the empty room.

She stood up, sniffing the air gingerly. The odor was gone. So was Dr. Bachman.

She walked toward the door. "Doctor?" she tried once more.

There was no answer. There never had been an answer, not from seventeen psychiatrists, Aber through Bachman. There was no doubt about it. The monster did like psychiatrists.

It was a truly terrifying situation she was in, certainly through no fault of her own, and a girl had to do the best she could. She could console herself with the thought that the monster would never take her for food.

She was the trap door it needed into this world. Eat her, and feeding time was over.

She was perfectly safe.

As long as she didn't run out of psychiatrists.

# Feeding Time

By Robert Sheckley

Treggis felt considerably relieved when the owner of the bookstore went front to wait upon another customer. After all, it was essentially nerve-racking, to have a stooped, bespectacled, fawning old man constantly at one's shoulder, peering at the page one was glancing at, pointing here and there with a gnarled, dirty finger, obsequiously wiping dust from the shelves with a tobacco-stained handkerchief. To say nothing of the exquisite boredom of listening to the fellow's cackling, high-pitched reminiscences.

Undoubtedly he meant well, but really, there was a limit. One couldn't do much more than smile politely and hope that the little bell over the front of the store would tinkle—as it had.

Treggis moved toward the back of the store, hoping the disgusting little man wouldn't try to search him out. He passed half a hundred Greek titles, then the popular sciences section. Next, in a strange jumble of titles and authors, he passed Edgar Rice Burroughs, Anthony Trollope, Theosophy, and the poems of Longfellow. The farther back he went the deeper the dust became, the fewer the naked light bulbs suspended above the corridor, the higher the piles of moldy, dog-eared books.

It was really a splendid old place, and for the life of him Treggis couldn't understand how he had missed it before. Bookstores were his sole pleasure in life. He spent all his free hours in them, wandering happily through the stacks.

Of course, he was just interested in certain types of books.

At the end of the high ramp of books there were three more corridors, branching off at absurd angles. Treggis followed the center path, reflecting that the bookstore hadn't seemed so large from the outside; just a door half-hidden between two buildings, with an old hand-lettered sign in its upper panel. But then, these old stores were deceptive, often extending to nearly half a block in depth.

At the end of this corridor two more book-trails split off. Choosing the one on the left, Treggis started reading titles, casually scanning them up and down with a practiced glance. He was in no hurry; he could, if he wished, spend the rest of the day here—to say nothing of the night.

He had shuffled eight or ten feet down the corridor before one title struck him. He went back to it.

It was a small, black-covered book, old, but with that ageless look that some books have. Its edges were worn, and the print on the cover was faded.

"Well, what do you know," Treggis murmured softly.

The cover read: *Care and Feeding of the Gryphon.* And beneath that, in smaller print: *Advice to the Keeper.*

A gryphon, he knew, was a mythological monster, half lion and half eagle.

"Well, now," Treggis said to himself. "Let's see now." He opened the book and began reading the table of contents.

The headings went: 1. *Species of Gryphon.* 2. *A Short History of Gryphonology.* 3. *Subspecies of Gryphon.* 4. *Food for the Gryphon.* 5. *Constructing a Natural Habitat for the Gryphon.* 6. *The Gryphon During Moulting Season.* 7. *The Gryphon and . . .*

He closed the book.

"This," he told himself, "is decidedly—well, unusual." He flipped through the book, reading a sentence here and there. His first thought, that the book was one of the "unnatural" natural history compilations so dear to the Elizabethan heart, was clearly wrong. The book wasn't old enough; and there was nothing euphuistic in the writing, no balanced sentence structure, ingenious antithesis and the like. It was straightforward, clean-cut, concise. Treggis flipped through a few more pages and came upon this:

"The sole diet of the Gryphon is young virgins. Feeding time is once a month, and care should be exercised—"

He closed the book again. The sentence set up a train of thought all its own. He banished it with a blush and looked again at the shelf, hoping to find more books of the same type. Something like *A Short History of the Affairs of the Sirens,* or perhaps *The Proper Breeding of Minotaurs.* But there was nothing even remotely like it. Not on that shelf nor any other, as far as he could tell.

"Find anything?" a voice at his shoulder asked. Treggis gulped, smiled, and held out the black-covered old book.

"Oh yes," the old man said, wiping dust from the cover. "Quite a rare book, this."

"Oh, is it?" murmured Treggis.

"Gryphons," the old man mused, flipping through the book, "are quite rare. Quite a rare species of—animal," he finished, after a moment's thought. "A dollar-fifty for this book, sir."

Treggis left with his possession clutched under his thin right arm. He made straight for his room. It wasn't every day that one bought a book on the *Care and Feeding of Gryphons.*

Treggis' room bore a striking resemblance to a secondhand bookstore. There was the same lack of space, the same film of gray dust over everything, the same vaguely arranged chaos of titles, authors, and types. Treggis didn't stop to gloat over his treasures. His faded *Libidinous Verses* passed unnoticed. Quite unceremoniously he pushed the *Psychopathia Sexualis* from his armchair, sat down and began to read.

There was quite a lot to the care and feeding of the gryphon. One wouldn't think that a creature half lion and half eagle would be so touchy. There was also an interesting amplication of the eating habits of the gryphon. And other information. For pure enjoyment, the gryphon book was easily as good as the Havelock Ellis lectures on sex, formerly his favorite.

Toward the end, there were full instructions on how to get to the zoo. The instructions were, to say the least, unique.

It was a good ways past midnight when Treggis closed the book. What a deal of strange information there was between those two black covers! One sentence in particular he couldn't get out of his head:

"The sole diet of the gryphon is young virgins."

That bothered him. It didn't seem fair, somehow.

After a while he opened the book again to the *Instructions for Getting to the Zoo.*

Decidedly strange they were. And yet, not too difficult. Not requiring, certainly, too much physical exertion. Just a few words, a few motions. Treggis realized suddenly how onerous his bank clerk's job was. A stupid waste of eight good hours a day, no matter how one looked at it. How much more interesting to be a keeper in charge of the gryphon. To use the special ointments during moulting season, to answer questions about gryphonology. To be in charge of feeding. "The sole diet . . ."

"Yes, yes, yes, yes," Treggis mumbled rapidly, pacing the floor of his narrow room. "A hoax—but might as well try out the instructions. For a laugh."

He laughed hollowly.

There was no blinding flash, no clap of thunder, but Treggis was nevertheless transported, instantaneously so it seemed, to a place. He staggered for a moment, then regained his balance and opened his eyes. The sunlight was blinding. Looking around, he could see that someone had done a very good job of constructing *The Natural Habitat of the Gryphon.*

Treggis walked forward, holding himself quite well considering the trembling in his ankles, knees, and stomach. Then he saw the gryphon.

At the same time the gryphon saw him.

Slowly at first, then with ever-gaining momentum, the gryphon advanced on him. The great eagle's wings opened, the talons extended, and the gryphon leaped, or sailed, forward.

Treggis tried to jump out of the way in a single uncontrollable shudder. The gryphon came at him, huge and golden in the sun, and Treggis screamed desperately, "No, no! The sole diet of the gryphon is young—"

Then he screamed again in full realization as the talons seized him.

## The Final Quest

By William F. Nolan

Here now, stand close, and let me weave
  A tale so eldritch you'll believe
Me mad. For never has been told
  This death-dark saga. Brave and bold
Was Arthur, bearing Britain's crown,
  A king of courage and renown.
Begat above a thundered sea,
  A just and stalwart lord was he.
In glittered armor, head to heel,
  He smote rogue knights with magic steel.

With Saxon blood upon his blade,
  He came from battle to a glade
Where demons did upon him cast
  A deep spell dark-designed to last
Ten thousand years or more they say.
  Till Merlin came at break of day

And found his lord in sleeping death.
   Then blew upon his cheek a breath
Which waked him full. Cried out the king:
   "The Earth shall ever of thee sing!
I vow upon sweet Jesu's name
   That you shall never want for fame."
But Merlin sighed and bowed his head,
   His waxen face deep-marked with dread.
"This fame, my king, that you bestow
   Avails me naught where I must go.
For though I saved thee on this day
   From Old King Death there is no stay."

"Not so!" cried Arthur, fist raised high,
   "I say that Death Himself shall die!"
"But surely, Sire, you speak in jest,
   No chance have we in such a quest."
But Arthur gripped good Merlin's arm.
   "I shall not let thee come to harm.
Death shall not pluck thee from my side.
   To his dominion we shall ride,
And there, I vow, shall king meet king.
   An end to Death's long reign I'll bring!"

And so began, as legends tell,
   A quest for Death where he might dwell.
On horse, Excalibur in hand,
   With Merlin, searched they land to land
Across the world. And years did pass
   Until, one morn, within a mass
Of stone from which no shadow's breath
   Was cast, at length they found Old Death.
Two kings, both bold, did thundrous reel
   Together, crashing, steel on steel.

And, sad by, watching Merlin wept,
   Aware that Arthur would be swept
From out this life. That even he
   Could not prevail now in the lee
Of Death's dark power. Yea, hour 'pon hour
   The marveled conflict hotly raged,
For never had the world seen staged
   Such awesome clash of mighty wills.

And ringing from the sky-tall hills
   Was word of battle swiftly sown
From castle wall to hut of stone.
   From moor and meadow, mountain, plain,
Fast came they all to see Death slain
   By Arthur. Duke, serf-slave, and lord
Were dazzled by his blazing sword.

A day, a night, a week passed by
   Without surcease. O'er land and sky
These titans met in frighted clash
   Of arms, to hew and maim and slash
Each one in turn, while moons did wane
   And blooded sunsets redly stain
The earth. And even those long dead
   Themselves raised from their graves, 'tis said,
And stood, stark-boned in silent rows,
   To watch these fearsome, dreaded foes.

Until, at long last, it was done.
   Incredibly, their knight had won!
And Death Himself was laid full out.
   Then, heavenward, the strangled shout
From Arthur's throat: "We'll have no more
   Of Death upon fair Britain's shore!"
But Death knew well the knightly code,
   And to victorious Arthur showed
A face of guile. And, from the ground,
   His voice a low and piteous sound,
He asked for mercy, loud implored,
   Till Arthur put away his sword
To help him stand. Then Merlin rushed
   Straight on, ash-eyed, his tone close-hushed
In Arthur's ear. He harshly warned
   That here all mercy must be scorned.

"This thing I cannot do, good friend,"
   Said he to Merlin. "For once bend
Our code, and it shall surely break
   And, with it, knightly honor take."
Thus, Arthur's fixed code could not yield.
   He laid aside his blade and shield,

While foul and fetid Death roared free.
  And not for all eternity
Would king meet king in such a fight
  As this. And Death, in turn, did blight
The world for his defeat. All died:
  E'en Arthur, Merlin at his side,
Sore-wounded now, his magic fled
  In this, their final leafy bed.

And later, all of Camelot,
  Knights of the Table Round could not
Evade that final darkling wood
  Where smiling, white-boned tall Death stood
Supreme. No further songs were sung
  Of chivalry. The knell had rung.

## Fish Night

By Joe R. Lansdale

It was a bleached-bone afternoon with a cloudless sky and a monstrous sun. The air trembled like a mass of gelatinous ectoplasm. No wind blew.

Through the swelter came a worn, black Plymouth, coughing and belching white smoke from beneath its hood. It wheezed twice, backfired loudly, died by the side of the road.

The driver got out and went around to the hood. He was a man in the hard winter years of life, with dead brown hair and a heavy belly riding his hips. His shirt was open to the navel, the sleeves rolled up past his elbows. The hair on his chest and arms was gray.

A younger man climbed out on the passenger side, went around front too. Yellow sweat-explosions stained the pits of his white shirt. An unfastened, striped tie was draped over his neck like a pet snake that had died in its sleep.

"Well?" the younger man asked.

The old man said nothing. He opened the hood. A calliope note of steam blew out from the radiator in a white puff, rose to the sky, turned clear.

"Damn," the old man said, and he kicked the bumper of the Plymouth as if he were kicking a foe in the teeth. He got little satisfaction out of the action, just a nasty scuff on his brown wingtip and a jar to his ankle that hurt like hell.

"Well?" the young man repeated.

"Well what? What do you think? Dead as the can opener trade this week. Deader. The radiator's chickenpocked with holes."

"Maybe someone will come by and give us a hand."

"Sure."

"A ride anyway."

"Keep thinking that, college boy."

"Someone is bound to come along," the young man said.

"Maybe. Maybe not. Who else takes these cutoffs? The main highway, that's where everyone is. Not this little no account shortcut." He finished by glaring at the young man.

"I didn't make you take it," the young man snapped. "It was on the map. I told you about it, that's all. You chose it. You're the one that decided to take it. It's not my fault. Besides, who'd have expected the car to die?"

"I did tell you to check the water in the radiator, didn't I? Wasn't that back as far as El Paso?"

"I checked. It had water then. I tell you, it's not my fault. You're the one that's done all the Arizona driving."

"Yeah, yeah," the old man said, as if this were something he didn't want to hear. He turned to look up the highway.

No cars. No trucks. Just heat waves and miles of empty concrete in sight.

They seated themselves on the hot ground with their backs to the car. That way it provided some shade—but not much. They sipped on a jug of lukewarm water from the Plymouth and spoke little until the sun fell down. By then they had both mellowed a bit. The heat had vacated the sands and the desert chill had settled in. Where the warmth had made the pair snappy, the cold drew them together.

The old man buttoned his shirt and rolled down his sleeves while the young man rummaged a sweater out of the backseat. He put the sweater on, sat back down. "I'm sorry about this," he said suddenly.

"Wasn't your fault. Wasn't anyone's fault. I just get to yelling sometime, taking out the can-opener trade on everything but the can openers and myself. The days of the door-to-door salesman are gone, son."

"And I thought I was going to have an easy summer job," the young man said.

The old man laughed. "Bet you did. They talk a good line, don't they?"

"I'll say!"

"Make it sound like found money, but there ain't no found money, boy. Ain't nothing simple in this world. The company is the only one ever makes any money. We just get tireder and older with more holes in our shoes. If I had any sense I'd have quit years ago. All you got to make is this summer—"

"Maybe not that long."

"Well, this is all I know. Just town after town, motel after motel, house after house, looking at people through screen wire while they shake their heads. No. Even the cockroaches at the sleazy motels begin to look like little fellows you've seen before, like maybe they're door-to-door peddlers that have to rent rooms too."

The young man chuckled. "You might have something there."

They sat quietly for a moment, welded in silence. Night had full grip on the desert now. A mammoth gold moon and billions of stars cast a whitish glow from eons away.

The wind picked up. The sand shifted, found new places to lie down. The undulations of it, slow and easy, were reminiscent of the midnight sea. The young man, who had crossed the Atlantic by ship once, said as much.

"The sea?" the old man replied. "Yes, yes, exactly like that. I was thinking the same. That's part of the reason it bothers me. Part of why I was stirred up this afternoon. Wasn't just the heat doing it. There are memories of mine out here," he nodded at the desert, "and they're visiting me again."

The young man made a face. "I don't understand."

"You wouldn't. You shouldn't. You'd think I'm crazy."

"I already think you're crazy. So tell me."

The old man smiled. "All right, but don't you laugh."

"I won't."

A moment of silence moved in between them. Finally the old man said, "It's fish night, boy. Tonight's the full moon and this is the right part of the desert if memory serves me, and the feel is right—I mean, doesn't the night feel like it's made up of some soft fabric, that it's different from other nights, that it's like being inside a big dark bag, the sides sprinkled with glitter, a spotlight at the top, at the open mouth, to serve as a moon?"

"You lost me."

The old man sighed. "But it feels different. Right? You can feel it too, can't you?"

"I suppose. Sort of thought it was just the desert air. I've never camped out in the desert before, and I guess it is different."

"Different, all right. You see, this is the road I got stranded on twenty years back. I didn't know it at first, least not consciously. But down deep in my gut I must have known all along I was taking this road, tempting fate, offering it, as the football people say, an instant replay."

"I still don't understand about fish night. What do you mean, you were here before?"

"Not this exact spot, somewhere along in here. This was even less of a road back then than it is now. The Navajos were about the only ones who traveled it. My car conked out, like this one today, and I started walking instead of waiting. As I walked the fish came out. Swimming along in the starlight pretty as you please. Lots of them. All the colors of the rainbow. Small ones, big ones, thick ones, thin ones. Swam right up to me . . . *right through me!* Fish just as far as you could see. High up and low down to the ground.

"Hold on, boy. Don't start looking at me like that. Listen: You're a college boy, you know something about these things. I mean, about what was here before we were, before we crawled out of the sea and changed enough to call ourselves men. Weren't we once just slimy things, brothers to the things that swim?"

"I guess, but—"

"Millions and millions of years ago this desert was a sea bottom. Maybe even the birthplace of man. Who knows? I read that in some science books. And I got to thinking this: If the ghosts of people who have lived can haunt houses, why can't the ghosts of creatures long dead haunt where they once lived, float about in a ghostly sea?"

"Fish with a soul?"

"Don't go small-mind on me, boy. Look here: Some of the Indians I've talked to up North tell me about a thing they call the manitou. That's a spirit. They believe everything has one. Rocks, trees, you name it. Even if the rock wears to dust or the tree gets cut to lumber, the manitou of it is still around."

"Then why can't you see these fish all the time?"

"Why can't we see ghosts all the time? Why do some of us never see them? Time's not right, that's why. It's a precious situation, and I figure it's like some fancy time lock—like the banks use. The lock clicks open at the bank, and there's the money. Here it ticks open and we get the fish of a world long gone."

"Well, it's something to think about," the young man managed.

The old man grinned at him. "I don't blame you for thinking what you're thinking. But this happened to me twenty years ago and I've never forgotten it. I saw those fish for a good hour before they disappeared. A Navajo came along in an old pickup right after and I bummed a ride into town with him. I told him what I'd seen. He just looked at me and grunted. But I could tell he knew what I was talking about. He'd seen it too, and probably not for the first time.

"I've heard that Navajos don't eat fish for some reason or another, and I bet it's the fish in the desert that keep them from it. Maybe they hold them sacred. And why not? It was like being in the presence of the Creator; like crawling back inside your mother and being unborn again, just kicking around in the liquids with no cares in the world."

"I don't know. That sounds sort of . . ."

"Fishy?" The old man laughed. "It does, it does. So this Navajo drove me to town. Next day I got my car fixed and went on. I've never taken that cutoff again—until today, and I think that was more than accident. My subconscious was driving me. That night scared me, boy, and I don't mind admitting it. But it was wonderful too, and I've never been able to get it out of my mind."

The young man didn't know what to say.

The old man looked at him and smiled. "I don't blame you," he said. "Not even a little bit. Maybe I am crazy."

They sat awhile longer with the desert night, and the old man took his false teeth out and poured some of the warm water on them to clean them of coffee and cigarette residue.

"I hope we don't need that water," the young man said.

"You're right. Stupid of me! We'll sleep awhile, start walking before daylight. It's not too far to the next town. Ten miles at best." He put his teeth back in. "We'll be just fine."

The young man nodded.

No fish came. They did not discuss it. They crawled inside the car, the young man in the front seat, the old man in the back. They used their spare clothes to bundle under, to pad out the cold fingers of the night.

Near midnight the old man came awake suddenly and lay with his hands behind his head and looked up and out the window opposite him, studied the crisp desert sky.

And a fish swam by.

Long and lean and speckled with all the colors of the world, flicking its tail as if in good-bye. Then it was gone.

The old man sat up. Outside, all about, were the fish—all sizes, colors, and shapes.

"Hey, boy, wake up!"

The younger man moaned.

"Wake up!"

The young man, who had been resting face down on his arms, rolled over. "What's the matter? Time to go?"

"The fish."

"Not again."

"Look!"

The young man sat up. His mouth fell open. His eyes bloated. Around and around the car, faster and faster in whirls of dark color, swam all manner of fish.

"Well, I'll be . . . *How?*"

"I told you, I told you."

The old man reached for the door handle, but before he could pull it a fish swam lazily through the back window glass, swirled about the car, once, twice, passed through the old man's chest, whipped up and went out through the roof.

The old man cackled, jerked open the door. He bounced around beside the road. Leaped up to swat his hands through the spectral fish. "Like soap bubbles," he said. "No. Like smoke!"

The young man, his mouth still agape, opened his door and got out. Even high up he could see the fish. Strange fish, like nothing he'd ever seen pictures of or imagined. They flitted and skirted about like flashes of light.

As he looked up, he saw, nearing the moon, a big dark cloud. The only cloud in the sky. That cloud tied him to reality suddenly, and he thanked the heavens for it. Normal things still happened. The whole world had not gone insane.

After a moment the old man quit hopping among the fish and came out to lean on the car and hold his hand to his fluttering chest.

"Feel it, boy? Feel the presence of the sea? Doesn't it feel like the beating of your own mother's heart while you float inside the womb?"

And the younger man had to admit that he felt it, that inner rolling rhythm that is the tide of life and the pulsating heart of the sea.

"How?" the young man said. "Why?"

"The time lock, boy. The locks clicked open and the fish are free.

Fish from a time before man was man. Before civilization started weighing us down. I know it's true. The truth's been in me all the time. It's in us all."

"It's like time travel," the young man said. "From the past to the future, they've come all that way."

"Yes, yes, that's it . . . Why, if they can come to our world, why can't we go to theirs? Release that spirit inside of us, tune into their time?"

"Now wait a minute . . ."

"My God, that's it! They're pure, boy, pure. Clean and free of civilization's trappings. That must be it! They're pure and we're not. We're weighted down with technology. These clothes. That car."

The old man started removing his clothes.

"Hey!" the young man said. "You'll freeze."

"If you're pure, if you're completely pure," the old man mumbled, "that's it . . . yeah, that's the key."

"You've gone crazy."

"I won't look at the car," the old man yelled, running across the sand, trailing the last of his clothes behind him. He bounced about the desert like a jackrabbit. "God, God, nothing is happening, nothing," he moaned. "This isn't my world. I'm of that world. I want to float free in the belly of the sea, away from can openers and cars and—"

The young man called the old man's name. The old man did not seem to hear.

"I want to leave here!" the old man yelled. Suddenly he was springing about again. "The teeth!" he yelled. "It's the teeth. Dentist, science, foo!" He punched a hand into his mouth, plucked the teeth free, tossed them over his shoulder.

Even as the teeth fell the old man rose. He began to stroke. To swim up and up and up, moving like a pale pink seal among the fish.

In the light of the moon the young man could see the pooched jaws of the old man, holding the last of the future's air. Up went the old man, up, up, up, swimming strong in the long-lost waters of a time gone by.

The young man began to strip off his own clothes. Maybe he could nab him, pull him down, put the clothes on him. Something . . . God, something. . . . But, what if *he* couldn't come back? And there were the fillings in his teeth, the metal rod in his back from a motorcycle accident. No, unlike the old man, this was his world and he was tied to it. There was nothing he could do.

A great shadow weaved in front of the moon, made a wriggling slat of darkness that caused the young man to let go of his shirt buttons and look up.

A black rocket of a shape moved through the invisible sea: a shark, the granddaddy of all sharks, the seed for all of man's fears of the deeps.

And it caught the old man in its mouth, began swimming upward toward the golden light of the moon. The old man dangled from the creature's mouth like a ragged rat from a house cat's jaws. Blood blossomed out of him, coiled darkly in the invisible sea.

The young man trembled. "Oh God," he said once.

Then along came that thick dark cloud, rolling across the face of the moon.

Momentary darkness.

And when the cloud passed there was light once again, and an empty sky.

No fish.

No shark.

And no old man.

Just the night, the moon and the stars.

## The Four-Fingered Hand

By Barry Pain

Charles Yarrow held fours, but as he had come up against Brackley's straight flush they only did him harm, leading him to remark—by no means for the first time—that it did not matter what cards one held, but only when one held them. 'I get out here,' he remarked, with resignation. No one else seemed to care for further play. The two other men left at once, and shortly afterwards Yarrow and Brackley sauntered out of the club together.

'The night's young,' said Brackley; 'if you're doing nothing you may as well come round to me.'

'Thanks, I will. I'll talk, or smoke, or go so far as to drink; but I don't play poker. It's not my night.'

'I didn't know,' said Brackley, 'that you had any superstitions.'

'Haven't. I've only noticed that, as a rule, my luck goes in runs, and that a good run or a bad run usually lasts the length of a night's play. There is probably some simple reason for it, if I were enough of a mathematician to worry it out. In luck as distinct from arithmetic I have no belief at all.'

'I wish you could bring me to that happy condition. The hard-headed man of the world, without a superstition or a belief of any kind, has the best time of it.'

They reached Brackley's chambers, lit pipes, and mixed drinks. Yarrow stretched himself in a lounge chair, and took up the subject again, speaking lazily and meditatively. He was a man of thirty-eight, with a clean shaven face; he looked, as indeed he was, travelled and experienced.

'I don't read any books,' he remarked, 'but I've been twice round the world, and am just about to leave England again. I've been alive for thirty-eight years and during most of them I have been living. Consequently, I've formed opinions, and one of my opinions is that it is better to dispense with superfluous luggage. Prejudices, superstitions, beliefs of any kind that are not capable of easy and immediate proof are superfluous luggage; one goes more easily without them. You implied just now that you had a certain amount of this superfluous luggage, Brackley. What form does it take? Do you turn your chair—are you afraid of thirteen at dinner?'

'No, nothing of that sort. I'll tell you about it. You've heard of my grandfather—who made the money?'

'Heard of him? Had him rubbed into me in my childhood. He's in *Smiles* or one of those books, isn't he? Started life as a navvy, educated himself, invented things, made a fortune, gave vast sums in charity.'

'That is the man. Well, he lived to be a fair age, but he was dead before I was born. What I know of him I know from my father, and some of it is not included in those improving books for the young. For instance, there is no mention in the printed biography of his curious belief in the four-fingered hand. His belief was that from time to time he saw a phantom hand. Sometimes it appeared to him in the daytime, and sometimes at night. It was a right hand with the second finger missing. He always regarded the appearance of the hand as a warning. It meant, he supposed, that he was to stop anything on which he was engaged; if he was about to let a house, buy a horse, go on a journey, or whatever it was, he stopped if he saw the four-fingered hand.'

'Now, look here,' said Yarrow, 'we'll examine this thing rationally. Can you quote one special instance in which your grandfather saw this maimed hand, broke off a particular project, and found himself benefited?'

'No. In telling my father about it he spoke quite generally.'

'Oh, yes,' said Yarrow, drily. 'The people who see these things do speak quite generally as a rule.'

'But wait a moment. This vision of the four-fingered hand appears to have been hereditary. My father also saw it from time to time. And here I can give you the special circumstances. Do you remember the Crewe disaster some years ago? Well, my father had intended to travel by the train that was wrecked. Just as he was getting into the carriage he saw the four-fingered hand. He at once got out and postponed his journey until later in the day. Another occasion was two months before the failure of Varings'. My father banked there. As a rule he kept a comparatively small balance at the bank, but on this occasion he had just realized an investment, and was about to place the result—six thousand pounds—in the bank, pending re-investment. He was on the point of sending off his confidential clerk with the money, when once more he saw the four-fingered hand. Now at that time Varings' was considered to be as safe as a church. Possibly a few people with special means of information may have had some slight suspicion at the time, but my father certainly had none. He had always banked with Varings', as his father had done before him. However, his faith in the warning hand was so great that instead of paying in the six thousand he withdrew his balance that day. Is that good enough for you?'

'Not entirely. Mind, I don't dispute your facts, but I doubt if it requires the supernatural to explain them. You say that the vision appears to be hereditary. Does that mean that you yourself have ever seen it?'

'I have seen it once.'

'When?'

'I saw it tonight.' Brackley spoke like a man suppressing some strong excitement. 'It was just as you got up from the card-table after losing on your fours. I was on the point of urging you and the other two men to go on playing. I saw the hand distinctly. It seemed to be floating in the air about a couple of yards away from me. It was a small white hand, like a lady's hand, cut short off at the wrist. For a second it moved slowly towards me, and then vanished. Nothing would have induced me to go on playing poker tonight.'

'You are—excuse me for mentioning it—not in the least degree under the influence of drink. Further, you are by habit an almost absurdly temperate man. I mention these things because they have to be taken into consideration. They show that you were not at any rate the victim of a common and disreputable form of illusion. But what service has the hand done you? We play a regular point at the club. We are not the excited gamblers of fiction. We don't increase the points, and we never play after one in the morning. At the moment when the hand appeared to you, how much had you won?'

'Twenty-five pounds—an exceptionally large amount.'

'Very well. You're a careful player. You play best when your luck's worst. We stopped play at half-past eleven. If we had gone on playing till one, and your luck had been of the worst possible description all the time, we will say that you might have lost that twenty-five and twenty-five more. To me it is inconceivable, but with the worst luck and the worst play it is perhaps possible. Now then, do you mean to tell me that the loss of twenty-five pounds is a matter of such importance to a man with your income as to require a supernatural intervention to prevent you from losing it?'

'Of course it isn't.'

'Well, then, the four-fingered hand has not accomplished its mission. It has not saved you from anything. It might even have been inconvenient. If you had been playing with strangers and winning, and they had wished to go on playing, you could hardly have refused. Of course, it did not matter with us—we play with you constantly, and can have our revenge at any time. The four-fingered hand is proved in this instance to have been useless and inept. Therefore, I am inclined to believe that the appearances when it really did some good were coincidences. Doubtless your grandfather and father and yourself have seen the hand, but surely that may be due to some slight hereditary defect in the seeing apparatus, which, under certain conditions, say, of the light and of your own health creates the illusion. The four-fingered hand is natural and not supernatural, subjective and not objective.'

'It sounds plausible,' remarked Brackley. He got up, crossed the room, and began to open the card-table. 'Practical tests are always the most satisfactory, and we can soon have a practical test.' As he put the candles on the table he started a little and nearly dropped one of them. He laughed drily. 'I saw the four-fingered hand again just then,' he said. 'But no matter—come—let us play.'

'Oh, the two game isn't funny enough.'

'Then I'll fetch up Blake from downstairs; you know him. He never goes to bed, and he plays the game.'

Blake, who was a youngish man, had chambers downstairs. Brackley easily persuaded him to join the party. It was decided that they should play for exactly an hour. It was a poor game; the cards ran low, and there was very little betting. At the end of the hour Brackley had lost a sovereign, and Yarrow had lost five pounds.

'I don't like to get up a winner, like this,' said Blake. 'Let's go on.'

But Yarrow was not to be persuaded. He said that he was going off to bed. No allusion to the four-fingered hand was made in speaking in the presence of Blake, but Yarrow's smile of conscious superiority had its meaning for Brackley. It meant that Yarrow had overthrown a superstition, and was consequently pleased with himself. After a few minutes' chat Yarrow and Blake said good-night to Brackley, and went downstairs together.

Just as they reached the ground floor they heard, from far up the staircase, a short cry, followed a moment afterwards by the sound of a heavy fall.

'What's that?' Blake exclaimed.

'I'm just going to see,' said Yarrow, quietly. 'It seemed to me to come from Brackley's rooms. Let's go up again.'

They hurried up the staircase and knocked at Brackley's door. There was no answer. The whole place was absolutely silent. The door was ajar; Yarrow pushed it open, and the two men went in.

The candles on the card-table were still burning. At some distance from them, in a dark corner of the room, lay Brackley, face downwards, with one arm folded under him and the other stretched wide.

Blake stood in the doorway. Yarrow went quickly over to Brackley, and turned the body partially over.

'What is it?' asked Blake, excitedly. 'Is the man ill? Has he fainted?'

'Run downstairs,' said Yarrow, curtly. 'Rouse the porter and get a doctor at once.'

The moment Blake had gone, Yarrow took a candle from the card-table, and by the light of it examined once more the body of the dead man. On the throat there was the imprint of a hand—a right hand with the second finger missing. The marks, which were crimson at first, grew gradually fainter.

Some years afterwards, in Yarrow's presence, a man happened to tell some story of a warning apparition that he himself had investigated.

'And do you believe that?' Yarrow asked.

'The evidence that the apparition was seen—and seen by more than one person—seems to me fairly conclusive in this case.'

'That is all very well. I will grant you the apparition if you like. But why speak of it as a warning? If such appearances take place, it still seems to me absurd and disproportionate to suppose that they do so in order to warn us, or help us, or hinder us, or anything of the kind. They appear for their own unfathomable reasons only. If they seem to forbid one thing or command another, that also is for their own purpose. I have an experience of my own which would tend to show that.'

## A Ghost Story

By Mark Twain

I took a large room, far up Broadway, in a huge old building whose upper stories had been wholly unoccupied for years until I came. The place had long been given up to dust and cobwebs, to solitude and silence. I seemed groping among the tombs and invading the privacy of the dead, that first night I climbed up to my quarters. For the first time in my life a superstitious dread came over me; and as I turned a dark angle of the stairway and an invisible cobweb swung its slazy woof in my face and clung there, I shuddered as one who had encountered a phantom.

I was glad enough when I reached my room and locked out the mold and the darkness. A cheery fire was burning in the grate, and I sat down before it with a comforting sense of relief. For two hours I sat there, thinking of bygone times; recalling old scenes, and summoning half-forgotten faces out of the mists of the past; listening, in fancy, to voices that long ago grew silent for all time, and to once familiar songs that nobody sings now. And as my reverie softened down to a sadder and sadder pathos, the shrieking of the winds outside softened to a wail, the angry beating of the rain against the panes diminished to a tranquil patter, and one by one the noises in the street subsided, until the hurrying footsteps of the last belated straggler died away in the distance and left no sound behind.

The fire had burned low. A sense of loneliness crept over me. I arose and undressed, moving on tiptoe about the room, doing stealthily what I had to do, as if I were environed by sleeping enemies whose slumbers it would be fatal to break. I covered up in bed, and lay listening to the rain and wind and the faint creaking of distant shutters, till they lulled me to sleep.

I slept profoundly, but how long I do not know. All at once I found myself awake, and filled with a shuddering expectancy. All was still. All but my own heart—I could hear it beat. Presently the bedclothes began to slip away slowly toward the foot of the bed, as if some one were pulling them! I could not stir; I could not speak. Still the blankets slipped deliberately away, till my breast was uncovered. Then with a great effort I seized them and drew them over my head. I waited, listened, waited. Once more that steady pull began, and once more I lay torpid a century of dragging seconds till my breast was naked again. At last I roused my energies and snatched the covers back to their place and held them with a strong grip. I waited. By and by I felt a faint tug, and took a fresh grip. The tug strengthened to a steady strain—it grew stronger and stronger. My hold parted, and for the third time the blankets slid away. I groaned. An answering groan came from the foot of the bed! Beaded drops of sweat stood upon my forehead. I was more dead than alive. Presently I heard a heavy footstep in my room—the step of an elephant, it seemed to me—it was not like anything human. But it was moving *from* me—there was relief in that. I heard it approach the door—pass out without moving bolt or lock—and wander away among the dismal corridors, straining the floors and joists till they creaked again as it passed—and then silence reigned once more.

When my excitement had calmed, I said to myself, "This is a dream—simply a hideous dream." And so I lay thinking it over until I convinced myself that it *was* a dream, and then a comforting laugh relaxed my lips and I was happy again. I got up and struck a light; and when I found that the locks and bolts were just as I had left them, another soothing laugh welled in my heart and rippled from my lips. I took my pipe and lit it, and was just sitting down before the fire, when—down went the pipe out of my nerveless fingers, the blood forsook my cheeks, and my placid breathing was cut short with a gasp! In the ashes on the hearth, side by side with my own bare footprint, was another, so vast that in comparison mine was but an infant's! Then I had *had* a visitor, and the elephant tread was explained.

I put out the light and returned to bed, palsied with fear. I lay a long time, peering into the darkness, and listening. Then I heard a grating noise overhead, like the dragging of a heavy body across the floor; then the throwing down of the body, and the shaking of my windows in response to the concussion. In distant parts of the building I heard the muffled slamming of doors. I heard, at intervals, stealthy footsteps creeping in and out among the corridors, and up and down the stairs. Sometimes these noises approached my door, hesitated, and went away again. I heard the clanking of chains faintly, in remote passages, and listened while the clanking grew nearer—while it wearily climbed the stairways, marking each move by the loose surplus of chain that fell with an accented rattle upon each succeeding step as the goblin that bore it advanced. I heard muttered sentences; half-uttered screams that seemed smothered violently; and the swish of invisible garments, the rush of invisible wings. Then I became conscious that my chamber was invaded—that I was not alone. I heard sighs and breathings about my bed, and mysterious whisperings. Three little spheres of soft phosphorescent light appeared on the ceiling directly over my head, clung and glowed there a moment, and then dropped—two of them upon my face and one upon the pillow. They spattered, liquidly, and felt warm. Intuition told me they had turned to gouts of blood as they fell—I needed no light to satisfy myself of that. Then I saw pallid faces, dimly luminous, and white uplifted hands, floating bodiless in the air—floating a moment and then disappearing. The whispering ceased, and the voices and the sounds, and a solemn stillness followed. I waited and listened. I felt that I must have light or die. I was weak with fear. I slowly raised myself toward a sitting posture, and my face came in contact with a clammy hand! All strength went from me apparently, and I fell back like a stricken invalid. Then I heard the rustle of a garment—it seemed to pass to the door and go out.

When everything was still once more, I crept out of bed, sick and feeble, and lit the gas with a hand that trembled as if it were aged with a hundred years. The light brought some little cheer to my spirits. I sat down and fell into a dreamy contemplation of that great footprint in the ashes. By and by its outlines began to waver and grow dim. I glanced up and the broad gas-flame was slowly wilting away. In the same moment I heard that elephantine tread again. I noted its approach, nearer and nearer, along the musty halls, and dimmer and dimmer the light waned. The tread reached my very door and paused—the light had dwindled to a sickly blue, and all things about me lay in a spectral twilight. The door did not open, and yet I felt a faint gust of air fan my cheek, and presently was conscious of a huge, cloudy presence before me. I watched it with fascinated eyes. A pale glow stole over the Thing; gradually its cloudy folds took shape—an arm appeared, then legs, then a body, and last a great sad face looked out of the vapor. Stripped of its filmy housings, naked, muscular and comely, the majestic Cardiff Giant loomed above me!

All my misery vanished—for a child might know that no harm could come with that benignant countenance. My cheerful spirits returned at once, and in sympathy with them the gas flamed up brightly again. Never a lonely outcast was so glad to welcome company as I was to greet the friendly giant. I said:

"Why, is it nobody but you? Do you know, I have been scared to death for the last two or three hours? I am most honestly glad to see you. I wish I had a chair— Here, here, don't try to sit down in that thing!"

But it was too late. He was in it before I could stop him, and down he went—I never saw a chair shivered so in my life.

"Stop, stop, you'll ruin ev—"

Too late again. There was another crash, and another chair was resolved into its original elements.

"Confound it, haven't you got any judgment at all? Do you want to ruin all the furniture on the place? Here, here, you petrified fool—"

But it was no use. Before I could arrest him he had sat down on the bed, and it was a melancholy ruin.

"Now what sort of a way is that to do? First you come lumbering about the place bringing a legion of vagabond goblins along with you to worry me to death, and then when I overlook an indelicacy of costume which would not be tolerated anywhere by cultivated people except in a respectable theater, and not even there if the nudity were of *your* sex, you repay me by wrecking all the furniture you can find to sit down on. And why will you? You damage yourself as much as you do me. You have broken off the end of your spinal column, and littered up the floor with chips of your hams till the place looks like a marble yard. You ought to be ashamed of yourself—you are big enough to know better."

"Well, I will not break any more furniture. But what am I to do? I have not had a chance to sit down for a century." And the tears came into his eyes.

"Poor devil," I said, "I should not have been so harsh with you. And you are an orphan, too, no doubt. But sit down on the floor here—nothing else can stand your weight—and besides, we cannot be sociable with you away up there above me; I want you down where I can perch on this high counting-house stool and gossip with you face to face."

So he sat down on the floor, and lit a pipe which I gave him, threw one of my red blankets over his shoulders, inverted my sitz-bath on his head, helmet fashion, and made himself picturesque and comfortable. Then he crossed his ankles, while I renewed the fire, and exposed the flat, honeycombed bottoms of his prodigious feet to the grateful warmth.

"What is the matter with the bottom of your feet and the back of your legs, that they are gouged up so?"

"Infernal chilblains—I caught them clear up to the back of my head, roosting out there under Newell's farm. But I love the place; I love it as one loves his old home. There is no peace for me like the peace I feel when I am there."

We talked along for half an hour, and then I noticed that he looked tired, and spoke of it.

"Tired?" he said. "Well, I should think so. And now I will tell you all about it, since you have treated me so well. I am the spirit of the Petrified Man that lies across the street there in the museum. I am the ghost of the Cardiff Giant. I can have no rest, no peace, till they have given that poor body burial again. Now what was the most natural thing for me to do, to make men satisfy this wish? Terrify them into it!—haunt the place where the body lay! So I haunted the museum night after night. I even got other spirits to help me. But it did no good, for nobody ever came to the museum at midnight. Then it occurred to me to come over the way and haunt this place a little. I felt that if I ever got a hearing I must succeed, for I had the most efficient company that perdition could furnish. Night after night we have shivered around through these mildewed halls, dragging chains, groaning, whispering, tramping up and down stairs, till, to tell you the truth, I am almost worn out. But when I saw a light in your room to-night I roused my energies again and went at it with a deal of the old freshness. But I am tired out—entirely fagged out. Give me, I beseech you, give me some hope!"

I lit off my perch in a burst of excitement, and exclaimed:

"This transcends everything! everything that ever did occur! Why you poor blundering old fossil, you have had all your trouble for nothing—you have been haunting a *plaster cast* of yourself—the real Cardiff Giant is in Albany![1] Confound it, don't you know your own remains?"

I never saw such an eloquent look of shame, of pitiable humiliation, overspread a countenance before.

The Petrified Man rose slowly to his feet, and said:

"Honestly, *is* that true?"

[1] A fact. The original fraud was ingeniously and fraudfully duplicated, and exhibited in New York as the "only genuine" Cardiff Giant (to the unspeakable disgust of the owners of the real colossus) at the very same time that the latter was drawing crowds at a museum in Albany.

"As true as I am sitting here."

He took the pipe from his mouth and laid it on the mantel, then stood irresolute a moment (unconsciously, from old habit, thrusting his hands where his pantaloons pockets should have been, and meditatively dropping his chin on his breast), and finally said:

"Well—I *never* felt so absurd before. The Petrified Man has sold everybody else, and now the mean fraud has ended by selling its own ghost! My son, if there is any charity left in your heart for a poor friendless phantom like me, don't let this get out. Think how *you* would feel if you had made such an ass of yourself."

I heard his stately tramp die away, step by step down the stairs and out into the deserted street, and felt sorry that he was gone, poor fellow—and sorrier still that he had carried off my red blanket and my bathtub.

# Give Her Hell

By Donald A. Wollheim

It's no good making a deal with the devil. He's a cheat. He's all they say he is and more. The effete modern books like to present him as a smiling red devil, all clean and slick. Or as some cagey, witty peddler, or a tophat-and-tails city slicker. But the monks of the Middle Ages knew better. They described him as a beast; a stinking, foul-breathed, corrupt, and totally loathsome abomination.

Take my word for it. He is. I know, for I was fool enough to make such a pact. I saw him and dealt with him and from beginning to end, it was never worth it.

It was desperate, and like all whom fate had played crooked, I was sore about it. Things were not going well with me, and it was all their fault. My wife and my daughter's. I refuse to take the blame in spite of what the devil may claim. I know when I'm right. My daughter had run away from my home—that was the shock that made me realize what was happening.

That girl ran away and she was only sixteen, and she'd stolen the contents of my wallet and took some of my wife's jewelry and ran away. My wife wasn't so shocked. She had the nerve to say it served me right. I didn't "understand the child."

What's to understand about a disobedient daughter who doesn't listen to her father, and who makes dates after eight o'clock at night, who sneaks magazines into her bedroom, actually talks to some of those uncouth common kids from across the tracks, and has been seen in soda parlors after dark. Sure, I had to beat her. I've been doing that since she was seven. I've had to be stricter and stricter with her. Spare the rod and spoil the child—that's the slogan I was raised on and I did my best. But the girl was rotten—something from her mother's side of the family, no doubt—and she had the nerve to try to run away.

I called the police. I'm not going to be thought of as the father of a wild kid. I sent out an alarm. My wife objected, but I put her in her place. Slap across the face shut her up—I'd taught her long ago who was master. Me, the way it was meant to be. I locked her up in our bedroom, and later on I gave her a lesson with the strap, face down on the bed with her clothes off. Women know only one master. My mother never complained; she didn't dare, not even when she was dying after my father threw her down the stairs that night.

My father's ways were right and I was right. The cops brought the girl back to me the next day. I gave her a hiding she'd not forget, and then I arranged to have her committed to a corrective institution. One of those private sanitariums for disturbed children, you know. Exclusive, well-guarded, and well-disciplined. All right, they made life hell for her, but how else can you teach a wayward child how to do right. Better for the family name than to have her in public vision.

They had my orders and the extra payments I made were generous enough to enforce them—she'd not get out until she was good if they had to nearly kill her to do it. They kept her in a straitjacket for months at a time at my insistence, and in restraining cuffs and belts at all other times. A series of regular electric shocks taught her a few things. The doctor says now she's faking insanity, that she shrieks night and day, and they keep her by herself in a padded, locked cell. But I think she's faking. She's just a disobedient girl and she's got to learn who's master.

As for my wife, she had the nerve to leave me. She climbed out of a window the night I bribed the doctors to start my bad daughter's shock treatments. She ran to my business partner, that skunk, and he helped her hide. Next day he dared put it up to me. He said he thought I was the one who was cracking up. Me! The nerve of him.

Obviously he was scheming to steal my wife away from me. And he must have been double-booking my firm. I was sure of it. I could see it all from his faking, sly ways. He must have been plotting my ruin the way he must have been scheming after my wife.

So I took steps to sell him out. But the skunk had covered his tracks. He had acted first. He had an order taken out against me, charging me with deceit and having my wife charge me with mental cruelty and suing to get custody of my child and my business.

I could see I'd get no help from the courts and the lawyers. They're all corrupt, unable to see how a man must be stern with his own. These are decadent times. No wonder the world is going to hell.

I was in a jam. They'd cornered me, boxed me with legal chicaneries, tied up my funds. I was furious that night as I stalked up and down my house. The windows were shut and the shades down. I don't stand for curious eyes. I was alone and the next day they'd be closing in from all directions. That's when I turned to Satan.

I figured if Satan had been maligned as much as I was, he must be all right. Just a victim of the same errors. I called on him. When you really mean it, the devil will come. I gave him a sacrifice—I tossed the Bible into the fire; I got hold of my wife's cat—that snarling, fuzzy beast—and I cut its throat on the living room rug and called Satan.

He stank. The place stank and he was there—a foul sort of thing. He was crawly and slimy and toady. He belched rot, and his voice would give you the willies. But I don't go for appearances. I knew he had to have the stuff to stand up to all those dirty do-gooders and Gospel pounders.

I told him I wanted to get out of my jam. I wanted my wife back under my control, my daughter where I wanted her, and my partner in hell.

Satan agreed. He could do the first two things, and while the judgment of my partner would be up to That Other One, maybe he'd get his soul in the end, too. Anyway, he'd die, and what did he want of me?

My soul, of course. I'd trusted him for that. What good would it do him? I believe in reincarnation, anyway. I struck a hard bargain. I said first I had to have a chance to be reborn again and live a whole new life from the start. Then he could have my soul afterward.

Because if he got my whole soul but only gave me the last half of my life as I wanted it, that wasn't fair, was it? No. I drove a hard bargain. He had to give me an entire life from start to finish.

He whined and he threatened and he bellowed, but he agreed. On my deathbed, he said, he'd reappear and give me the word on the whole new life I was going to get to live. There were certain rules he had to go by in that sort of thing. Okay, I said, I trust you. You and me, we think alike, we think right. An iron hand in a velvet glove, that's the rule.

He stank, that no-good bum. He gave me his word, and I say he cheated, but he didn't think so.

My partner died that same night. His furnace exploded in his house. The place was a seething mass of flames. He tried to get down the stairs, got splashed with flaming oil, was scorched from head to foot, ran out in flames and died in agony. Served him right. The firm's ledgers were in his house for his auditors, and they burned up, too, putting me entirely in the clear.

He died in scandal, too, because my wife was caught in his house. She had a room upstairs, and she jumped from the window and the newspapers snapped her picture in her torn nightgown on the lawn coming away from that man's house. That queered any divorce case for her. She came home, and she had to keep her mouth shut. There'd never be a chance for her to get custody of our runaway daughter or any divorce.

I've never let her forget the scandal, even though she claims there was nothing between them—he was just being hospitable. Ha! I showed her. She's not allowed out of the house now, and I beat her black and blue whenever I think of it. She hasn't got a legal leg to stand on, not after those newspaper photos and stories.

My daughter is still in the padded cell I arranged for her. If she's going to fake insanity, I'll make it so hot for her she'll learn the error of her ways. She's been there ten years now and the kid is stubborn. But the doc and his strongarms have been well paid. They use the leather mitts on her and the rubber sheets and the shocks. She'll stop her act or else.

Unfortunately I won't live to see it. I'm dying now, and I've arranged in my will to see that her cure and treatment continues. I got this cancer of the throat, from inhaling some kind of poison gases or something years ago. I think it was that evening with that stinking cheat. His bad smell burned my throat, it did. I told you he cheats.

And he's been back, just now. He's been back and he gave me the full dope on our deal. I'm to get a full life, from birth to maturity and eventually death. Only he's cheated.

He can't give me a life that hasn't been lived yet. He can't reincarnate me in a future year. No, he hasn't any control over future lives. He has only control over lives that have been lived, he said, the cheat—why couldn't he have said that when we first made the deal?

And it seems to be a rule in this kind of transaction that he can't take life over in the same sex. Something about positive and negative polarity in souls. If you live twice, then you got to see life from first one sex and then the other. Makes the soul rounded, he says, the cheat.

And it's also got to be somebody who's a blood relation, he tells me, the stinking, slimy no-good crook.

I'm dying, and in a few minutes more I'm going to be dead. And then I'll open my eyes again, a newborn baby, and start living through all the long, long years of another person's life. I got to experience everything, every darn, horrible, painful, frustrated, mean minute of it.

I'm going to be reborn as my own daughter.

It's going to be hell.

## The Giveaway

By Steve Rasnic Tem

If you don't cut that out something real bad's gonna happen to you!"

Six-year-old Marsha dropped the second handful of mud she was about to smear on seven-year-old Alice Kennedy's party dress. "Like what?"

Alice made a thinking face for a little while. "Well . . . I might tell your daddy about it and he just might give *you* away!"

"Uh-uh," Marsha grunted. She proceeded to gather another handful of mud. Some of it spattered onto her shoes and she had to twist each foot just so to wipe them in the grass. It was hard to do that and still hold onto the slippery mud. Then she walked carefully over to where Alice was sitting making mud pies and raised both hands.

"Stop it, Marsha! I told you what I'd do! I'll *tell* and he'll just give you away!"

Marsha didn't understand why Alice didn't want her to smear mud on the dress anyway; it was nice and cool and besides, Alice's dress was already muddy from making mud pies all afternoon. But she was even more confused about this giveaway stuff. She'd never heard of that before.

"What do you mean, give me away?"

"I'll tell him you've been real bad to me, Marsha, and he'll give you away to some other family, or even worse!"

Marsha just looked at her in confusion. "Moms and dads don't give their kids away," she said seriously.

Alice looked up from her mud pie and smiled. "That's what your daddy did with your brother Billy."

"That's not true, Alice Kennedy; Billy died and went to heaven!"

"How do you know? Did you see him go?"

"Well, no. But Daddy told me he did."

"They *have* to say that, stupid! They don't want you crying and making trouble."

"Don't call me stupid!" Marsha watched her shoes squishing into the mud. "Why did they give Billy away?" she asked softly.

"I heard your daddy tell my daddy that Billy was too small and that he'd never be very big, ever. He sounded real sad about that. So I guess he just gave him away so he can get a bigger boy later on."

Marsha nodded her head solemnly.

"Know who else got given away?"

"Who?"

"Johnny Parker."

"I 'member him! He was like a grownup 'cept he had something funny wrong with his head made him want to play with kids all the time. But he went to a special school! My aunt said so and she's a teacher!"

"Well, he was gonna go to one of them schools, but they gave him away instead. Know who else?"

"Uh-uh."

"Shelly Cox. She kept breaking things and being mad and real mean and one night her daddy had them take her away."

"Who's them?"

Alice looked back over her shoulder at the backyard of her house. "I don't know for *sure*. Guess who else?"

"Who?"

"*You,* Marsha, 'cause you got my party dress *all* muddy and my daddy's probably gonna want to give *me* away so I'm gonna have to tell on *you.*"

"Tattletale!" Marsha cried, tears streaming down her face.

"Crybaby!" Alice yelled, running toward her house.

Marsha threw a handful of mud after Alice in frustration. "Uh-uh," she grunted as she began the long walk home.

There were loud voices coming from the kitchen when Marsha got home. She could hear her mother crying, her father shouting. He sounded real mad. Marsha hated it when they had a fight. She sat down in a chair in the living room, picked up one of her books, and pretended to read. But she could only pretend because they were too loud.

"Can't you do anything so simple as enter a check properly, Jennie? I bet Marsha could do that and she's only six years old!"

"I'm sorry, Ted. I just forgot! Will you leave me alone!"

"If I let you alone we'd be broke within the month! Last week you took out the grocery money twice and caused six checks to bounce! And you *say* you don't know what happened to the money! You're driving me crazy, Jennie! I can't take it! I tell you I can't take it anymore!"

"I've *tried* to be a good wife to you . . ." Her mom started to cry and cough, and Marsha couldn't tell what she said anymore. She wanted to go in and see her mom, but she was too afraid. Her daddy was shouting louder than ever now.

"You haven't *been* a wife to me, Jennie, since Billy's been gone!"

Her mom was crying louder than before. Marsha could hardly understand her. "The doctor says . . . you know the doctor said I can't have *any more!*"

"You're lying, Jennie; you're lying through your teeth. I know that quack's nurse! You've been lying to me, lying all the time. You just *don't want to,* Jennie. *You just don't want to!*"

Marsha went upstairs until dinner. She thought her daddy noticed the dried mud on her shoes when she got up from the table, but he didn't say anything.

Marsha woke up with it still dark outside. Something told her she should go to the window. She was afraid, because it was real dark out there, but she thought she should probably go. She tiptoed as softly as she could, afraid she might wake up her dad.

A funny-looking car was parked out in front of the house. It was long and black, the longest and blackest car she had ever seen. And there was a long silver thing, jagged like lightning, that went from one end of the car to the other. This lightning was brighter than the streetlights and hurt her eyes.

The car windows were gray. They looked dirty. She couldn't see through them at all.

Marsha didn't want to see the big black car anymore, but she was more afraid not to see it. She didn't know why she was more afraid of not seeing it, but she was.

Marsha tiptoed down the stairs in her pajamas, scared to death that her father would catch her and maybe give her away like he had Billy. She went into the dark living room. The front door was wide open; she could see the long black car by standing in front of the open door.

She stepped carefully onto the front sidewalk and started walking to the car. She tried to be as quiet as a mouse like her aunt had told her once. She was scared of the car, but she had to keep walking toward it. She couldn't understand that at all.

When she got to the side of the car she held her hands up to her eyes and leaned against the window, trying to see what was inside. But it was too gray, too dirty, too dark. She started to walk around the front of the car and to the other side to look in the windows there, when the tall man stepped in front of her.

He was tall with black shadows all over him and he had a big white bow tie and a big white flower on his chest, but she couldn't see his coat, he was so black, so she didn't know how the flower stayed on.

The tall man bent over. He had no face, just a head full of white fog, like his face hadn't made itself yet.

Marsha began to cry in a soft voice, scared to death she'd wake up her daddy and he'd give her away for spoiling his sleep. But she couldn't help crying, and it kept getting louder and louder until she was sure he'd wake up and want to give her away. Her pajamas felt suddenly wet and warm and she knew she'd wet herself and he'd want to give her away for that too.

She turned around to run back into the house.

Two men with no faces were standing there, carrying a long thing between them. Marsha was so surprised she stopped crying.

For some reason she wasn't so afraid now, so she walked up to the long thing they were carrying to see what it was.

Her mommy was tied to the thing and she was looking up with her eyes all funny and her mouth open and oh she knew her mommy was dead oh dead dead dead!

She ran screaming into the house and they grabbed her and she was screaming and they put something into her mouth—

Only "they" was her daddy. He was sitting with her on the sofa now, looking all serious like when she'd done something real bad.

"You saw the car?"

She nodded her head tearfully.

"Your mommy went away in the car?"

"Ye-es," her voice broke and she cried a little.

"Okay, I want you to listen, Marsha." He held her chin up and made her look into his eyes. "Your mommy didn't do things right, Marsha; she wasn't *good* enough. So you know what happened?"

Marsha nodded her head solemnly.

"I had to *give* your mommy *away*. That's what happens to people who mess up, Marsha. You've got to do your *best,* do your best for *me, all the time.*"

Again she nodded her head, but then her father was gone, as quickly as he had arrived, and she was all alone on the couch in the darkened living room. She looked out the window but there was nothing there. She knew everything was all over, then.

Marsha sleepily climbed off the sofa and stumbled around trying to find a light switch. She couldn't find one so she had to make her way to the kitchen in the dark. She would have cried then, but she really didn't feel like crying anymore.

The kitchen light switch was too high, so she had to work in the dark. It was hard to find the pans or the turner in the dark, but she finally did. At least the refrigerator light let her see the eggs, and she kept the door open afterward so she could see better.

She knew she'd better start her daddy's breakfast now if she was to get it finished on time. The stove and counters were real high for her, so it would take a long time for her to use them.

Daddy liked big breakfasts, and more than anything else in the whole wide world, she wanted to please her daddy.

## The Glove

By Fritz Leiber

My most literally tangible brush with the supernatural (something I can get incredibly infatuated with yet forever distrust profoundly, like a very beautiful and adroit call girl) occurred in connection with the rape by a masked intruder of the woman who lived in the next apartment to mine during my San Francisco years. I knew Evelyn Mayne only as a neighbor and I slept through the whole incident, including the arrival and departure of the police, though there came a point in the case when the police doubted both these assertions of mine.

The phrase "victim of rape" calls up certain stereotyped images: an attractive young woman going home alone late at night, enters a dark street, is grabbed . . . or, a beautiful young suburban matron, mother of three, wakes after midnight, feels a nameless dread, is grabbed . . . The truth is apt to be less romantic. Evelyn Mayne was sixty-five long divorced, neglected, and thoroughly detested by her two daughters-in-law and only to a lesser degree by their husbands, lived on various programs of old age, medical and psychiatric assistance, was scrawny, gloomy, alcoholic, waspish, believed life was futile, and either overdosed on sleeping pills or else lightly cut her wrists three or four times a year.

Her assailant at least was somewhat more glamorous, in a sick way. The rapist was dressed all in rather close-fitting gray, hands covered by gray gloves, face obscured by a long shock of straight silver hair falling over it. And in the left hand, at first, a long knife that gleamed silver in the dimness.

And she wasn't grabbed either, at first, but only commanded in a harsh whisper coming through the hair to lie quietly or be cut up.

When she was alone again at last, she silently waited something like the ten minutes she'd been warned to, thinking that at least she hadn't been cut up, or else (who knows?) wishing she had been. Then she went next door (in the opposite direction to mine) and roused Marcia Everly, who was a buyer for a department store and about half her age. After the victim had been given a drink, they called the police and Evelyn Mayne's psychiatrist and also her social worker, who knew her current doctor's number (which she didn't), but they couldn't get hold of either of the last two. Marcia suggested waking me and Evelyn Mayne countered by suggesting they wake Mr. Helpful, who has the next room beyond Marcia's down the hall. Mr. Helpful (otherwise nicknamed Baldy, I never remembered his real name) was someone I loathed because he was always prissily dancing around being neighborly and asking if there was something he could do—and because he was six foot four tall, while I am rather under average height.

Marcia Everly is also very tall, at least for a woman, but as it happens I do not loathe her in the least. Quite the opposite in fact.

But Evelyn Mayne said I wasn't sympathetic, while Marcia (thank goodness!) loathed Mr. Helpful as much as I do—she thought him a weirdo, along with half the other tenants in the building.

So they compromised by waking neither of us, and until the

police came Evelyn Mayne simply kept telling the story of her rape over and over, rather mechanically, while Marcia listened dutifully and occupied her mind as to which of our crazy fellow-tenants was the best suspect—granting it hadn't been done by an outsider, although that seemed likeliest. The three most colorful were the statuesque platinum-blond drag queen on the third floor, the long-haired old weirdo on six who wore a cape and was supposed to be into witchcraft, and the tall, silver-haired, Nazi-looking lesbian on seven (assuming she wore a dildo for the occasion as she was nuttier than a five-dollar fruit cake).

Ours really is a weird building, you see, and not just because of its occupants, who sometimes seem as if they were all referred here by mental hospitals. No, it's eerie in its own right. You see, several decades ago it was a hotel with all the rich, warm inner life that once implied: bevies of maids, who actually used the linen closets (empty now) on each floor and the round snap-capped outlets in the baseboards for a vacuum system (that hadn't been operated for a generation) and the two dumbwaiters (their doors forever shut and painted over). In the old days there had been bellboys and an elevator operator and two night porters who'd carry up drinks and midnight snacks from a restaurant that never closed.

But they're gone now, every last one of them, leaving the halls empty-feeling and very gloomy, and the stairwell an echoing void, and the lobby funereal, so that the mostly solitary tenants of today are apt to seem like ghosts, especially when you meet one coming silently around a turn in the corridor where the ceiling light's burned out.

Sometimes I think that, what with the smaller and smaller families and more and more people living alone, our whole modern world is getting like that.

The police finally arrived, two grave and solicitous young men making a good impression—especially a tall and stalwart (Marcia told me) Officer Hart. But when they first heard Evelyn Mayne's story, they were quite skeptical (Marcia could tell, or thought she could, she told me). But they searched Evelyn's room and poked around the fire escapes and listened to her story again, and then they radioed for a medical policewoman, who arrived with admirable speed and who decided after an examination that in all probability there'd been recent sex, which would be confirmed by analysis of some smears she'd taken from the victim and the sheets.

Officer Hart did two great things, Marcia said. He got hold of Evelyn Mayne's social worker and told him he'd better get on over quick. And he got from him the phone number of her son who lived in the city and called him up and threw a scare into his wife and him about how they were the nearest of kin, goddamn it, and had better start taking care of the abused and neglected lady.

Meanwhile the other cop had been listening to Evelyn Mayne, who was still telling it, and he asked her innocent questions, and had got her to admit that earlier that night she'd gone alone to a bar down the street (a rather rough place) and had one drink, or maybe three. Which made him wonder (Marcia said she could tell) whether Evelyn hadn't brought the whole thing on herself, maybe by inviting some man home with her, and then inventing the rape, at least in part, when things went wrong. (Though I couldn't see her inventing the silver hair.)

Anyhow the police got her statement and got it signed and then took off, even more solemnly sympathetic than when they'd arrived, Officer Hart in particular.

Of course, I didn't know anything about all this when I knocked on Marcia's door before going to work that morning, to confirm a tentative movie date we'd made for that evening. Though I was surprised when the door opened and Mr. Helpful came out looking down at me very thoughtfully, his bald head gleaming, and saying to Marcia in the voice adults use when children are listening. "I'll keep in touch with you about the matter. If there is anything I can do, don't hesitate . . ."

Marcia, looking at him very solemnly, nodded.

And then my feeling of discomfiture was completed when Evelyn Mayne, empty glass in hand and bathrobe clutched around her, edged past me as if I were contagious, giving me a peculiarly hostile look and calling back to Marcia over my head, "I'll come back, my dear, when I've repaired my appearance, so that people can't say you're entertaining bedraggled old hags."

I was relieved when Marcia gave me a grin as soon as the door was closed and said, "Actually she's gone to get herself another drink, after finishing off my supply. But really, Jeff, she has a reason to this morning—and for hating any man she runs into." And her face grew grave and troubled (and a little frightened too) as she quickly clued me in on the night's nasty events. Mr. Helpful, she explained, had dropped by to remind them about a tenants' meeting that evening and, when he got the grisly news, to go into a song and dance about how shocked he was and how guilty at having slept through it all, and what could he do?

Once she broke of to say, almost worriedly, "What I can't understand, Jeff, is why any man would want to rape someone like Evelyn."

I shrugged. "Kinky some way, I suppose. It does happen, you know. To old women, I mean. Maybe a mother thing."

"Maybe he *hates* women," she speculated. "Wants to punish them."

I nodded.

She had finished by the time Evelyn Mayne came back, very listless now, looking like a woebegone ghost, and dropped into a chair. She hadn't got dressed or even combed her hair. In one hand she had her glass, full and dark, and in the other a large, pale gray leather glove, which she carried oddly, dangling it by one finger.

Marcia started to ask her about it, but she just began to recite once more all that had happened to her that night, in an unemotional mechanical voice that sounded as if it would go on forever.

Look, I didn't like the woman—she was a particularly useless, venemous sort of nuisance (those wearisome suicide attempts!)—but that recital got to me. I found myself hating the person who would deliberately put someone into the state she was in. I realized, perhaps for the first time, just what a vicious and sick crime rape is and how cheap are all the easy jokes about it.

Eventually the glove came into the narrative naturally: ". . . and in order to do that he had to take off his glove. He was particularly excited just then, and it must have got shoved behind the couch and forgotten, where I found it just now."

Marcia pounced on the glove at once then, saying it was important evidence they must tell the police about. So she called them and after a bit she managed to get Officer Hart himself, and he told her to tell Evelyn Mayne to hold on to the glove and he'd send someone over for it eventually.

It was more than time for me to get on to work, but I stayed until she finished her call, because I wanted to remind her about our date that evening.

She begged off, saying she'd be too tired from the sleep she'd lost and anyway she'd decided to go to the tenants' meeting tonight. She told me, "This has made me realize that I've got to begin to take some responsibility for what happens around me. We may make fun of such people—the good neighbors—but they've got something solid about them."

I was pretty miffed at that, though I don't think I let it show. Oh, I didn't so much mind her turning me down—there were reasons enough—but she didn't have to make such a production of it and drag in "good neighbors." (Mr. Helpful, who else?) Besides, Evelyn

Mayne came out of her sad apathy long enough to give me a big smile when Marcia said "No."

So I didn't go to the tenants' meeting that night, as I might otherwise have done. Instead I had dinner out and went to the movie—it was lousy—and then had a few drinks, so that it was late when I got back (no signs of life in the lobby or lift or corridor) and gratefully piled into bed.

I was dragged out of the depths of sleep—that first blissful plunge—by a persistent knocking. I shouted something angry but unintelligible and when there was no reply made myself get up, feeling furious.

It was Marcia. With a really remarkable effort I kept my mouth shut and even smoothed out whatever expression was contorting my face. The words one utters on being suddenly awakened, especially from that matchless first sleep that is never recaptured, can be as disastrous as speaking in drink. Our relationship had progressed to the critical stage and I sure didn't want to blow it, especially when treasures I'd hoped to win were spread out in front of my face, as it were, under a semitransparent nightgown and hastily thrown on negligee.

I looked up, a little, at her face. Her eyes were wide.

She said in a sort of frightened little-girl voice that didn't seem at all put on, "I'm awfully sorry to wake you up at three o'clock in the morning, Jeff, but would you keep this 'spooky' for me? I can't get to sleep with it in my room."

It is a testimony to the very high quality of Marcia's treasures that I didn't until then notice what she was carrying in front of her—in a fold of toilet paper: the pale gray leather glove Evelyn Mayne had found behind her couch.

"Huh?" I said, not at all brilliantly. "Didn't Officer Hart come back, or send someone over to pick it up?"

She shook her head. "Evelyn had it, of course, while I was at my job—her social worker did come over right after you left. But then at suppertime her son and daughter-in-law came (Officer Hart did scare them!) and bundled her off to the hospital, and she left the glove with me. I called the police, but Officer Hart was off duty and Officer Halstead, whom I talked to, told me they'd be over to pick it up early in the morning. Please take it, Jeff. Whenever I look at it, I think of that crazy sneaking around with the silver hair down his face and waving the knife. It keeps giving me the shivers."

I looked again at her "spooky" in its fold of tissue (so that she wouldn't have to touch it, what other reason?) and, you know, it began to give *me* the shivers. Just an old glove, but now it had an invisible gray aura radiating from it.

"OK," I said, closing my hand on it with an effort, and went on ungraciously, really without thinking, "Though I wondered you didn't ask Mr. Helpful first, what with all his offers and seeing him at the meeting."

"Well, I asked *you,*" she said a little angrily. Then her features relaxed into a warm smile. "Thanks, Jeff."

Only then did it occur to me that here I was passing up in my sleep-soddenness what might be a priceless opportunity. Well, that could be corrected. But before I could invite her in, there came this sharp little cough, or clearing of the throat. We both turned and there was Mr. Helpful in front of his open door, dressed in pajamas and a belted maroon dressing gown. He came smiling and dancing toward us (he didn't really dance, but he gave that impression in spite of being six foot four) and saying, "Could I be of any assistance, Miss Everly? Did something alarm you? Is there . . . er . . . ?" He hesitated, as if there might be something he should be embarrassed at.

Marcia shook her head curtly and said to me quite coolly, "No, thank you, I needn't come in, Mr. Winters. That will be fine. Good night."

I realized Baldy *had* managed to embarrass her and that she was making it clear that we weren't parting after a rendezvous, or about to have one. (But to use my last name!)

As she passed him, she gave him a formal nod. He hurried back to his own door, a highlight dancing on the back of his head. (Marcia says he shaves it; I, that he doesn't have to.)

I waited until I heard her double-lock her door and slide the bolt across. Then I looked grimly at Baldy until he'd gone inside and closed his—I had that pleasure. Then I retired myself, tossed the glove down on some sheets of paper on the table in front of the open window, threw myself into bed, and switched out the light.

I fully expected to spend considerable time being furious at my hulking, mincing officious neighbor, and maybe at Marcia too, before I could get to sleep, but somehow my mind took off on a fantasy about the building around me as it might have been a half century ago. Ghostly bellboys sped silently with little notes inviting or accepting rendezvous. Ghostly waiters wheeled noiseless carts of silver-covered suppers for two. Pert, ghostly maids whirled ghostly sheets through the dark air as they made the bed, their smiles suggesting they might substitute for nonarriving sweethearts. The soft darkness whirlpooled. Somewhere was wind.

I woke with a start as if someone or something had touched me, and I sat up in bed. And then I realized that something *was* touching me high on my neck, just below my ear. Something long, like a finger laid flat or—oh God!—a centipede. I remembered how centipedes were supposed to cling with their scores of tiny feet—and *this* was clinging. As a child I'd been terrified by a tropical centipede that had come weaving out of a stalk of newbought bananas in the kitchen, and the memory still returned full force once in a great while. Now it galvanized me into whirling my hand behind my head and striking my neck a great brushing swipe, making my jaw and ear sting. I instantly turned on the light and rapidly looked all around me without seeing anything close to me that might have brushed off my neck. I thought I'd felt something with my hand when I'd done that, but I couldn't be sure.

And then I looked at the table by the window and saw that the glove was gone.

Almost at once I got the vision of it lifting up and floating through the air at me, fingers first, or else dropping off the table and inching across the floor and up the bed. I don't know which was worse. The thing on my neck *had* felt leathery.

My immediate impulse was to check if my door was still shut. I couldn't tell from where I sat. A very tall clothes cabinet abuts the door, shutting the view off from the head of the bed. So I pushed my way down the bed, putting my feet on the floor after looking down to make sure there was nothing in the immediate vicinity.

And then a sharp gust of wind came in the window and blew the last sheet of paper off the table and deposited it on the floor near the other sheets of paper *and the glove* and the tissue now disentangled from it.

I was so relieved I almost laughed. I went over and picked up the glove, feeling a certain revulsion, but only at the thought of who had worn it and what it had been involved in. I examined it closely, which I hadn't done earlier. It was a rather thin gray kid, a fairly big glove and stretched still further as if a pretty big hand had worn it, but quite light enough to have blown off the table with the papers.

There were grimy streaks on it and a slightly stiff part where some fluid had dried and a faintly reddish streak that might have been lipstick. And it looked old—decades old.

I put it back on the table and set a heavy ashtray on top of it and got back in bed, feeling suddenly secure again.

It occurred to me how the empty finger of a gray leather glove is really very much like a centipede, some of the larger of which are the same size, flat and yellowish gray (though the one that had come out of the banana stalk had been bright red), but these thoughts were no longer frightening.

I looked a last time across the room at the glove, pinioned under the heavy ashtray, and I confidently turned off the light.

Sleep was longer in coming this time, however. I got my fantasy of hotel ghosts going again, but gloves kept coming into it. The lissome maids wore work ones as they rhythmically polished piles of ghostly silver. The bellboys' hands holding the ghostly notes were gloved in pale gray cotton. And there were opera gloves, almost armpit length, that looked like spectral white cobras, especially when they were drawn inside-out off the sinuous, snake-slender arms of wealthy guesting ladies. And other ghostly gloves, not all hotel ones, came floating and weaving into my fantasy: the black gloves of morticians, the white gloves of policemen, the bulky fur-lined ones of polar explorers, the trim dark gauntlets of chauffeurs, the gloves of hunters with separate stalls only for thumb and trigger finger, the mittens of ice-skaters and sleigh riders, old ladies' mitts without any fingers at all, the thin, translucent elastic gloves of surgeons, wielding flashing scalpels of silver-bright steel—a veritable whirlpool of gloves that finally led me down, down, down to darkness.

Once again I woke with a start, as if I'd been touched, and shot up. Once again I felt something about four inches long clinging high on my neck, only this time under the other ear. Once again I frantically slashed at my neck and jaw, stinging them painfully, only this time I struck upward and away. I *thought* I felt something go.

I got the light on and checked the door at once. It was securely shut. Then I looked at the table by the open window. The heavy ashtray still sat in the center of it, rock firm.

But the rapist's glove that had been under it was gone.

I must have stood there a couple of minutes, telling myself this could not be. Then I went over and lifted the ashtray and carefully inspected its underside, as if the glove had somehow managed to shrink and was clinging there.

And all the while I was having this vision of the glove painfully humping itself from under the ashtray and inching to the table's edge and dropping to the floor and then crawling off . . . almost anywhere.

Believe me, I searched my place then, especially the floor. I even opened the doors to the closet and the clothes cabinet, though they had been tightly shut, and searched the floor there. And of course I searched under and behind the bed. And more than once while I searched, I'd suddenly jerk around thinking I'd seen something gray approaching my shoulder from behind.

There wasn't a sign of the glove.

It was dawn by now—had been for sometime. I made coffee and tried to think rationally about it.

It seemed to boil down to three explanations that weren't widely farfetched.

First, that I'd gone out of my mind. Could be, I suppose. But from what I'd read and seen, most people who go crazy know damn well ahead of time that something frightening is happening to their minds, except maybe paranoics. Still, it remained a possibility.

Second, that someone with a duplicate or master key had quietly taken the glove away while I was asleep. The apartment manager and janitor had such keys. I'd briefly given my duplicate to various people. Why, once before she got down on me, I'd given it to Evelyn Mayne—matter of letting someone in while I was at work. I *thought* I'd got it back from her, though I remember once having a second duplicate made—I'd forgotten why. The main difficulty about this explanation was motive. Who'd want to get the glove?—except the rapist, maybe.

Third, of course, there was the supernatural. Gloves are ghostly to start with, envelopes for hands—and if there isn't a medieval superstition about wearing the flayed skin of another's hand to work magic, there ought to be. (Of course, there was the Hand of Glory, its fingers flaming like candles, guaranteed to make people sleep while being burgled, but there the skin is still on the dried chopped-off hand.) And there are tales of spectral hands a-plenty—pointing out buried treasure or hidden graves, or at guilty murderers, or carrying candles or daggers—so why not gloves? And could there be a kind of telekinesis in which a hand controls at a distance the movements and actions of a glove it has worn? Of course that would be psionics or whatnot, but to me the parapsychological is supernatural. (And in that case what had the glove been trying to do probing at my neck?—strangle me, I'd think.) And somewhere I'd read of an aristocratic Brazilian murderess of the last century who wore gloves woven of spider silk, and of a knight blinded at a crucial moment in a tourney by a lady's silken glove worn as a favor. Yes, they were eerie envelopes, I thought, gloves were, but I was just concerned with one of them, a vanishing glove.

I started with a jerk as there came a measured *knock-knock.* I opened the door and looked up at the poker faces of two young policemen. Over their shoulders Mr. Helpful was peering down eagerly at me, his lips rapidly quirking in little smiles with what I'd call questioning pouts in between. Back and a little to one side was Marcia, looking shocked and staring intently at me through the narrow space between the second policeman and the doorjamb.

"Jeff Winters," the first policeman said to me, as if it were a fact that he was putting into place. It occurred to me that young policemen look very *blocky* around their narrow hips with all that equipment they carry snugly nested and cased in black leather.

"Officer Hart—" Marcia began anxiously.

The second policeman's eyes flickered toward her, but just then the first policeman continued, "Your neighbor Miss Everly says she handed you a glove earlier this morning," and he stepped forward into the private space (I think it's sometimes called) around my body, and I automatically stepped back.

"We want it," he went on, continuing to step forward, and I back.

I hesitated. What was I to say? That the glove had started to spook me and then disappeared? Officer Hart followed the first policeman in. Mr. Helpful followed *him* in and stopped just inside my door, Marcia still beyond him and looking frantic. Officer Hart turned, as if about to tell Mr. Helpful to get out, but just then Officer Halstead (that was the other name Marcia had mentioned) said, "Well, you've still got it, haven't you? She gave it to you, didn't she?"

I shook and then nodded my head, which must have made me look rattled. He came closer still and said harshly and with a note of eagerness, "Well, where is it, then?"

I had to look up quite sharply at him to see his face. Beyond it, just to one side of it, diagonally upward across the room, was the top of the tall clothes cabinet, and on the edge of that there balanced that damned gray glove, flat fingers dripping over.

I froze. I could have sworn I'd glanced up there more than once when I was hunting the thing, and seen nothing. Yet there it was, as if it had flown up there or else been flicked there by me the second time I'd violently brushed something from my face.

Officer Halstead must have misread my look of terror, for he ducked his head forward toward mine and rasped. "Your neighbor Mr. Angus says that it's *your* glove, that he saw you wearing gray gloves night before last! What do you say?"

But I didn't say anything, for at that moment the glove slid off its precarious perch and dropped straight down and landed on Mr. Helpful's (Angus's) shoulder close to his neck, just like the hand of an arresting cop.

Now it may have been that in ducking his head to look at it, he trapped it between his chin and collarbone, or it may have been (as it looked to me) that the glove actively clung to his neck and shoulder, resisting all his frantic efforts to peel it off, while he reiterated, his voice mounting in screams, "It's not my glove!"

He took his hands away for a moment and the glove dropped to the floor.

He looked back and forth and saw the dawning expressions on the faces of the two policemen, and then with a sort of despairing sob he whipped a long knife from under his coat.

Considerably to my surprise I started toward him, but just then Officer Hart endeared himself to us all forever by wrapping his arms around Mr. Angus like a bear, one hand closing on the wrist of the hand holding the knife.

I veered past him (I vividly recall changing the length of one of my strides so as not to step on the glove) and reached Marcia just in time to steady her as, turned quite white, she swayed, her eyelids fluttering.

I heard the knife clatter to the floor. I turned, my arms around Marcia, and we both saw Mr. Angus seem to shrink and collapse in Officer Hart's ursine embrace, his face going gray as if he were an empty glove himself.

That was it. They found the other glove and the long silver wig in a locked suitcase in his room. Marcia stayed frightened long enough, off and on, for us to become better acquainted and cement our friendship.

Officer (now Detective) Hart tells us that Mr. Angus is a model prisoner at the hospital for the criminally insane and has gone very religious, but never smiles. And he—Hart—now has the glove in a sort of Black Museum down at the station, where it has never again been seen to move under its own power. If it ever did.

One interesting thing. The gloves had belonged to Mr. Angus's father, now deceased, who had been a judge.

## The Grab

By Richard Laymon

My old college roomie, Clark Addison, pulled into town at sundown with a pickup truck, a brand-new gray Stetson, and a bad case of cowboy fever.

"What kind of nightlife you got in this one-hearse town?" he asked after polishing off a hamburger at my place.

"I see by your outfit you don't want another go at the Glass Palace."

"Disco's out, pardner. Where you been?"

With that, we piled into his pickup and started scouting for an appropriate night spot. We passed the four blocks of downtown Barnesdale without spotting a single bar that boasted of country music or a mechanical bull. "Guess we're out of luck," I said, trying to sound disappointed.

"Never say die," Clark said.

At that moment, we bumped over the railroad tracks and Clark punched a forefinger against the windshield. Ahead, on the far side of the grain elevator, stood a shabby little clapboard joint with a blue neon sign: THE BAR NONE SALOON.

Short of a bucking machine, the Bar None had all the trappings needed to warm the heart of any yearning cowpoke: sawdust heaped on the floor, Merle Haggard on the juke box, Coors on tap, and skin-tight jeans on the lower half of every gal. We mosied up to the bar.

"Two Coors," Clark said.

The bartender tipped back his hat and turned away. When the mugs were full, he pushed them toward us. "That's one-eighty."

"I'll get this round," Clark told me. Taking out his wallet, he leaned against the bar. "What kind of action you got here?" he asked.

"We got drinking, dancing, carousing, and The Grab."

"The Grab?" Clark asked. "What is it?"

The bartender stroked his handlebar moustache as if giving the matter lots of thought. Then he pointed down the bar at a rectangular metal box. The side I could see, painted with yellow letters, read, TEST YER GUTS.

"What's it do?" Clark asked.

"Stick around," the bartender said. With that advice, he moved on.

Clark and I wandered over to the metal box. It stood more than two feet high, its sides about half as wide as its height. THE GRAB was painted on its front in sloppy red letters intended, no doubt, to suggest dripping blood. Its far side was printed with green: PAY $10 AND WIN.

"Wonder what you win?" Clark said.

I shrugged. Leaning over the bar, I took a peek at the rear of the box. It was outfitted with a pound of hardware and padlocked to the counter.

While I checked out the lock, Clark was busy hopping and splashing beer. "No opening on top," he concluded.

"The only way in is from the bottom," I said.

"Twas ever thus," he said, forgetting to be a cowboy. He quickly recovered. "Reckon we oughta grab a couple of fillies and raise some dust."

As we started across the room toward a pair of unescorted females, the juke box stopped. There were a few hushed voices as everyone looked toward the bartender.

"Yes," he cried, raising his arms, "the time is now! Step on over and face The Grab. But let me warn you, this ain't for the faint of heart, it ain't for the weak of stomach. It ain't a roller coaster or a tilt-a-whirl you get off, laughing, and forget. This is a genuine test of grit, and any that ain't up to it are welcome to vamoose. Any that stay to watch or participate are honor bound to hold their peace about what takes place here tonight. Alf's curse goes on the head of any who spill the beans."

I heard Clark laugh softly. A pale girl, beside him, looked up at Clark as if he were a curiosity.

"Any that ain't up to it, go now," the bartender said.

The bartender lowered his arms and remained silent while two couples headed for the door. When they were gone, he removed a thin chain from around his neck. He held it up for all to see. A diamond ring and a small key hung from it. He slid them free, and raised the ring.

"This here's the prize. Give it to your best gal, or trade it in for a thousand dollars if you're man enough to take it. So far, we've gone three weeks with The Grab, and not a soul's shown the gumption to make the ring his own. Pretty thing, isn't it? Okay, now gather

’round. Move on in here and haul out your cash, folks. Ten dollars is all it takes.”

We stepped closer to the metal box at the end of the bar, and several men reached for their wallets—Clark included.

“You going to do it?” I whispered to him.

“Sure.”

“You don’t even know what it is.”

“Can’t be that bad. *They’re* all gonna try it.”

Looking around at the others as they took out their money, I saw a few eager faces, some wild, grinning ones, and several that appeared pale and scared.

The bartender used his key to open the padlock at the rear of the metal box. He held up the lock, and somebody moaned in the silence.

“Dal,” a woman whispered. She was off to my left, tugging on the elbow of a burly, bearded fellow. He jerked his arm free and sneered at her. “Then go ahead, fool,” she said, and ran. The muffled thud of her cowboy boots was the only sound in the room. Near the door, she slipped on the sawdust and fell, landing on her rump. A few people laughed.

“Perverts!” she yelled as she scurried to her feet. She yanked open the door and slammed it behind her.

“Gal’s got a nervous stomach,” Dal said, grinning around at the rest of us. To the bartender, he said, “Let’s get to it, Jerry!”

Jerry set aside the padlock. He climbed onto the bar and stood over the metal container. Then he raised it. The cover slid slowly upward, revealing a glass tank like a tall, narrow aquarium. All around me, people gasped and moaned as they saw what lay at the bottom, barely visible through its gray, murky liquid. A stench of formaldehyde filled my nostrils, and I gagged.

Face up at the bottom of the tank was a severed head, its black hair and moustache moving as if stirred by a breeze, its skin wrinkled and yellow, its eyes wide open, its mouth agape.

“Well, well,” Clark muttered.

Jerry, kneeling beside the glass tank, picked up a straight-bent coat hanger with one end turned up slightly to form a hook. He slipped the diamond ring over it. Standing, he lowered the wire into the tank. The ring descended slowly, the brilliance of its diamond a dim glow in the cloudy solution. Then it vanished inside the open mouth. Jerry flicked the hanger a bit, and raised it. The ring no longer hung from its tip.

I let out a long-held breath, and looked at Clark. He was grinning.

"All you gotta do, for the thousand dollar ring, is to reach down with one hand and take it out of the dead man's mouth. Who'll go first?"

"That's me!" said Dal, the bearded one whose girl had just run off. He handed a ten-dollar bill to Jerry, then swung himself onto the bar. Standing over the tank, he unbuttoned his plaid shirt.

"Let me just say," Jerry continued, "nobody's a loser at the Bar None Saloon. Every man with grit enough to try The Grab gets a free beer afterwards, compliments of the house."

Throwing down his shirt, Dal knelt behind the tank. Jerry tied a black blindfold over his eyes.

"All set?"

Dal nodded. He lowered his head and took a few deep breaths, psyching himself up like a basketball player on the free-throw line. Nobody cheered or urged him on. There was dead silence. Swelling out his chest, he held his breath and dipped his right hand into the liquid. It eased lower and lower. A few inches above the face, it stopped. The thick fingers wiggled, but touched nothing. The arm reached deeper. The tip of the middle finger stroked the dead man's nose. With a strangled yelp, Dal jerked his arm from the tank, splashing those of us nearby with the smelly fluid. Then he sighed, and shook his head as if disgusted with himself.

"Good try, good try!" Jerry cried, removing the blindfold. "Let's give this brave fellow a hand!"

A few people clapped. Most just watched, hands at their sides or in pockets, as Jerry filled a beer mug and gave it to Dal. "Try again later, pardner. Everyone's welcome to try as often as he likes. It only costs ten dollars. Ten little dollars for a chance at a thousand. Who's next?"

"Me!" called the pale girl beside Clark.

"Folks, we have us a first! What's your name, young lady?"

"Biff," she said.

"Biff will be the very first lady ever to try her hand at The Grab."

"Don't do it," whispered a chubby girl nearby. "Please."

"Lay off, huh?"

"It's not worth it."

"Is to me," she muttered, and pulled out a ten-dollar bill. She handed her purse to the other girl, then stepped toward the bar.

"Thank you, Biff," Jerry said, taking her money.

She removed her hat, and tossed it onto the counter. She was wearing a T-shirt. She didn't take it off. Leaning forward, she stared down into the tank. She looked sick.

Jerry tied the blindfold in place. "All set?" he asked.

Biff nodded. Her open hand trembled over the surface of the fluid. Then it slipped in, small and pale in the murkiness. Slowly, it eased downward. It sunk closer and closer to the face, never stopping until her fingertips lit on the forehead. They stayed there, motionless. I glanced up. She was tight and shaking as if naked in an icy wind.

Her fingers moved down the head. One touched an open eye. Flinching away, her hand clutched into a fist.

Slowly, her fingers fluttered open. They stretched out, trembled along the sides of the nose, and settled in the moustache. For seconds, they didn't move. The upper lip wasn't visible, as though it had shrunken under the moustache.

Biff's thumb slid along the edges of the teeth. Her fingertips moved off the moustache. They pressed against the lower teeth.

Biff started to moan.

Her fingers trembled off the teeth. They spread open over the gaping mouth, and started down.

With a shriek, she jerked her hand from the tank. She tugged the blindfold off. Face twisted with horror, she shook her hand in the air and gazed at it. She rubbed it on her T-shirt and looked at it again, gasping for air.

"Good try!" Jerry said. "The little lady made a gutsy try, didn't she, folks?"

A few of the group clapped. She stared out at us, blinking and shaking her head. Then she grabbed her hat, took the complimentary beer, and scurried off the bar.

Clark patted her shoulder. "Good going," he said.

"Not good enough," she muttered. "Got spooked."

"Who'll be next?" Jerry asked.

"Yours truly," Clark said, holding up a pair of fives. He winked at me. "It's a cinch," he said, and boosted himself onto the bar. Grinning, he tipped his hat to the small silent crowd. "I have a little surprise for y'all," he said in his thickest cowboy drawl. "You see, folks . . ." He paused and beamed. "Not even my best friend, Steve, knows about this, but I work full time as a mortician's assistant."

That brought a shocked murmur from his audience, including me.

"Why, folks, I've handled more dead meat than your corner butcher. This is gonna be a sure cinch."

With that, he skinned off his shirt and knelt behind the tank. Jerry, looking a bit amused, tied the blindfold over his eyes.

"All set?" the bartender asked.

"Ready to lose your diamond ring?"

"Give it a try."

Clark didn't hesitate. He plunged his arm into the solution and drove his open hand downward. His fingers found the dead man's hair. They patted him on the head. "Howdy pardner," he said.

Then his fingers slid over the ghastly face. They tweaked the nose, they plucked the moustache. "Say ahhhh."

He slipped his forefinger deep between the parted teeth, and his scream ripped through the silence as the mouth snapped shut.

His hand shot upward, a cloud of red behind it. It popped from the surface, spraying us with formaldehyde and blood.

Clark jerked the blindfold down and stared at his hand. The forefinger was gone.

"My *finger!*" he shrieked. "My God, my *finger!* It bit . . . it . . ."

Cheers and applause interrupted him, but they weren't for Clark.

"Look at him go!" Dal yelled, pointing at the head.

"Go, Alf, go!" cried another.

"Alf?" I asked Biff.

"Alf Packer," she said without looking away from the head. "The famous cannibal."

The head seemed to grin as it chewed.

I turned to Biff, "You knew?"

"Sure. Any wimp'll make The Grab, if he doesn't know. When you know, it takes real guts."

"Who's next?" Jerry asked.

"Here's a volunteer," Biff called out, clutching my arm. I jerked away from her, but was restrained by half a dozen mutilated hands. "Maybe you'll get lucky," she said. "Alf's a lot more tame after a good meal."

# The Haunted Mill or the Ruined Home

By Jerome K. Jerome

## Introduction

It was Christmas Eve.

I begin this way, because it is the proper, orthodox, respectable way to begin, and I have been brought up in a proper, orthodox, respectable way, and taught to always do the proper, orthodox, respectable thing; and the habit clings to me.

Of course, as a mere matter of information it is quite unnecessary to mention the date at all. The experienced reader knows it was Christmas Eve, without my telling him. It always is Christmas Eve, in a ghost story.

Christmas Eve is the ghosts' great gala night. On Christmas Eve they hold their annual fête. On Christmas Eve everybody in Ghostland who *is* anybody—or rather, speaking of ghosts, one should say, I suppose, every nobody who *is* any nobody—comes out to show himself or herself, to see and to be seen, to promenade about and display their winding-sheets and grave-clothes to each other, to criticize one another's style, and sneer at one another's complexion.

'Christmas Eve Parade,' as I expect they themselves term it, is a function, doubtless, eagerly prepared for and looked forward to throughout Ghostland, especially by the swagger set, such as the murdered Barons, the crime-stained Countesses, and the Earls who came over with the Conqueror, and assassinated their relatives, and died raving mad.

Hollow moans and fiendish grins are, one may be sure, energetically practised up. Blood-curdling shrieks and marrow-freezing gestures are probably rehearsed for weeks beforehand. Rusty chains and gory daggers are overhauled, and put into good working order; and sheets and shrouds, laid carefully by from the previous year's show, are taken down and shaken out, and mended, and aired.

Oh, it is a stirring night in Ghostland, the night of December the twenty-fourth!

Ghosts never come out on Christmas night itself, you may have noticed. Christmas Eve, we suspect, has been too much for them; they are not used to excitement. For about a week after Christmas Eve, the gentlemen ghosts, no doubt, feel as if they were all head, and go about making solemn resolutions to themselves that they will stop in next Christmas Eve; while the lady spectres are contradictory and snappish, and liable to burst into tears and leave the room hurriedly on being spoken to, for no perceptible cause whatever.

Ghosts with no position to maintain—mere middle-class ghosts—occasionally, I believe, do a little haunting on off-nights: on All-hallows Eve, and at Midsummer; and some will even run up for a mere local event—to celebrate, for instance, the anniversary of the hanging of somebody's grandfather, or to prophesy a misfortune.

He does love prophesying a misfortune, does the average British ghost. Send him out to prognosticate trouble to somebody, and he is happy. Let him force his way into a peaceful home, and turn the whole house upside down by foretelling a funeral, or predicting a bankruptcy, or hinting at a coming disgrace, or some terrible disaster, about which nobody in their senses would want to know sooner than they could possibly help, and the prior knowledge of which can serve no useful purpose whatsoever, and he feels that he is combining duty with pleasure. He would never forgive himself if anybody in his family had a trouble and he had not been there for a couple of months beforehand, doing silly tricks on the lawn, or balancing himself on somebody's bed-rail.

Then there are, besides, the very young, or very conscientious ghosts with a lost will or an undiscovered number weighing heavy on their minds, who will haunt steadily all the year round; and also the fussy ghost, who is indignant at having been buried in the dustbin or in the village pond, and who never gives the parish a single night's quiet until somebody has paid for a first-class funeral for him.

But these are the exceptions. As I have said, the average orthodox ghost does his one turn a year, on Christmas Eve, and is satisfied.

Why on Christmas Eve, of all nights in the year, I never could myself understand. It is invariably one of the most dismal of nights to be out in—cold, muddy, and wet. And besides, at Christmas time, everybody has quite enough to put up with in the way of a houseful of living relations, without wanting the ghosts of any dead ones mooning about the place, I am sure.

There must be something ghostly in the air of Christmas—something about the close, muggy atmosphere that draws up the ghosts, like the dampness of the summer rains brings out the frogs and snails.

And not only do the ghosts themselves always walk on Christmas Eve, but live people always sit and talk about them on Christmas Eve. Whenever five or six English-speaking people meet round a fire on Christmas Eve, they start telling each other ghost stories. Nothing satisfies us on Christmas Eve but to hear each other tell authentic anecdotes about spectres. It is a genial, festive season, and we love to muse upon graves, and dead bodies, and murders, and blood.

There is a good deal of similarity about our ghostly experiences; but this of course is not our fault but the fault of the ghosts, who never will try any new performances, but always will keep steadily to the old, safe business. The consequence is that, when you have been at one Christmas Eve party, and heard six people relate their adventures with spirits, you do not require to hear any more ghost stories. To listen to any further ghost stories after that would be like sitting out two farcical comedies, or taking in two comic journals; the repetition would become wearisome.

There is always the young man who was, one year, spending the Christmas at a country house, and, on Christmas Eve, they put him to sleep in the west wing. Then in the middle of the night, the room door quietly opens and somebody—generally a lady in her nightdress—walks slowly in, and comes and sits on the bed. The young man thinks it must be one of the visitors, or some relative of the family, though he does not remember having previously seen her, who, unable to go to sleep, and feeling lonesome, all by herself, has come into his room for a chat. He has no idea it is a ghost: he is so unsuspicious. She does not speak, however; and, when he looks again, she is gone!

The young man relates the circumstance at the breakfast table next morning, and asks each of the ladies present if it were she who was the visitor. But they all assure him that it was not, and the host, who has grown deadly pale, begs him to say no more about the matter, which strikes the young man as a singularly strange request.

After breakfast the host takes the young man into a corner, and explains to him that what he saw was the ghost of a lady who had been murdered in that very bed, or who had murdered somebody else there—it does not really matter which: you can be a ghost by murdering somebody else or by being murdered yourself, whichever you prefer. The murdered ghost is, perhaps, the more popular; but, on the other hand, you can frighten people better if you are the murdered one, because then you can show your wounds and do groans.

Then there is the sceptical guest—it is always 'the guest' who gets let in for this sort of thing, by-the-bye. A ghost never thinks much of his own family: it is 'the guest' he likes to haunt who after listening to the host's ghost story, on Christmas Eve, laughs at it, and says that he does not believe there are such things as ghosts at all; and that he will sleep in the haunted chamber that very night, if they will let him.

Everybody urges him not to be so reckless, but he persists in his foolhardiness, and goes up to the Yellow Chamber (or whatever colour the haunted room may be) with a light heart and a candle, and wishes them all good-night, and shuts the door.

Next morning he has got snow-white hair.

He does not tell anybody what he has seen: it is too awful.

There is also the plucky guest, who sees a ghost, and knows it is a ghost, and watches it, as it comes into the room and disappears through the wainscot, after which, as the ghost does not seem to be coming back, and there is nothing, consequently, to be gained by stopping awake, he goes to sleep.

He does not mention having seen the ghost to anybody, for fear of frightening them—some people are so nervous about ghosts,—but determines to wait for the next night, and see if the apparition appears again.

It does appear again, and, this time, he gets out of bed, dresses himself and does his hair, and follows it; and then discovers a secret passage leading from the bedroom down into the beer-cellar,—a passage which, no doubt, was not unfrequently made use of in the bad old days of yore.

After him comes the young man who woke up with a strange sensation in the middle of the night, and found his rich bachelor uncle standing by his bedside. The rich uncle smiled a weird sort of smile and vanished. The young man immediately got up and looked at his watch. It had stopped at half-past four, he having forgotten to wind it.

He made enquiries the next day, and found that, strangely enough, his rich uncle, whose only nephew he was, had married a widow with eleven children at exactly a quarter to twelve, only two days ago.

The young man does not attempt to explain the extraordinary circumstance. All he does is to vouch for the truth of his narrative.

And, to mention another case, there is the gentleman who is returning home late at night, from a Freemasons' dinner, and who, noticing a light issuing from a ruined abbey, creeps up, and looks through the keyhole. He sees the ghost of a 'grey sister' kissing the ghost of a brown monk, and is so inexpressibly shocked and frightened that he faints on the spot, and is discovered there the next morning, lying in a heap against the door, still speechless, and with his faithful latch-key clasped tightly in his hand.

All these things happen on Christmas Eve, they are all told of on Christmas Eve. For ghost stories to be told on any other evening than the evening of the twenty-fourth of December would be impossible in English society as at present regulated. Therefore, in introducing the sad but authentic ghost story that follows, I feel that it is unnecessary to inform the student of Anglo-Saxon literature that the date on which it was told and on which the incidents took place was—Christmas Eve.

Nevertheless, I do so.

## The Haunted Mill

Well, you all know my brother-in-law, Mr Parkins (began Mr Coombes, taking the long clay pipe from his mouth, and putting it behind his ear: we did not know his brother-in-law, but we said we did, so as to save time), and you know of course that he once took a lease on an old mill in Surrey, and went to live there.

Now you must know that, years ago, this very mill had been occupied by a wicked old miser, who died there, leaving—so it was rumoured—all his money hidden somewhere about the place. Naturally enough, everyone who had since come to live at the mill had tried to find the treasure; but none had ever succeeded, and the local wiseacres said that nobody ever would, unless the ghost of the miserly miller should, one day, take a fancy to one of the tenants, and disclose to him the secret of the hiding-place.

My brother-in-law did not attach much importance to the story, regarding it as an old woman's tale, and, unlike his predecessors, made no attempt whatever to discover the hidden gold.

'Unless business was very different then from what it is now,' said my brother-in-law, 'I don't see how a miller could very well have saved anything, however much of a miser he might have been: at all events, not enough to make it worth the trouble of looking for it.'

Still, he could not altogether get rid of the idea of that treasure.

One night he went to bed. There was nothing very extraordinary about that, I admit. He often did go to bed of a night. What *was* remarkable, however, was that exactly as the clock of the village church chimed the last stroke of twelve, my brother-in-law woke up with a start, and felt himself quite unable to go to sleep again.

Joe (his Christian name was Joe) sat up in bed, and looked around.

At the foot of the bed something stood very still, wrapped in shadow.

It moved into the moonlight, and then my brother-in-law saw that it was the figure of a wizened little old man, in knee-breeches and a pigtail.

In an instant the story of the hidden treasure and the old miser flashed across his mind.

'He's come to show me where it's hid,' thought my brother-in-law; and he resolved that he would not spend all this money on himself, but would devote a small percentage of it towards doing good to others.

The apparition moved towards the door: my brother-in-law put on his trousers and followed it. The ghost went downstairs into the kitchen, glided over and stood in front of the hearth, sighed and disappeared.

Next morning, Joe had a couple of bricklayers in, and made them haul out the stove and pull down the chimney, while he stood behind with a potato-sack in which to put the gold.

They knocked down half the wall, and never found so much as a fourpenny bit. My brother-in-law did not know what to think.

The next night the old man appeared again, and led the way into the kitchen. This time, however, instead of going to the fireplace, it stood more in the middle of the room, and sighed there.

'Oh, I see what he means now,' said my brother-in-law to himself; 'it's under the floor. Why did the old idiot go and stand up against the stove, so as to make me think it was up the chimney?'

They spent the next day in taking up the kitchen floor; but the only thing they found was a three-pronged fork, and the handle of that was broken.

On the third night, the ghost reappeared, quite unabashed, and for a third time made for the kitchen. Arrived there, it looked up at the ceiling and vanished.

'Umph! he don't seem to have learned much sense where he's been to,' muttered Joe, as he trotted back to bed; 'I should have thought he might have done that at first.'

Still, there seemed no doubt now where the treasure lay, and the first thing after breakfast they started pulling down the ceiling. They got every inch of ceiling down, and they took up the boards of the room above.

They discovered about as much treasure as you would expect to find in an empty quart pot.

On the fourth night, when the ghost appeared, as usual, my brother-in-law was so wild that he threw his boots at it; and the boots passed through the body, and broke a looking-glass.

On the fifth night, when Joe awoke, as he always did now at twelve, the ghost was standing in a dejected attitude, looking very miserable. There was an appealing look in its large sad eyes that quite touched my brother-in-law.

'After all,' he thought, 'perhaps the silly chap's doing his best. Maybe he has forgotten where he really did put it, and is trying to remember. I'll give him another chance.'

The ghost appeared grateful and delighted at seeing Joe prepare to follow him, and led the way into the attic, pointed to the ceiling, and vanished.

'Well, he's hit it this time, I do hope,' said my brother-in-law; and next day they set to work to take the roof off the place.

It took them three days to get the roof thoroughly off, and all they found was a bird's nest; after securing which they covered up the house with tarpaulins, to keep it dry.

You might have thought that would have cured the poor fellow of looking for treasure. But it didn't.

He said there must be something in it all, or the ghost would never keep on coming as it did; and that, having gone so far, he would go on to the end, and solve the mystery, cost what it might.

Night after night, he would get out of his bed and follow that spectral old fraud about the house. Each night, the old man would indicate a different place; and, on each following day, my brother-in-law would proceed to break up the mill at the point indicated, and look for the treasure. At the end of three weeks, there was not a room in the mill fit to live in. Every wall had been pulled down, every floor had been taken up, every ceiling had had a hole knocked in it. And then, as suddenly as they had begun, the ghost's visits ceased; and my brother-in-law was left to rebuild the place at his leisure.

'What induced the old image to play such a silly trick upon a family man and a ratepayer?' Ah! that's just what I cannot tell you.

Some said that the ghost of the wicked old man had done it to punish my brother-in-law for not believing in him at first; while others held that the apparition was probably that of some deceased local plumber and glazier, who would naturally take an interest in seeing a house knocked about and spoilt. But nobody knew anything for certain.

## He Kilt It with a Stick

By William F. Nolan

A summer night in Kansas City.

Ellen away, visiting her parents. The house on Forest empty, waiting.

Warm air.

A high, yellow moon.

Stars.

Crickets thrumming the dark.

Fireflies.

A summer night.

Fred goes to the Apollo on Troost to see a war film. It depresses him. All the killing. He leaves before it has ended, walking up the aisle and out of the deserted lobby and on past the empty glass ticket booth. Alone.

The sidewalk is bare of pedestrians.

It is late, near midnight, and traffic is very sparse along Troost. The wide street is silent. A truck grinds heavily away in the distance.

Fred begins to walk home.

He shouldn't. It is only two blocks: a few steps to the corner of 33rd, then down the long hill to Forest, then right along Forest to his house at the end of the block, near 34th. Not quite two blocks to walk. But too far for him. Too far.

Fred stops.

A gray cat is sleeping in the window of Rae's Drugstore. Fred presses the glass.

*I could break the window—but that would be useless. The thing would be safe by then; it would leap away and I'd never find it in the store. The police would arrive and . . . No. Insane. Insane to think of killing it.*

The gray cat, quite suddenly, opens its eyes to stare at Fred Baxter. Unblinking. Evil.

He shudders, moves quickly on.

The cat continues to stare.

*Foul thing knows what I'd like to do to it.*

The hill, sloping steeply toward Forest, is tinted with cool moonlight. Fred walks down this hill, filled with an angry sense of frustration: he would very much have enjoyed killing the gray cat in the drugstore window.

Hard against chest wall, his heart judders. Once, twice, three times. Thud thud thud. He slows, removes a tissue-wrapped capsule from an inside pocket. Swallows the capsule. Continues to walk.

Fred reaches the bottom of the hill, crosses over.

Trees now. Big fat-trunked oaks and maples, fanning their leaves softly over the concrete sidewalk. Much darker. Thick tree-shadow midnight dark, broken by three street lamps down the long block. Lamps haloed by green night insects.

Deeper.

Into the summer dark . . .

When Fred Baxter was seven, he wrote: "Today a kitty cat bit me at school and it sure hurt a lot. The kitty was bad, so I kilt it with a stick."

When he was ten, and living in St. Louis, a boy two houses up told Fred his parents wanted to get rid of a litter. "I'll take care of it," Fred assured him—and the next afternoon, in Miller Lake, he drowned all six of the kittens.

At fifteen, in high school, Fred trapped the janitor's Tabby in the gymnasium locker room, choked it to death, and carried it downstairs to the furnace. He was severely scratched in the process.

As a college freshman, in Kansas City, Fred distributed several pieces of poisoned fish over the Rockhurst campus. The grotesquely twisted bodies of seven cats were found the next morning.

Working in the sales department of Hall Brothers, Fred was invited to visit his supervisor at home one Saturday—and was seen in the yard playing with Frances, a pet Siamese. She was later found crushed to death, and it was assumed a car had run over the animal. Fred quit his job ten days later because his supervisor had cat hands.

Fred married Ellen Ferber when he was thirty, and she wanted to have children right away. Fred said no, that babies were small and furry in their blankets, and disturbed him. Ellen bought herself a small kitten for company while Fred was on the road. He didn't object—but a week after the purchase, he took a meat knife and dismembered the kitten, telling Ellen that it had "wandered away." Then he bought her a green parakeet.

*ZZZZZZZ Click*

This is Frederick Baxter speaking and I . . . wait, the sound level is wrong and I'll— There, it's all right now. I can't tell anyone about this—but today I found an old Tom in an alley downtown, and I got hold of the stinking, wretched animal and I . . .

*ZZZZZZZ Click*

The heart trouble started when Fred was thirty-five.

"You have an unusual condition," the doctor told him. "You are, in effect, a medical oddity. Your chest houses a quivering-muscled heart—fibrillation. Your condition can easily prove fatal. Preventive measures must be taken. No severe exercise, no overeating, plenty of rest."

Fred obeyed the man's orders—although he did not really trust a doctor whose cat eyes reflected the moon.

*ZZZZZZZ Click*

. . . awful time with the heart. Really awful. The use of digitalis drives me to alcohol, which sends my heart into massive flutters. Then the alcohol forces me into a need for more digitalis. It is a deadly circle and I . . .

I have black dreams. A nap at noon and I dream of smothering. This comes from the heart condition. And because of the cats. They all fear me now, avoid me on the street. They've *told* one another about me. This is fact. Killing them is becoming quite difficult . . . but I caught a big, evil one in the garden last Thursday and buried it. Alive. As I am buried alive in these black dreams of mine. I got excited, burying the cat—and this is bad for me. I must go on killing them, but I must *not* get excited. I must stay calm and not—here comes Ellen, so I'd better . . .

*ZZZZZZZ Click*

"What's wrong, Fred?"

It was 2 A.M. and Ellen had awakened to find him standing at the window.

"Something in the yard," he said.

The moon was flushing the grass with pale gold—and a dark shape scuttled over the lawn, breaking the pattern. A cat shape.

"Go to sleep," said his wife, settling into her pillow.

Fred Baxter stared at the cat, who stared back at him from the damp yard, its head raised, the yellow of the night moon now brimming the creature's eyes. The cat's mouth opened.

"It's sucking up the moonlight," Fred whispered.

Then he went back to bed.

But he did not sleep.

Later, thinking about this, Fred recalled what his mother had often said about cats. "They perch on the chest of a baby," she'd said, "place their red mouth over the soft mouth of the baby, and draw all the life from its body. I won't have one of the disgusting things in the house."

Alone in the summer night, walking down Forest Avenue in Kansas City, Fred passes a parked car, bulking black and silent in its gravel driveway. The closed car windows gleam deep yellow from the eyes inside.

Fred stops, looks back at the car.

*How many? Ten . . . a dozen. More . . . twenty, maybe. All inside the car, staring out at me. Dozens of foul, slitted yellow eyes.*

Fred can do nothing. He checks all four doors of the silent automobile, finds them locked. The cats stare at him.

*Filthy creatures!*

He moves on.

The street is oddly silent. Fred realizes why: the crickets have stopped. No breeze stirs the trees; they hang over him, heavy and motionless in the summer dark.

The houses along Forest are shuttered, lightless, closed against the night. Yet, on a porch, Fred detects movement.

Yellow eyes spark from porch blackness. A big, dark-furred cat is curled into a wooden swing. It regards Fred Baxter.

*Kill it!*

He moves with purposeful stealth, leans to grasp a stout tree limb which has fallen into the yard. He mounts the porch steps.

The dark-furred cat has not stirred.

Fred raises the heavy limb. The cat hisses, claws extended, fangs balefully revealed. It cries out like a wounded child and vanishes off the porch into the deep shadow between houses.

*Missed. Missed the rotten thing.*

Fred moves down the steps, crosses the yard toward the walk. His head is lowered in anger. When he looks up, the walk is thick with cats. He runs into them, kicking, flailing the tree club. They scatter, melting away from him like butter from a heated blade.

Thud thud thud. Fred drops the club. His heart is rapping, fisting his chest. He leans against a tree, sobbing for breath. The yellow-eyed cats watch him from the street, from bushes, from steps and porches and the tops of cars.

*Didn't get a one of them. Not a damn one . . .*

The fireflies have disappeared. The street lamps have dimmed to smoked circles above the heavy, cloaking trees. The clean summer sky is shut away from him—and Fred Baxter finds the air clogged with the sharp, suffocating smell of cat fur.

He walks on down the block.

The cats follow him.

He thinks of what fire could do to them—long blades of yellow crisping flame to flake them away into dark ash. But he cannot burn them; burning them would be impossible. There are *hundreds.* That many at least.

They fill driveways, cover porches, blanket yards, pad in lion-like silence along the street. The yellow moon is in their eyes, sucked from the sky. Fred, his terror rising, raises his head to look upward.

*The trees are alive with them!*

His throat closes. He cannot swallow. Cat fur cloaks his mouth.

Fred begins to run down the concrete sidewalk, stumbling, weaving, his chest filled with a terrible winged beating.

A sound.

The scream of the cats.

Fred claps both hands to his head to muffle the stab and thrust of sound.

*The house . . . must reach the house.*

Fred staggers forward. The cat masses surge in behind him as he runs up the stone walk to his house.

A cat lands on his neck. Mutely, he flings it loose—plunges up the wooden porch steps.

*Key. Find your key and unlock the door. Get inside!*

Too late.

Eyes blazing, the cats flow up and over him, a dark, furry, stifling weight. As he pulls back the screen, claws and needle teeth rip at his back, arms, face, legs . . . shred his clothing and skin. He twists wildly, beating at them. Blood runs into his eyes. . . .

The door is open. He falls forward, through the opening. The cats swarm after him in hot waves, covering his chest, sucking the breath from his body. Baxter's thin scream is lost in the sharp, rising, all-engulfing cry of the cats.

A delivery boy found him two days later, lying face down on the living room floor. His clothes were wrinkled, but untorn.

A cat was licking the cold, white, unmarked skin of Frederick Baxter's cheek.

## Heading Home

By Ramsey Campbell

Somewhere above you can hear your wife and the young man talking. You strain yourself upward, your muscles trembling like water, and manage to shift your unsteady balance onto the next stair.

They must think he finished you. They haven't even bothered to close the cellar door, and it's the trickle of flickering light through the crack that you're striving toward. Anyone else but you would be dead. He must have carried you from the laboratory and thrown you down the stairs into the cellar, where you regained consciousness on the dusty stone. Your left cheek still feels like a rigid plate slipped into your flesh where it struck the floor. You rest on the stair you've reached and listen.

They're silent now. It must be night, since they've lit the hall lamp whose flame is peeking into the cellar. They can't intend to leave the house until tomorrow, if at all. You can only guess what they're doing now, thinking themselves alone in the house. Your numb lips crack again as you grin. Let them enjoy themselves while they can.

He didn't leave you many muscles you can use; it was a thorough job. No wonder they feel safe. Now you have to concentrate yourself in those muscles that still function. Swaying, you manage to raise yourself momentarily to a position from which you can grip the next higher stair. You clench on your advantage. Then, pushing with muscles you'd almost forgotten you had, you manage to lever yourself one step higher.

You maneuver yourself until you're sitting upright. There's less risk that way of your losing your balance for a moment and rolling all the way down to the cellar floor where, hours ago, you began climbing. Then you rest. Only six more stairs.

You wonder again how they met. Of course you should have known that it was going on, but your work was your wife and you couldn't spare the time to watch over the woman you'd married. You should have realized that when she went to the village she would meet people and mightn't be as silent as at home. But her room might well have been as far from yours as the village is from the house; you gave little thought to the people in either.

Not that you blame yourself. When you met her—in the town where you attended the University—you'd thought she understood the importance of your work. It wasn't as if you'd intended to trick her. It was only when she tried to seduce you from your work, both for her own gratification and because she was afraid of it, that you barred her from your companionship by silence.

You can hear their voices again. They're on the first floor. You don't know whether they're celebrating or comforting each other as guilt settles on them. It doesn't matter. So long as he didn't close the laboratory door when he returned from the cellar. If it's closed you'll never be able to open it. And if you can't get into the laboratory he has killed you after all. You raise yourself, muscles shuddering with the effort, your cheek chafing against the wood of the stair. You won't relax until you can see the laboratory door.

You're reaching for the top stair when you slip. Your chin comes down on it, and slides back. You grip the wooden stair with your jaws, feeling splinters lodge between your teeth. Your neck scraped the lower stair, but it has lost all feeling save an ache fading slowly into dullness. Only your jaws prevent you from falling back where you started, and they're throbbing as if nails are being driven through their hinges with measured strokes. You close them tighter, pounding with pain, then you overbalance yourself onto the top stair. You teeter for a moment, then you're secure.

But you don't rest yet. You edge yourself forward and sit up so that you can peer out of the cellar. The outline of the laboratory door billows slightly as the lamp flickers. It occurs to you that they've lit the lamp because she's terrified of you, lying dead beyond the main staircase—as she thinks. You laugh silently. You can afford to. When the flame steadies you can see darkness gaping for inches around the laboratory door.

You listen to their voices upstairs and rest. You know he's a butcher, because once he helped one of the servants carry the meat from the village. In any case, you could have told his profession from what he has done to you. You're still astonished that she should have taken up with him. From the little you knew of the village people you were delighted that they always avoided the house.

You remember the day the new priest visited the house. You could tell he'd heard all the wildest village tales about your experiments; you were surprised he didn't try to ward you off with a cross. When he found you could argue his theology into a corner he left, a twitch pulling his smile awry. He'd tried to persuade you both to attend the church, but your wife had sat silent throughout. It had been then that you decided to trust her to go to the village. You'd dismissed the servants, but you told yourself she would be less likely to talk. You grin fiercely. If you'd been as inaccurate in your experiments you would be dead.

Upstairs they're still talking. You rock forward and try to wedge yourself between the cellar door and its frame. With your limited control it's difficult, and you find yourself leaning in the crack with no purchase on the wood. Your weight hasn't moved the door, which is heavier than you have ever before had cause to realize. Eventually you manage to wedge yourself in the crack, gripping the frame with all your strength. The door rests on you, and you nudge your weight clumsily against it.

It creaks away from you a little, then swings back, crushing you. It has always hung unevenly and persisted in standing ajar; it never troubled you before. Now the strength he left you, even focused like light through a burning-glass, seems unequal to shifting the door. Trapped in the crack, you relax for a moment. Then, as if to take it unawares, you close your grip on the frame and shove against the door, pushing yourself forward as it swings away. It returns, answering the force of your shove, and you aren't clear. But you're still falling into the hall, and as the door chops into the frame you fall on your back, beyond the sweep of the door.

You're free of the cellar, but on your back you're helpless. The slowing door is more mobile than you. All the muscles you've been using can only work aimlessly and loll in the air. You're laid out on the hall floor like a laboratory subject, beneath the steadying flame.

Then you hear the butcher call to your wife, "I'll see," and start downstairs.

You begin to twitch all the muscles on your right side frantically. You roll a little toward that side, then your wild twitching rocks you back. About you the light shakes, making your shadow play the cruel trick of achieving the roll you're struggling for. He's at the halfway landing now. You work your right side again and hold your muscles still as you begin to turn that way. Suddenly you've swung over your point of equilibrium and are lying on your right side. You strain your aching muscles to inch you forward, but the laboratory is feet away, and you are by no means moving in a straight line. His footsteps resound. You hear your wife's terrified voice, entreating him to return to her. There's a long pondering silence. Then he hurries back upstairs.

You don't let yourself rest until you're inside the laboratory, although by then your ache feels like a cold stiff surface within your flesh, and your mouth like a dusty hole in stone. Once beyond the door you sit still, gazing about. Moonlight is spread from the window to the door. Your gaze seeks the bench where you were working when he found you. He hasn't cleared up any of the material that was thrown to the floor by your convulsion. Glinting on the floor you see a needle, and nearby the surgical thread which you never had occasion to use. You relax to prepare for the next concerted effort, remembering.

You recall the day you perfected the solution. As soon as you'd quaffed it you felt your brain achieve a piercing alertness, become precisely and continually aware of the messages of each nerve and preside over them, making minute adjustments at the first hint of danger. You knew this was what you'd worked for, but you couldn't prove it to yourself until the day you felt the stirrings of cancer. Then your brain seemed to condense into a keen strand of energy that stretched down and burned out the cancer. That was proof. You were immortal.

Not that some of the research hadn't been unpleasant. It had taken you a great deal of furtive expenditure at the mortuaries to discover that some of the extracts you needed for the solution had to be taken from the living brain. The villagers thought the children had drowned, for their clothes were found on the river bank. Medical progress, you told yourself, had always involved suffering.

Perhaps your wife suspected something of this stage of your work or perhaps they'd simply decided to rid themselves of you. You were working at your bench, trying to synthesize your discovery when you heard him enter. He must have rushed at you, for before you could turn you felt a blazing slash gape at the back of your neck. Then you awoke on the cellar floor.

You edge yourself forward across the laboratory. Your greatest exertion is past, but this is the most exacting part. When you're nearly touching your prone body you have to turn round. You move yourself with your jaws and steer with your tongue. It's difficult, but less so than tonguing yourself upright on your neck to rest on the stairs. Then you fit yourself to your shoulders, groping with your perfected mind until you feel the nerves linking again.

Now you'll have to hold yourself unflinching or you'll roll apart. With your mind you can do it. Gingerly, so as not to part yourself, you stretch out your arm and touch the surgical needle and thread.

## The Hollow of the Three Hills

By Nathaniel Hawthorne

In those strange old times, when fantastic dreams and madmen's reveries were realized among the actual circumstances of life, two persons met together at an appointed hour and place. One was a lady, graceful in form and fair of feature, though pale and troubled, and smitten with an untimely blight in what should have been the fullest bloom of her years; the other was an ancient and meanly-dressed woman, of ill-favored aspect, and so withered, shrunken, and decrepit, that even the space since she began to decay must have exceeded the ordinary term of human existence. In the spot where they encountered, no mortal could observe them. Three little hills stood near each other, and down in the midst of them sunk a hollow basin, almost mathematically circular, two or three hundred feet in breadth, and of such depth that a stately cedar might but just be visible above the sides. Dwarf pines were numerous upon the hills, and partly fringed the outer verge of the intermediate hollow, within which there was nothing but the brown grass of October, and here and there a tree trunk that had fallen long ago, and lay mouldering with no green successor from its roots. One of these masses of decaying wood, formerly a majestic oak, rested close beside a pool of green and sluggish water at the bottom of the basin. Such scenes as this (so gray tradition tells) were once the resort of the Power of Evil and his plighted subjects; and here, at midnight or on the dim verge of evening, they were said to stand round the mantling pool, disturbing its putrid waters in the performance of an impious baptismal rite. The chill beauty of an autumnal sunset was now gilding the three hill-tops, whence a paler tint stole down their sides into the hollow.

"Here is our pleasant meeting come to pass," said the aged crone, "according as thou hast desired. Say quickly what thou wouldst have of me, for there is but a short hour that we may tarry here."

As the old withered woman spoke, a smile glimmered on her countenance, like lamplight on the wall of a sepulchre. The lady trembled, and cast her eyes upward to the verge of the basin, as if meditating to return with her purpose unaccomplished. But it was not so ordained.

"I am a stranger in this land, as you know," said she at length. "Whence I come it matters not; but I have left those behind me with whom my fate was intimately bound, and from whom I am cut off forever. There is a weight in my bosom that I cannot away with, and I have come hither to inquire of their welfare."

"And who is there by this green pool that can bring thee news from the ends of the earth?" cried the old woman, peering into the lady's face. "Not from my lips mayst thou hear these tidings; yet, be thou bold, and the daylight shall not pass away from yonder hill-top before thy wish be granted."

"I will do your bidding though I die," replied the lady desperately.

The old woman seated herself on the trunk of the fallen tree, threw aside the hood that shrouded her gray locks, and beckoned her companion to draw near.

"Kneel down," she said, "and lay your forehead on my knees."

She hesitated a moment, but the anxiety that had long been kindling burned fiercely up within her. As she knelt down, the border of her garment was dipped into the pool; she laid her forehead on the old woman's knees, and the latter drew a cloak about the lady's face, so that she was in darkness. Then she heard the muttered words of prayer, in the midst of which she started, and would have arisen.

"Let me flee—let me flee and hide myself, that they may not look upon me!" she cried. But, with returning recollection, she hushed herself, and was still as death.

For it seemed as if other voices—familiar in infancy, and unforgotten through many wanderings, and in all the vicissitudes of her heart and fortune—were mingling with the accents of the prayer. At first the words were faint and indistinct, not rendered so by distance, but rather resembling the dim pages of a book which we strive to read by an imperfect and gradually brightening light.

In such a manner, as the prayer proceeded, did those voices strengthen upon the ear; till at length the petition ended, and the conversation of an aged man, and of a woman broken and decayed like himself, became distinctly audible to the lady as she knelt. But those strangers appeared not to stand in the hollow depth between the three hills. Their voices were encompassed and reëchoed by the walls of a chamber, the windows of which were rattling in the breeze; the regular vibration of a clock, the crackling of a fire, and the tinkling of the embers as they fell among the ashes, rendered the scene almost as vivid as if painted to the eye. By a melancholy hearth sat these two old people, the man calmly despondent, the woman querulous and tearful, and their words were all of sorrow. They spoke of a daughter, a wanderer they knew not where, bearing dishonor along with her, and leaving shame and affliction to bring their gray heads to the grave. They alluded also to other and more recent wo, but in the midst of their talk their voices seemed to melt into the sound of the wind sweeping mournfully among the autumn leaves; and when the lady lifted her eyes, there was she kneeling in the hollow between three hills.

"A weary and lonesome time yonder old couple have of it," remarked the old woman, smiling in the lady's face.

"And did you also hear them?" exclaimed she, a sense of intolerable humiliation triumphing over her agony and fear.

"Yea; and we have yet more to hear," replied the old woman. "Wherefore, cover thy face quickly."

Again the withered hag poured forth the monotonous words of a prayer that was not meant to be acceptable in heaven; and soon, in the pauses of her breath, strange murmurings began to thicken, gradually increasing so as to drown and overpower the charm by which they grew. Shrieks pierced through the obscurity of sound, and were succeeded by the singing of sweet female voices, which, in their turn, gave way to a wild roar of laughter, broken suddenly by groanings and sobs, forming altogether a ghastly confusion of terror and mourning and mirth. Chains were rattling, fierce and stern voices uttered threats, and the scourge resounded at their command. All these noises deepened and became substantial to the listener's ear, till she could distinguish every soft and dreamy accent of the love songs that died causelessly into funeral hymns. She shuddered at the unprovoked wrath which blazed up like the spontaneous kindling of flame, and she grew faint at the fearful merriment raging miserably around her. In the midst of this wild scene, where unbound passions jostled each other in a drunken career, there was one solemn voice of a man, and a manly and melodious voice it might once have been. He went to and fro continually, and his feet sounded upon the floor. In each member of that frenzied company, whose own burning thoughts had become their exclusive world, he sought an auditor for the story of his individual wrong, and interpreted their laughter and tears as his reward of scorn or pity. He spoke of woman's perfidy, of a wife who had broken her holiest vows, of a home and heart made desolate. Even as he went on, the shout, the laugh, the shriek, the sob, rose up in unison, till they changed into the hollow, fitful, and uneven sound of the wind, as it fought among the pine-trees on those three lonely hills. The lady looked up, and there was the withered woman smiling in her face.

"Couldst thou have thought there were such merry times in a mad-house?" inquired the latter.

"True, true," said the lady to herself; "there is mirth within its walls, but misery, misery without."

"Wouldst thou hear more?" demanded the old woman.

"There is one other voice I would fain listen to again," replied the lady faintly.

"Then, lay down thy head speedily upon my knees, that thou mayst get thee hence before the hour be past."

The golden skirts of day were yet lingering upon the hills, but deep shades obscured the hollow and the pool, as if sombre night were rising thence to overspread the world. Again that evil woman began to weave her spell. Long did it proceed unanswered, till the knolling of a bell stole in among the intervals of her words, like a clang that had travelled far over valley and rising ground, and was just ready to die in the air. The lady shook upon her companion's knees as she heard that boding sound. Stronger it grew and sadder, and deepened into the tone of a death bell, knolling dolefully from some ivy-mantled tower, and bearing tidings of mortality and wo to the cottage, to the hall, and to the solitary wayfarer, that all might weep for the doom appointed in turn to them. Then came a measured tread, passing slowly, slowly on, as of mourners with a coffin, their garments trailing on the ground, so that the ear could measure the length of their melancholy array. Before them went the priest, reading the burial service, while the leaves of his book were rustling in the breeze. And though no voice but his was heard to speak aloud, still there were revilings and anathemas, whispered but distinct, from women and from men, breathed against the daughter who had wrung the aged hearts of her parents—the wife who had betrayed the trusting fondness of her husband—the mother who had sinned against natural affection, and left her child to die. The sweeping sound of the funeral train faded away like a thin vapor, and the wind, that just before had seemed to shake the coffin pall, moaned sadly round the verge of the Hollow between three Hills. But when the old woman stirred the kneeling lady, she lifted not her head.

"Here has been a sweet hour's sport!" said the withered crone, chuckling to herself.

## The Hollow Man

By Norman Partridge

Four. Yes, that's how many there were. Come to my home. Come to my home in the hills. Come in the middle of feast, when the skin had been peeled back and I was ready to sup. Interrupting, disrupting. Stealing the comfortable bloat of a full belly, the black scent of clean bones burning dry on glowing embers. Four.

Yes. That's how many there were. I watched them through the stretched-skin window, saw them standing cold in the snow with their guns at their sides.

The hollow man saw them too. He heard the ice dogs bark and raised his sunken face, peering at the men through the blue-veined window. He gasped, expectant, and I had to draw my claws from their fleshy sheaths and jab deep into his blackened muscles to keep him from saying words that weren't mine. Outside, they shouted, *Hullo! Hullo in the cabin!* and the hollow man sprang for the door. I jumped on his back and tugged the metal rings pinned into his neck. He jerked and whirled away from the latch, but I was left with the sickening sound of his hopeful moans.

Once again, control was mine, but not like before. The hollow man was full of strength that he hadn't possessed in weeks, and the feast was ruined.

They had ruined it.

"Hullo! We're tired and need food!"

The hollow man strained forward, his fingers groping for the door latch. My scaled legs flexed hard around his middle. His sweaty stomach sizzled and he cried at the heat of me. A rib snapped. Another. He sank backward and, with a dry flutter of wings, I pulled him away from the window, back into the dark.

"Could we share your fire? It's so damn cold!"

"We'd give you money, but we ain't got any. There ain't a nickel in a thousand miles of here . . ."

Small screams tore the hollow man's beaten lips. There was blood. I cursed the waste and twisted a handful of metal rings. He sank to his knees and quieted.

"We'll leave our guns. We don't mean no harm!"

I jerked one ring, then another. I cooed against the hollow man's skinless shoulder and made him pick up his rifle. When he had it loaded, cocked, and aimed through a slot in the door, I whispered in his ear and made him laugh.

And then I screamed out at them, "You dirty bastards! You stay away! You ain't comin' in here!"

Gunshots exploded. We only got one of them, not clean but bad enough. The others pulled him into the forest, where the dense trees muffled his screams and kept us from getting another clear shot.

The rifle clattered to the floor, smoking faintly, smelling good. We walked to the window. I jingled his neck rings and the hollow man squinted through the tangle of veins, to the spot where a red streak was freezing in the snow.

I made the hollow man smile.

So four. Still four, when night came and moonlight dripped like melting wax over the snow-capped ridges to the west. Four to make me forget the one nearly drained. Four to make me impatient while soft time crept toward the leaden hour, grain by grain, breath by breath . . .

The hour descended. I twisted rings and plucked black muscles, and the hollow man fed the fire and barred the door. I released him and he huddled in a corner, exhausted.

I rose through the chimney and thrust myself away from the cabin. My wings fought the biting wind as I climbed high, searching the black forest below. I soared the length of a high mountain glacier and dove away, banking back toward the heart of the valley. Shadows that stretched forever, and then, deep in a jagged ravine that stabbed at a river, a sputtering glimmer of orange. A campfire.

So bold. So typical of their kind. I extended my wings and drifted down like a bat, coming to rest in the branches of a giant redwood. Its live green stench nearly made me retch. Huddling in my wings for warmth, I clawed through the bark with a wish to make the ancient monster scream. The tree quivered against the icy wind. Grinning, satisfied, I looked down.

Two strong, but different. One weak. One as good as dead.

Three.

Grizzly sat in silence, his black face as motionless as a tombstone. Instantly, I liked him best. Mammoth, wrapped in a bristling grizzly coat he looked even bigger, almost as big as a grizzly. He sat by the fire, staring at his reflection in a gleaming ax blade. He made me anxious. He could last for months.

Across from Grizzly, Redbeard turned a pot and boiled coffee. He straightened his fox-head cap and stroked his beard, clearing it of ice. I didn't like him. His milky squint was too much like my own. But any fool could see that he hated Grizzly, and that made me smile.

Away from them both, crouching under a tree with the whimpering ice dogs, Rabbit wept through swollen eyes. He dug deep in his plastic coat and produced a crucifix. I almost laughed out loud.

And in a tent, wrapped in sweaty wool and expensive eiderdown that couldn't keep him warm anymore, still clinging to life, was the dead man, who didn't matter.

But maybe I could make him matter.

And then there would only be two.

When the clouds came, when they suffocated the unblinking moon and brought sleep to the camp, I swept down to the dying fire and rolled comfortably in the crab-colored coals. The hush of the river crept over me as I decided what to do.

To make three into two.

Three men, and the dead man. Two tents: Grizzly and Redbeard in one, Rabbit and the dead man in the other. Easy. No worries, except for the dogs. (For ice dogs are wise. Their beast hearts hide simple secrets . . .)

The packed snow sizzled beneath my feet as I crept toward Rabbit's tent. The dead man's face pressed against one corner of the tent, molding his swollen features in yellow plastic. Each rattling breath gently puffed the thin material away from his face, and each weak gasp slowly drew it back. It was a steady, pleasant sound. I concentrated on it until it was mine.

No time for metal rings. No time for naked muscle and feast. Slowly, I reached out and took hold of Rabbit's mind, digging deep until I found his darkest nightmare. I pulled it loose and let it breathe. At first it frightened him, but I tugged its midnight corners straight and banished its monsters, and soon Rabbit was full of bliss, awake without even knowing it.

I circled the tent and pushed against the other side. The dead man rolled across, cold against the warmth of Rabbit's unbridled nightmare.

"Jesus, you're freezin', Charlie," whispered Rabbit as he moved closer. "But don't worry. I'll keep you warm, buddy. I've gotta keep you warm."

But in the safety of his nightmare, that wasn't what Rabbit wanted at all.

I waited in the tree until Grizzly found them the next morning, wrapped together in the dead man's bag. He shot Rabbit in the head and left him for the ice dogs.

Redbeard buried the dead man deep in a silky snowdrift.

That day was nothing. Grizzly and Redbeard sat at the edge of the clearing and wasted their only chance. Grizzly stared hungrily at the cabin, seeing only what I wanted him to see. Thick, safe walls. A puffing chimney. A home. But Redbeard, damned Redbeard, wise with fear and full of caution, sensed other things. The dead man's fevered rattle whispering through the trees. An ice dog gnawing a fresh, gristly bone. And bear traps, rusty with blood.

Redbeard rose and walked away. Soon Grizzly followed.

And then there was only the hollow man, rocking gently in his chair. The soles of his boots buffed the splintery floor as his legs swung back and forth, back and forth.

Two. Now two, as the second night was born, a silent twin to the first. Only two, as again I twisted rings and plucked muscles and put the hollow man to sleep. Just two, as my wings beat the night and I flew once more from the sooty chimney to the ravine that stabbed a river.

There they sat, as before, grizzly and fox. And there I watched, waiting, with nothing left to do but listen for the sweet arrival of the leaden hour.

Grizzly chopped wood and fed the fire. Redbeard positioned blackened pots and watched them boil. Both planned silently while they ate, and afterwards their mute desperation grew, knotting their minds into coils of anger. Grizzly charged the dying embers with whole branches and did not smile until the flames leaped wildly. The heat slapped at Redbeard in waves, harsh against the pleasant brandy-warmth that swam in his gut and slowed his racing thoughts.

"Tomorrow mornin'," blurted Redbeard, "we're gettin' away from here. I'm not dealin' with no crazy hermit."

Grizzly stared at his ax-blade reflection and smiled. "We're gonna kill us a crazy hermit," he said. "Tomorrow mornin'."

Soon the old words came, taut and cold, and then Grizzly sprang through the leaping flames, his black coat billowing, and Redbeard's fox-head cap flew from his head as he whirled around. Ax rang against knife. A white fist tore open a black lip, and the teeth below ripped into a knuckle. Knife split ebony cheek. Blood hissed through the flames and sizzled against burning embers. A sharp crack as the ax sank home in a tangle of ribs. Redbeard coughed a misty breath past Grizzly's ear, and the bigger man spun the smaller around, freed his ax, and watched his opponent stumble backward into the fire.

I laughed above the crackling roar. The ice dogs scattered into the forest, barking, wild with fear and the sour smell of death.

So Grizzly had survived. He stood still, his singed coat smoking, his cut cheek oozing blood. His mind was empty—there was no remorse, only a feeling that he was the strongest, he was the best.

Knowing that, I flew home happy.

There was not much in the cabin that I could use. I found only a single whalebone needle, yellow with age, and no thread at all. I watched the veined window as I searched impatiently for a substitute, and at last I discovered a spool of fishing line in a rusty metal box. Humming, I went about my work. First I drew strips of the hollow man's pallid skin over his shrunken shoulder muscles, fastening them along his backbone with a cross stitch. Then I bunched the flabby tissue at the base of his skull and made the final secret passes with my needle.

Now he was nothing. I tore the metal rings out of his neck and the hollow man twitched as if shocked.

A bullet ripped through the cabin door. "I'm gonna get you, you bastard," cried Grizzly, his voice loud but worn. "You hear me? I'm gonna *get* you!"

The hollow man sprang from the rocker; his withered legs betrayed him and he fell to the floor. I balanced on the back of the chair and hissed at him, spreading my wings in mock menace. With a laughable scream, he flung himself at the door.

Grizzly must have been confused by the hollow man's ravings, for he didn't fire again until the fool was nearly upon him. An instant of pain, another of relief, and the hollow man crumpled, finished.

And then Grizzly just sat in the snow, his eyes fixed on the open cabin door. I watched him from a corner of the veined window, afraid to move. He took out his ax and stared at his reflection in the glistening blade. After a time Grizzly pocketed the ax, and then he pulled his great coat around him, disappearing into its bristling black folds.

In the afternoon I grew fearful. While the redwoods stretched their heavy shadows over the cabin, Grizzly rose and followed the waning sun up a slight ridge. He cleaned his gun. He even slept for a few moments. Then he slapped his numb face awake and rubbed snow over his sliced cheek.

Grizzly came home.

I hid above the doorway. Grizzly sighed as he crossed the threshold, and I bit back my laughter. The door swung shut. Grizzly stooped and tossed a thick log onto the dying embers. He grinned as it crackled aflame.

I pushed off hard and dove from the ceiling. My claws ripped through grizzly hide and then into human hide. Grizzly bucked awfully, even tried to smash me against the hearth, but the heat only gave me power and as my legs burned into his stomach Grizzly screamed. I drove my claws into a shivering bulge of muscle and brought him to his knees.

The metal rings came next. I pinned them into his neck: one, two, three, four.

After I had supped, I sat the hollow man in the rocker and whispered to him as we looked through the veined window. A storm was rising in the west. We watched it come for a long time. Soon, a fresh dusting of snow covered the husk of man lying out on the ridge.

I told Grizzly that he had been my favorite. I told him that he would last a long time.

## Holly, Don't Tell

By Juleen Brantingham

I was eleven. That's probably the reason for it. You don't know or understand *yourself* when you're eleven.

Daddy had been gone two years and Mom had just been fired

from the grocery. She took a job as a cocktail waitress. At the time I thought the name had something to do with the skirt that showed off her legs clear up to here. That's the trouble with being eleven. You know there are secret things you are supposed to understand but no one has taken the trouble to explain them to you yet so sometimes you see something and the world flips completely over and you think, Oh, *that's* what she meant when she—"

But anyway, I was eleven and mostly I was alone at night. People think too much when they're alone. Mom does it. She sits and drinks and thinks. Of course, I'm there but to Mom that's the same as being alone. She thinks about something I did or something Daddy did and how much I'm like him and pretty soon it gets all mixed up in her head and she hits me. So I know how dangerous it is to be alone and thinking.

Our rented house was pretty run-down. There were cracks around the window frames and up under the roof. We had bats. Sometimes I'd get up at night to go to the bathroom or get a drink of water and when I'd turn on the light, one would swoop down at me. I'd heard all of Pinky Johnston's stories, the ones about vampire bats that suck your blood and the one about a woman who got a bat caught in her hair and went crazy and now her family has to keep her locked up in the attic. So when a bat swooped at me I'd do the thing that Pinky said was the only thing you *could* do to save yourself—I'd run back to bed and pull the blanket over my head and tuck everything down tight so the bat couldn't get at me.

As I listened to the bat banging into walls and furniture and it got hard to breathe under that blanket, I'd wonder if Pinky was standing outside the bedroom window, looking at me and laughing. That's part of the trouble about being eleven. People will tell you all kinds of crazy things and some of them turn out to be true and some of them they just said as a joke so they could laugh at you when you believed them. Especially people like Pinky, who left his brain behind in second grade. He's older than me but the only way it shows is in size.

It almost made *me* laugh to think of the crazy way Pinky said babies are made.

Sometimes there were things besides bats that scared me when I was alone. Oh, I don't mean things like lightning or branches that tap at the window or shadows in the corner. That's baby stuff and eleven is too old for that. Anyway, I remember being scared of those things and it was all pretend. I made myself scared so Daddy would sit with me for a while and maybe tell me a story.

There was no sense scaring myself when I was alone in the

house. Mom said if I called her at work one more time she'd have the phone taken out and *then* what would I do if the house caught fire. I had to listen to the story of the boy who cried wolf about a hundred thousand times.

The things that scared me then weren't baby things. One of them was Daddy's footlocker. After he went away, it was the only thing I had left that belonged to him. I wouldn't let Mom touch it or sell it or throw it away. When she wasn't around I'd go upstairs to the storage room and just look at it. At first I did it because it made me feel better to think about Daddy and that he loved me once. But that was before I was eleven, before it started scaring me. Then I would go look at it to be sure the lid was shut and it wasn't leaking blood.

I guess if Daddy hadn't gone away, he and Mom would have gotten a divorce. Or maybe they wouldn't. Pinky said that when his mother divorced his father she took all his money. Daddy never had any money so maybe he couldn't get a divorce.

Even when I was little I knew Mom didn't like Daddy very much. I used to run home as soon as I saw Daddy's car turn into our street. He always got there first and Mom would be at the front door. By the time I reached the prickly bush by the porch, I'd stop and hold my breath because that's when we'd find out if Mom was in a bad mood. Usually she would be. She'd yell at him for losing an account or saying the wrong thing to a customer. She was friends with one of the secretaries at the office and she always knew what was going on.

I'd stop at the prickly bush and I'd hear him open the screen door and walk through the house to the kitchen to get a glass of milk or upstairs to change his clothes. I always knew where he was by the sound of her voice. It was like her words were a balloon that floated above his head. She followed him all over the house. He couldn't get away from her. The only place she didn't follow him was the bathroom and even there she'd stand outside and yell through the keyhole.

Sometimes when he got home she didn't yell at him. She'd just say "Hello" and "Did you pick up that loaf of bread I asked for?" Then I knew it was all right and I'd run around and up the steps and Daddy would hold me up in the air and say, "How's my princess today?" That's the way I remember Daddy best, holding me up in the air and smiling at me and making me feel special.

Mom didn't like *me* very much either. She said I was like him. After he went away she couldn't be mad at him anymore so she took it all out on me.

I asked her one time what kind of work Daddy did. She said he was a businessman. So then I asked what kind of businessman.

"A *nothing* businessman," she said. "In a *nothing* business."

That was kind of funny though Mom never meant to be funny. If someone had asked me what kind of work Daddy did I would have said he was a magician. Isn't it the business of a magician to turn nothing into something?

Daddy did real magic. Lots of people know one or two card tricks but that's not real magic. Daddy used to tear a piece of paper to small bits and put it in a little bag. Then he would say some magic words and give the bag to me and when I'd open it, there would be the exact same piece of paper only now it was all in one piece.

He could pull fifty-cent pieces out of ears and noses. He used to do that when I wanted to go to the movies on Saturday. He'd look through all his pockets and say, "I'm sorry, Holly, but I don't have any money." Then he would look at me as if he just noticed something. "Why are you asking me for money? You have some right here," he would say. Then he would reach up to my ear and pull out a fifty-cent piece. Sometimes he'd pull a fifty-cent piece out of my ear and another one out of my nose and he'd go with me to the matinee. That was more fun than going alone.

When Mom said he was in a nothing business, she wasn't talking about magic. He just did that for his friends. Once he put on a show for my birthday party and Pinky was so surprised that he didn't tease me for a whole week.

Mom didn't even *like* his magic. She said it was childish. Daddy kept his magic stuff in a footlocker and he asked me not to touch it. So I never did. But Mom "cleaned" it once in a while and threw out some of his best tricks. When that happened, Daddy would get this funny, sick look in his eyes but he never said anything to her.

After he went away Mom said she was going to call the trash man and have him pick up the footlocker. Mostly I just let Mom do what she wanted to do and tried to stay out of her way. But not that time. I told her I'd kill her if she touched that footlocker. I got a beating for it but she left it alone.

I didn't start being scared of it until I was eleven. That was when Pinky told me about a man who chopped up his wife and put the pieces in a trunk and mailed it to a made-up name in a town he'd never been to. That was when I started thinking it was funny that Daddy went away without saying good-bye to me. And wondering if Mom could have done that to him.

It wasn't fun anymore to sit on the footlocker and think about

Daddy. I couldn't go near the footlocker. But I couldn't stay away, either. I'd go to the door of the storage room and look at it. Sometimes after I'd stared at it for a while, the sides would seem to bulge, as if someone inside was trying to get out. Sometimes the shadows on the floor would look like pools of blood. Other times I could almost hear something, like someone calling my name but I couldn't quite make it out because I was listening too hard.

When that happened I'd get really scared and run away. Next day I'd be mad at myself for running away from nothing and I'd decide that tonight I would—

But I never did.

When I was eleven I spent a lot of time being scared. After Mom left for work I'd think about the footlocker leaking blood. And I'd hear noises, like people creeping through the house. I'd think about the last time Mom had beat me and wonder if tomorrow would be the day she'd do it again—because she'd *always* do it again, sooner or later.

Sometimes when I'd been thinking about it too long and been scared for too long, I'd start getting mad at Daddy for going away. I guess I loved Daddy better than anyone in the world and I know he loved me more than anyone else did. That's what I mean about it being dangerous to sit alone and think. It wasn't Daddy's fault that Mom had no one to get mad at but me.

Another thing that scared me when I was eleven was the way the curtains at the front window didn't quite close all the way. So when I was watching television I'd get the feeling that someone was watching me through the crack. Usually I'd tell myself it was just Pinky being silly again. But sometimes I couldn't make myself believe it.

One night the crack between the curtains bothered me more than ever. A couple times I thought I saw someone moving around out there. I was too scared to go over and look to find out for sure. I thought about calling Mom but I didn't dare. Finally I turned off the television and, trying to act like I didn't think anything was wrong, I started for my bedroom. That's when he knocked.

I didn't open the door. "Who is it? What do you want?" I asked.

"It's Pinky," he said, real fast and excited. "I just saw someone pick the lock on your back door and sneak inside. Let me in quick! It's probably the sex maniac that just escaped from the county jail!"

Well, I didn't like Pinky but he'd never tried to hurt me, just kiss me. And a sex maniac sounded like a pretty awful thing to be locked up in the house with. Besides, I listened real hard and I thought I could hear a slithery sound from the kitchen. It was hard to get the door unlocked because I was hurrying too much.

He walked into the house, grinning. Then I knew it was another one of his tricks but he was too big to push out the door.

"Hi, there. I was kidding about a sex maniac escaping from jail. It's only me," he said.

I looked up at him and though I knew it was Pinky, I couldn't stop being scared. He was different somehow. I tried yelling at him to leave and I tried crying but he just stood there and grinned at me. I ran for the phone. He ran after me and knocked it out of my hand.

I backed away. He followed me. He started talking, staring into my eyes, telling me things, crazy things that he was going to do to me. I didn't know whether to believe him or not but I knew that whatever this new Pinky had planned, I wouldn't like it.

I ran and dodged but he was right behind me. I tried for the front door but he had snapped the lock as he closed it and my frozen fingers just slid over the catch.

The only way left to run was up the stairs. He tried to follow but his feet got tangled in the phone cord and he fell hard. When he got up he was saying the same words without the ugly laugh. Now he sounded mad. It was almost better that way.

The sound of my breathing was louder than the sound of his voice. This was all the scary things rolled into one and doubled because I didn't know why Pinky was acting this way. I reached the end of the hall before he was halfway up the stairs. I was inside the storage room before I remembered that it didn't have a lock on it like the bedroom doors.

There was no place left to run and no one to call for help. There was just me in that dusty room with Daddy's footlocker.

I opened the lid. I don't remember now if I was going to hide in there or just try to jam it against the door. But there wasn't time for either of those things. I opened the lid.

After a frozen minute, the storage room door crashed against the wall and Pinky came up behind me. He laughed as he tried to grab me. I pointed behind him and screamed, "Bat!" He ducked and stumbled against the footlocker. When he was pulled inside, I slammed the lid and sat down on it. But he didn't try to push his way out or even make a noise.

I was eleven when I stopped thinking about being scared. I didn't stop *being* scared, just thinking about it. I didn't want to understand what happened that night. So I locked it away in my head and wouldn't think about it. But I was still scared, back there behind the locked-up place.

There was nothing inside the footlocker. No magic props. No body. Not even the bottom and sides. It was a lot of nothing, like opening a door into a night without stars. I couldn't see him when he took Pinky away. But I could hear him. He sounded scared. Now that I think of it, Daddy was always scared. Just like I used to be.

Things are different now. See, Mom found this new apartment over on the other side of town and she says we're going to move there. She gave me Daddy's footlocker and told me to pack all my stuff. She really got mad this morning and hit me because I hadn't done it yet. That was the next to the last mistake Mom ever made.

It's too bad about Daddy. But he never should have left me. "Holly, don't tell," he had said from the nothing-space of the footlocker. "Please don't tell your mother where I am."

I wonder how far she will follow him. . . .

## The Hound

By H. P. Lovecraft

In my tortured ears there sounds unceasingly a nightmare whirring and flapping, and a faint, distant baying as of some gigantic hound. It is not dream—it is not, I fear, even madness—for too much has already happened to give me these merciful doubts.

St John is a mangled corpse; I alone know why, and such is my knowledge that I am about to blow out my brains for fear I shall be mangled in the same way. Down unlit and illimitable corridors of eldritch phantasy sweeps the black, shapeless Nemesis that drives me to self-annihilation.

May heaven forgive the folly and morbidity which led us both to so monstrous a fate! Wearied with the commonplaces of a prosaic world; where even the joys of romance and adventure soon grow stale. St John and I had followed enthusiastically every aesthetic and intellectual movement which promised respite from our devastating ennui. The enigmas of the symbolists and the ecstasies of the pre-Raphaelites all were ours in their time, but each new moon was drained too soon, of its diverting novelty and appeal.

Only the sombre philosophy of the decadents could help us, and this we found potent only by increasing gradually the depth and diabolism of our penetrations. Baudelaire and Huysmans were soon exhausted of thrills, till finally there remained for us only the more direct stimuli of unnatural personal experiences and adventures. It was this frightful emotional need which led us eventually to that detestable course which even in my present fear I mention with shame and timidity—that hideous extremity of human outrage, and abhorred practice of grave-robbing.

I cannot reveal the details of our shocking expeditions, or catalogue even partly the worst of the trophies adorning the nameless museum we prepared in the great stone house where we jointly dwelt, alone and servantless. Our museum was a blasphemous, unthinkable place, where with the satanic taste of neurotic virtuosi we had assembled a universe of terror and decay to excite our jaded sensibilities. It was a secret room, far, far, underground; where huge winged daemons carven of basalt and onyx vomited from wide grinning mouths weird green and orange light, and hidden pneumatic pipes ruffled into kaleidoscopic dances of death the lines of red charnel things hand in hand woven in voluminous black hangings. Through these pipes came at will the odours our moods most craved; sometimes the scent of pale funeral lilies, sometimes the narcotic incense of imagined Eastern shrines of the kingly dead, and sometimes—how I shudder to recall it!—the frightful, soul-upheaving stenches of the uncovered grave.

Around the walls of this repellent chamber were cases of antique mummies alternating with comely, lifelike bodies perfectly stuffed and cured by the taxidermist's art, and with headstones snatched from the oldest churchyards of the world. Niches here and there contained skulls of all shapes, and heads preserved in various stages of dissolution. There one might find the rotting, bald pates of famous noblemen, and the fresh and radiantly golden heads of new-buried children.

Statues and paintings there were, all of fiendish subjects and some executed by St John and myself. A locked portfolio, bound in tanned human skin, held certain unknown and unnamable drawings which it was rumoured Goya had perpetrated but dared not acknowledge. There were nauseous musical instruments, stringed, brass, and wood-wind, on which St John and I sometimes produced dissonances of exquisite morbidity and cacodaemoniacal ghastliness; whilst in a multitude of inlaid ebony cabinets reposed the most incredible and unimaginable variety of tomb-loot ever assembled by human madness and perversity. It is of this loot in particular that I must not speak—thank God I had the courage to destroy it long before I thought of destroying myself!

The predatory excursions on which we collected our unmentionable treasures were always artistically memorable events. We were no vulgar ghouls, but worked only under certain conditions of mood, landscape, environment, weather, season, and moonlight. These pastimes were to us the most exquisite form of aesthetic expression, and we gave their details a fastidious technical care. An inappropriate hour, a jarring lighting effect, or a clumsy manipulation of the damp sod, would almost totally destroy for us that ecstatic titillation which followed the exhumation of some ominous, grinning secret of the earth. Our quest for novel scenes and piquant conditions was feverish and insatiate—St John was always the leader, and he it was who led the way at last to that mocking, accursed spot which brought us our hideous and inevitable doom.

By what malign fatality were we lured to that terrible Holland churchyard? I think it was the dark rumour and legendry, the tales of one buried for five centuries, who had himself been a ghoul in his time and had stolen a potent thing from a mighty sepulchre. I can recall the scene in these final moments—the pale autumnal moon over the graves, casting long horrible shadows; the grotesque trees, drooping sullenly to meet the neglected grass and the crumbling slabs; the vast legions of strangely colossal bats that flew against the moon; the antique ivied church pointing a huge spectral finger at the livid sky, the phosphorescent insects that danced like death-fires under the yews in a distant corner; the odours of mould, vegetation, and less explicable things that mingled feebly with the night-wind from over far swamps and seas; and, worst of all, the faint deep-toned baying of some gigantic hound which we could neither see nor definitely place. As we heard this suggestion of baying we shuddered, remembering the tales of the peasantry; for he whom we sought had centuries before been found in this self-same spot, torn and mangled by the claws and teeth of some unspeakable beast.

I remember how we delved in the ghoul's grave with our spades, and how we thrilled at the picture of ourselves, the grave, the pale watching moon, the horrible shadows, the grotesque trees, the titanic bats, the antique church, the dancing death-fires, the sickening odours, the gentle moaning nightwind, and the strange, half-heard directionless baying of whose objective existence we could scarcely be sure.

Then we struck a substance harder than the damp mould, and beheld a rotting oblong box crusted with mineral deposits from the long undisturbed ground. It was incredibly tough and thick, but so old that we finally prized it open and feasted our eyes on what it held.

Much—amazingly much—was left of the object despite the lapse of five hundred years. The skeleton, though crushed in places by the jaws of the thing that had killed it, held together with surprising firmness, and we gloated over the clean white skull and its long, firm teeth and its eyeless sockets that once had glowed with a charnel fever like our own. In the coffin lay an amulet of curious and exotic design, which had apparently been worn around the sleeper's neck. It was the oddly conventionalized figure of a crouching winged hound, or sphinx with a semi-canine face, and was exquisitely carved in antique Oriental fashion from a small piece of green jade. The expression of its features was repellent in the extreme, savouring at once of death, bestiality, and malevolence. Around the base was an inscription in characters which neither St John nor I could identify; and on the bottom, like a maker's seal, was given a grotesque and formidable skull.

Immediately upon beholding this amulet we knew that we must possess it; that this treasure alone was our logical pelt from the centuried grave. Even had its outlines been unfamiliar we would have desired it, but as we looked more closely we saw that it was not wholly unfamiliar. Alien it indeed was to all art and literature which sane and balanced readers know, but we recognized it as the thing hinted of in the forbidden *Necronomicon* at the mad Arab Abdul Alhazred; the ghastly soul-symbol of the corpse-eating cult of inaccessible Leng, in Central Asia. All too well did we trace the sinister lineaments described by the old Arab demonologist; lineaments, he wrote, drawn from some obscure supernatural manifestation of the souls of those who vexed and gnawed at the dead.

Seizing the green jade object, we gave a last glance at the bleached and cavern-eyed face of its owner and closed up the grave as we found it. As we hastened from the abhorrent spot, the stolen amulet in St John's pocket, we thought we saw the bats descend in a body to the earth we had so lately rifled, as if seeking for some cursed and unholy nourishment. But the autumn moon shone weak and pale, and we could not be sure.

So, too, as we sailed the next day away from Holland to our home, we thought we heard the faint distant baying of some gigantic hound in the background. But the autumn wind moaned sad and wan, and we could not be sure.

Less than a week after our return to England, strange things began to happen. We lived as recluses; devoid of friends, alone, and without servants in a few rooms of an ancient manor-house on a bleak and unfrequented moor; so that our doors were seldom disturbed by the knock of the visitor.

Now, however, we were troubled by what seemed to be a frequent fumbling in the night, not only around the doors but around the windows also, upper as well as lower. Once we fancied that a large, opaque body darkened the library window when the moon was shining against it, and another time we thought we heard a whirring or flapping sound not far off. On each occasion investigation revealed nothing, and we began to ascribe the occurrences to imagination which still prolonged in our ears the faint far baying we thought we had heard in the Holland churchyard. The jade amulet now reposed in a niche in our museum, and sometimes we burned a strangely scented candle before it. We read much in Alhazred's *Necronomicon* about its properties, and about the relation of ghosts' souls to the objects it symbolized; and were disturbed by what we read.

Then terror came.

On the night of September 24th, 19—, I heard a knock at my chamber door. Fancying it St John's, I bade the knocker enter, but was answered only by a shrill laugh. There was no one in the corridor. When I aroused St John from his sleep, he professed entire ignorance of the event, and became as worried as I. It was the night that the faint, distant baying over the moor became to us a certain and dreaded reality.

Four days later, whilst we were both in the hidden museum, there came a low, cautious scratching at the single door which led to the secret library staircase. Our alarm was now divided, for, besides our fear of the unknown, we had always entertained a dread that our grisly collection might be discovered. Extinguishing all lights, we proceeded to the door and threw it suddenly open; whereupon we felt an unaccountable rush of air, and heard, as if receding far away, a queer combination of rustling, tittering, and articulate chatter. Whether we were mad, dreaming, or in our senses, we did not try to determine. We only realized, with the blackest of apprehensions, that the apparently disembodied chatter was beyond a doubt *in the Dutch language*.

After that we lived in growing horror and fascination. Mostly we held to the theory that we were jointly going mad from our life of unnatural excitements, but sometimes it pleased us more to dramatize ourselves as the victims of some creeping and appalling doom.

Bizarre manifestations were now too frequent to count. Our lonely house was seemingly alive with the presence of some malign being whose nature we could not guess, and every night that daemoniac baying rolled over the wind-swept moor, always louder and louder. On October 29 we found in the soft earth underneath the library window a series of footprints utterly impossible to describe. They were as baffling as the hordes of great bats which haunted the old manor-house in unprecedented and increasing numbers.

The horror reached a culmination on November 18, when St John, walking home after dark from the dismal railway station, was seized by some frightful carnivorous thing and torn to ribbons. His screams had reached the house, and I had hastened to the terrible scene in time to hear a whir of wings and see a vague black cloudy thing silhouetted against the rising moon.

My friend was dying when I spoke to him, and he could not answer coherently. All he could do was to whisper, "The amulet—that damned thing—"

Then he collapsed, an inert mass of mangled flesh.

I buried him the next midnight in one of our neglected gardens, and mumbled over his body one of the devilish rituals he had loved in life. And as I pronounced the last daemoniac sentence I heard afar on the moor the faint baying of some gigantic hound. The moon was up, but I dared not look at it. And when I saw on the dim-lighted moor a wide nebulous shadow sweeping from mound to mound, I shut my eyes and threw myself face down upon the ground. When I arose, trembling, I know not how much later, I staggered into the house and made shocking obeisances before the enshrined amulet of green jade.

Being now afraid to live alone in the ancient house on the moor, I departed on the following day for London, taking with me the amulet after destroying by fire and burial the rest of the impious collection in the museum. But after three nights I heard the baying again, and before a week was over felt strange eyes upon me whenever it was dark. One evening as I strolled on Victoria Embankment for some needed air, I saw a black shape obscure one of the reflections of the lamps in the water. A wind, stronger than the night-wind, rushed by, and I knew that what had befallen St John must soon befall me.

The next day I carefully wrapped the green jade amulet and sailed for Holland. What mercy I might gain by returning the thing to its silent, sleeping owner I knew not; but I felt that I must try any step conceivably logical. What the hound was, and why it had pursued me, were questions still vague; but I had first heard the baying in that ancient churchyard, and every subsequent event including St John's dying whisper had served to connect the curse with the stealing of the amulet. Accordingly I sank into the nethermost abysses of despair when, at an inn in Rotterdam, I discovered that thieves had despoiled me of this sole means of salvation.

The baying was loud that evening, and in the morning I read of a nameless deed in the vilest quarter of the city. The rabble were in terror, for upon an evil tenement had fallen a red death beyond the foulest previous crime of the neighbourhood. In a squalid thieves' den an entire family had been torn to shreds by an unknown thing which left no trace, and those around had heard all night a faint, deep, insistent note as of a gigantic hound.

So at last I stood again in the unwholesome churchyard where a pale winter moon cast hideous shadows, and leafless trees drooped sullenly to meet the withered, frosty grass and cracking slabs, and the ivied church pointed a jeering finger at the unfriendly sky, and the night-wind howled maniacally from over frozen swamps and frigid seas. The baying was very faint now, and it ceased altogether as I approached the ancient grave I had once violated, and frightened away an abnormally large horde of bats which had been hovering curiously around it.

I know not why I went thither unless to pray, or gibber out insane pleas and apologies to the calm white thing that lay within; but, whatever my reason, I attacked the half-frozen sod with a desperation partly mine and partly that of a dominating will outside myself. Excavation was much easier than I expected, though at one point I encountered a queer interruption; when a lean vulture darted down out of the cold sky and pecked frantically at the grave-earth until I killed him with a blow of my spade. Finally I reached the rotting oblong box and removed the damp nitrous cover. This is the last rational act I ever performed.

For crouched within that centuried coffin, embraced by a close-packed nightmare retinue of high, sinewy, sleeping bats, was the bony thing my friend and I had robbed; not clean and placid as we had seen it then, but covered with caked blood and shreds of alien flesh and hair, and leering sentiently at me with phosphorescent sockets and sharp ensanguined fangs yawning twistedly in mockery of my inevitable doom. And when it gave from those grinning jaws a deep, sardonic bay as of some gigantic hound, and I saw that it held in its gory filthy claw the lost and fateful amulet of green jade, I merely screamed and ran away idiotically, my screams soon dissolving into peals of hysterical laughter.

Madness rides the star-wind . . . claws and teeth sharpened on centuries of corpses . . . dripping death astride a bacchanale of bats from night-black ruins of buried temples of Belial . . . Now, as the baying of that dead fleshless monstrosity grows louder and louder, and the stealthy whirring and flapping of those accursed web-wings circles closer and closer, I shall seek with my revolver the oblivion which is my only refuge from the unnamed and unnamable.

## The Hour and the Man

By Robert Barr

Prince Lotarno rose slowly to his feet, casting one malignant glance at the prisoner before him.

'You have heard,' he said, 'what is alleged against you. Have you anything to say in your defence?'

The captured brigand laughed.

'The time for talk is past,' he cried. 'This has been a fine farce of a fair trial. You need not have wasted so much time over what you call evidence. I knew my doom when I fell into your hands. I killed your brother; you will kill me. You have proven that I am a murderer and a robber; I could prove the same of you if you were bound hand and foot in my camp as I am bound in your castle. It is useless for me to tell you that I did not know he was your brother, else it would not have happened, for the small robber always respects the larger and more powerful thief. When a wolf is down, the other wolves devour him. I am down, and you will have my head cut off, or my body drawn asunder in your courtyard, whichever pleases your Excellency best. It is the fortune of war, and I do not complain. When I say that I am sorry I killed your brother, I merely mean I am sorry you were not the man who stood in his shoes when the shot was fired. You, having more men than I had, have scattered my followers and captured me. You may do with me what you please. My consolation is that killing me will not bring to life the man who is shot; therefore conclude the farce that has dragged through so many weary hours. Pronounce my sentence. I am ready.'

There was a moment's silence after the brigand had ceased

speaking. Then the Prince said, in low tones, but in a voice that made itself heard in every part of the judgement-hall—

'Your sentence is that on the fifteenth of January you shall be taken from your cell at four o'clock, conducted to the room of execution, and there beheaded.'

The Prince hesitated for a moment as he concluded the sentence, and seemed about to add something more, but apparently he remembered that a report of the trial was to go before the King, whose representative was present, and he was particularly desirous that nothing should go on the records which savoured of old-time malignity; for it was well known that his Majesty had a particular aversion to the ancient forms of torture that had obtained heretofore in his kingdom. Recollecting this, the Prince sat down.

The brigand laughed again. His sentence was evidently not so gruesome as he had expected. He was a man who had lived all his life in the mountains, and he had had no means of knowing that more merciful measures had been introduced into the policy of the Government.

'I will keep the appointment,' he said jauntily, 'unless I have a more pressing engagement.'

The brigand was led away to his cell. 'I hope,' said the Prince, 'that you noted the defiant attitude of the prisoner.'

'I have not failed to do so, your Excellency,' replied the ambassador.

'I think,' said the Prince, 'that under the circumstances, his treatment has been most merciful.'

'I am certain, your Excellency,' said the ambassador, 'that his Majesty will be of the same opinion. For such a miscreant beheading is too easy a death.'

The Prince was pleased to know that the opinion of the ambassador coincided so entirely with his own.

The brigand Toza was taken to a cell in the northern tower, where, by climbing on a bench, he could get a view of the profound valley at the mouth of which the castle was situated. He well knew its impregnable position commanding, as it did, the entrance to the valley. He knew also that if he succeeded in escaping from the castle he was hemmed in by mountains practically unscalable, while the mouth of the gorge was so well guarded by the castle that it was impossible to get to the outer world through that gateway. Although he knew the mountains well, he realized that, with his band scattered, many killed, and the others fugitives, he would have a better chance of starving to death in the valley than of escaping out of it. He sat on the bench and thought over the situation. Why had the Prince been so merciful? He had expected torture, whereas he was to meet the easiest death that a man could die. He felt satisfied there was something in this that he could not understand. Perhaps they intended to starve him to death, now that the appearance of a fair trial was over. Things could be done in the dungeon of a castle that the outside world knew nothing of. His fears of starvation were speedily put to an end by the appearance of his gaoler with a better meal than he had had for some time; for during the last week he had wandered a fugitive in the mountains until captured by the Prince's men, who evidently had orders to bring him in alive. Why then were they so anxious not to kill him in a fair fight if he were now to be merely beheaded?

'What is your name?' asked Toza of his gaoler.

'I am called Paulo,' was the answer.

'Do you know that I am to be beheaded on the fifteenth of the month?'

'I have heard so,' answered the man.

'And do you attend me until that time?'

'I attend you while I am ordered to do so. If you talk much I may be replaced.'

'That, then, is a tip for silence, good Paulo,' said the brigand. 'I always treat well those who serve me well; I regret, therefore, that I have no money with me, and so cannot recompense you for good service.'

'That is not necessary,' answered Paulo. 'I receive my recompense from the steward.'

'Ah, but the recompense of the steward and the recompense of a brigand chief are two very different things. Are there so many pickings in your position that you are rich. Paulo?'

'No; I am a poor man.'

'Well, under certain circumstances, I could make you rich.'

Paulo's eyes glistened, but he made no direct reply. Finally he said in a frightened whisper, 'I have tarried too long, I am watched. By-and-by the vigilance will be relaxed, and then we may perhaps talk of riches.'

With that the gaoler took his departure. The brigand laughed softly to himself. 'Evidently,' he said, 'Paulo is not above the reach of a bribe. We will have further talk on the subject when the watchfulness is relaxed.'

And so it grew to be a question of which should trust the other. The brigand asserted that hidden in the mountains he had gold and jewels, and these he would give to Paulo if he could contrive his escape from the castle.

'Once free of the castle, I can soon make my way out of the valley,' said the brigand.

'I am not so sure of that,' answered Paulo. 'The castle is well guarded, and when it is discovered that you have escaped, the alarm-bell will be rung, and after that not a mouse can leave the valley without the soldiers knowing it.'

The brigand pondered on the situation for some time, and at last said, 'I know the mountains well.'

'Yes,' said Paulo; 'but you are one man, and the soldiers of the Prince are many. Perhaps,' he added, 'if it were made worth my while, I could show you that I know the mountains even better than you do.'

'What do you mean?' asked the brigand, in an excited whisper.

'Do you know the tunnel?' inquired Paulo, with an anxious glance towards the door.

'What tunnel? I never heard of any.'

'But it exists, nevertheless; a tunnel through the mountains to the world outside.'

'A tunnel through the mountains? Nonsense!' cried the brigand. 'I should have known of it if one existed. The work would be too great to accomplish.'

'It was made long before your day, or mine either. If the castle had fallen, then those who were inside could escape through the tunnel. Few knew of the entrance; it is near the waterfall up the valley, and is covered with brushwood. What will you give me to place you at the entrance of that tunnel?'

The brigand looked at Paulo sternly for a few moments, then he answered slowly, 'Everything I possess.'

'And how much is that?' asked Paulo.

'It is more than you will ever earn by serving the Prince.'

'Will you tell me where it is before I help you to escape from the castle and lead you to the tunnel?'

'Yes,' said Toza.

'Will you tell me now?'

'No; bring me a paper tomorrow, and I will draw a plan showing you how to get it.'

When his gaoler appeared, the day after Toza had given the plan, the brigand asked eagerly, 'Did you find the treasure?'

'I did,' said Paulo quietly.

'And will you keep your word?—will you get me out of the castle?'

'I will get you out of the castle and lead you to the entrance of the tunnel, but after that you must look to yourself.'

'Certainly,' said Toza, 'that was the bargain. Once out of this accursed valley, I can defy all the princes in Christendom. Have you a rope?'

'We shall need none,' said the gaoler. 'I will come for you at midnight, and take you out of the castle by the secret passage; then your escape will not be noticed until morning.'

At midnight his gaoler came and led Toza through many a tortuous passage, the two men pausing now and then, holding their breaths anxiously as they came to an open court through which a guard paced. At last they were outside of the castle at one hour past midnight.

The brigand drew a long breath of relief when he was once again out in the free air.

'Where is your tunnel?' he asked, in a somewhat distrustful whisper of his guide.

'Hush!' was the low answer. 'It is only a short distance from the castle, but every inch is guarded, and we cannot go direct; we must make for the other side of the valley and come to it from the north.'

'What!' cried Toza in amazement, 'traverse the whole valley for a tunnel a few yards away?'

'It is the only safe plan,' said Paulo. 'If you wish to go by the direct way, I must leave you to your own devices.'

'I am in your hands,' said the brigand with a sigh. 'Take me where you will, so long as you lead me to the entrance of the tunnel.'

They passed down and down around the heights on which the castle stood, and crossed the purling little river by means of stepping-stones. Once Toza fell into the water, but was rescued by his guide. There was still no alarm from the castle as daylight began to break. As it grew more light they both crawled into a cave which had a low opening difficult to find, and there Paulo gave the brigand his breakfast, which he took from a little bag slung by a strap across his shoulder.

'What are we going to do for food if we are to be days between here and the tunnel?' asked Toza.

'Oh, I have arranged for that, and a quantity of food has been placed where we are most likely to want it. I will get it while you sleep.'

'But if you are captured, what am I to do?' asked Toza. 'Can you not tell me now how to find the tunnel, as I told you how to find my treasure?'

Paulo pondered over this for a moment, and then said, 'Yes: I think it would be the safer way. You must follow the stream until you reach the place where the torrent from the east joins it. Among the hills there is a waterfall, and halfway up the precipice on a shelf of rock there are sticks and bushes. Clear them away, and you will find the entrance to the tunnel. Go through the tunnel until you come to a door which is bolted on this side. When you have passed through, you will see the end of your journey.'

Shortly after daybreak the big bell of the castle began to toll, and before noon the soldiers were beating the bushes all around them. They were so close that the two men could hear their voices from their hiding-place, where they lay in their wet clothes, breathlessly expecting every moment to be discovered.

The conversation of two soldiers, who were nearest them, nearly caused the hearts of the hiding listeners to stop beating.

'Is there not a cave near here?' asked one. 'Let us search for it!'

'Nonsense,' said the other. 'I tell you that they could not have come this far already.'

'Why could they not have escaped when the guard changed at midnight?' insisted the first speaker.

'Because Paulo was seen crossing the courtyard at midnight, and they could have had no other chance of getting away until just before daybreak.'

This answer seemed to satisfy his comrade, and the search was given up just as they were about to come upon the fugitives. It was a narrow escape, and, brave as the robber was, he looked pale, while Paulo was in a state of collapse.

Many times during the nights and days that followed, the brigand and his guide almost fell into the hands of the minions of the Prince. Exposure, privation, semi-starvation, and, worse than all, the alternate wrenchings of hope and fear, began to tell upon the stalwart frame of the brigand. Some days and nights of cold winter rain added to their misery. They dare not seek shelter, for every habitable place was watched.

When daylight overtook them on their last night's crawl through the valley, they were within a short distance of the waterfall, whose low roar now came soothingly down to them.

'Never mind the daylight,' said Toza; 'let us push on and reach the tunnel.'

'I can go no farther,' moaned Paulo; 'I am exhausted.'

'Nonsense,' cried Toza; 'it is but a short distance.'

'The distance is greater than you think; besides, we are in full view of the castle. Would you risk everything now that the game is nearly won? You must not forget that the stake is your head; and remember what day this is.'

'What day is it?' asked the brigand, turning on his guide.

'It is the fifteenth of January, the day on which you were to be executed.'

Toza caught his breath sharply. Danger and want had made a coward of him, and he shuddered now, which he had not done when he was on his trial and condemned to death.

'How do you know it is the fifteenth?' he asked at last.

Paulo held up his stick, notched after the method of Robinson Crusoe.

'I am not so strong as you are, and if you will let me rest here until the afternoon, I am willing to make a last effort, and try to reach the entrance of the tunnel.'

'Very well,' said Toza shortly.

As they lay there that morning neither could sleep. The noise of the waterfall was music to the ears of them both; their long toilsome journey was almost over.

'What did you do with the gold that you found in the mountains?' asked Toza suddenly.

Paulo was taken unawares, and answered, without thinking, 'I left it where it was. I will get it after.'

The brigand said nothing, but that remark condemned Paulo to death. Toza resolved to murder him as soon as they were well out of the tunnel, and get the gold himself.

They left their hiding-place shortly before twelve o'clock, but their progress was so slow, crawling, as they had to, up the steep side of the mountain, under cover of bushes and trees, that it was well after three when they came to the waterfall, which they crossed, as best they could, on stones and logs.

'There,' said Toza, shaking himself, 'that is our last wetting. Now for the tunnel!'

The rocky sides of the waterfall hid them from view of the castle, but Paulo called the brigand's attention to the fact that they could be easily seen from the other side of the valley.

'It doesn't matter now,' said Toza; 'lead the way as quickly as you can to the mouth of the cavern.'

Paulo scrambled on until he reached a shelf about halfway up the cataract; he threw aside bushes, brambles, and logs, speedily disclosing a hole large enough to admit a man.

'You go first,' said Paulo, standing aside.

'No,' answered Toza; 'you know the way, and must go first. You cannot think that I wish to harm you—I am completely unarmed.'

'Nevertheless,' said Paulo, 'I shall not go first. I did not like the way you looked at me when I told you the gold was still in the hills. I admit I distrust you.'

'Oh, very well,' laughed Toza, 'it doesn't really matter.' And he crawled into the hole in the rock, Paulo following him.

Before long the tunnel enlarged so that a man could stand upright.

'Stop!' said Paulo; 'there is the door near here.'

'Yes,' said the robber, 'I remember that you spoke of a door,' adding, however, 'What is it for, and why is it locked?'

'It is bolted on this side,' answered Paulo, 'and we shall have no difficulty in opening it.'

'What is it for?' repeated the brigand.

'It is to prevent the current of air running through the tunnel and blowing away the obstruction at this end,' said the guide.

'Here it is,' said Toza, as he felt down its edge for the bolt.

The bolt drew back easily, and the door opened. The next instant the brigand was pushed rudely into a room, and he heard the bolt thrust back into its place almost simultaneously with the noise of the closing door. For a moment his eyes were dazzled by the light. He was in an apartment blazing with torches held by a dozen men standing about.

In the centre of the room was a block covered with black cloth, and beside it stood a masked executioner, resting the corner of a gleaming axe on the black draped block, with his hands crossed over the end of the axe's handle.

The Prince stood there surrounded by his ministers. Above his head was a clock, with the minute hand pointed to the hour of four.

'You are just in time!' said the Prince grimly; 'we are waiting for you!'